PRAISE FOR **ADVENTURES OF V**

With a few brush strokes, Reid creates a whole world. It's like magic –
the reader is sucked into that world, instantaneously. V swirls us into an
extravaganza, a detailed, delightful, dystopic, alien, familiar future – primal,
ferocious, and gratifying.
– Susan S. Senstad, author of *Milk and Venom* and *Music for the Third Ear*

Vivacious, vampish, victorious, voluptuous, vibrant, villainous … An
eternal 19-year-old, gorgeous vampire, monster-vixen named "V" – a pagan
Goddess, reborn as a super-heroine beauty who lives off the blood of the
bad, to rescue the souls of the good. Irresistible hijinks!
– Ed Cowen, producer, impresario

A wild ride into adventure, fantasy, and chills, V gifted me with glimpses of
arcane current and historical knowledge. Not for years have novels been as
much fun and enlightening.
– Chuck Shamata, actor

Utterly engrossing, rich, dark, and deep, Gilbert Reid creates worlds within
worlds of vivid, bold adventure.
– Bernice Landry, artist

Gilbert Reid's prose is so sensuous and evocative! When he takes you down
unfamiliar paths, and into situations that excite suspension of disbelief, you
follow him because the energy of V's personality is so witty and alluring, she
charms you into the universe the author has created. Vivid, complex, wildly
imaginative.
– Diana Leblanc, actor, director

PRAISE FOR OTHER BOOKS BY GILBERT REID

PRAISE FOR OTHER BOOKS BY GILBERT REID

PRAISE FOR *LAVA AND OTHER STORIES*

Very powerful, poetic and nasty and tough.
– Anna Porter, writer, publisher

The writing is terrific. The characters are glamorous, decayed, old, young, loved, unloved. Reid inhabits each one. His raw, elegant prose, his vivid and sensuous images leave one breathless, with recognition and terror.
– Diana Leblanc, actor, director

The women, how they speak, what they confide, and omit, what they expose about each other! It's as if only sexuality happened that summer.
– Susan S. Senstad, author of *Milk and Venom* and *Music for the Third Ear*

PRAISE FOR SO *THIS IS LOVE: LOLLIPOP AND OTHER STORIES*

Reid's stories are in the great traditions of Alice Munro or Mavis Gallant.
– Margaret Macmillan, historian, writer

Powerfully rendered and suspenseful.
– Joyce Carol Oates, critic, publisher, writer

An unerring and compelling examination of aggression and compassion.
– *The Vancouver Sun*

One of the 100 best books of the year.
– *The Globe & Mail*

EXTINCTION

BOOK 1
GIRL WITH THE GOLDEN EYES

ADVENTURES OF V: VOLUME 5
"The Goddess is back. Her hour has come."
– Jules Cashford

EXTINCTION

BOOK 1
GIRL WITH THE GOLDEN EYES

by
GILBERT REID

TWIN RIVERS
PRODUCTIONS

Issused in print and electronic formats
ISBN 978-1-7771580-5-7: *Extinction Book 1, Girl with the Golden Eyes:* Paperback
ISBN 978-1-7771580-4-0: *Extinction Book 1, Girl with the Golden Eyes:* EPUB
ISBN 978-1-9994790-4-6: *Extinction Book 1, Girl with the Golden Eyes:* Kindle
ISBN 978-1-7773141-4-9: *Extinction Book 1, Girl with the Golden Eyes:* Amazon paperback

Cover and text design by Counterpunch Inc. / Linda Gustafson
Illustrations by Niki9door

Published by
Twin Rivers Productions
20 Bloor Street East
PO Box 75070
Toronto, Ontario, M4W 3T3

To receive a free book or novella, sign up at:
https://gilbertreid.com

For Jenny Hambleton & Julia Hambleton

The Garden of Eden is no more. We are in a new age: the Age of Humans.
— DAVID ATTENBOROUGH

Everyone, deep in their hearts, is waiting for the end of the world.
— HARUKI MURAKAMI

Evil comes from a failure to think. … That is the banality of evil.
— HANNAH ARENDT

CONTENTS

CAST OF CHARACTERS

Beaver – talking, beaver-like surface mutant

Bear Hans – bear-like mutant, member of the Bear Guard

Bear Peter – bear-like mutant, member of the Bear Guard

Bear Yan – bear-like mutant, member of the Bear Guard

Bear Yorick – bear-like mutant, member of the Bear Guard

Boy – The Boy, also El Niño, prophet, emanation of the Force of Evil

Brother Rat – celebrant in the Cult of Dolly

Brother Toad – celebrant in the Cult of Dolly

Caliban – Prince of the Mutant Kingdom, aka Tarzan of the Desert

Claire V Jacobs – V's clone, model, fashion designer

Clown – A preacher-clown apparition, a Cyber-Ghost

Colonel Edwards – Commander of the Cosmos Centurion Column

Corporal Garrison – Cosmos Centurion snipper

Cyril Bedford – classmate of Miranda Hughes

Dolly – the first cloned mammal, Goddess of the mutants

Fanny Dakin – Kit Candy's Sub neighbor and friend down in Sub Land

Great High Priest – Mutant Ruler, Chief celebrant, the Religion of Dolly

Henry Cook – survivor from an outpost village conquered by the Boy

Ida Bones – glossy, fur-covered mutant

Janet Wong – flight attendant on Presidential Super-Liner 47

Kat M Jackson – lieutenant in the elite Cosmos Centurion Force

Kit Candy – 16-year-old Sub, cleaning girl for Nikki Hughes

Lemur Ball – small, affectionate, bouncy mutant

Major Emily Rodriguez – V's alias as a Centurion Cosmos officer

Major Gauss – Cosmos Centurion officer

Master Fluff – three-foot-high, friendly, furry mutant

Miranda Hughes – 13-year-old ultra-privileged elite Cosmos

Mr. Bounce – ghoul, the son of the ghoul family

Mrs. Daisy – ghoul, matriarch of the ghoul family

Mr. Deep – ghoul, patriarch of the ghoul family

Nikki Hughes – graphic designer, ex-star, mother of Miranda Hughes

Old Melody – owner of a café, isolated in the Deadlands

President-Leader – the Leader of the American Cosmos Imperium

Rodent – friendly surface rodent who gives Miranda advice

Scav – Scavenger, a toad-like mutant, friend of Caliban

Shimmer Lazar – pig-like girl mutant with two-fingered hands

Sniggy Propane – Kit Candy's Sub boyfriend

Tara Capricorn – keeper of the sacred bathtub in the Cult of Dolly

Tracy Plume – feather-covered, bird-girl mutant

Valda Weber – Nikki's best friend at university, Paris, deep past

Weasel – talking, weasel-like, surface mutant

PROLOGUE – LOST SOULS

6: 00 PM, December 24, 2157 CE.

"You're one of *them*." The old woman stared at V.

Outside, on the rickety porch of Old Melody's Café, the thermometer, an antiquated rusty contraption that used a column of mercury to register temperature, said it was a cool 110 degrees Fahrenheit.

"You *are* one of them, aren't you?" The old lady's elbows rested on the wooden tabletop, her thin fingers clutched tight around the coffee mug – so tight the flesh looked transparent. Her clear blue eyes fixed V with a penetrating stare. "You *are* one of them, aren't you?"

It was dusk. The light of day, a livid, yellow glow, dimmed by rippling streams of sand, was dying over the vast arid plain of the American Central Desert, the Unpeopled Dead Lands – nothing and nobody for miles and miles. "You're one of them, aren't you," the old woman licked her lips, "one of those creatures, one of them, one of the –"

"*Hybrids*, one of the alien-human hybrids, you mean," V lifted the mug to her lips. "This is excellent coffee."

Outside, the wind that so often comes at twilight was picking up. A shutter banged. A windowpane rattled. Yellow sand hissed, streaming under the loose wooden door.

The old woman's clear-eyed stare didn't flinch. She took a careful sip and wiped her mouth with the back of her hand "I get it contraband. Mexican gangs bring it in, the ones that smuggle people and drugs and body parts and DNA and bio-bricks and such-like. They bounty hunt for mutants too, you know. The mutants, really weird creatures, have colonies, underground, out that way; it's not far." She motioned with her chin.

"Yes, I know."

"So, tell me, are you one of those creatures – those hybrid reptile things?" The old lady's stare was more intense now, her eyes bright like glass. "I thought they were all dead, all murdered, all disappeared – *todos desaparecidos!*" She revealed her teeth – fine, bright, even teeth – in what V took for a smile, a friendly smile. "But you *are* one of them. I can feel it. You're more than human: you're too beautiful even for a Cosmos. You can kill me, if that is what you need to do. I'm old. I'm ready to die."

"Yes, I am one of them," V said, again lifting the mug to her lips, and thinking that, yes, she would now perhaps kill the old lady, which would be a real shame, since the old lady had been so kind, so frank, so helpful – and she was brave too, holding on, keeping her café running, out here, all alone, just for the smugglers, the gangs, the mutants, and a few adventurers.

The old lady, leaned forward, and put her cup down, "And you came here to … do what, exactly?"

V allowed herself a thin smile. "You already had that figured out this morning, Melody, right after I got here." V paused. Melody's gaze didn't flicker. V cleared her throat, "I came to find my brothers and sisters," she hesitated again, drank another sip of the coffee, "all my fellow hybrids; when they disappeared, years ago, they've …" She stopped and swallowed. She put down her mug; her gaze almost wavered – fighting back tears.

"Well, they killed them," the old lady said, the light in her eyes hardening, "The military, the Cosmos Centurions, they killed them. I saw it, one night, I saw the mercenaries too. Almost fourteen years ago, it must be … that night … I saw what they did."

"Yes, out there in the field, where I went this afternoon, where you told me to look. I found them – in the remains of that old Cosmos Centurion bivouac from fourteen years back, the one you told me about." V took another slow sip, staring over the edge of the mug. The old lady's eyes were blue, clear cornflower blue; and, yes, it was truly fine coffee, a rarity really, a pleasure.

"That's right," said the old lady, "out there, where you went this afternoon, that's where it happened. Like I said, there were lots of mercenaries too."

"Yes, they did kill them," V repeated. She was absent now, her voice almost dreamy. She put the coffee cup down. She already knew that the Centurions – and mercenaries – had killed the hybrids, of course, but out there in the field, she had *seen* it, *smelled* it, *felt* it.

That afternoon, four miles east of Melody's Café, V knelt in the hot dust. The sun glared down, a huge burning oyster-gray splotch. The humidity was 90 percent, temperature 120 Fahrenheit, 49 Celsius.

She dug with her hands, with a spade, with a trowel; and, finally, closing in on her prey, and using a fine-pointed, soft-bristle archaeologist's brush, she carefully cleaned away the dry encrusted earth and sand; she lifted up bones and fragments of bones – a collarbone, a jaw bone, a tibia … And with the bones, came visions – voices …

She could *see* it; she could *feel* it; she could *smell* it.

Not only hybrids – people too, dissidents, and children, human children.

And SINs too – *Synthetic Individuals*, never harmed anybody.

All dead.

And she knew who had done it, the mind behind it.

The Leader, the President.

The Hero of Cosmos.

The handsome, irresistible …

The man who …

The man …

V clenched her fists: It was her fault, it was certainly her fault; he did it because of her, he did it because they … because he saw … because he truly understood … because he truly knew what she was …

Or maybe not …

Now, in Old Melody's Café, the images – the *visions* – came back, her brothers and sisters, murdered, in cold blood, a helpless hapless stream of bloody images. "That night, that night fourteen years ago …"

"The night you all disappeared," said the old lady, sighing. "*Los desaparecidos* … You see, I'm old, I have memories. I know what everybody has forgotten, what no longer can be spoken about – even *thought* about. I know what has been *erased*." She waved her hand towards V, wafting her into nothingness. "You see, my dear, *you* no longer exist! And never have existed."

"Yes, I no longer exist, *we* no longer exist," V repeated in a whisper. She swallowed. "We aren't now, and have never been." Her eyes had become wet, glossy, the ache of loss, the temptation of tears. She hated emotions. *Emotions were human!*

The night of *the Culling* – all the hybrids and SINs suddenly disappeared, banished from the face of the earth, massacred: *obliterated*. That night – *we were erased*.

It was as if we had never been – even the memory was gone.

It was clear the old lady understood this. She understood all of it. Yes, perhaps she would have to kill the old lady. V smiled and said. "I think I'll have another cup of your excellent coffee."

"I thought you might, dear. I thought you might," the old lady returned V's smile as she pushed herself up from the chair to get the coffee pot, "You know, I don't think they killed all of them. Some they took with them – into the Dead Lands, out there, beyond the first mutant colonies – hundreds of miles, there's nothing there, just sand and rattlers and scorpions, and mutants of course."

"Yes, and I will find them," V said, "The survivors, I mean. Some must have survived. I will find them, and I will free them – and I will take my revenge." She watched the old lady – her graceful, precise movements, her crisp blue-and-white striped shirt and the silver quarter moon on a chain at her neck, the clear tanned skin, only slightly mottled by age.

Melody brought the coffee pot to their table. V gazed at her. If I kill her, I will do it softly, I will do it quickly, I will do it … with love.

A shutter banged. The wind rose. It was night. There was not a light for miles. The window of the café was as dark as slate.

Yes, V glanced at the window: once upon a time this country was alive. Now they call it "The Dead Lands."

Three months later …

PART ONE – LOST SOULS

THE DEAD LANDS: NORTH AMERICAN DUST BOWL – 2158 CE

CHAPTER 1 – MAROONED

"Shoo! Damn! Shoo!" Miranda Hughes batted a floating string of burning human flesh. "Go away!"

Explosions echoed.

Death was everywhere.

The string of sizzling skin drifted in the smoky air – points sparkling like rubies, bubbles of burning fat. It hovered near Miranda's cheek. "Damn! Go away!"

Huge fires lit up the crash site.

"They are going to *eat* us, mother," Miranda sniffed the air and glanced around at the wreckage.

"Eat us? Who's going to eat us, darling?" Nikki Hughes stretched, arms up in the air. She wiggled her shoulders, working out the stiffness.

"Mutants. They're getting close." Miranda stared at the granite walls of the ravine, lit up by the burning wreckage of Presidential Super-Liner Airship 47. Beyond that cliff, Miranda somehow knew, weird creatures, strange misshapen shapes, were hurrying toward them, hobbling, leaping, hopping, crawling, and slithering – ever closer.

Death was a heartbeat away.

"Sorry, Miranda. I was distracted. Who is coming to eat us?"

"Mutants! They're coming fast."

"Ah, mutants!" Nikki Hughes glanced at her daughter, narrowed her eyes, and smiled. "So, these mutants intend to eat us?"

"Yes, mother."

"You don't say!"

"Yes. I do say!"

Nikki, her hands her on hips, nodded, and with a thin smile, said, "Well, just let them try!"

"Mother! This is serious!" Miranda fumed. Such casual insouciance was so typical of Nikki! She was ultra-cool. About absolutely everything! It was infuriating. Miranda frowned and kicked a pebble. What a puzzle! *Why* did she know mutants were galloping towards them? *How* she did she know they were eager to feast on her and her mother's élite Cosmos first-class flesh, and drink their élite, champagne-quality, first-class Cosmos blood? She had absolutely no idea how she knew all this. But she knew it – she *felt* it. She could *see* it. She *heard* them, their growling acidic stomachs, their drooling jaws, their clamorous inchoate whispery thoughts, like the rustling of leaves.

It was *weird*, totally *weird!*

Miranda and Nikki Hughes were the only survivors of the crash, just the two of them, alone, in the Dead Land Desert, a thousand miles from civilization. How could such a thing happen?

Miranda was just two weeks short of her fourteenth birthday. She stared at the burning wreckage: Well, on one level, *how had it happened* was a stupid question!

They had crashed – as simple as that!

Around them was burning wreckage. Miranda suddenly had a *vision* – of what the last few seconds must have looked like from the ground. It was awesome, this *vision*, that's what it was!

The monster aircraft, Presidential Super Liner 47, screamed out of the night, its engines aflame, its wings dark, like immense shadows, swooping earthward at a shallow angle – out of control, doomed.

When the wings touched the walls of the gully, they snapped off, scything, somersaulting – giant knives.

The motors flew away, skittered, careened along the stony escarpment, and plowed into the ground, smashing out huge waves of flame, coating the floor of the ravine with a flood of liquid fire.

The fuselage thumped, belly down, skidded, and exploded, breaking into four giant pieces. Fragments smashed into rocks and outcroppings. Metal spun, rocketing everywhere. Behind the hurtling hunks of fuselage came the wall of fire.

On first impact, two titanium safety pods shot out of the fuselage, soaring up into the air. Mini-parachutes billowed. Mini-jets fired. The pods fell back, slowed, landed with a thud, and spun along the sandy bottom of the ravine. Finally, both pods came to rest, upright, next to each other, unscathed.

The two largest sections of fuselage skidded past the pods, and smashed against the valley wall. They exploded in an inferno of flame as the fuel tanks spread an ocean of fire. Red-hot fragments of metal showered down.

And so that was it – the crash.

Miranda sniffed the air. It must have happened ten minutes ago.

Maybe it had been fifteen minutes ago.

It was difficult to tell. Miranda glanced at her wristwatch: it indicated one o'clock in the morning, Central Standard Time.

The burning wreckage of Presidential Super Liner 47 was awesome. But it was horrible too – and it wasn't a video game!

Miranda Hughes was a Fully Certified Human Being, a Cosmos First Class Full Citizen, an inhabitant of Elysium Domed City-Ancient-Manhattan, and a full member in good standing of the World Elite – the rarefied elite of the elite, the *Cosmos*, the cream of the 0.000001 percent, who ruled with an iron fist over the whole planet.

She resisted admitting it, even to herself – since Cosmos, and in particular, Cosmos Elite Storm Trooper Girl Scouts are *never* supposed to show weakness, not under *any* circumstances – but she did feel just a tiny bit dazed – and confused.

She shook her head. And she wiped her eyes which stung from the heat and the waves of oily smoke. It was clear that she and Nikki were the only ones who had survived the crash.

How could that be?

Was it a miracle?

Miranda did not believe in miracles. No way! Ancient superstitions – religion and mumbo jumbo and voodoo and witchcraft and divine bells-and-whistles and swinging pots of incense and various other black arts – such things were encouraged among the slavish vulgar unwashed barbarian *Burbites* in the Burbs, as a means of controlling them, and among *Subs*, who were the inferior subservient Urban Class, allowed to live inside special segregated lower-class neighborhoods in the Domed Cities, but such archaic superstitions, opioids for the masses, were not for the elite Cosmos, and, most particularly, not for Miranda Hughes, who was a star performer in the Cosmos Scout Top Science Seminar Olympics.

Miranda looked down at her hands. This was another troubling puzzle. Her hands should be scarred and burnt to a crisp. Her clothes should be reduced to ribbons of smoking fiber.

Just a few moments before, demonstrating exemplary Cosmos Elite Storm Trooper Scout Courage, Miranda had fought her way through the flames into a burning section of fuselage, desperately trying to save Janet Wong, one of the flight attendants. The protective pod had split open. Janet was trapped in her seat. Miranda cut her arm on a sharp twisted piece of smoking metal. And while she struggled to free Janet, Miranda had been in the middle of the flames, the very middle.

She hadn't felt any pain – no pain at all!

And now, two or three minutes later, her hands were intact, the skin unmarked, not even redness; and the cut, which ran up the inside of her forearm – it was healing before her eyes – the skin joined, then closed, then wound was invisible – it was gone

What in the world …?

True, Miranda Hughes never got sick. Any bruise or scratch healed quickly. But this apparent invulnerability was really a bit much – really spooky – however useful it might be.

What is happening to me?

Maybe I'm dead; maybe we're dead.

Maybe mother and I are dead.

But I don't feel dead.

She was about to ask Nikki. "*Do you think we are dead, mother?*"

But she was interrupted. A burst of fire flared up. Bits of wreckage exploded. A smaller wall of flame rolled down the widening gully, and out into the valley below. Sparks rocketed into the sky. The boom echoed in the enflamed and starry night.

All down the stony slope of the ravine, fires were still burning; flames flickered around the shattered fragments of fuselage, scattered over at least 300 meters, maybe more.

It was at that precise moment – after the last explosion – that Miranda *sensed* something. She had no idea how she sensed it, but she did. She sensed *mutants!*

Mutants were coming – and they were hungry.

"They're coming, mother; they're coming!"

Nikki Hughes turned to inspect her daughter. Yes, Miranda was intact. She was okay, definitely okay, her golden tan glowing, blond hair as if just shampooed – not even Miranda's clothes had been singed; the skintight black shorts, white running shoes, and synthetic-silk black halter-top embroidered with the letter "M" – and with the *Cosmos Youth Medal First Class* pinned just above her heart – all were just as if they had come fresh and pressed from the laundry. It was beginning. Nikki frowned. The *change* was beginning.

"Who is coming?" she asked, rather absently, as she turned to squint through the wavering air, through the walls of flame and red-hot air, searching for any other signs of life.

"Mutants, mother," Miranda said, "mutants – and they want to eat us!"

"Mutants, ah, Miranda, well, let them come!" Nikki took a swipe at a floating strip of burning plastic, pushing it away from her daughter, "As for eating *us* – well, just let them try!"

Just let them try! Miranda sighed. That was *so* mother – *so* imperturbable, *so* unflappable. Miranda looked around. It was a scene from Dante's Inferno.

Yes, Dante's bloody Inferno.

Miranda had a "Platinum Quality for Cosmos Only" education. And, mentally empowered by her various culture mind implants, and by lots of hard work, she could evoke a vast range of images and references. She was considered, even by some of her ultra-élite Cosmos classmates, to be a prodigy. "The beautiful geek," Eddie Schmidt called her, "The Beautiful Geek with golden stars in her eyes."

Those bloody golden stars Eddie admired were annoying. They frightened Miranda, if the truth be told.

Yes, all around, it was like an image from Dante's vision of hell.

O'er all the sand-waste, with a gradual fall
Were raining down dilated flakes of fire,
Thus was descending the eternal heat,
Whereby the sand was set on fire, like tinder

Nikki and Miranda were standing in the midst of rubble and wreckage: Giant wheels torn from the undercarriage, torn passenger seats, broken and shattered bodies, fragments of metal and twisted smoking ribbons and lengths of plastic. The debris stretched up the ravine and down into what, in the flickering darkness, looked like a wide, flat-bottomed valley. The stench of burning fuel, plastic and metal, and roasted human flesh, made Miranda's nostrils quiver. A glowing haze filled the air.

Miranda looked up. Above, through the vibrant flaming heated air, stars shone down out of an ink-black sky.

Never before had Miranda seen such a sky.

She had never seen stars before, not real stars, not real sky!

Awesome!

Her whole life had been lived under the protective Dome of Elysium City.

Awesome! Stars shimmering and constellations – Taurus and Aries!

Miranda returned her gaze to earth. Janet Wong, the stewardess – she had such a beautiful smile and she'd served Miranda fresh apple juice and told Miranda about her two kids who lived in Hawaii – where they were headed – Janet was now a charred smoldering statue of black carbon. She was still sitting in the safety seat, the cadaver bent forward slightly from when Miranda had tried to pull Janet free.

Without even thinking, Miranda had pushed her way into the flames and had managed to open Janet's seat buckle – it was red hot – and she somehow managed to pull the belt loose. And she tried to pull Janet free. But the fire had welded Janet to the seat, only part of the torso ripped apart and tipped forward when Miranda pulled.

Janet was already dead. The gorgeous wide-open Eurasian southern belle smile was a skeletal rictus, all the teeth and the jawbone showing, a silent last scream of horror and pain; the flesh was melting and steaming, burning away, visibly dissolving, like wax. There was nothing to be done. Miranda backed out of the flames, her eyes wet with tears and smoke.

Now, three minutes later, she looked away from the smoking cadaver and stared into the darkness, beyond the burning fires, beyond the edge of the ravine, up towards the rocky crest above her, lit by the fires and outlined against the darkness of the night sky.

Yes, the stars shone down; the moon was not yet up.

Miranda had never left the Elysium City Dome. She had never been anywhere like this. This was the Dust Bowl Central Desert – the great continental wasteland – the Dead Lands – created by a hundred years of drought, invasion, gang wars, mutant infestation, nuclear accidents, civil war, and revolution. And it was weird, but she really could sense, beyond the ridge of the valley, the onrush of weird and alien creatures – the mutants. She'd never even seen a mutant before. Mutants were forbidden in Elysium Domed City – they were obscene, unclean, and unnatural.

Mutants were dangerous.

Mutants were freakish.

And these particular mutants were hungry, really hungry.

And, for her, it was spooky, uncanny. It was as if she could *read* their minds and *sense* their feelings – as if she were *one of them*.

Impossible!

The mutants, Government Text Blips continually explained, were misshapen creatures that lived in the Dust Bowl and the Dead Lands, wild beings, and products, as Miranda had learned in her Platinum Confidential-For-Cosmos-Only History of the 2085-2106 Civil Wars, of perverted science and wild religion. They lived beyond the rule of law and beyond civilization; they were even beyond the reach of the government of the World Elite, of the Cosmos, beyond the reach of the Government of the Imperial Cosmos United Imperial States of America, even beyond the reach of the President, the Leader. Just the thought of the Leader stirred Miranda's heart and brought tears to her eyes.

All hail the Leader!

All hail the Leader!

Yes, she could sense it: the mutants and others – perhaps even renegade humans – were coming towards the crash site, hurrying, jostling through the dark, hopping, skipping, jumping, slithering, crawling and running.

She knew too that they carried weapons – guns, knives, wrenches, crowbars, clubs, machetes. They grunted and shouted and slobbered. Some of them were humanoid; and some were not. *And all of them were hungry.*

"So, they're coming," said Nikki, wiping a streak of dust from her jacket, "You sense them."

One half of Nikki's face was smudged with burnt rubber from when she tried to pull a steward from a burning safety seat.

Nikki had gotten the man unbuckled and out and away from the fire; but it was too late; the steward had gulped, sputtering blood, "Thank you, Ms. Hughes, thank you," and died in Nikki's arms.

Standing in the firelight, Nikki looked like a harlequin, a beautiful clown; there was a perfectly round black clown-like smudge on the end of her nose.

"Yes, they're coming."

"Well, then, we shall meet them."

"Yes, mother! And we shall fight to the last, as Cosmos should," Miranda saluted, stretching her arm up at a forty-five-degree angle, and she stood up even straighter. "We will stand heroically, our backs to the wall, flag flying, we shall slay as many as we can, and we shall never surrender! Victory or Death! Long live the Leader! Long live the Leader. Hail! Hail!"

Oh, say, can you see, by the dawn's early light …

Nikki gave her daughter a thoughtful look. "Well, I'm not sure, Miranda – perhaps we could try diplomacy first."

"But, mother, we Cosmos never surrender, never negotiate, never palaver, never shilly-shally, never fudge, never … A day as a lion is worth a lifetime as a lamb! Our President-Leader says –"

"True, true, Miranda, our Glorious Leader says lots of things," Nikki smiled, "But let us take one thing at a time, shall we!"

Miranda looked down, then she looked up, and she blinked at her mother. Nikki seemed totally unconcerned. Miranda was pretty sure these mutant creatures would not be friendly – after all, she and her mother were part of the elite, the despised and feared elite, the Cosmopolitans – or "Cosmos" – and Full Citizens, Certified Fully Human, living in the privileged Domed City, the greatest city of all North America, Elysium City, floating over urban ruins, on the élite fortress island of Manhattan, where mutants and non-humans were forbidden entry and where Subs were kept – mostly – firmly in their place.

It was a well-known fact: Everyone who wasn't one, hated the Cosmos.

"I wish we could have saved someone, at least one," said Nikki. There were five dead bodies in view, burnt, broken, torn apart; one, another stewardess, lying on her back, was still smoldering. "Damn it!"

"You did everything you could, mother."

"Yes," Nikki sighed, "I guess we did, both of us. You are a heroine, Miranda, a true heroine."

"Cosmos duty," Miranda said. She again raised her right arm, perfect forty-five-degree-angle, fist clenched, in the Cosmos Imperial Salute.

Hail the Leader. Oh, Hail, Hail, Hail!

"Oh, Miranda," Nikki pulled Miranda to her and stroked her hair. Miranda was as if untouched – not a smudge, not a trace, and not a burn or even a flush on her golden skin. Nikki was relieved. But she was not totally surprised. The *change* had begun. The poor girl had no idea what awaited her!

A fluttering sound interrupted Nikki's thought: the two giant engines were still smoking, inner blades still turning, lazily.

A large circular section of the fuselage was smashed up against the rock face which trailed a huge black smear from the fire that had followed the explosion.

"They're closer, they're coming faster," Miranda said again, "And they're really hungry."

"And you and I are choice morsels." Nikki was smiling, teeth bright in the flickering firelight. Her eyes had a strange light in them – a hard light.

"Yes, we are," whispered Miranda. This was real, not a virtual game. She took her mother's hand. Perhaps, secretly, her mother was a warrior Cosmos, a killer, a hunter. Maybe she'd been a Cosmos Centurion.

Nothing fazed Nikki. And she was always ultra-quick to take decisions, decisive and fearless, as the Glorious Leader said they all should be.

But this was not Elysium City; this was a whole new world – scary and awesome and mysterious. Miranda tightened her grip on her mother's hand. Nikki squeezed back.

Presidential Super-Liner 47 had been carrying Nikki Hughes and her daughter – they were the only passengers.

Twenty minutes earlier, Miranda had been staring out her own personal super-liner window.

Thirty thousand feet below, there was nothing. Just thinking about it made her dizzy. Down there, were ruins and desert – the poisoned Dead Lands, once the heart of the now almost mythical – and much lamented – Great Republic, the United States of America, *the land of the free and the home of the brave ...*

The suave female Info Voice was saying, "We are now passing over the heart of the Unpeopled Dead Lands, a section of the Great South Central Dust Bowl."

"Nikki, this is awesome!" Miranda turned to her mother and then back to the window. The window was a real window, not a video frame. It looked out onto the real world. It was the earth, the earth outside the Dome of Elysium City!

It was dark, no lights; no lights at all. Miranda was electric with excitement. She had never been outside Elysium.

"What is awesome, darling?"

"Mutants and land pirates live down there. It's totally awesome!" Miranda imagined land pirates might be like the pirates of old, like the pirates of the 17th and 18th centuries. Just yesterday, she had been playing war games as a cyber-game pirate, with a wooden leg, a beard, and a patch over one eye, and a parrot on her shoulder and mascara on her eyes, and an open unbuttoned white silk shirt under her blue velvet corduroy jacket, and she had cut off the heads of slave traders, and she had captured slave ships, and liberated handsome dark slaves and beautiful aristocratic ladies from really bad rival pirates or slave-dealers; and, then, feeling it was time for a change, she had played an aristocratic lady in need of rescue – a damsel in distress. Sometimes, she would play the game in one leading role and then take the other leading role – or sometimes she would even play a bit part, say a bystander, or a sailor or a cabin boy, or a slave, or a British redcoat, or a French bluecoat, or a cute, alluring kitchen maid, that is, if she was feeling particularly lazy, and just wanted to witness the main action.

But, when playing the heroine, she had fallen, often, oh, so often, into the arms of her liberator, who looked rather like herself, or sometimes like that soccer guy she was in love with – was it love, really, really love? – Cyril Bedford, or Eddie Schmidt, her rival in biochemistry class, or sometimes like her Sub Non-Cosmos girlfriend Kit Candy – whom she also rescued from slavery on occasion – and Miranda herself had, as the French or Spanish girl aristocrat captured by evil pirates, been sold in the slave market of Algiers or Casablanca; and, once liberated, either through her own ingenuity and pluck, or aided by some dark handsome swashbuckler, she had set up her own business and run a plantation in the ancient West Indies, striding around, a pistol in the belt of her skirt or jodhpurs, her blond hair held up high by a pin, giving orders left, right, and center, and she had been, in the games, both slave-owner, and slave, black and white, Chinese or Indian merchant, Vietnamese sailor, down-on-his-luck Scottish prospector for gold, or escapee blasphemous irreverent Cockney thief, talented pickpocket and locksmith …

And so she thought, maybe down on the barrens and the Dead Lands, the pirates – who kidnapped people and held them for ransom and often killed them, so the plane's brochure said – would be something like those pirates of old, those romantic swashbucklers, vagabonds of the vast, frothy, unpolluted, oxygen-drenched, ancient blue seas that teamed with fish, except that these pirates, today's pirates, the 22nd century land pirates, would sail across the desert wastes in wild, rusty, hydrogen-powered, ramshackle desert buggies – Dust Bugs – and often they were, in fact, mutants, blood-thirsty, dirty, ignorant, ugly, evil – cannibalistic, and sworn enemies of Cosmos …

"Oh, land pirates …" Nikki was flipping through a Hologram Net fashion magazine. "You know, Miranda, I rather like this one." She indicated a rotating hologram model cocktail dress and pushed a button, ordering the black, nano-synthetic, bespoke, skin-clinging, sleeveless, short-hemmed number directly from the Pierre Bruni Design Studio in Cosmos Domed City Paris. The designer firm, one of Nikki's favorites, and for whom she occasionally modeled or created designs and logos, was based in Cosmos Domed City in France, and had her measurements on record, updated monthly, though they never changed, as Miranda had noticed: Nikki never varied in the slightest, was never sick, never overweight, never depressed, never had a headache, never even had a pimple or rash – *weird!*.

Courtesy of the Cloud and the Net, aka the Cosmos World Mind, which knew and controlled and communicated everything, the dress would be conjured up, nano-built, in clinging, skin-caressing, synthetic latex silk, in Hawaii and would be hanging in their pre-booked luxury suite – which, the Cloud had informed them, overlooked a newly created beach and a picturesque drowned city – when they landed.

"I think I'll wear it to that dinner the Military Governor, General Herzog, will be giving tomorrow night." Nikki flipped to another page – featuring gossip about a Moscow-based starlet who had been found naked swimming by moonlight in the sunken ruins of the British Houses of Parliament – a tourist attraction, but normally closed at night and out-of-bounds to all but Cosmos – in the company of the British Prime Minister, also naked, Sir Humphrey Davies OBE ...

Miranda did sometimes wonder about her mother's cultural tastes – which were eclectic to say the least – and about her mother's calm, phlegmatic Cosmos sang-froid which, even for a Cosmos, seemed just too perfect. Everything about her mother was surrounded by an aura of ... well ... of mystery.

Even why they were on the flight and how they got to be on it was strange, a puzzle which had part of Miranda's mind buzzing with speculation and hypotheses. She ran over it in her mind.

They were at home, in their Cosmos First Class luxury apartment floating above the artificial clouds, in the kitchen, watching the evening InfoFlow. The news that day had been more than weird; the World Mind and its attendant Cloud had partially collapsed, and no one seemed to know why. Then they started to function again.

Then, there was another flash: Domed Los Angeles – the part of the city that was protected by a giant dome and still inhabited by Cosmos – had suffered a massive blackout and was incommunicado for several hours – No Net, no Cloud, no anything. Riots were rumored among the Non-Cosmos, wicked, vulgar, semiliterate Burbites, who thronged the chaotic, unhygienic Burbs outside the L.A. Dome.

The same had happened to Domed San Francisco, Domed San Diego, and to the upper, militarized, partly submerged colonies of Seattle and Vancouver. All of them flickered, went dark, and disappeared.

Some of the cities and outposts stayed dark.

Maybe they would never be heard from again!

Strange winged creatures had been reported moving through the great inland salt lake of what was once the Napa Valley, dark, man-sized bat-like beings, though the "sightings could not be confirmed."

Riots by Non-Cosmos humans, vulgar Burbites and some Subs, due in part to high food prices, were sweeping through the Burbs on the fringes of all the domed cities.

Religious prophets and crackpots were spewing nonsense on all the illegal airwaves – preaching the Apocalypse and the End of Time, revolt against the World Order and against the Cosmos. Here and there, all over the planet, the appearance of messiahs had been reported.

One news item even claimed that mutants had assaulted the Appalachian frontier barrier, the wall which was meant to keep mutants from invading the East Coast Cosmos Empire. They had been driven back by drones and Cosmos Centurions. No human or Cosmos Centurion casualties were reported.

"It does rather look, Miranda, as if the world is finally coming to an end," said Nikki, "It's about time."

"What? You can't mean that, mother!"

"Maybe I do, maybe I don't," Nikki was munching on a celery stick; it stuck out of her mouth as she talked and wagged up and down like a cigar. She was mashing up garlic to make a pesto sauce and looking up at the InfoFlow news. "Pass me that little packet of basil, will you, darling?"

Miranda frowned and passed the basil.

They ate together, watching the stream of strange news. "What are those winged creatures out in the west, I wonder?" said Miranda.

"Maybe a new kind of mutant," said Nikki, suddenly turning, leaning close and tousling Miranda's hair. She stared at Miranda with that intense dark hungry gaze that made Miranda feel weak with love for her mother – for that strange, loving, enigmatic woman, for Nikki.

"Your eyes are flaring gold again," Nikki pushed a strand of gold-blond hair away from Miranda's eyes.

"Yuk! I hate it when they do that!" Miranda closed and opened her eyes. Those golden star-like flares in her eyes didn't hurt – in fact, they gave her a voluptuous shivery feeling, but she felt they made her ... different ... they were weird, really weird, even if Cyril Bedford said he adored them and Karen Pak said they made her utterly green with envy.

"They're beautiful," said Nikki, caressing Miranda's hair, "They're part of you."

An hour later, at about ten-thirty, there was a knock on the door.

"Who could that be – at this hour?"

Nikki walked to the door and opened it.

"Hail the President, Hail the Leader!" The five agents raised their right arms in the ritual salute.

"Hail, all Hail!"

"Hail, all Hail!"

Standing just inside the door, Nikki returned the salute lazily, her arm only going halfway up. "Hail, All Hail," she said, in a very soft voice.

It was Military Cosmos Police, with Presidential Secret Service agents, and, standing in the entry, they told Nikki and Miranda that they were to pack and leave immediately.

"The President is worried for your safety, Ms. Hughes," the woman agent – who seemed to be the leader – said. "He wants you and your daughter to leave for the Presidential Compound in Hawaii – now."

"The President, the Leader?" said Miranda. She adored the President; she worshiped the President; but what did Nikki or what did she have to do with the President, the Glorious Leader?

"Now? He wants us to leave now?" Nikki raised an eyebrow. She had been in her studio working on a graphic design for a new bio T-shirt logo and had two colored pencils – a red and a black pencil – tucked behind one ear. She touched her throat and her collarbone, just above the open white shirt.

"Yes, immediately, now," The agent handed Nikki a folded sealed piece of paper, "It's an order from the Leader-President Himself, personally!"

"Hail, all Hail!"

"Hail, all Hail!"

Nikki broke the seal, opened the paper, glanced at it, and said, "It's that serious? The president really thinks it's that serious?" She glanced at Miranda and then handed the paper back to the agent.

"Yes, he does. And it *is* that serious, Ms. Hughes, the situation could change at any moment. The president wanted you to go to Europe. But transatlantic guidance systems are down. It must be Hawaii."

"Hawaii?"

"You'll be safe there."

"It's fully militarized, Ms. Hughes," one of the muscle-bound male agents said, "Full Cosmos control guaranteed."

"Yes, martial law," said the female, "Twenty years of martial law. There are no deviants or mutants or SINs, no Burbites, and only a few well-controlled constantly monitored Subs."

"Well …" Nikki turned to Miranda.

"We have no time to lose; it must be now!" The agent glanced at her watch and then at the muscled guys standing around her. Their arms were folded over their chests; they all wore dark glasses and you couldn't see their eyes.

Miranda grinned and fluttered her eyelashes at the muscled guys. But she didn't get any response – whatever was going on, they didn't think it was a joke.

"Then it shall be now," said Nikki with a crisp smile. She turned to Miranda, "Miranda, check your little valise – most of what you need will be in it. The toiletries are already packed."

That was one little thing that Miranda had noticed – Nikki always had a set of bags packed, for herself and for Miranda, as if they might leave at any moment; but, up until a few hours ago, they never had left anywhere. Every week or so Nikki checked the bags; sometimes she made a few changes, adding new emergency food pouches, electro packs, stuff you'd need if you went to the moon or some outlandish place beyond Cosmos Civilization.

And so, a few minutes later, they were escorted from their flat, down the express elevator, suddenly reserved just for them, with guards standing on both sides.

Miranda wondered whether they were being arrested.

Down and down they went, seventy-eight floors, in the glass-walled elevator, past the luxury suites – like theirs – past the gymnasiums and swimming pools, where she'd played water polo with Eddie Schmidt and ended up falling into his arms and then wrestling him underwater and pinning him down against the bottom until he signaled he'd given up, bubbles rising deliciously all around them; past the restaurant and patio level, where she and Nikki had celebrated Miranda's birthdays; past the Elysium university campus – where Miranda attended classes and seminars – past the high school level, where she first fell for Cyril Bedford during the advanced math class, and where she'd first felt the funny tickling feeling in her tummy that came back to her now, and she remembered the voice of the Professor, Martina Popova, saying, with that cute French accent, "Daydreaming are we, Miranda?" For some reason, Miranda suddenly felt she was saying goodbye to everything and to everybody – to her whole life!

Yes, maybe they were being arrested!

Would they be killed?

Would they be erased?

What had they done?

Then, at Level 1-B, they were hurried outside; Miranda noticed there were guards with guns in the lobby, and they were ushered into a vehicle that seemed to be part of a column of four vehicles.

And in the vehicles, which all had dark tinted windows, they were taken right to the airport, and out onto the launch pad, and into the plane – where, to her astonishment, Miranda discovered that they were the only passengers – and they were treated like royalty.

It was one of the President's planes.

It had The Leader's logo everywhere.

Nikki, Miranda noticed, did not seem in the least surprised by all of this. But Miranda certainly was: Why would the President be interested in Nikki and Miranda Hughes?

Had Nikki and the President been lovers?

Nikki had starred in some films and been a model, and had been famous in a way, but that was years ago, and there were a lot of other stars and ex-stars. Miranda was eager to ask questions, but she could see in Nikki's eyes – in spite of the classic Nikki smile – the clear message: Now, dear Miranda, is *not* the time to ask questions!

And there was even – Janet Wong the stewardess told them – a program for what they would be doing in Hawaii – in the Presidential Compound! They would be meeting the Military Governor, General Herzog, and having dinner in his Mansion! Everything was totally weird!

And so, now, here they were, flying over the Dead Lands.

"It says here," Miranda frowned, "in the brochure, that …"

"If you will now look out your window," the suave female Info Voice began, "you can see fires burning where mining pits and oil wells exploded seven decades ago; and also from where shale and clay structures fractured and began to smolder."

"Wow," Miranda blinked, "This is awesome!"

The smooth voice whispered: "Now, seventy years later, underground fires are still burning. You will note that, at this moment, the fires are reflected in the smoke to beautiful effect. Infrared sensors will give you an impression of the heat being generated. If you push your personal in-depth button, you can see a holographic map of the region. Or you can request a direct personalized live infra-red map and overlay vision from your window."

Miranda whispered "infrared" to the window and the window said, "Yes, Miranda," and gave her – floating just above her lap and also superimposed on the window, infrared mappings of the land below; yes, it definitely looked like something from Dante's inferno! Miranda stared out the window: huge flares shot upwards and flickering blotches of fiery red glowed, reaching many layers down under the desert floor.

The Info Voice went on: "This section of the Dead Lands is inhabited by mutants who live mostly underground in caverns and abandoned mineshafts and who are active as land pirates and smugglers."

Awesome! Miranda's eyes went wide.

"It is rumored the mutants capture people for cell and organ harvesting and DNA piracy, and that they occasionally practice cannibalism, eating those who cannot pay sufficient ransom – or who lack pirate insurance – or whose bodies are not sufficiently healthy for antique mutant medical harvesting techniques. Efforts to tame or police the Dead Lands have been discontinued for some decades as uneconomic, though Cosmos Centurion Forces still venture into the Badlands for special peace-keeping and rescue operations."

"Not terribly sporting," said Nikki, who had been eavesdropping on the Info Voice and who was turning the hologram fashion pages, "Eating your guests – I rather imagine these mutants are not terribly pleasant. I dare say they need a lesson in civility – or a good brain-washing."

"I'll bet they're interesting," said Miranda.

Nikki glanced at her, turned a page, and smiled, "Yes, I'll bet they are."

Miranda had read about mutants and seen video mock-ups of mutant battles and played a few mutant games. When she was not studying – she already had the equivalent of three university degrees – and she was a top volleyball and water polo player – Capitan of the Elysium City Girl's Champion Cosmos Team – she amused herself by constructing virtual mock-mutants by transforming herself or some of her virtual friends and avatars into monsters. She liked being a furry – four or two-legged – sometimes with wings – or a scaly or a slippery or a crawly.

She had tried to transform herself into a *hybrid* – for some reason she had a real desire, a perfect itch, to do so. *Hybrids* were obscene, totally wicked creatures, that she, Miranda, would love to fight, subdue and slay. But they were off-limits even to full citizen Cosmos imagination and full citizen Cosmos thought.

In fact, official policy seemed to be that hybrids didn't exist and never had. Miranda was informed of this by the automatic video censor that transmitted to her, directly, a feeling of deep shame. "Any attempt to emulate or impersonate or construct – or even to do battle with – a *hybrid* will lead to severe punishment," the Cloud-Thought-Wave said. The screen flashed a warning in Big Red Letters: "Off-limits, off-limits, Miranda Hughes, repeat: off-limits." Miranda whispered "Ouch" as the *Shame Wave* hit. She sighed in frustration.

The officially *Permitted Mind Range* – PMR – for Cosmos was large; but there were barriers, beyond which none but rebels and perverts desired to go; and they could be punished, Miranda had discovered, by loss of Cosmos status, by decertification as a human being, or, even worse, by partial or total mind erasure, or by death.

Hybrids were one of those off-limits topics.

Still, there was something about *hybrids* that Miranda found … enticing. She really wanted to do battle with a hybrid – it would be like slaying a real dragon.

She kept this thought strictly to herself. Except once she had mentioned to her mother that she thought *hybrids* were fascinating. "But they are absolutely evil, weren't they, mother? And, I mean, maybe they are just mythical creatures, that's what the World Mind Encyclopaedia says."

"Well …" Nikki frowned.

"I mean, according to legend, *hybrids* eat people, and they possess our bodies, like those SINs, those really weird freaky *Synthetic Individuals*, and they want to take over the world and turn us into slaves, I mean, I've read all about it, and I saw a documentary about how they drink blood and eat babies and practice human sacrifice in their religious rituals, and …"

Nikki, strangely, looked upset – something she never seemed to be – there were tears in her eyes.

"What did I say?" Miranda was shocked. "Mother, what did I say?"

Nikki held up her hand and then laid her hands gently on Miranda's shoulders, kissed her on the lips, and stared at her, tears glistening in her eyes, little silver lights sparkling in the dark iris and pupil, a silver drop or two on the fine dark lashes. "Don't believe everything you are told, Miranda. We live in a funny world. It's topsy-turvy in some ways." Nikki gazed at her daughter. Then she changed the subject, "Now, darling, I think you and I should go shopping! There is a new Non-Virtual Prada shop on the fifth level; we should go and explore."

And so that was that – they went shopping – virtual and real – and there was no more mention of *hybrids* or those horrendous *Synthetic Individuals* or *SINs*.

It left Miranda wondering. She sometimes caught glimpses of a different personality inside her mother, a more emotional, but also a much more serious, tougher, acute character. It was a personality quite unlike the surface Nikki, the flawless fashion icon and scrupulously affectionate mother, the Nikki she knew and loved. Miranda couldn't find the right words for the suspicion – but somehow she thought *Nikki was playing at being Nikki.*

And why did Nikki get upset at the talk about *hybrids* and SINs? Everybody knew about hybrids and SINs – *Synthetic Individuals*! If hybrids did exist, they were evil, utterly dangerous – the worst enemies of the Glorious Leader – *Hail, All Hail* – and of Cosmos and of Humanity.

Sometimes, too, Nikki became positively goofy, with a ridiculous, daring sense of humor – like that time they had the wild pillow fight, or the time she insisted they try on clown costumes, or the time they splashed around in the wading pool and fell over each other, laughing, or the time she tickled Miranda so much Miranda could just not stop laughing and …

Maybe Nikki was really somebody else – but who? Maybe Nikki was more than one person. Miranda frowned. That was an inebriating possibility, depths, and more depths, and yet more depths.

Miranda's bedroom was on the 78th floor of the Sky Dreamer Complex in Elysium Dome City, built over the ruins of ancient Gotham, once known as New York City, much of which – the old streets, the subways, the sewage and water systems, the museums and office buildings – had been blown up in terrorist attacks and in the civil war of the late 21st century, and was now rusting and rotting under the water of the Atlantic Ocean which had risen by 155 feet.

In her bedroom, Miranda could flip a switch so the window unveiled, revealing the other Elysium towers, dreamily reaching upward, ribbons of mist drifting between them, the sunlight filtered by the Elysian Dome that protected Elysium City from the atmosphere which people said had become poisoned and virtually unbreathable, though when Miranda mentioned this to Nikki, Nikki had given her a crooked little smile and said, "Utter rubbish! They just don't want Cosmos and Citizens and Shoppers to go outside."

"Oh?"

"Yes," Nikki, in black silk pajamas, was sitting at a screen designing a new product – she had become famous for her graphic work after ending her acting and modeling career. "Elysium City is a gilded cage, and all of us, darling, are birds of paradise, trapped inside, fluttering, fluttering, and shopping, shopping ..."

"Oh." Miranda frowned, went back to her room and looked up references to "gilded cage" and "birds of paradise" and frowned. Was it possible her mother was a subversive, a revolutionary? And to question the value of *shopping*, Oh-My-God, *nobody* did that! Was mother a traitor to Cosmos? Should Miranda report her? And to whom would she report her?

Should she report her mother to the President, the Glorious Leader?

Hail, all Hail!

Hail, all Hail!

Or maybe she could report Nikki to a Centurion if she saw one?

And wasn't it dangerous – very dangerous?

She decided after tossing and turning all night that she would not denounce Nikki.

After all, I love her – and she is my mother.

Nikki was not the only problem. Sometimes Miranda had a really weird feeling that she was not really herself, not really Miranda Hughes. One day, Miranda had been playing a scaly, a scary dragon with fangs and claws, in one of the International Video Tournaments, and she wanted to check that she was still herself, the effects had been so stunningly real; she had fought with some Chinese guy, an Upper Cosmos, in Domed Floating City Singapore who played a furry, and she had won, and he had demanded, and she had said, yes, that they could have a rematch. She liked him – he was really cute in his projected self-image – and she thought that maybe some time in the real space-time matrix they should meet – though this in truth rarely happened. Real travel was hazardous and rare – most fully elite certified human citizens or Cosmos stayed safely tucked within their own hygienic segregated Domed City, wherever it happened to be.

When the Tournament was over, she wanted to make sure that she was still Miranda and fully human – Miranda Hughes, Upper Cosmos, Class #1-A. So, she went into the bathroom and looked in the mirror – yes, the golden skin – her own skin not dragon scales – and the luxuriant blond hair which her mother called honey-gold – the dragon had no hair, just scales. "So, yes, I am me," thought Miranda, "I am human. I am still me."

But, suddenly, in her eyes the golden stars appeared – it was the first time she had seen them. She almost fainted. She took a deep breath and leaned close to the mirror. "Magnify please, five times." And, yes, there in her eyes were golden stars: they burst and exploded and put on a splendid display of fireworks! One last super-nova flare and they disappeared. *It was like they were inside her and wanted out.* Miranda frowned. They were beautiful, okay. But they were scary. They gave her the shivers.

Maybe I'm going blind!

She ran to her mother.

Nikki, who was sitting, neatly poised on her mobile floating backless graphic designer chair, swiveled around and asked what precisely the flares looked like. She listened carefully to Miranda's breathless description, and then said, with a big reassuring smile, "Oh, I wouldn't worry about them, darling! They sound beautiful!"

And so Miranda had gotten used to them – the golden flares, nebulae and supernovas and golden stars in her eyes. One particular pattern, if she enlarged it twenty times, looked precisely like the Andromeda galaxy. Weird!

Now, flying over the Dead Lands towards the exotic place called Hawaii, and wondering why in the world they were going there – in a Presidential airliner no less – Miranda glanced at her mother. Nikki had jet-black hair, chalk-white skin, while Miranda was blond, with blue eyes, and with permanently tanned skin – a sort of warm golden tone all over everywhere. Hmm! The whole thing was more than strange.

Miranda sometimes suspected that her mother was not her real mother.

As for her father – she had no idea who he might be. She was sure he must be a knight in shining armor, somebody bold, heroic, beautiful, brave, generous, and handsome!

But Nikki said that he was "gone": that was what she said "gone," just "gone." This was, evidently, a *non-subject*, one of the few; because Nikki was generally open to anything, more than open to anything.

Miranda often thought that someday, like a girl detective in an old story, she would get to the bottom of it. She would delve into ancient dusty archives, with yellow brittle paper piled up to the ceiling, she would cruise deep into the World Cloud Mind, she would visit exotic places – *real* places – hotels on beaches with palm trees, desert oases, and she would bribe servants, and peep through keyholes, she would ...

She would discover who her father was.

Miranda leaned against the window in her 78th-floor bedroom and watched an airship touch gently down on a platform on Sky Garden Tower, about a kilometer away.

She sighed. She had never been outside of the Dome of Elysium City, and she dreamed that someday she would be on an airship that would lift off, leave the dome, travel over the Dead Lands, and that she would see some of the great ruined and devastated world that was said to exist out there beyond the dome. It was a weird yearning, really.

She wondered where such strange thoughts – such exotic dreams – came from. They reminded her of ancient songs from her "Pop Cult of the Past" course, part of the platinum "Primitive America Culture" mind implant number 178-34, series B: There were two in particular that she really liked "Come Fly with Me" and "Beyond the Blue Horizon."

She pressed her face against the window of her studio-bedroom. Out there, the airships flew, beyond the Protective Dome of Elysium City, free, like the pirates of old who sailed in wooden ships on the frothy, blue, dolphin-rich seas, and landed on beaches among palm trees crowded with brilliantly flashy talkative parrots.

Miranda twitched her nose. She could almost smell those ancient tropical seas, those bronzed sweaty pirates, and, as she pressed her face against the glass, she frowned. In truth, life was not as adventurous as it should be. In Elysium City, even the air, even the air outside, which was not really outside since it was enclosed by the Dome, was filtered, purified, perfumed.

"This environment is totally controlled to assure your security and comfort."

That slogan of Elysium Dome City made Miranda grit her teeth. She wanted to scream. There was something so – she didn't know how to put it – something so cowardly, so mediocre, and *so unadventurous* about it.

It didn't seem to be like real life at all.

Life should be an adventure!

Life should be unpredictable and … heroic!

She mentioned her annoyance to Nikki who was reading a book – a real, antique book – by an old 20th century American author, Ernest Hemingway, *For Whom the Bell Tolls*.

"Everything is so controlled, mother, it's driving me crazy!"

"It's a bubble, darling," said Nikki, "It will burst."

"Elysium City will burst?"

"Everything does, sooner or later," said Nikki; she got up, came over, kissed Miranda on the forehead, tousled her hair, and went back, sat down, and returned to her book.

"Haven't you read that already?"

"Many times," said Nikki, and turned a page.

In truth, Nikki was certainly a mystery for Miranda, and in more than one way.

Nikki would stand to attention when the giant image of the President hovered over the city and when the anthem – *Hail to the Leader* – was played, and she would raise her right arm in the Leader's Salute, but she seemed to be less enthusiastic about it than Miranda would have liked.

Miranda stood to attention, her hand on her breast.

Miranda raised her right arm, stiffly extended, in The Leader's Salute.

Her heart swelled with pride.

The President, she thought, the Leader, the President who rules over us, who protects us, who lives only for us, who is the very image of Cosmos!

True, the President was extraordinarily handsome – tanned, and blue-eyed, with thick curly blond hair. The giant images and the smaller images, that were everywhere showed how handsome he was, and the huge statue that was on the New Broadway Square. In the holograms that floated in the air, day and night, he was the ideal image – a truly manly man – pure Cosmos!

And she had met him!

And her hand had touched his!

And his eyes had stared into hers!

And he had spoken to her, almost as if she were an old friend!

"Now, Miranda Hughes, you have won the highest youth medal there is – what do you think of that?"

"I am honored, Mr. President!"

"Well, this is just the beginning, Miranda Hughes. I am sure you will go on to greater and greater things."

And he patted her on the shoulder and went on to the next medal winner, another girl from Miranda's class.

He was the most glamorous man in the whole wide world Miranda could possibly think of. "Don't you think he is wonderful, mother? Isn't he wonderful?!"

"I suppose he's okay," Nikki said, once, "But there is a lot of blood on his hands."

"What?"

"And he's really divided, Miranda, he's almost a split personality."

"What?"

"Ignore that, sweet Miranda, I didn't say that, okay?"

"Yes, of course, mother, but ..."

How did her mother know these things about the President? And what did she mean by saying he was *divided*? What could that possibly mean?

Yes, Nikki was mysterious – and unpredictable.

Like, there was the time Nikki had surprised Miranda and Kit Candy in *flagrante delicto*, in red hot, burning, blazing sexual misbehavior – the punishment for such interclass Cosmos-Sub monkey business should have been – and officially was – death or loss of Cosmos status, or mind erasure.

Kit Candy was their cleaning girl, a cute tattooed Sub with some neat piercings and who came from the proletarian and sub-zones, in the lower depths of Elysium City.

The funny thing was – Kit had been Nikki's idea.

Miranda hated having a cleaning girl – *a Sub – Ugh! – Triple Ugh!* – enter their lives. She was furious, she was insulted – she was violated. It was disgusting! Miranda had *never* met a Sub and she didn't *want* to meet one!

"She's a Sub, mother, why are we letting a Sub into our home?"

"Subs are human too, Miranda."

"Subs are not Cosmos, mother, Subs are Subs."

"There's very little difference, Miranda."

"What?"

"You heard me, Miranda; there is very little difference between a Cosmos and a Sub."

"Subs are *poor*, Mother! They are filthy and uncouth; they *pollute* everything they touch! They pollute people. They are like the plague!"

"Poverty is not a crime, Miranda."

"This is outrageous, Mother, this is unspeakable, this is unorthodox; this is against the very *Credo of Cosmos*! Poverty is unclean; it is pollution. Poverty is *taboo*!"

"Calm down, Miranda."

"Subs are *filthy*. I will not have a Sub in my room!"

"Not all Subs are filthy, and my mind is made up!"

"Machines and nanorobots can do the work, mother!"

"Of course, machines and nanorobots and mini drones can do the work, Miranda, but I, personally, like the human touch," Nikki turned to concentrate on her work, "Just bear with me, Miranda."

"This is disgusting! This is obscene! I don't like this! This is Un-Cosmos!" Miranda pouted and stamped her feet; she went off into her room and steamed; she sat in front of her study-and-game console and fumed, in fact, she fumed so much it felt like smoke was coming out of her ears; she couldn't concentrate; she tried to focus on an interesting video about plate tectonics and the newest developments in the earth's electromagnetic field, but she couldn't; she fumed some more; she knew she was a snob; more than anything, she was proud of being a Cosmos, a conqueror, one of the elite, the rulers.

Cosmos are meant to rule, not to mingle!

Miranda's heart soared when she sang the Cosmos Anthem!

She headed back to Nikki's studio, her head buzzing with arguments of why they should not allow a Sub into their apartment, into their lives. All the kids despised Subs, and made jokes about them! It would be horrible to admit to Cyril Bedford or Greta Sampson or Karen Pak or Betty Ho that she and Nikki had allowed a Sub into their home; Miranda would never live it down! She'd be *polluted* by the filth; she'd bear the *stigmata of contact* with a Sub; she'd be an *outcast*!

"Mother …!" Miranda stormed into the studio.

"You'll like her, Nikki said, swiveling on her chair, infuriatingly calm, "Besides, you'll learn things from her."

"*Learn?* Whatever could I, Miranda Hughes, a Cosmos First Class, a Storm

Trooper Scout, a Presidential Medal Cosmos Girl Youth, learn from a Sub? The very idea is ridiculous, inappropriate, and insulting!"

"You will have responsibilities someday, Miranda, so you have to learn how the world works – and what people, real people, are like."

"How the world works! How will I ever learn that from a Sub! The whole idea is grotesque!"

"You'll see."

"No, I won't see!"

"Yes, I believe you will, see, I mean," and Nikki gave Miranda one of her seraphic, imperturbable Nikki smiles.

"Mother! Oh, you are terrible! I can't stand this! I hate you!" Miranda stormed away. "I hate you!"

And so it was: Miranda Hughes met Kit Candy.

Kit was a very tricky person, it turned out.

At first, Kit seemed to be a normal Sub, without big words or complex thoughts and she perfectly mimicked the mindless totally immersed in the cliché-drenched Sub-Consumer-Vulpine-Volpe language that was said to be the lingo of Subs. Kit was really something, with her short thick fine black hair, chalk-white skin, her entirely, scrupulously hairless body, her big grey eyes, finely sculpted, rather boyish face, sometimes her head shaved, just the pale stubble, often covered in tattoos and pierced in the most interesting places with rings and little chains and plugs.

It was the most disgusting thing Miranda had ever seen!

Yuk! Yuk! And double Yuk!

The Cosmos Youth Movement motto was "The Body is Sacred; not to be scarred, pierced, or doodled upon!"

Yuk, how could anyone, *even* a Sub, do such things!

Only later did Miranda discover that the tattoos could be easily removed and that the rings and chains and plugs could too.

One afternoon when Kit had finished her chores, doing the garden seasonal shrubbery and floral refit on the balcony, Kit took off her clothes and showed Miranda the whole array of markings, tattoos, piercings, and the metal rings, loops, and plugs.

"Gosh," said Miranda; she was fascinated and appalled. She decided she should try to communicate with Kit. After all, "A Cosmos Storm Trooper Scout is never at a loss in any situation!"

Miranda knew that with Kit you had to talk about styles and the newest sub fashions. Miranda thought that if she used really short simple words and simple linear declarative sentences, Kit might just understand.

Kit said she was going to do body sculpture too. "It's the newest new thing. Holly Holiday changed her nose, her breasts, her lips, her eyes, her ears, her hips. So, like, I think I'll, like, try it, like, you know, like."

"Who is Holly Holiday?" Miranda knew she was totally ignorant of Sub Cult. It was really embarrassing. Kit had a dragon down all of her back, and she had flames coming up from her sex, and flooding over her belly, and she had a steel ring in her belly-button.

"Can I touch?"

"Sure, kid, go ahead, do it! I'm here to be touched."

Kit also had rather big breasts. Miranda asked if they were real.

"Yeah, I haven't had an enhancement yet, but Hot Doggy got hers enhanced it was on the Foxy Reel Tinsel Net so I'll enhance too, it's like, it's, like cool." Kit said.

Miranda felt the breasts. "Awesome," she said.

"You use big words, Miranda," said Kit, "I don't always understand you."

"I don't understand you either," said Miranda, "Who is Hot Doggy?"

"Hot Doggy, you don't know who Hot Doggy is? Why girl, where you been hanging? She's, like, cool. Hot doggy is dry ice. She steams you up, numbs your fingers, gels your tongue, & freezes your lips. She's the latest cool."

"Oh," said Miranda. Subs were usually limited in their vocabularies. They were not supposed to have over 2,000 active-use words, roughly. Fashion words that came and went didn't count.

"Words carry ideas like shit carries diseases," Robber Mudcock of the Vulpine Volpe Gutter Slime Net had once declared, "So we keep intelligent words away from the Subs. We spy on them too, to tailor our shit to theirs, and vice-versa, naturally. If you build an outhouse people will sit in it."

The Sub sub-culture was designed to exclude reflection. The *Past* was a forbidden subject for Subs; what went before was of no interest. The Past was not cool. It was, like, history, man! It was, like, obscene, vaguely obscene, like dirty, like *pollution* somehow, like in bad taste, really not cool, not sexy, a downer, like wearing last season's T-shirt, it was obscene like old age and like a leaky anus, dribbling shit, is obscene.

By accident, Miranda overheard Kit talk on her sub mob phone.

"Yeah, so I was like, fuck you, and she was like, how can he fucking do this?

Like, and he, the fucker, he was like, fuck off, you fucking bitch, you fucking fornicating cow ..."

...

"Yeah, he actually fucking said 'fucking fornicating cow,' the fucker."

...

"Yeah, I know, it's a fucking bitch."

...

"No, so like, I go, I'm fucking gone, and he's, like, fucking really? *Like fucking, really?* he fucking says, and I go: *Yeah, fucking really,* and I say, 'So *you* fuck off,' which means he's got to fuck literally off in real space-time because it's my fucking pod pad he's fucking camping his fucking ass in, so out he fucking goes and he turns his fucking skinny ass at me, and farts."

...

"Yeah, I fucking swear, he fucking did."

...

"A real fucking real fart, a gigantic fucking ripple tidal wave of a fart, it was like awesome and awful! Like so total – last year's garlic!"

...

"Last thing I see is his buck-naked, sweaty back, pimples, and blackheads, and those cool tattoos up the spine. It all, like, makes me, looking back, like, sad – tattoos, his tattoos, my tattoos, disappearing down the fucking stairs, his pimple-and-rash-packed, acne-splattered, fucking back, and then, like all that fucking stuff we did it together, like, I like to remember stuff, like him leaving like that – gone, gone, and gone!"

...

"I know fucking memories are fucking sick!"

...

"Yeah, I know! Don't I know! Doctor Professor Herr Ort on the Volpe says, like, remembering stuff is, like, *bad*, if you don't transcend, you remember, and if you remember, you don't fucking well *transcend*, like there's no, like, fucking *closure*, like, you get what I mean, you gotta slam the fucking door on the fucking past, which is so, so totally yesterday, which is a true bugger, you fucking well see what I fucking mean, right?"

...

Miranda thought: how awful, how horrible, how limited Sub Talk and Sub Minds were! Ugh! It might be infectious! This was unhygienic; this was a health hazard! She was in a rage. She could feel the smoke spurting out her ears like in a cartoon: *I'm going to ask Nikki to fire this creature right away, but right away, like so now! Like yesterday!*

Kit blipped the conversation off. She spotted Miranda who had been too hypnotized to move – and whose disgust was clearly visible, shimmering and simmering on her face; and whose thought was clear: *We really must get rid of this creature. She would talk to her mother, she would …*

Kit winked. "So, eavesdropping, are we, then, Oh, Divine Cosmos Child?"

"I … ah … I …" Miranda blushed.

"Ah, dear Cosmos," Kit declaimed, standing up, and striking a very theatrical pose, like something Miranda had seen in a hologram performance of *Richard III*, "Dear Cosmos, do you understand one iota of that of which I just now spoke – the loss of true love, the haunting memories, the recurring tears, the desperate gnashing of teeth, the sick yearning, the vertigo-like nostalgia, and how it weaves in, this spiritual sickness I mean, this aching absence, with the endless irrevocable passage of time – the autumn leaves tumbling – youthful beauty fading – a tapestry of memory and regret and craving, such as Marcel Proust might have danced an arabesque upon – where there are so many paths in the dark deep woods not taken, so many promises denied, as the snow falls and deep-fraught, scary, infinite night draws in, so many lives not chosen, so many selves that never came to be, stillborn in the mind, hunches that faded, intimations never explored, so many experiences forever forgone, so many things, too, and loved ones, too, yes, loved ones too, golden lads and lasses, that shone so bright, beacons of promise, now all gone to ashes, and that are nevermore, and, trapped in one's own mind are these memories, that can never be shared, entombed in the solitary anguish of beauty seen, and of longing, each of us being, essentially, solipsistic. Such is love, right – huh?"

Miranda stood there with her mouth open, "I …"

"You want the back story – admit it, Cosmos, you're curious!"

"I, well, I thought that maybe .."

"Cool it, kid. I can fess up. It was all about when I broke up with Sniggy Propane. That's the back story. He was a jerk. He was the jerk of jerks, the Absolute Supremo in the Jerk Department. Why I fall for total jerks I'll never understand! Sniggy tried to feel up Fanny Dakin, my neighbor down in Sub Land. Fanny told me. She said he had an extremely *vulgar* – 'crude' I think was the word she used – she might even have said '*inept*' – way of going about it, the feeling up, I mean. I wanted an excuse to dump Sniggy Propane anyway. His conversation – when he *had* any – was *boring*: I mean *boring* beyond belief, mind-fucking numbing, paralyzing, like talking to an ice cube. And you can only stare at a beautiful case of bubbly acne and scarlet adolescent rash for so long. So, there it was – the perfect excuse to terminate with Sniggy: the Fanny-feel-up. But I felt I should display some emotion. I mean after all it was the disintegration of a meaningful relationship, both carnal and spiritual, right? 'Fuck,' by the way, is common currency, down in Sub-Land, you know, an intensifier, it sounds good if you put 'fuck' in everywhere, especially if you don't know what to say. It's a place-holder too; it takes the place of an utter vacuum of feeling and cogitation and culture. It spares the trouble of thinking. Where no thought is, Fuck is bound to be! It makes up 90% of the lexicon out in the Burbs among Burbites too, I'm told."

"Oh," said Miranda.

"Now, like a good little Sub, I've got to get back to work." Kit turned her back and began washing the windows. The windows, of course, could wash themselves, but, as Nikki had declared, she wanted the *human touch*.

Miranda watched Kit stretch up and sweep the cloth back and forth and she listened to the dry clean squeak of the bio-sponge against the glass. A string of foam dribbled down Kit's arm. Kit's vertebrae and shoulder-blades were visible, straining, under her thin white T-shirt; the nape of her neck seemed, oh so fragile and delicate and fine. Her hot pants molded her bum, neatly, curves worthy of a Cherubim. It was like Kit's body was sculpted in clay or pen or pencil or something and it was worming its way – *dark, secret love* – into Miranda's tummy and heart: *the lineaments of desire …*

Breathless!

Miranda held her breath; she was feeling something strange.

What was it?

Breathless – and an extra heartbeat too!

Doctor Professor Herr Ort gave advice on the Volpe Screen so Miranda knew about sex and romance though she suspected that much of what Doctor Ort preached was pure Volpe Bull Shit designed specifically for Subs and Outer Darkness Burbites. Miranda was atremble. She wanted to touch Kit all over; she suddenly found Kit really sexy, one-dimensional maybe, but maybe not, indeed, maybe Kit was the reverse of one-dimensional – an exponentially increasing probability – and she was certainly passionate, edgy, and risky. Miranda wanted Kit to like her – and, just maybe, to touch her all over too. It gave her a funny tickly feeling just to think about it.

In a way, Miranda was jealous, and she realized she was jealous and she disapproved of jealousy – how confusing! And what was she jealous of – Kit's relationship with pimply Sniggy Propane?

Was this sex?

Was this about sex?

Lots of Subs were sterilized and regularly inspected and continuously monitored – sexual truants were permanently tagged with monitor implants transmitting continuous data and setting off body alarm bells – a pulsating bright red warming light emanating from the Sub's pubis and the end of the Sub's nose if anything unhygienic or socially untoward was about to happen – so sex would not be dangerous, anyway, or, rather, the sex they might have, as girls, would not be dangerous; girl-on-girl sex was not dangerous, though the *Mind-Sex For Young Cosmos Instruction Booklet Implant* said you gotta be careful about all contacts with bio-beings of whatever kind and class – *Merely touch a Sub and you may become a Sub!*

Nikki was right.

Miranda did like Kit Candy and she did learn lots and lots of things from Kit, perhaps too many things.

Late one afternoon, with the air outside just turning that delicious rose and pink pre-dusk color, Nikki had come home and had surprised Miranda and Kit "making out."

Disaster! Catastrophe! Apocalypse!

It was all because Miranda had expressed an interest in sex.

And this is how that particular total disaster came about:

Miranda had expressed an interest in sex because Miranda was really impressed with Cyril Bedford – on the boy-girl Cosmos First Class soccer team – Cyril was the most beautiful creature on the whole team and once after practice he had pinned Miranda down on the soccer field – she'd let him – and he had kissed her on the lips – in full view of everybody! And he said, "I love you, Miranda" and then he got up, turned red in the face, and ran away. Miranda wanted to be able to really impress Cyril if another magic moment were to present itself.

When Miranda confessed all of this to Kit, Nikki was out at some important business meeting and not due back until dusk. Miranda was alone with Kit. The apartment was all theirs.

"Okay, I get it, I see your problem," said Kit, who that day was utterly – and mysteriously – without tattoos or piercings, a totally pure chalk-white ephebe, with that shock of jet-black hair, cut short pixie style, "I do see your problem. Well, here's what we do!"

And she had obliged by giving Miranda a detailed demonstration, about kissing and about various ways one body could make another body quiver and tremble, and it was a pretty encyclopedic demonstration, really, at least so it seemed to Miranda.

"He's called Cyril?" Kit grinned.

"Yes," for some reason Miranda blushed.

"Cyril," Kit was almost laughing, "Does he wear an ascot or what?"

"Well …"

"Okay, I'm Cyril and you're you."

Then, later on:

"Now, you're Cyril; and I'm you," Kit grinned, "Cyril, Cyril, Cyril: If you say it over enough it almost sounds normal."

And so, the lesson had begun:

"Okay," said Kit, "take off your clothes. No, better idea, I'll take off your clothes for you."

"Okay," said Miranda.

"Unpeeling the fruit is a very important part of the ritual."

"Oh."

"Utmost respect must be shown." Kit's lips moved along Miranda's collarbone. Kit's jet-black hair smelt like sweet gold lemons.

"Oh."

"Each tantalizing feature and detail must have its moment." Kit slipped Miranda's T-shirt off one shoulder, slowly, millimeter by millimeter, creeping, creeping, and creeping, tiny bits of skin being uncovered, with a tender exploratory nibble here and there.

"I see." Miranda shivered.

"Moments of high drama must be allowed for," in one swift move Kit suddenly tore Miranda's T-shirt away, tossed it over her shoulder, and took Miranda's face between her hands, and kissed her.

"Oh," Miranda breathed, kissing and then nibbling back.

"It takes two to tango."

"Yes, oh, yes."

"Clichés, darling First-Class Cosmos Child, are the spice of life," Kit was now using her tongue to considerable effect; the dark gray eyes narrowed like those of a cat, she looked up at Miranda.

"Yes, Kit, oh, yes."

"Without mottos, sayings, aphorisms, and platitudes, we would be lost," the dark gray eyes blinked, and, under the charcoal eyebrows, they sparkled – *Mischief perhaps?*

"Yes, Kit, oh, yes."

"We would be adrift in a vast uncoded sea, no signs – no stars to guide us."

"Yes, really, yes, I mean, I see; I do see."

So, Kit had taken off Miranda's clothes very slowly, one item at a time, with kisses and touching in between, and a few moments of carefully chosen accelerated drama. It had been quite an experiment and very exciting and Miranda had had what she considered must be her first real interpersonal orgasm, or maybe, a ripple of orgasms – three or four – is that possible? – because it happened a couple of times and one of them didn't stop for quite a while – she screamed several times – and it left her feeling almost dizzy and like she was limp all over and wanted to go to sleep, and while they were still lying there, Kit stroking Miranda's hair and Miranda lazily stroking and occasionally kissing Kit's breasts, Kit saying, "You are good, Cosmos Girl, you are really good," both of them naked on the rug in Miranda's bedroom studio when …

"Well …"

Then they were lying on their tummies, side by side; then on their sides, staring into each other's eyes.

"You have these golden sparkles that suddenly appear in your eyes," Kit said, touching Miranda's forehead. "They're like stars and comets! They are really cool, absolutely awesome!"

"They give me the shivers," Miranda blushed.

"They're utterly beautiful," Kit's hand was caressing with the tips of her fingers Miranda's eyebrows, her forehead, playing with strands of golden hair.

"My mother told me not to worry about them."

"Your mother is right."

Then, minutes later, both of them were there, Kit and Miranda, stark naked, on their knees, face to face, nipples just touching, lips brushing against lips, on the rug in Miranda's bedroom-studio, when – surprise!

There was a knock on the door and, without waiting for an answer, the door opened, and Nikki was standing there, "Miranda, I just wanted to …"

"Oh!" Miranda turned crimson.

"Well …" said Nikki, gazing at them, her briefcase still in her hand.

Oh, my God! Miranda's mind went into a tailspin of dreadful possibilities, I'm going to be grounded, definitely grounded, forever grounded, grounded for all of eternity!

"Ms. Hughes, ah," Kit was struggling to stand up, "Ms. Hughes, I, ah, I can explain … It's not Miranda. It's my fault. It's absolutely all my fault, I –"

Nikki raised a hand, which clearly meant: Silence!

There followed a dramatic pause. Miranda held her breath; she noticed that Kit's face – usually so pale, so composed – was turning crimson.

Nikki tilted her head to one side, "I've had a rather busy day. I'm going to make some coffee, would either of you girls like some? Or tea – tea is also a distinct possibility. It's very refreshing – tea …"

Both girls – now crouching on all fours – nodded, wide-eyed, and solemn and, to tell the truth, stunned.

Nikki exited, and, softly, closed the door behind her.

"Wow," said Kit, her eyes still round.

"Yes," said Miranda, "that's the way Nikki is."

"Maybe she's going to put poison in my coffee," said Kit.

"No," Miranda was thoughtful, "No, that's not really mother's style."

"Maybe she'll fire me, get me erased."

"No, I don't think so."

Ten minutes later, they were fully dressed and having coffee and biscuits, sitting on Nikki and Miranda's private terrace by their private swimming pool, looking out over the misty spires and towers of Elysium City. The breeze was slightly lemon-flavored – truly poetic – "*Courtesy of Givenchy*" said the blinking, flirting Hologram Bio Float-Bys – and Nikki didn't mention the sex scene at all. And she never mentioned it again, except, occasionally she would give Miranda a sly, knowing look. Well, once she did say, "Sex and love are like high explosives, Miranda – handle with care: people can get hurt; even you can get hurt – and of course you can hurt other people."

"Like Kit?"

"Exactly – like Kit."

"You don't want me to hurt Kit."

"Yes, I don't want you to hurt Kit."

That afternoon, with the three of them sitting on the terrace, like Kit was a real person and a Cosmos just like them, as if Kit was a friend and equal and not a Sub and Dollar Token Slave (DTS), Nikki asked Kit – not at all in a patronizing way – lots of questions, probing questions, about Kit's life, about the life of a Sub, about what Kit did for entertainment, about what her flat was like, about Kit's adventures in the Sin Zone, about …

"Why don't you show Miranda some of the places you know best, Kit, I think it would broaden her horizons."

Kit stared, and gulped some coffee, almost dribbling it on her chin, and said, "You think so, Ms. Hughes?"

"Call me Nikki, Kit." Nikki refilled Kit's coffee cup.

Nikki actually suggested that Kit show Miranda some of the parts of Elysium City Cosmos rarely admitted to having visited and rarely did visit – the Sin Zone, the Religious Bazaar, and some of the plumbing, like the sewers, and the old drowned canals and subway lines, mythical dead places like Soho, and Tribeca, and a narrow sunken festering canal lined with rats which was once called Wall Street.

And so, one day and far into one night Kit took Miranda on a guided tour of the sub-worlds of Elysium City.

It turned out Kit knew every nook and cranny, every secret tunnel, every elevator shaft, service elevator, freight elevator, and ventilation shaft and cable tunnel, and, well, just about everything.

"I'm a sewer rat," said Kit, "It's my hobby."

"This is … awesome!" Miranda didn't know what else to say, and she had discovered that Kit had a big vocabulary and knew a whole lot of stuff – and not only about the sewers.

"It's like being an explorer, sort of," said Kit.

"Like Magellan or Columbus."

"Yeah, or like Captain Cook or Ibn Battuta, the Muslim guy; he covered about 75,000 miles, 30 years of travel, camel, horse, or on foot."

"It's sort of like going down into caves, like with stalactites and stalagmites," said Miranda, staring up at the low stone arches and concrete ceilings of the tunnel, dripping with moss and lichen and strange humid life forms.

"Yeah, we're speleologists – maybe anthropologists and biologists too, I mean there are so many unique life forms down here."

"There sure are!"

"But, lower down," Kit put her hand on Miranda's arm, "lower down, way below the Sex Zone, and down under the Religion Bazaar, it gets dangerous – they say there are mutants – dangerous mutants, not cute ones – and things like *ghouls* – not nice cuddly ghouls, but nasty cannibal ghouls – in the sewers and the drowned subway system. I went down there a couple of times, but that was enough. I got back out fast. It was really spooky."

"Wow!" Miranda thought this was awesome – there was adventure here in Elysium City, not just in the past, not just in books or videos, and not just out in the Burbs and Badlands.

"It's even rumored that the Control Center of the World Cloud Mind has its main lair down here somewhere," Kit said, "You'd think the Cloud would be up in the sky, but it's actually, so the rumor goes, deep under Elysium City; it is huge, the Cloud, and they say it's alive, a bio-silicon synthesis, organic and nonorganic, and it's evolving, its tentacles are spreading out. I'm not even sure anybody controls it anymore. I've heard whispers that it's gone AWOL, it's become its own master."

"Wow!"

"But that is, if true, obviously totally classified, I mean totally, we could be erased or neutered just for whispering about it," Kit shot Miranda a sly conspiratorial glance, "but," and here she whispered, "I think I even know where the World Mind Cloud is!"

"You do?"

"Yes," Kit leaned close, "But, don't mention this to anyone. It could get us erased or neutered."

"Erased or neutered, wow," Miranda was amazed. Kit was extraordinarily intelligent for a Sub – they were supposed to have restricted and censored thoughts and limited vocabularies – but Kit spoke like a Cosmos, only even better, she used colorful language when she wanted to, with jargon and argot and swear words and technical stuff, and she seemed to know everything about the lower depths, it was thrilling!

There were types of people down in the Sin Zone, for example, that Miranda had never seen, or even imagined – people designed, or redesigned, to give other people erotic – or sexual – pleasure.

"They are weird," she was staring at a Sex Toy Clown Woman.

"Body redesign is usually punishment," Kit said, "They get mind-erased, their personalities and memories gone, and redesigned, mentally, physically, and their desires are remolded too, a total refit and retrofit. It's not only punishment – it's also profit. They get re-designed, so they can be used to make money. There are *no free lunches*, you know, or so they say in *Indoctrination 101*."

Miranda gaped at the passing parade. It was fascinating. There were clowns and acrobats, and geishas, and musclemen, and snake ladies, and guys called gigolos, and, tattooed monsters, and pole-dancer strippers, and dominatrixes, and French cafés, and Oriental Harems, and, gosh, it was just endless.

As for the Religious Bazaar, four levels further down, deep under the surface, that was even more weird!

"There's a guy down here I really like," Kit said, as they entered a deep, arched, smoky tunnel, where the damp dark walls leaned in close.

"Oh, who's he?" Miranda was drinking it all in – the musty smells, the dripping walls, the candles, the crazies of all kinds, the hawkers, the preachers, the nudists, the tents, the nuns, the turbans, the niqabs, the burqas, the flat-rimmed black hats, the shaven heads, the hairy heads, the curls, the long stringy locks, the Iroquois cuts – black garb, orange garb, crimson garb, pointed hats, skullcaps. It was the total opposite of sanitized, hygienic, agnostic, aesthetically controlled, secular life up in the towers of Elysium. Life was much bigger and richer than anyone could conceive!

"He's a bearded guy, thin, dark, and really gentile – but he's mad underneath – I don't mean mad crazy, I mean, mad furious – mad about the way things are, about the way people are, but he hides it. He keeps his cool. He talks in parables and aphorisms and stuff. He's awesome," Kit was leading Miranda along the bank of a dark dark underground canal, "But I don't see him anywhere right now."

"He does sound cool," said Miranda.

"He is, but you know who's also cool – really cool – your mother is really cool," said Kit, stopping, leaning over and giving Miranda a kiss on the lips while a conga line of Buddhist monks swayed past them, chanting and holding up candles which made smoky whirling circles on the ceiling of the old underground canal; in the distance, echoing, someone was wailing something sacred in Latin – or maybe it was Greek.

"Yes, she is," said Miranda, catching her breath.

"In fact," said Kit, taking Miranda's hand, "Nikki's more than cool – she's mysterious. There's something about her …"

Another group was passing by, jingling bells, chanting something about Hairy Krishna, Hairy Krishna, Hairy Krishna …

"Yes, there is – something about her," said Miranda, "She may be my mother, but I haven't got her figured out at all – but I'm glad she's what she is, whatever that is."

"So am I," said Kit, "I mean, just think, she could have killed us!"

"Yes," Miranda covered her mouth; she had to giggle at the memory: the two of them on the rug, stark naked, and Nikki, in her synthetic black silk business suit, impeccable, looking at the two of them, and not blinking, not for a nanosecond – stern-looking at first, then flashing that sudden, bright, all-encompassing smile.

Miranda came back from the tour of the lower depths with a bit more of a crush on Kit Candy – it was almost love, yes, in a way, it was love – Kit knew so many weird things and she was so ... so exotic, with the on-again-off-again tattoos and piercings and that perfect pale skin and those sweet lips.

"It was good?" Nikki looked up from her drawing board.

"It was fantastic, really fantastic!"

"Kit is a fine girl," said Nikki a couple of days later, "She's a good influence. You and she should hang out more. She knows things we don't know."

Well, this was weirder and weirder, thought Miranda, who really was a Cosmos, and the proudest of Cosmos.

She actually couldn't understand how she, Miranda Hughes, a Cosmos First Class – and a Super Cosmos Girl Scout – could have a Sub as her friend, her best friend, and maybe even more, like, in some ways, it was, yes, it was love ...

Yes, it was love; they were lovers.

Kit Candy and Miranda Hughes – creatures from two entirely different worlds – had become really close friends, and they shared lots of stuff – like mind-implant lessons, skill implants, courses on the history of science, on biology, on Shakespeare's plays, on the history of Pop, the music of the Spiced Up Mushrooms, a few extra sessions of sex instruction, really spicy, totally thrilling, and unbridled fun, and just about everything.

Miranda was enthralled with Kit. She secretly thought Kit should be upgraded and become a Cosmos, but she didn't know whether such a thing was possible, and she didn't mention the idea. She vaguely suspected that Kit might be insulted. She was going to ask Nikki what she thought of the idea, but for some reason, she was shy about doing so.

So, Kit had helped Miranda discover life. There was so much adventure in the world – even in Elysium City, though you had to go down into the lower depths to find it.

Outside Elysium City, it would be even better.

But you needed special permission – a whole lot of "bureaucratic nonsense"

Nikki called it – to leave the protection of the Domed City and Miranda was not old enough to go on her own.

She often wished she could escape from the Dome and go out into the badlands; she wished she could meet one of those pirates face-to-face! She'd show them! And now …

And, now, here she was, in the Dead Lands – she and Nikki, alone, dead people lying all around them – Janet Wong, the really kind stewardess with the southern accent and big smile, the gruff pilot who told jokes, the other pretty young woman, Kathy Sanchez, who offered them drinks – and now hungry mutants and maybe pirates were headed their way. This, Miranda suspected, would not be a game.

In fact, it even seemed, now that Miranda had time to think about it, that the crash was part of something bigger.

Maybe something really big – a real adventure – was going on, like the end of the world Nikki had talked about.

During the flight, the pilot came on the speaker to talk to them – to Nikki directly, as if she *owned* the President's plane!

And that was when there were the first hints of trouble.

"Ms. Hughes, we're heading south to evade what looks like some difficulty on our flight path," said the pilot's voice; then Janet came back and gave the news personally.

"I see, I guess we'll be over Mexico then," Nikki didn't seem disturbed by this news.

"Yes, Ms. Hughes, we'll be traveling along the old border, or close to it."

"Interesting – call me Nikki, by the way, Janet. And Miranda is Miranda."

Miranda looked up and grinned.

Janet smiled, "Thank you, Ms. Hughes – I mean, Nikki, thank you, Miranda."

Janet left them and walked forward.

A few minutes later there was another announcement by the pilot, "The World Mind Cloud is down, Ms. Hughes."

"What – how can that be?" Nikki had noticed that, just a few moments earlier, her fashion magazine hologram – an article about the newest in Bangladeshi swimsuits – had faded into sparks and then nothing; but she thought it was just a local blip; she had a real, old-fashioned book with her, so she just slipped it out of her purse, and began to flip the pages …

Miranda's Info Voice had faded away too; she was listening to the pilot's voice; maybe this was the beginning of a *real* adventure!

"Does this sound like it might be exciting, Miranda?" Nikki turned to Miranda and smiled, "A real adventure?"

"Yes, it is exciting. Maybe it's dangerous!"

"Yes, you're right – maybe it's dangerous." Nikki smiled again and picked up her book, *A History of Renaissance Art*.

Then, about five minutes later, the pilot's voice came on again, "L.A. and San Francisco are no longer responding."

"Really," Nikki said, "that happened earlier, didn't it, yesterday; and –"

The pilot's voice, which sounded strange, said, "They say a wave of darkness is sweeping over the land."

"*A wave of darkness is sweeping over the land* ... Whatever does that mean?" Nikki for the first time seemed concerned. Her eyebrow arched; she bit her lip; she put the book back in its pouch, "The man is talking poetry or metaphysics; I don't like this."

A few minutes later Nikki was invited up to speak to the Captain.

Miranda asked, "What did he tell you? What did he say?"

"He thinks we're in trouble," Nikki said, sitting down, "He would have headed back to Elysium City, but it's too late now, he says."

"Too late ...?"

"Yes. He was very strange, the co-pilot too. Janet says she's never seen them like this. Janet thinks they are frightened, actually, 'terrified' was the word she used," Nikki put her hand on Miranda's hand. "The pilot said, and the words really struck me, he said, 'We are headed into the heart of darkness, Ms. Hughes, we are headed into the heart of darkness.'"

"It sounds," Miranda frowned, "like the man is possessed."

"Yes, it does, doesn't it," Nikki gave Miranda a sharp little smile. "Brooding evil spirits are rising up from the dark backward abyss of time."

"Gosh."

"Yes, you're quite right – Gosh!"

A few moments later, Janet brought them a snack. Orange juice, water, coffee, and lobster and chicken salad sandwiches.

Nikki glanced up, "So, Janet, what do you think is really going on?"

Janet paused and then she said in a really low voice, "I really don't know what I think, Ms. Hughes – I mean, Nikki – I really don't know. Usually, the pilots leave everything to the Cloud. But now nothing is working: nothing at all. Something very strange is happening. We are on our own."

"Presidential Super-Liner 47," it said on the big piece of wreckage that had careened over the sand dunes, cart-wheeled and exploded, and was now leaning against the steep granite wall of the valley.

It had all exploded …

It had all exploded and Miranda, still strapped in her seat, blinked, thinking, maybe this is death, death finally come! But it's not supposed to, not for me, not yet, I'm young, I'm thirteen, not quite fourteen.

It had happened so fast, there was hardly any time to think.

Not even seconds, maybe nanoseconds …

"Please fasten your seat belts," the smooth female emergency voice had said, "and please lower your body protection pods. Thank you. The Presidential Special Super-Liner 47 hopes you have a pleasant landing. All Hail, the Leader, All Hail, the Leader! Now, please fasten your seat belts …"

Then, through static, some mike must have been left open, and Miranda heard the pilot's voice: "This is unprecedented. I don't know …"

"Damned guidance systems have just failed!"

"Action the automatic crash beacon, now!"

"Yes, yes, beacon actuated. I mean if we don't crash, it –"

"Look at that … and you doubt we're going to crash?"

"Right! God help us!"

"Left motor – it's not responding."

"What about manual …?"

"No response … Manual won't engage …"

The pilot's voice came on the Intercom, "Ms. Hughes, we've lost computer controls and we are getting contradictory information from all the sensors, please get ready to … we can no longer … I'm sorry … but …"

His voice was replaced by static.

Janet came into their compartment. "Ms. Hughes, Nikki, Miranda – we seem to have lost all our electronic controls, please lower your body shield pods and put yourself in the safety position. Thank you!" She gave them her bright smile and disappeared.

"This does sound serious." Nikki was not smiling.

Miranda looked out the window. The engines were on fire. She leaned forward. She could see flames. It was awesome!

This was an *adventure*!

Everything rattled. The coffee cup danced across the tray. The pages of the book – yes, book, an old-fashioned book, she had been reading before she became hypnotized by the sights out the window, fluttered. The book took off, flew up, smashed against the ceiling, and dropped straight to the floor.

Outside the window, it was night, it was dark, they were still over the Dead Lands – no lights below and no signs of civilization; in fact, there was no civilization, only bandits, smugglers, mutants, slaves.

It rattled, luggage bounced in the luggage compartments.

"Miranda, lower your body pod," said Nikki.

Outside the compartment, a trolley broke loose, ran down the aisle, and exploded, almost exploded, everything flying every which way. It was all happening so fast. Miranda was fascinated.

"Miranda!"

"Yes, mother, I'll lower my body pod."

"Now! Miranda!"

Miranda fastened her seat belt. She pushed the button, lowering the body pod, a titanium Plexiglas Ultra capsule that totally enclosed her. She gripped the armrests. Through the translucent body shield, she could see concern in her mother's eyes, her mother's beautiful eyes.

"Miranda, it will be fine." Nikki smiled, as she lowered her own body shield.

There was another explosion.

Everything was a blur.

Through a wave of static, the pilot's voice said, "I'm sorry Ms. Hughes, but we're going down."

"Lower your head, Miranda. Put your head down, on your knees. You know, the way Janet showed you. And push the high-pressure button – Now!"

"I love you, mother," Miranda said.

"I love you too, Miranda, and I always will."

Everything exploded – Miranda was caught in a whirling maelstrom, twirling around, upside down, right side up, sideways, upside down, dizzying vertigo, then thundering darkness. She blinked.

And here we are …

How it happened, she had no idea. But she and Nikki were still alive, unless of course, she was dreaming, or already dead, and having a dream of life, now that she was dead, but she had no idea whether the dead dreamed or not;

she suspected that, really, the dead probably did nothing at all, just lazed and lolled away the centuries and millennia in pure oblivion, conscious of nothing, non-existent, not even a whiff of French fries or perfume of lilies or glimmer of neon or touch of a warm hand or soft lips to make them conscious.

It could, of course, be a dream that was only taking a second – while seeming to last for hours, a dream caught in the instant of death, the illusion of a whole life contained in a nanosecond!

But right now, it didn't feel like a dream. It felt messy and real and physical and slow-moving and not at all symbolic, not like a dream.

Once the thunder of the crash subsided, and the whirling stopped and everything was still, Miranda had unbuckled herself from the ejection seat and pulled the lever unlocking the Body Pod – she had read the instructions carefully. She paused for a second and pushed it open. The Body Pod had somehow landed right side up.

She stepped out, stretched, and looked around. They were in a wide, flat-bottomed ravine or valley, with sharp granite cliffs on both sides that ran all the way down the ravine, which widened out into a valley; beyond the flaming wreckage, sand dunes and low pebbled ridges stretched away into darkness. The sky was dark, high above, veiled by dust and flames.

Nikki was a few meters away, sitting, eyes open and blinking, inside her Body Pod, still strapped in. Nikki looked undamaged, even unruffled. "Mother, are you alright?"

"Yes, darling, I'm fine." Nikki's voice came, muffled, through the Body Pod shield. Nikki unbuckled the seat belt, pulled the manual lever, pushed open the Body Pod shield, stepped out, and stood up, stretched, murmuring, "Ouch," and then saying "Oh, no"

The body of a stewardess – it was Kathy Sanchez – lay a few feet away, sprawled spread-eagled stomach down; Kathy's head was missing.

Farther away, Janet was buckled in, her pod smashed open, and the safety seat on fire.

Closer by, a steward, Guy, was burning to death, flames still flickering.

Nikki and Miranda tried to save Janet and Guy – in vain.

And, strangely, after plunging into the infernos of fire, neither Miranda nor Nikki had been harmed by the flames.

"Miranda," Nikki knelt in front of her daughter. Half of Nikki's face was masked in charcoal; there was a thick round black clown-like smudge on the end of her nose. "Miranda," Nikki hugged Miranda, holding her close, pressing her face against Miranda's tummy, "Miranda!"

Later Nikki and Miranda explored the ravine, poking into the wreckage. No one else had survived.

"We were in the high-security compartment, and we had the special Body Pods," said Nikki, crouching over the body of a steward, a very friendly young man. His body was unmarked, but dead, definitely dead. Nikki took her finger off his neck. "He was so young!" She stood up, "It is unfair, but … we are alive."

"Yes." Miranda wiped away a tear. She hardly felt anything. She was not yet in mourning. Feeling would come later, she figured, when she had time to sit down and think. Right now, everything was unreal. Like, this could not really have happened, could it?

Nikki took a Kleen-Koth out of her purse and cleared away the smudge of burnt rubber from her cheek and the blob from the point of her nose. "Did I get it all?"

"Yes, mother, you look perfect." And it was true. Nikki had done a perfect job; the face that had starred in movies and been up on huge electro-posters covering whole mobile walls and airships and Float-Bys was once again perfect – just as it always had been.

The fire had had no effect on either of them – no effect whatsoever!

Miranda took her mother's hand; then she sniffed the air; her nostrils seemed to quiver; she once again had that overpowering feeling – the mutants! They were closer now.

"You sense them," Nikki gazed into Miranda's eyes, "You sense that they are closer."

"Yes, I sense them. They're close now."

Miranda moved to her mother, and clung to her. Nikki stroked her hair. "You are not afraid, Miranda, are you?"

"No, we are Cosmos," Miranda straightened up, a fierce look in her eyes. "We are Cosmos. We can conquer anything!"

"Miranda …" Nikki gave Miranda the look.

"We are to prefer diplomacy to force?" Miranda frowned, bit and twisted her lip. Her Cosmos warrior instincts bubbling up.

"Yes, Miranda, diplomacy – we give diplomacy a chance," Nikki smiled, "So, what are you feeling? Aside from ferocious patriotic Cosmos battle fever, of course."

"I'm more curious than afraid," said Miranda, "at least I think that's what I am."

"You're not sure?"

"No, not really; I'm not sure of anything."

"Well, we shall see what we shall see," said Nikki.

The moon was now up, finally: just peeking over the high dark ridge of granite.

Miranda stared at it – a big fat round silver-white thing in the sky, slowly emerging into sight above the rock face; she'd lived all her life under the Elysium Dome. She had never seen the moon, not the real moon, out here in the open, where the real moon really lived.

Awesome!

This was an adventure – definitely an adventure!

A few minutes later, the moon cleared the ridge. It was big and perfectly round, a full moon, and with it came strange music – the beating of drums and tambours, the whistling of flutes, the clanging of bells. Silhouettes, monstrous silhouettes, appeared at the top of the ridge, an alien army, outlined against the star-filled sky. The mutants were singing.

Jingle Jangle
Tingle Tangle
What a treat
Raw flesh to eat
Stir the pot
And eat a lot
We are the woven web
Where Cosmos fear to tread

Metal clanged on metal, wood beat on animal skin, round tubes emitted squeals and throaty melodies. The ominous chant echoed, deep and spooky, in the ravine.

"Well, there they are," said Nikki, nodding towards the craggy ridge that rose up over the ravine. "There are your mutants."

The first creatures were now lit up by the burning wreckage, outlined brightly on the crest of the ridge. One of them looked human but it had wrinkled toad-like skin and it scurried along the ridge on all fours, only standing up from time to time to sniff and glance around. Then there were others, peeking up over the crest of rock. In the moonlight, they looked like cari-catures, cut-out silhouettes: frogs, foxes, feathery creatures, furry creatures. Again, they took up the chant, clanging pieces of metal, spikes and knives and swords, and trashcan lids together.

Jingle Jangle
Tingle Tangle
What a treat
Raw flesh to eat
Stir the pot
And eat a lot
We are the woven web
Where Cosmos fear to tread

"They could do better. Dreadful lack of harmony," said Nikki.

Firelight from burning wreckage flickered over silhouettes and grotesque faces that looked like carnival masks, and weird, distorted bodies, hobgoblins, gnome-like monkeys, feather-covered females, some of them half-human, half-animal, in many different combinations. Behind them shone the moon, a vast yellow peaceful harvest moon, slowly rising.

"Gosh," said Miranda, "I wonder what's going to happen now! I wonder what they want. Are they really going to try to eat us?" This would be inter-esting, really interesting!

"We'll soon see what they want," Nikki put her arm around Miranda's shoulders, "And, yes, Miranda, it certainly will be interesting!"

The mutants came streaming down the cliff face and down into the wreckage-strewn ravine.

When they got to the bottom, some of them stopped to sniff at pieces of metal and parts of the aircraft. They sniffed at the dead bodies. One dog-like creature began to rip a stewardess to bits, and several dog-like creatures fought over the body of the steward.

"Distasteful," said Nikki, "but no use trying to stop them, I think."

"And what will they do to us?"

"Well, we shall see, Miranda." And, as the chanting mutants, dancing, and cavorting, gathered in a tightening circle round them, Nikki pulled her daughter closer to her side.

Jingle Jangle
Tingle Tangle
What a treat
Raw flesh to eat
Stir the pot
And eat a lot
We are the woven web
Where Cosmos fear to tread.

CHAPTER 2 – CENTURIONS

The Dead Lands: 245 kilometers to the east.

V gazed at the reflection in Lieutenant K.M. Jackson's smooth, dark, bullet-proof wraparounds; she saw her own Centurion helmet and neck-armor, her dark InfoFlow wraparound glasses, her cheekbones, lips, and chin, all reflected in the lieutenant's wraparounds.

Below the opaque wraparounds, Lieutenant K.M. Jackson had full lips, skin like fine dark chocolate, a perfect chin, and, as V noticed when Jackson's lips parted, bright even teeth.

I'll bet she's got a beautiful smile.

Lieutenant Jackson is probably watching me too.

With the wraparounds, it's impossible to tell.

V and Lieutenant Jackson had not yet exchanged a word. They were seated, facing each other, their knees almost touching, jostled by the movement of the Cosmos Centurion Troop Carrier as it sped over the cracked and broken asphalt of an ancient Interstate Highway.

It was a sweltering December day in the South-Central Dead Lands, on the edge of the Great Dust Bowl. The temperature in the shade – and there was no shade – was already 104 degrees Fahrenheit.

"Forty degrees," thought V, translating into Celsius. She turned her gaze away from Lieutenant Jackson's lips and wraparounds, and focused on the landscape outside the tinted armored windows, an unfolding panorama of endless desolation, ruins, and desert sands.

V allowed herself to nod off, lulled by the gentle vibration of the troop carrier, by the streaming whispering InfoFlow in her wraparounds, and by the occasional gentle nudge of Lieutenant Jackson's knees against her knees.

Dozing, sitting there, V thought about how she had purposely placed herself amidst her mortal enemies – the elite Presidential Cosmos Centurions, the strongest force of Cosmos Civilization, the greatest enemy of hybrids and SINs.

Fourteen years ago, commanded by their Leader – now the President of Cosmos America – the Cosmos Centurions and their allies had carried out the *Culling*, the systematic world-wide elimination of V's tribe, of her children, of hybrids and of SINs.

On Cosmos World Vision, in a brilliant speech worthy of the greatest of demagogues, the President declared that he had *cleansed* – and saved – Cosmos and Human Civilization from alien invasion and from biological contamination. He instantly became *The Leader* – and soon he was President for Life. His image was everywhere.

That such a man should do what he did was … beyond … understanding …

V started awake, blinking.

That he should do what he did …

Lieutenant Jackson's knees jostled hers, gently. V looked up. The lieutenant drew back and shifted her position. Her lips, again revealing bright even teeth, mimed a discreet, silent "*sorry.*"

V nodded and took a deep breath, absorbing the smell of new machinery and polished weapons – oil, and paint, and high-tech compounds, electro- and bio-components, all the best weapons and intelligence machinery that money could buy.

The perfume of power.

When the Cosmos Human Imperium dies, V mused, the last to suffer would be its Centurion Legions, the last rampart between mankind and chaos, the last barrier against the rising tide of disorder and catastrophe.

And, strange to admit it, even strange to think it, but the Centurions will never know that they and I are on the same side!

She glanced outside the tinted windows. What she saw was a pageant of ruination. The column of eight armored Centurion transports raced through devastated suburbs, desolate countryside, and burnt-out towns. Everything had morphed into desert – few people lived here in this desolation now, vagrants, eccentrics, vagabonds, criminals.

Except for a few outposts, the humans had left because of the mutants, the radiation, the poisoned water, and the seventy-year drought had destroyed all agriculture and emptied all the cities and towns.

This mission – the mission she had infiltrated – V knew from hacking into secret documents – was to "protect Top-Secret Bio-Resources."

Those "bio-resources" were hybrids – carriers of a unique mix of alien and human DNA, V was certain of it. Those "bio-resources" were her brothers and sisters, a treasure house, a powerhouse of strength and ingenuity, and perhaps humanity's last chance of redesign and survival – if the hybrids were still alive.

Even the Centurions did not know where they were going, but somewhere, out there, beyond the dusty horizon, V was certain she would find them, the hybrids, after fourteen years of solitude and exile and searching.

Perhaps they were all dead.

No, I can't even think that!

But it was strange – no mind signals, no intimations, no hints ...

Usually Claire Jacobs, her clone and first sister, and Sabrina Jacobs – once her deadliest enemy now her close friend – sent little mind ripples, little signals, little suggestions of love, and reminders of presence, almost every day.

But for fourteen years nothing – total mind silence.

Part of her soul – and part of her mind – murdered, gone ...

The InfoFlow inside the wraparounds gave her continuous updates – latitude, longitude, speed of the transports, and scanning schematics from the bio-drones that flew ahead of the column and on either side – monitoring for threats, and dangerous life forms, mines, hidden weapons ...

Temperature: 104 F, 40 C.

Relative humidity: 90%

Bio-Threats: nothing to report.

Mines & IED: nothing to report.

Nothing to report!

But, in spite of the present calm, something big was definitely going on. Rumors had it – but this had not been confirmed – that the 104th Airborne Regiment had been destroyed two days before while attempting to reach the ruins of Houston, Texas. There were, the rumors said, no survivors.

Rumors also had it that several satellites had been knocked out, and that part of the World Net and of the World Mind had been mysteriously compromised. Static and interruptions were certainly crisscrossing communications lines.

The Domed Cosmos Cities of the West Coast – Los Angeles up to Vancouver and Prince Rupert had briefly been disconnected.

Strange creatures had been reported in the Napa Valley, flying over the Great Napa Salt Lake.

Rumors also had it that the True Believers or Zealots were responsible – a fanatical religious movement that had risen up in the western Dead Lands and in some of the frontier re-settlements of California. Mention was made of a Messiah, called *El Niño*, or The Boy.

Sitting, buckled in, opposite the mysterious Special Ops Cosmos Centurion officer, Cosmos Centurion Lieutenant Kat M Jackson ran through the possibilities. What was their mission? – Was it a punitive mission against the mutants? Was it a quick strike against the religious zealots (whatever they were)? Or was it a rescue operation to extract resources – humans and Cosmos – from one of the high-security mines or forward bases in the Dead Lands Dust Bowl?

She stared out the tinted armored window. The remains of Ancient American Civilization streamed past – a ruined suburb – a burnt-out mall – a rusting industrial park.

It was depressing – the immensity of the waste.

But, at least, thanks to the Glorious Leader – something had been saved: Cosmos and the Domed Cities. Still, it was appalling; it would be nice to have a magic wand and wave all the mistakes of the human race away – forever – and kick-start history all over again, recreate paradise, recreate civilization. Well, it was a nice dream, but that was all it was – a dream.

Kat glanced at the mysterious Special Ops Cosmos Centurion officer – an Anti-Insurgency Major to judge by the electro badge – sitting opposite her.

Their knees, jostling with the movement of the vehicle, were almost touching, sometimes brushing, skintight ultra-smooth black synthetic armored synthetic leather bodysuits, almost like being naked; but they had not spoken; they might as well have been on different planets.

Much of the woman's face was hidden by her helmet, high armored collar, and her dark wraparounds.

The stranger's wraparounds reflected smeared fragments of the landscape as they streamed by – and a shadowy caricature of Kat's own helmet, dark wraparounds, neck guard, lips and cheekbones.

Kat looked away – she didn't want to be seen staring at the woman – who was quite probably staring at her.

They were now moving into pure dust bowl desert territory, almost totally uninhabited, a result of the latest 70-year drought and of the break-down in law-and-order, the Cosmos-Heartland Civil War, and the spread of armed bands, and of the spillover of the Great Mexican Drug War of 2122, as well as of various accidents, atomic and biological, plus the Oklahoma nano-tech catastrophe of 2136.

Kat took a deep breath. She really didn't like venturing into the Dead Lands. Once, on a two-man mission, she and her partner – the guy had been killed two years ago – had hunted and trapped a SIN who had somehow escaped the Culling. Kat and Adam killed the SIN; neither of them were happy about it and it was not easy. the SIN was beautiful – auburn hair, hazel eyes, beautiful skin, looked to be about 18 – and even shot seven times, the SIN wouldn't die; she stared at Kat, blood dripping from her mouth, and said, "You Cosmos are really stupid, you know. We are not the enemy!" In the end, while Adam held her down, Kat had to chop off the girl's head. SINs were resilient.

Kat was black, 23-years-old, a graduate of the elite Cosmos Centurion Academy, a top sniper and trained intelligence expert – fluent in four languages and adept at advanced logistics, planning, and vector analysis.

She had been destined to be a Presidential Guard Centurion since she was 12. That was after her parents, who were both Cosmos, disappeared on a vacation to Russia – kidnapped by mutant outlaws, so it was said; their bodies were never found. Sometimes she wondered … if they had had *enemies*. Sometimes, she wondered if they were still alive, imprisoned somewhere.

So, age 12, Kat was an orphan, which automatically jeopardized her Cosmos status. The Military was the only option open – unless she wanted to be re-classified as a lower class Sub, or as an unemployable Burbite Proletarian, or sold for child prostitution in Russia or Brazil, or terminated, and broken up, and sold in pieces, for DNA and organ harvesting; Kat was valuable; her genetics were rated triple-A.

So, she became a Centurion.

From age 16, she had participated in "special kill" operations – hunting down and eliminating the few SINs that had escaped the Culling.

Age 18, she had fought in the Fifth Mexican Drug War and won the Presidential Cosmos Centurion Cross – First Class – with Oak Leaves.

V was eavesdropping – just the surface – on the young lieutenant's thoughts, just a run of superficial, random thoughts about the mission, about hunting SINs, and about the *Culling*. She picked up on the young lieutenant's curiosity about the mysterious Special Ops Anti-Insurgency Major sitting across from her.

"Lieutenant K.M. Jackson," said the lieutenant's electro badge. She was maybe 23-years-old, V thought. They were knee to knee, just the two of them together, separated from the others by an internal anti-blast wall.

Jackson's dark wraparounds reflected the midday desert glare as the convoy headed deeper and deeper into the Dead Lands. White dust rose around the eight vehicles, clouding the view.

The InfoFlow inside V's wraparounds continued to give her a running commentary:

Temperature: 108 F, 42 Celsius.

Humidity: 88%

Bio Threats: nothing to report.

Mines & IED: nothing to report.

National Alert: Massive power failure reported from Los Angeles; in San Francisco communications are down.

Interim: Limited failure in some sectors of World Cloud Mind reported.

Interim: Zealot forces reported gathering in the Dead Lands.

Interim: Twelve frontier outpost InfoFlows have ceased reporting.

A state of heightened anti-terrorist alert had been declared in Elysium City.

Even in Elysium City! Well, thought V, even the center cannot hold. Perhaps the end was coming. Sooner than she expected.

Beyond the wraparound InfoFlow, through the tinted glass, the desolate landscape rolled by; abandoned malls, half-buried in sand, skeletons of burnt-out automobiles sticking out of drifts of dust.

Dark vultures perched on the roofs of ruined suburban bungalows and on sagging and broken lampposts. One tall, isolated, gray cement apartment building stood out, its gutted windows staring like empty eyes; and then it too was left behind, disappearing into the swirling wake of dust.

They were moving through a range of hills and soon they would be heading into the vast desert, the heart of the badlands – the desolate heart of what was once the United States of America.

V's electro badge said, "Major Emily Rodriguez, Centurion Cosmos Special Forces," one of the identities V had been able to build out of the wreckage of the last fourteen years – the pitiless war against hybrids and SINs.

V was conscious of the others around her: young men and women who were the best and brightest young warriors, out to defend the rich citizens of the Dome Cities, the Cosmos, from the outlanders. The warriors were handsome, intelligent, and in superb physical shape. They were the cutting-edge of Cosmos, and all of Cosmos was an elite militarized society. Even the children of the most privileged Cosmos families learned to fight – and to fight to the death.

The Centurions were true believers, isolated from society, and trained to see themselves as an elite, a killer elite, whose capacity for violence and cruelty served the greater good.

So, V was alone, among the finest and most skilled of her enemies. She allowed her mind to drift. Boredom is the soldier's lot; interrupted by moments, as someone once remarked, of pure terror.

V's reverie was interrupted by the Info-Voice, the commanding colonel speaking.

"This is Colonel Edwards …" There was a bit of static on the line. Lieutenant Jackson sat upright, attentive, listening.

"This is Colonel Edwards. I think we can put on a little show here. We have hostiles – two klicks, two o'clock."

We've got hostiles! V heard the mind murmurs of the young Centurions; they were excited; their muscles tensed; adrenaline began to flow; boredom was ending; the time for killing had come.

"It looks like we have some mutants," the colonel's voice continued, "It looks like … they're in there, behind the burned-out school, two clicks, two o'clock, on the right."

"Colonel, let's show those critters what we can do!" a voice clattered over the Info-Voice."

"Colonel, we could let the drones do it," said another voice. The Centurions had a camaraderie V found endearing; they spoke to each other as if they were equals; except in extreme situations, they seemed to ignore hierarchy.

"No," said the colonel, and he sounded like he was enjoying himself, "let's do it the traditional way – fire and brimstone."

"Damn right!"

"Damn right!"

"Okay, ladies and gentlemen, this is Colonel Edwards again. We're going to make a little demonstration."

V watched with interest as the radar and sensor locations were being flashed on the InfoFlow screens inside the wraparounds.

"We got them locked with drones," said the colonel's voice.

The image from a nano-drone camera took up a corner of V's visual field inside the wraparound – she could see a herd or group of what looked like monkeys, but they were a mixture of human and simian, running from something – and they were pointing up towards the screen.

They sensed the fly-sized drones; there were babies and mothers and children. Some of them were wearing clothing, odd mixtures, of styles and fragments – a shirt here, trousers there, a gym outfit, a cowboy hat, an old straw boater.

Most were naked.

A few held pistols and guns, old material – ancient stuff, shotguns, AK-47s, old laser guns. The drone picked up sound; these mutants could speak; their voices sounded like growls.

"Coming …"

"Humans …"

"Run, run …"

"No, fight, we fight!"

"We can no fight, fool, we run."

"Help! Get females and littles in shelter!"

"What shelter you talk, freak, what you talk? No shelter from Cosmos."

A child screamed. The drone camera zoomed in. The child was snatched up by a female – albino, white-blond, covered in hair or fur, silver-white, as was the child. The female's face was hairless, and so far as V could judge from the InfoFlow image, perfectly human, exquisite, in a classic, elongated, melancholic haunting way, a sketch by Modigliani.

The female swept the child up in her arms – she had five-fingered, webbed hands, V noticed. Holding the child, the creature looked upwards. Her pale baleful round eyes – arched thick black eyebrows – looked straight at the camera.

The image zoomed back. The drone was rising; it showed the mutants scattering, running for the ruined school building, only a few walls remained, and the football field that was just a dust field now, an asphalt court, that had basketball hoops up on one wall, and the asphalt was cracked and melted. V glanced at the external temperature flow – 106 degrees Fahrenheit.

A few of the mutants were wheeling what looked like an old piece of artillery into place; they were going to fight; it was absurd, of course. They didn't stand a chance.

"Okay, no sentiment here, folks," the colonel's voice had hardened, "We take them; this is part of the purification program; if you find mutants, wherever you find them, you take them out – you all know the drill! We will eliminate them quickly – it's more hygienic that way."

"They're vermin," someone shouted, "they should all be eliminated, vermin, they are vermin. I mean look at them, they're filthy; it's genetic pollution, for Christ's sake! They're a threat to the purity of the race!"

"Right, right, that's right! Okay – now we show them!"

The Centurion column swerved, bounced off the road, smashed through a half-ruined bungalow, and shot across a crumbling side street.

Jostled by the rapid acceleration, and the bouncing across uneven ground, V's knees rubbed against those of Lieutenant Jackson.

V noted the lieutenant's expressionless face; her lips were set; she didn't seem that enthusiastic for this little hunting caper.

Lieutenant Jackson bared her teeth, "I guess, Major, we'll just be spectators for this one."

It's bold of her, V thought, breaking the ice with a superior officer, a Centurion Special Forces outsider she doesn't know: the girl is spunky; she's got a mind, maybe even a mind of her own. "Yes, Lieutenant, I think we'll sit this one out. I imagine they will manage quite well without us."

The Centurion column smashed through a series of dustbowl backyards, backyards of houses in what had once been a suburb; a small graveyard of the dreams of the extinct middle class of the long-dead Great Republic. They raced past a gutted swimming pool, with glints of flaking aquamarine paint, a barbecue grill on a flagstone platform, and what looked like what might have once been a tennis court.

The vehicles bounced out into a small park – now just a valley of dust. The skeleton of a large gazebo flashed up – mostly dismantled, cannibalized certainly by mutants or gangs. Once it must have housed a school band. V thought she heard the ghost of a Sousa march – maybe *Semper Fidelis*."

They raced across a small ravine which certainly once contained a stream and was now a bed of bleached pebbles and dirty brown drifts of sand.

Then, bouncing out of the ravine, racing up its side, they were out onto the former football field where the drones had spotted the mutants.

The vehicles swerved smartly around, offering their sides full-on, like old ships of the line, V thought, so they can use all their guns, like the canons of old, in a sort of 22nd century broadside.

"Fire at will," the colonel's voice came, slightly throaty, excited by the smell and taste of the chase.

The guns and grenade launchers and long-distance flame throwers opened up.

A raw high-pitched voice shouted, "Let's give these pesky mutant folk hell, let's totalize them!"

Excited school children, V thought. She clenched her teeth; she wanted to scream. These elite killers are excited school children.

The school building exploded in a towering roar of flame; the mutants were caught in walls of fire or whooshes of explosion. Above them, as they scattered and ran, the drones hovered, swerved, zipped back and forth, and darted here and there, getting the best angles, the best actionable information, the most enticing, exciting images.

The Centurions were ecstatic.

Most of these elite soldiers, V figured, were maybe 18 or 19 years old, just kids, high testosterone (even the women), muscle-bound orphans; their lives had been spent in barracks, ruthless training, and monastic deprivation. Their only family was the Centurion Corps. They needed an outlet. Murder was that outlet.

"Whoopee!"

"Atta boy!"

"Oh, go, boy, go!"

"Kill them critters!"

"Get the vermin!"

"Hell's bells, this is cool!"

The InfoFlow showed individual mutants going up in columns of smoke and fire. The pretty silver-white female and her child were running, the slender mother turned, looked up, her beautiful mournful eyes seeming to meet those of V directly; then she was hit by a spray of flame and both mother and child were burned, crisped, and vaporized. They were still holding hands and turned to ash in a second. The afterimage lingered.

It only took a few minutes.

"Okay, ladies and gentlemen, we go around and look for stragglers and mop them up."

"That was quick," Lieutenant Jackson muttered, a statement meant for nobody. Jackson wasn't smiling.

"Yes, it was quick," V said in a low voice. She glanced out the tinted window as the column sped over the old football field, past the smoking ruins of the school.

Soon the convoy was back on the road.

"Well, that was fun," the colonel's voice insinuated itself into V's earpiece.

"It was quick," said Lieutenant Jackson said out loud this time, but with the Info-Voice turned off. Only V could hear her.

"Yes," V enunciated clearly, slowly, "It was quick."

The convoy raced on, sending up a trail of dust, leaving the little town and the dead smoking bodies far behind. The sun was low, hovering just above a line of barren treeless hills. Soon it would be night.

V nodded off. But she was still aware of Lieutenant Jackson's knees jostling against hers, still aware of the heat of the lowering sun on the tinted glass, still aware of the vehicles, the machinery of death, still aware of the smells of bodies, of oil and of machinery, still aware of whispered wisecracks: *Oh, that was great! Did you see the fat one? Did you see that white leopard lady, with the kid – whoosh! Ha, ha, ha! – Vermin, they are vermin!!*

The column raced through a few abandoned towns and rusting ancient oil fields into the desert – towards the heart of the Dead Lands.

What would they find when they got to their destination – whatever that was? V's mission, of course, was not the same as theirs.

The InfoFlow continued, lazily: Los Angeles was without power; all contact had been lost with Vancouver, Seattle and other west coast fortified Cosmos outposts … World Communications were troubled. The rump state of Canada East and the European Union had declared a state of emergency in response to an outbreak of, an outbreak of, an outbreak of … cf … a highly infectious … a highly infectious … infectious …

The InfoFlow flickered and stopped.

"InfoFlow has stopped," Lieutenant Jackson said.

"Yes," V nodded, blinking, lulled by the movement of the vehicle.

"I'll bet all hell is fucking well breaking loose," Lieutenant Jackson murmured, half to herself, "Everywhere."

"Yes," said V, suddenly wide awake.

"We've got a problem," said the colonel's voice, "We've got a posse of problems …"

The InfoFlow had woken up; now it was sending a stream of blinking red letters across the wraparound: but the info was *local only*, from inside the column only, "Lost contact with Base 10 and Base 3."

The colonel cleared his throat, "We've lost satellite feeds and satellite contact." His InfoFlow voice sputtered and was gone. The InfoFlow inside V's wraparounds blinked, went dark, then it lit up again.

The colonel's voice returned. "We've … across wave-bands …we've tried to access land-based tower connections, but with, ah, no result. There's some sort of electromagnetic storm … ah … maybe … I'm not sure."

His voice dissolved into static-filled silence.

"We got a report," the colonel's voice was back. It hesitated, "that … that before the connections closed down, ah – we got a report that almost all the com towers in the Dead Lands have been destroyed. I repeat: terrorists have apparently destroyed all the old com towers."

So that meant non-satellite backup was gone. Hmm. V shifted her legs.

The colonel cleared his throat. "There was a last flash that Cosmos Los Angeles has fallen. I repeat – Cosmos Los Angeles has fallen."

V noticed that Lieutenant Jackson's lips twitched at that last bit of news, she looked at V, intently from behind her dark wraparounds. "Major, but how the hell, could a whole city fall to the True Believers? I mean they're just a minority religious sect, aren't they? I mean how could they overthrow …?"

"Faith moves mountains, they say, Lieutenant, for good or for evil." V shifted her knees. This was proof that the Evil Force was loose in the world, a Force she had met before – and now she was going to meet it again. That new Messiah, the Boy, *El Niño*, he sounded dangerous; perhaps he was the one … Since the beginning of the human adventure, the end had been predicted, again and again; and now …

V bit her lip. This would complicate her own mission.

"Major! Major! Look!"

"Yes …" V shook her head, she had been absent, daydreaming, thinking about the past, and about how to confront the looming threat – and find her sister and brother hybrids. Lieutenant Jackson was talking. V blinked and turned her head – encased in the helmet and wraparounds – to follow the lieutenant's gloved hand, which was pointing.

"Look at that."

"What is that?" V said, though she already knew.

Lieutenant Jackson's lips moved; it seemed to V as if Lieutenant Jackson was speaking from very far away, "That's what's left of the 125th airborne regiment that came in nine hours ago."

V scanned the wreckage. "No survivors, I presume," she said, thinking that this was more than human; this was –

The colonel's voice came again, through static. "That is the 125th Airborne.

We are not to stop. Nobody got in touch after the attack. Communications with them were cut off just as this was happening – whatever it was that happened." The colonel cleared his throat; his static-riddled voice ceased; the earphones fell silent.

It was night, already; the moon shone on the ruins of a small town – a main street, with two-storied houses and storefronts and the remains of wrought iron lamp-posts, probably lovingly restored decades ago – a model little gentrified 21st century town pretending to be in the 19th century.

The main street was filled with drifting sand and, strung out along the street and sidewalks as if they had been ambushed, there were burnt-out tanks and military vehicles and jeeps and smashed up army troop transports, regular, not Centurion. Smoke was still rising from some of the vehicles; one shop, a drug store, was still burning.

"As I said, our orders were not to stop," the colonel's voice sounded tired, "I'm going to stick with that order. There's nothing we can do here."

The Info-Feed in the wraparounds was still only giving communications from within the column. So, V thought, we are out of touch too, out of touch, just like the 125th Airborne.

As the convoy slowed, she noticed another thing – two soldiers lying twisted on the sidewalk had attacked each other – with bayonets! A least that's what it looked like. And several of the vehicles had smashed into each other and the canons of several of the ruined tanks were aimed at each other.

Whatever did this had caused the crews and soldiers to attack each other! What sort of force could do this? She remembered a quote from an old Greek play, from Euripides, from *Medea*: "*Those whom the gods would destroy, they first drive mad.*"

"Did you see that, Major, those two with their bayonets?"

"Yes, Lieutenant, I did see that."

"They killed each other."

"It looks like it."

Certainly, it was better not to stop; to see such suicidal self-destruction would be demoralizing; and, whatever it was, it might be contagious.

Whatever it was that was spreading over the land, it had found a way to drive people mad ...

If so ...

If so, they were heading into a trap.

Around her, V could feel the murmuring minds, fragments of thoughts:

What the fuck happened? Who or what did this? We should have stopped. Did you see those two guys, bayonets for Christ's sake, bayonets!

The Centurion column raced out of the little town and on into the desert, beyond what once had been suburbs into what had once been farmland, and onward, ever onward, all night. As the sun rose, the heat soared – now, at 10:00 am the thermometers indicated – in the little stream of the InfoFlow – that it was 115 degrees Fahrenheit.

46 degrees Celsius, V thought, too hot, really, for humans.

If all the humans died, and if only hybrids and SINs were left, would that be so bad? If all the Cosmos died, would that be such a loss?

But were there any other hybrids or SINs left alive?

Onward, ever onward.

It was midnight when the column stopped. Like in the old Wild West days, they circled the wagons, with the heavily-armed armored Desert Bugs facing outwards; nano-drones were on constant parole around and beyond the perimeter, sending in a steady stream of information and images to automatic alarm systems and to the one tired, sleepy, oversight officer.

They were camped about 200 meters from an ancient mall – a line of shops and stores and an ancient parking lot, the detritus and graveyard of a civilization that had died more than a century ago. Nearby was a row of ruined houses and an abandoned school.

Colonel Edwards had taken off his helmet and his wraparounds and was standing in the center of a small circle of officers – Gauss, Garrison, Jackson, and the fictional Emily Rodriguez –V.

"Without communications and with dangerous and mysterious things happening all around us, we'll do this the old-fashioned way, and go slow. Without the net and GPS and satellites, we're flying blind. We don't know what's in front of us. So that's why I ordered a stop."

They all nodded; they were spooked by what they'd seen.

The colonel glanced at each of them. "And maybe tomorrow the Mind-Cloud will be back up and operating." He gave them a sheepish smile. "Besides, I think we could all use a rest."

They lit bonfires, using bits and pieces from an abandoned house and the nearby school and schoolyard; chopping up the wood. The fires flared up, lighting up the faces. People rubbed their hands together for comfort – even though it was still about 95 degrees.

"It's like winter camp, isn't it, Major," Lieutenant Jackson glanced up from feeding sticks to the fire, pieces of a shattered pine rocking chair.

"Yes, Lieutenant, it is," V crouched down next to the lieutenant, wanting to probe Jackson's thoughts, see if she had any ulterior motive or was just friendly.

"I'll stay awake, Major, if you want to catch some shuteye."

"We'll take turns, Lieutenant. Thank you."

V pretended to sleep but really she was thinking of what had happened, retracing her steps, fourteen years ago.

The *Culling* had come shortly after she'd met the man, her escape had been narrow – he had obviously wanted her dead too, or did he?

She'd barely gotten away with her life. Centurions rappelling down the cliff, light-bombs and exploding gas tossed into her underground bedroom, the whole place, her home for over 100 years, blowing up – and she woke up to chaos, leaped from her bed, morphed in mid-air into alien form, smashed through the armored plate glass, grabbed a Centurion as a hostage – a young woman as it turned out – and in a flail of bullets plunged 60 meters down, straight into the Mediterranean, and then, still grasping her struggling drowning hostage, she swerved into an underwater cave and hid there for a day and a night, before coming out, with her half-conscious hostage in tow and swimming up the coast to ... to find that the world had changed.

In a few hours – two days – all SINs and hybrids had disappeared; they just were no more ... *they had disappeared ... into Night and Fog.*

Strange that they hadn't killed her; there was a window, when the light-bombs exploded, and ... it would have been easy.

Perhaps the Great Leader had let her survive.

"Major! Major!"

"Yes, Lieutenant?" V looked up from the fire, flickering flames, comforting even on a warm night.

"We have an alarm, Major."

"Right!" V shook herself, stood up, stretched, and she and Lieutenant Jackson walked to the perimeter, and peered out between two of the Armored Desert Bugs which circled the camp.

Beyond the perimeter, garishly lit up by the vehicle floodlights, a man was dancing a jig. He was barefoot and kicking up little spurts of dust and sand. He wore a black stovepipe top hat that had been smashed down sideways, crinkled like a lopsided accordion; he sported a ragged black-and-white checkered tweed jacket, and a crimson vest with large shiny brass buttons, and baggy trousers that swelled with creases at the knees.

He also had an unbuttoned clerical collar. He was a clown-preacher, or a preacher-clown.

This is not good, V thought. She put her hands on her hips. *This is not good at all.*

"Weirder and weirder," Lieutenant Jackson was right beside V, their elbows almost touching, "I mean, what is this … clown … this …?"

"Put your hands up!" The colonel spoke through a megaphone.

"The end is nigh!" The clown grinned, a black hole, a ghastly toothless grin, in the shape of a giant empty dark U. "Put your faith in the Lord; the world is about to end. The end is coming, the dark tide is racing in. Stop it can no man, no, nor woman neither! The end is nigh! The Boy is here, *El Niño*, the Saviour, our brand-new, spick-and-span Messiah!"

"Put your hands up and come forward!"

"Oh, beware, ye of little faith! Beware, Satan is among you, Satan speaks with honeyed words, Satan's lips drip pure grain corn sugar honey and luscious sweets, Satan's appearance lures with a beauteous exterior, beware this world of illusion, of pleasure and of sin. The Boy is coming I tell you! His word is wrath; his deeds are mighty."

"Put your hands up and come forward!"

The floodlights lit up the clown-preacher and the guns were trained on him. But he took no notice. His face glowed with the blotched bright red complexion of a long-time hard drinker, and displayed the swollen crimson lips and luminous bulbous nose of a clown. In his mouth, teeth appeared, giving him a fixed bright gargantuan grin, a big bite, as if he were wearing outsized, freshly polished dentures.

"He's crazy," Lieutenant Jackson whispered. "We should just arrest him."

"Crazy or not, Lieutenant, he's a security risk." The colonel put the bullhorn to his lips, but he hesitated.

"We're traveling light – no place to put prisoners," Major Gauss said.

V glanced at the man. Major Gauss had a tight, even grin, perfect extra-white teeth, a smooth copper tan, perfectly unblemished skin; he was the very image of the warrior as skillful, calculating killer; everything about him, V noted, was neat, perfectly harmonized, faultlessly planned, utterly logical; Major Gauss, V decided, was insane.

"True, true," the colonel murmured, still holding the bullhorn, he'd pushed up his wraparounds, revealing a handsome face, dark eyes, sharp cheekbones; the colonel was Native American, V thought, Navajo, maybe. "He's alone," the colonel said, "no other creatures out there – not a single bio-signature, no radar signs, and the drones say there's nothing there, just tumbleweed, maybe a few rattlers."

"Just let him rant, maybe," Lieutenant Jackson adjusted her wraparounds; she put her thumbs under her ammunition and weapons belt, shifted her weight, first one boot, then the other; the desert sand was soft. The air was close, humidity seeping in, against her skin, sticky under the skintight body-suit, a trickle running down her spine. Extending her mental antennae, V felt, intensely, what Lieutenant Jackson was feeling.

The colonel glanced at V. He blinked. "I don't know how the hell he got inside the two-kilometer perimeter – the drones didn't spot anything, the radar didn't pick up anything. He didn't show up on the biosensors and the infrared."

"Shoot him!" Corporal Garrison spat.

Garrison was a sniper, or so it said on his Electro badge. V saw that the guy was on edge, on the very edge of edge. Her intuition plunged into his whole history – He had seen too much fighting in Mexico, been captured and tortured, had humiliated himself, betrayed some of his fellow Centurions, was seething with half-suppressed self-hatred, and struggling to hold down homicidal hysteria.

"Yeah, kill the bastard!" Major Gauss grinned; gently he slapped his thigh, his hand flat; he let his hand rest, moving it slightly, a self-caress.

The preacher-clown did another little jig, took off his stove-pipe, and took a low, extravagantly theatrical bow, sweeping his arm under his waist; then he straightened up, settled the teetering stovepipe back on his head, and opened his mouth wide, a yawning abyss – all teeth, tongue, and tonsils. "God the Son died for you on the Cross and now he wants to be paid. The reckoning is on the table. The check is flapping in the wind. The feasts of the earth have been laid before you and you have supped and drunk in abundance and laid waste to all around you, squandering your heritage and your fortune. Now the divine waiter, the Boy, El Niño, the New Messiah, is here to present the bill. It is time to pay up and fess up. The souls of sinners will be reaped and harvested and angels will be separated from the chaff! The Boy – El Niño, folks, *El Niño* – remember that name, folks, remember that name – will make grain and hay of all that is, grinding and turning it and you to powder, and a feast shall begin in Heaven, bread and sausages unlimited, and for those few who heed the call, the feast shall be everlasting! As you sow, so shall you reap!"

"Good God," mumbled the colonel, "What is this shit?"

"Eh," the clown began to dance a soft shoe routine, kicking up little clouds of brightly lit dust, "And what shall become of those who preach false doctrines? Eh, what of them? You may well ask, folks, you may well ask! Well, friends and neighbors, I'll let you in on a little secret: I'll tell you what will become of them, those liars and miscreants, those rascals and fools, they shall be pitched at the speed of light into the deepest darkest iciest fieriest most horrible depths of Hell to writhe in utter eternal pestilential agony, limbs wracked with unimaginable pain, skin bursting with colorful putrescent bubble-like pustules, blood boiling like sulfuric acid, saliva as black and thick and clogged as treacle, forked and elongated snake-like tongues dripping venom and lolling out from shattered fang-like mouths, their minds darkened by sheer madness, their beauty turned hideous, hateful and unbearable even to their own cursed eyes, their limbs contorted in agony; and what of those who worship false idols, what of the elite, what of the Cosmos and the golden idols of Elysium, what of the Domed Cities, of Shopping and Intercourse and Fornication, of Science and Idolatry, of Darwin, of the false doctrine that all life is one, that I, yours truly, me for God's sake, that I am certified first cousin to a cabbage or a snail or an earthworm, such blasphemy is an affront to the face and beauty of the Lord in whose image we magnificent bipeds were divinely created and fashioned – are we not beautiful, folks, are we not divine? Do you not feel this in your heart? Has not our every feature been forged in the perfection of the Divine Image, by the Divinity Himself? Are you not a mirror of Heaven? Is this not so? Step right up folks! Exalt your divinity! Made by God, we are gods! Who can deny it? Why, we know who the guilty are: the deniers of Holy Writ, such abominations as biologists and paleontologists, such pox-ridden harlots as shoppers and latte-drinkers, they shall wander forever in the lowest depths of Hell as hoofed and horned and scaly-demons, far from any succor or soothing nervy caffeine, not a leafy terrace in sight, grotesque exiles, repulsive, outcasts even from themselves, hideous in slippery slimy excremental ugliness, exuding sulfurous vapours and steamy excremental goo, crouching, unredeemed, over piles of unstoppable smoky sulfurous shit, scaly tails wagging, crestfallen snouts hanging low, haunted by past ephemeral beauty and bygone hygiene – an illusion in itself for such sacks of excrement as we terrestrial bipeds, in fact, are, since being tossed out of Eden! For, to be honest, let us look upon ourselves: We are filth, ladies and gentlemen of the jury! We are utter unredeemable filth, copulation and excrement entwined, fallen and pestilential, a plague upon the earth itself – such are we! As for the latte sippers lolling in lotus land, their past beauty, however splendid, shall be forever gone, but forever remembered and regretted, and they, even onto the wealthy brilliant Cosmos, shall be plunged into writhing deformity, loathing every horny aspect of the odious self, regretting every instant wasted in Pagan Idolatry and Abominable Nail Salons, Shopping, and Beauty Parlors and Spas, brand name fetishism, sidewalk cafes, four-star restaurants, deckchairs on pleasure cruises, the emporia of Sodom and Gomorrah, pagan temples of false abundance, a cornucopia which is but an illusion, unsustainable, utterly unsustainable, and Yes, yes, 'tis true, 'tis all too true, all is vanity, all is vanity! And now, when it is already too late, now, you shall see! Why, you servants of evil, look upon yourselves! You have spread sterility and death and pollution everywhere, a holocaust of species; you have spawned monstrosities; you have spawned evil and excess in all its forms, mutant creatures, and abominations, hybrids and SINs, all abominations, in the name of our Lord. Amen!"

"Shoot him!" Garrison was sweating.

"Yes, shoot the bugger." Gauss looked disgusted. He wanted it over with. Big words and long sentences were more than annoying. Once, years ago, he'd heard a preacher preach; once was enough.

V stood very still.

Lieutenant Jackson said nothing. Her hands were on her hips and her teeth were bared in what looked like a smile and her wraparounds reflected the glare of the floodlights; and, in their dark smoky depths, they reflected the small dusty dancing clownish figure out there, in the desert.

V frowned. This preacher-clown was not real, not really real …. He was a warning, a messenger, a provocateur, a … She flipped up her wraparounds; suddenly, she felt tired. *Somebody or something very, very powerful is playing games with us.*

"Last warning, sir," the colonel's voice sounded drained, no energy; his eyes were rimmed with red. "You will put your hands up and you will come forward or we will be forced, with great regret I say it, sir, we will be forced to shoot you!"

"Oh, men and women of little faith, how little do you understand, you helots and servants of the Devil!"

"This is my last warning, sir!"

"Oh, feeble humans – you understand nothing – and yet, and yet, you have among you a demon who is also an angel, and who understands, but not even she can save you, not even she …"

"Enough! Enough of this bullshit! Jesus!" Garrison took off his helmet and ran his fingers through his hair.

"Oh, my, oh, dear, so we are losing our tempers now, are we?" The clown kicked his heels, "How sweet! How utterly divine!" His nose blinked, glowing bright red, then green, then blinked again, on, then off, then on, then off, red, green, red, like an old-fashioned traffic light.

"Just shoot him." Garrison was sweating heavily, silver pearls on his cheeks and neck; he smelt like raw meat. V shifted to the left. She felt her saliva rise, a tingling at the cutting edge of her teeth, rising hunger.

"Last warning!" the colonel barked through the bullhorn. He raised his arm. He indicated to the sharp-shooters that they should fire away when his hand dropped.

"You are nothing," the preacher clown shouted, waving his hat, "You are such things as dreams are made on! You are curdled milk; you are the brittle burnt crust on a *crème brûlée*, scum on a stagnant pond, you are dust, you are ashes, you are …"

"Fire!"

The volley of bullets fled off.

But there was no one there. The floodlights shone on an empty flatness of sand, only a dust devil swirled up, yellow, like a miniature tornado, and then that was gone.

"Jesus!" Garrison said, "Oh, the Lord Jesus!"

"Well, I'll be …"

"Hologram projection maybe," Gauss stroked his smooth, clean-shaven chin, "Maybe a decoy, distract us from what's really going on."

"Right, but the feeds don't show *anything* going on."

"Well, Colonel, the hologram detector didn't register any damned hologram or mind projections or simulacra of a damned preacher-clown either."

"Right, okay, well, double-check the perimeter! Real eyes, and real boots – see to it. And send out all the drones, and keep two drones overhead at all times."

"This is downright spooky."

"And what was all that gibberish about damnation and salvation, the thing was sputtering on about, what the hell was that? Damned well ruined my digestion!"

Far off to the left, a single bolt of lightning – splashing down on the ruined mall – about 200 meters away – lit up the carcass of an ancient Taco Bell. The sizzling white light bounced off the Taco rooftop, and then careened among the ruined and cannibalized carcasses of cars – Dodges, Hummers, SUVs, miniature FIATs, and one antique Mini Cooper.

"Jesus!" whispered the colonel. He slid his wraparound down, hiding his eyes, "Alright, folks. This show is over. Get some sleep. We have a big day tomorrow." He turned to V. "Major Rodriguez, you've had experience with religious warfare, I see from your résumé. What do you think? Follow me. Let's talk." The colonel walked off, away from the others. V followed.

The colonel bent forward, his hands clasped behind his back, "So, Major, what do you think?" Around them were the Heavy Armored Desert Bugs, hunkered down, and pointing outward, mobile metallic symbols of the might and of the reach of the Cosmos Centurion Imperium.

"Sir, I think this phenomenon – the clown-preacher – was some sort of electro mind-game that some sects use, like the drugs they feed to believers." V lifted her helmet, took off her wraparounds and turned to the colonel, so he could, when he looked up, see her eyes. "But, to tell you the truth, Colonel, it is better – higher definition and more flexible – more reactive – than any example I've seen."

"Right," the colonel stopped walking and stood stroking his jaw, not yet looking up.

"And I've never seen anything evade the whole range of detectors before. We are up against something new, sir, and I'm not sure what it is. El Niño, the Boy, as the preacher called him, must have some pretty complex toys. I think what is happening is extremely dangerous." That, V thought, was an understatement.

"So, whatever they have, it's very advanced."

"Yes, it is, Colonel, it's something I've never met before." This, V knew, was not quite true – but it would be too complicated – and dangerous – to explain that she had once – over 100 years ago – saved the president of the United States, and the United States itself, from …

"So, what you're saying, Major, is that we're all in the dark here, including you and me."

"That's about it, sir."

"And we'd better watch out." The colonel looked up, looked at her eyes, blinked, looked down, and looked up again, a hard curious look.

"Exactly," V bit her lip. She was being honest, as far as she could go, she, a hybrid, the Queen of the hybrids, talking to a kindly and well-meaning killer of hybrids – and of SINs and mutants.

"Thank you, Major. It's nice to talk to somebody who doesn't pretend to know what they don't know. Get some rest now." The colonel smiled and put his hand on V's shoulder. "I appreciate honesty, Major, you're good folk, I can tell. There's too much bullshit in this fallen sublunary world, is there not?"

"Yes, Colonel, you put it very poetically, if I may say so, Colonel."

"Thank you, Major, I think we should just remind ourselves, from time to time, that we are still just human, after all."

"Indeed, you are right, Colonel." V saluted and withdrew, walking away into the shadows.

The colonel watched her go, thinking that she had most unusual eyes – dark and intense like nothing he'd ever seen – drew you in – it was like she was a hypnotist – eyes with depths a man would never have enough time to explore, a lifetime would not be enough. And he mused that it was lucky in the present crisis that the Centurions could count on troopers of the quality of Rodriguez and Jackson, his intelligence officer, and that, if he were to think like a man in civvies, both women were almost too good-looking to be real – truly wonderful! Ah, it was one of the few remaining natural pleasures of life! He thought of his own ancestors and what the Americas might have been like had the Europeans never come, and if the Algonquin and Navajo and Haida, the Aztec and Inca and Maya had been able to develop on their own, without the pale-faced invaders interrupting the process, smashing history apart, shattering nascent civilizations. Well, that was the ancient past. The world at present was full of wonders, and most of them were not particularly nice wonders – in fact, they were horrors, hybrids (though they were probably all dead), SINs, (ditto, he'd executed quite a few himself, always feeling a pang of regret because they seemed so human and so – yes, goddamn it – so exquisitely beautiful and superbly intelligent, well-meaning too: when they were caught, they rarely fought back. One girl SIN told him, *I don't want to hurt anybody, Colonel, though I could, of course, I certainly could.* And she let him put her down – no fuss, no bother, polite all the way. And then there were the mutants – mutants everywhere, in every goddamn place, swarming and pullulating mutants of every shape and form, too many of them to ever put them all down. He reserved a particular hatred for mutants.

Another stroke of lightning flashed, this time farther away, and darkness returned and the silence echoed with the rippling thunder, and the aftershock of the lightning bolt, which then, slowly, died away.

The colonel tilted back his helmet, lifted it off and the wraparounds, and wiped his forehead with the back of his hand; and then there was the heat, the heat that never stopped.

"I'm getting old," the colonel sighed. He was forty-six.

"Fire is old-fashioned. It's primitive," said V, staring into the small bonfire.

"Yes, old-fashioned," Lieutenant Jackson was sitting cross-legged by the flames; she poked them with a long, crooked stick, "I'm old-fashioned too, in some ways at least, and primitive, certainly, I'm primitive."

V crouched down next to Jackson and shoved into the fire a few extra pieces of wood that she had scavenged from a shattered playground fence.

After talking to the colonel, she had spent a few minutes standing in the dark, dreaming of lives past, and of all the dead she had known; she stared at the ruined playground, at the empty swing, at the shattered miniature merry-go-round, and at the cracked and dry wading pools. She'd walked out, beyond the outer perimeter, and into the schoolyard. The school on the other side of the playground, visible in the reflected glare of the campsite lights, was a burned and charred hulk, just like the other school where they had killed – murdered – the mutants. She broke off a few pieces of wood from a sagging miniature toy castle, turned away from the playground, and walked back to Jackson, where, camped next to an Armored Dust Bug, they shared their own little fire.

"Major, do you mind if I ask you a question?" Jackson bared her teeth, bright white between dark lips, turned her reflecting wraparounds towards V.

"No, Lieutenant, go ahead."

"You have four bars – including the Russian campaign – you've had experience with fundamentalism, with fanatics ..."

"Yes, a bit," V glanced at the lieutenant and, protected by her own wraparounds, smiled evenly. She could see herself reflected in Jackson's wraparounds.

"Do you mind if …?"

"No, not at all, I can tell you some of what I've seen."

Lieutenant Jackson took off her helmet and lifted off her wraparounds, revealing big liquid eyes, a high forehead, short straight hair, clear chocolate skin, full lips, and now she had an even more beautiful smile.

V slipped up her wraparounds, took off her helmet, smoothed down her hair – which was jet-black and cut short – looked straight at Jackson, and deep into the woman's eyes, and began to tell her tale; she adapted her own real experiences to the biography of her fictional identity, Major Emily Rodriguez: She had fought in Europe during the Russian uprising, when the enslaved outlanders and mutants rose against the Moscow-based Cosmos oligarchs; she had fought against robots in the first human-robot conflict in eastern China and Japan …

While she talked – and poked thoughtfully at the fire – V thought about the young woman – Lieutenant Jackson had the crossed-rifles insignia of a sharp-shooter first class, and also the twisted gold braid of an intelligence analyst first class; and, yes, she was Intelligence Officer on this expedition.

V sighed inwardly: I'd better watch this one; she's curious and persistent and high-principled, and she's very bright.

While Lieutenant Jackson slept, V sat, legs crossed, staring into the fire. It seemed to V like a return into the distant past, when she had accompanied Roman Legions to the frontiers of Empire, and sat with the troops around a campfire, with the alien darkness out beyond the circled vehicles, with sentries pacing the perimeter, though, now, of course, there were electronic sentries – flying nano-drones, the size of a grasshopper or smaller, and various forms of land-based and vehicle-based sensors; all of this local Cosmos military machinery still worked even now that they were cut off from the Net and the World Mind.

But it was still the same thing: a group of soldiers out in what was, potentially, only partially known and very hostile territory – full of creatures and dangers that could only be imagined.

Only now, in the 22nd century, that territory was located in the heart of what had once been the United States of America.

V was up before dawn and before Lieutenant Jackson who was lying on her side in her chameleon camouflage SleepSkin, lips open slightly, breathing softly.

V gazed down at the young woman – Ah, yes, almost too attractive. No, *definitely* too attractive. She sighed, crouched down, and triggered two coffee pods – one for the lieutenant and one for herself. The coffee was ready in three seconds; it smelled delicious.

The lieutenant opened her eyes.

"Breakfast," V said. She handed the steaming coffee to Lieutenant Jackson who slipped out of the SleepSkin and stood up, "Thank you, Major," she said, looking V straight in the eye and smiling an open fresh smile as if they had been friends for years, comrades in arms since forever.

The Centurion column re-assembled just as dawn was breaking. still no outside communications. Even the old radios didn't work. Everything they tried resulted in static. The GPS was nonresponsive. It was as if the satellites had ceased to exist. "So – we go ahead," said V.

"Into the unknown," Jackson peered over the wasteland. The ruined mall looked even more desolate in the light of day. There was something tragic, too, about the playground, the hot breeze moving a dangling swing, squeaking it back and forth, back and forth.

"That's about it," V was tightening the breast armor of her black bodysuit, smoothing it down, skin-adhering, skintight.

"This is a true adventure, then, Major," Lieutenant Jackson, tilting her head, suddenly smiled, looking for just a second like a twelve-year-old girl.

"Yes," V returned the smile, "a true adventure."

Hours later, with the sun high up the cloudless desert sky, the clown preacher appeared out of nowhere, drifting along, high speed, beside the convoy, like a mirage, or like moonlight racing on water.

He wavered, he danced, just above the dust, as the convoy rushed onwards. Then he disappeared, fading away.

With the clown gone, there was empty desert and the blue cloudless sky. It seemed lonely somehow.

In the early afternoon, the clown appeared again, floating like a reflection, like a wavering hologram, right beside the column. His lips moved. But his words were not spoken aloud; they were audible, resonating inside everybody's head.

"He's inside our heads," Jackson leaned forward. Daylight reflected on her lips, on the gleaming, satin-black thighs of her skintight bodysuit.

"Yes, he is," V glanced at Jackson, and then out at the clown, floating along, at 100 miles an hour, a hazy illusion, just beside the convoy.

"Hallelujah! Hallelujah! Welcome, all sinners. The Gates of Hell are swinging open, right here, right now – and ready to welcome you, one and all, Hallelujah! Hallelujah!"

V stared at the creature, trying to divine its secret, to penetrate its mind, if it had one. He glowed. He grinned. He looked straight at her; and, worse, he stuck out his tongue, oversized, and dripping thick, tar-like, black saliva, and, for a moment, his grinning teeth were fangs.

The 88mm gun of one of the Armored Desert Bugs was swinging around towards the clown, and in one more second, it would …

Poof! He disappeared.

"This is the damnedest thing," muttered the colonel, his voice barely audible in static over the InfoFlow.

The Desert Bug swung its gun back to the rest position, "Too bad, that character was just too fast."

Without stopping or slowing, the column raced forward, churning up the dirt, leaving a long yellowish dust tail hanging in the air behind it.

The sun beat down.

V glanced at the ruined desert-like fields, at a few gutted farmhouses, and abandoned rusting hunks of farm machinery. In the burnished golden glare, the rusted machinery, reduced to burnt sienna, looked like it had been preserved in amber. Many of the machines had been torn apart; they were cannibalized hulks, wrecked, maybe by humans, or, more likely, by the mutants that had multiplied in the Dead Lands when the humans left. V closed her eyes and let the rhythm of movement and the murmur of motorized power carry her along.

Lieutenant Jackson laid her gloved hand on V's knee, and said, "Major, look."

The convoy slowed. V shook herself, opened her eyes, and glanced out the tinted windows. V blinked; it took her half a second to realize what it was.

Crucified, a body hung from a tall wooden cross; the corpse, the thing, that hung there was naked and withered – the charred parody of a human being, the arms outstretched, nailed to the crossbeam, the head tossed back in an open-mouthed scream.

"Is that real, is it real?" Jackson used her wraparound zoom, and then it was clear, "It's not a scarecrow! Damn it!"

"It's real. It was somebody real," said V.

Another crucified body surged up, a woman. She was naked, too, except for the fluttering, torn remains of a scarlet loincloth. Her feet had been nailed to a high wooden vertical column; her skinny arms – the palms of her hands skewered into the wood – sagged from the crossbeam.

There were more, on both sides of the road, rows of the crucified humans, as the column slowed, approaching a small town.

Smoke rose from some of the buildings.

"This is Seed's Bend," the colonel's voice announced. "It was a frontier colony, one of the efforts of the Government to re-colonize the Dead Lands with Subs and Burbites. Looks like it's been overrun – and not long ago. All drones in the air, I repeat all drones in the air."

V saw, on the InfoFlow of her wraparound, the drone pattern; the drones flew around the column, ahead, on the sides, behind, and overhead, others skimmed the ground, all sensors activated, all cameras scanning earth and air, infra-red, bio-detectors, and other specialized detectors spanning the whole range of electromagnetic radiation and bio-molecular sensitivities.

"There is a bio-form ahead, it is humanoid, it is alive; the bio-signatures indicate a human, 93 percent probability, not SIN or mutant."

A drone zoomed down towards the bio-form, it looked like the silhouette of a human being, a man, and then it was clearly a man, unless he was a SIN, but that was highly improbable given the bio-signatures.

V frowned: Temperature 111 degrees Fahrenheit, 44 Celsius, wind 20 knots, with gusts to 45 knots. Crucified bodies hanging in the wind.

Hell had come to the Dead Lands.

Henry Cook was 27 years old, but he had the weathered beaten look of an old man, his skin was tanned to the consistency of dark leather, mottled and scarred and liverish; his face was lined with deep reams, crevices clogged with dirt. He stood, alone, in the center of a circle of Centurions, his ragged jeans soaked in blood, torn to ribbons and scorched by fire, his white T-shirt drenched in sweat and dirt and blood and engine grease. In some places, his hair had been burnt to ash. Tears streamed down his riven cheeks. Henry Cook was crying.

"Now, calm down, man, calm down."

Henry Cook stared at the colonel. Cook's eyes – bright, pale blue shards of shattered glass – looked like they had been emptied of personality, emptied of sanity.

Standing in front of the man, the colonel felt as if the Cook's soul had been sucked out of his body; it gave the colonel a dizzy feeling, vertigo, as if he too were going to be sucked into a dark emptiness.

"You don't understand." Cook's voice was calm and flat – expressionless, as if he were dead – or a zombie. The lifeless tone was in total contrast to his scorched, disheveled, frantic appearance. His left arm shook. Tears, dirty and bloody tears streamed down his cheeks.

"Tell us! What don't we understand?"

"You don't understand!"

"We understand that we don't understand. But what are we to understand that we don't understand?"

V, standing next to the colonel, had been following the colonel's inner confusion and frustration. She thought it was pretty clear what the colonel and the Centurions didn't understand – not yet anyway.

"He killed everybody, women, children, the old, the young …"

"He? Who is he?"

"The Boy! El Niño! The Saviour!" Henry Cook fell to his knees and clasped his chapped, skinny, sun-burnt hands together. "He took away their souls, all of them, each and every one; he carried their souls into the sky, on wings, terrible wings."

"So, it's the Rapture."

"Yes, it is the Rapture, the beginning of the end, the Saviour has arrived, and now he is killing everybody – all, all, guilty and innocent, child and man and woman, all, all, all …"

Henry Cook glanced up, sudden cunning in his eyes, "He wanted you to know. He left me alive so I could tell you. He wanted you to know what he can do."

"And what can he do?" The colonel was beginning – V could sense it – to lose his temper. Such fanatics as this El Niño character were among the most dangerous enemies of Cosmos.

Henry Cook – his eyes were really too bright – suddenly spoke in a sing-song, as if he were chanting a lesson, something learned by heart. There was no sign he understood what he was saying, "He can mix and churn each mind to madness. He can burn up every personality and every being, man or animal, he can turn each soul into a pure flame that consumes itself. He can cause a man to kill his wife, wife to strike down her husband, children to kill their parents, and parents to kill their children."

"This doesn't sound like the Jesus I believe in," said the colonel, "God may be a jealous God, but He –"

"He can turn men and women into beasts."

"Beasts?"

"Beasts that can fly. Cannibals on wings."

"Now, listen –"

"He Who Has Come is madness, pure madness. And do you know what madness is? Madness is strength. Insanity is power. No one can withstand it. In its purity – for it is pure unlimited fathomless madness – it knows no limit. He will do anything, say anything, be anything, and he will destroy everything."

In the main square, in front of a toppled, half-melted statue of Dwight D. Eisenhower, there was a huge wooden cross, bigger than all the others. A body hung limp on the cross, nailed, feet, and hands, the neck tied to the crossbeam. It was a young woman. Nailed up was a scrawled sign, "School-teacher – Blasphemous Whore!"

The body and cross had been half burned. As dusk settled on the little town, the cross was still smoking, its embers still glowing ...

Most of the buildings had been burned to the ground. Dead children lay in what had been the schoolyard – some had been decapitated, others had been stabbed or shot.

V said, "I think Colonel, it might be best to take special precautions."

"What sort of extra precautions can we take?"

"Possibly put the arms away, so that if people do go crazy ..."

"That would leave us defenseless, Major."

"You are right, Colonel, there are no easy choices here."

"I know, Major, I know. I think, though, we'll keep our weapons. I appreciate the suggestion, and I can see the logic of it, if indeed this creature can control minds, but a Cosmos Centurion without his or her weapon, well ..."

"You are right, of course, Colonel," V saluted.

She liked the man. But, when the moment came, he would try to kill her and she would be forced to kill him. If that time came, she would be forced to kill the others, including her young friend and bunkmate, Lieutenant K Jackson.

The column hunkered down for the night, just on the edge of the devastated settlement.

The next morning, before light broke, the column moved out and moved on – through the desert, more and more arid, now truly a wasteland, the Dead Land, which had truly earned its name. The hours passed.

"Major, are you okay?"

"Yes, Lieutenant, I'm just thinking," V had been peering at the sandstorm; it looked like they were plunged underwater, into a sea of polluted yellow, the sun was almost invisible, just a vague golden halo.

They had been on the road for maybe five hours.

When the column had packed up and left the insane, empty-eyed Mr. Henry Cook and the ruined village with its rows of charred crosses and charred bodies, it was two hours before dawn.

V turned and smiled at Jackson. "I'm just musing, about fate, and about what is waiting for us up there – ahead."

"Hybrids?"

"Yes, hybrids."

Now she was close to her goal – finding the hybrids. And she had the first proof that they were alive – the hybrids were alive!

Before they left the "village of the damned," the colonel had opened the sealed coded electro-pack that which was to be unsealed at oh-four-hundred hours – Their objective was a place called Camp Terminus. "We are to evacuate ..." the colonel hesitated "... we are to evacuate preserved hybrids ... and we are to ... terminate ... to terminate . . . all human guardians ... and staff ... and eliminate all human dissident prisoners ..." The colonel wiped his brow, "Hybrids ... We are to evacuate hybrids."

At last, thought V, Camp Terminus – the bio-resources were, in fact, the hybrids, and their treasure of alien-human DNA.

But, then, why did she not feel their presence?

Hybrids transmitted mind-waves.

Had they been lobotomized?

Were they being kept in a deep freeze?

And how would a column of Cosmos Centurions – however powerful – expect to control a pack of hybrid prisoners?

The column was on its way.

Navigating without GPS was a challenge, but the column's own sensors, electronic maps, and drone radar and sonar helped guide them towards Camp Terminus, as they sped westwards.

"Mega dust storm approaching, ETA about two hours, I reckon," said the female voice of the Command and Communications vehicle.

Three hours after sunrise, the dust storm hit, sweeping over the column. Most of the vanguard drones had to be grounded, flying back to their nests in the vehicles, and snapping their covers shut, crouching, hunkering down.

Even the finest and most modern materials – wherever there is a moving part of any kind – don't like dust storms.

"This is a whopper of a storm, Major," Lieutenant Jackson's teeth were bright – that beautiful smile.

"Yes, it is, it certainly is," V stared out the armored glass at the blinding blizzard of sand. It could clog up and block anything – even the military Centurion Armored Transports were vulnerable.

After an hour, the sandstorm passed.

The wind dropped.

The temperature hovered at 102 Fahrenheit, 39 Celsius, relatively cool.

A yellow sun hung low in a blue, blue sky, and it did look beautiful, but everything out there was covered in sand. They were on flat land now and soon the sun would set and ...

Toward dusk, they slowed down, maybe 80 miles an hour.

Out there, V thought, not far away, maybe four hours away, was their objective: Camp Terminus – and the hybrids, her brothers and sisters.

"Well, Lieutenant, maybe we should try to get some shuteye ..." And just as she uttered the phrase, V noticed, on her wraparound, the video feeds flicker; the local in-convoy sensors flickered; it was a less than a nano-second; probably nobody else had noticed; strange, she thought, that is strange ...

V flipped her mike, "Colonel, something is trying to interfere with our command and control system."

And, now on high alert, V's mind radar picked up something else – a dark mental cloud, an inner fog, something prying, poking, tentacular, trying to enter her mind, snaking itself inwards, trying to wrap itself around her thoughts, trying to create darkness, trying to paralyze ...

"What, Major Rodriguez, what makes you say that? I don't see any –"

V pushed the invading darkness away; she spoke into the InfoFlow – to the vehicle's driver, "Corporal Trent, take over manual, take evasive action, immediately. We are about to be ..." But ... the mike was dead.

The vehicle swerved out of control.

All the electronics died; the lights went off, the …

WHAM!

At that moment came the ambush.

WHAM!

In theory, the ambush of such a column of armored Cosmos Centurion Desert Bugs was impossible. Radar scanned for missiles or projectiles or aircraft. Multiband sensors scanned the horizon. Miniature overhead drones surveyed the ground and surroundings for bio-signatures and chemical markers and electromagnetic signals. Sniffer drones moved ahead of the column – just a few feet about the surface of the road and spread out on both sides – looking for mines and explosive devices.

But somehow …

WHAM!

Out of nowhere …

No, not out of nowhere, V understood: the vehicles were exploding from within; their ammunition and fuel supplies were being triggered, and then – boom!

Lieutenant Jackson was drawing her laser pistol and …

Damn, she is going to shoot me! V slammed the lieutenant's pistol aside. A sizzling purple ray shot past her, burning through the metal back of her seat; V grabbed Jackson's arm, twisting it, forcing her to drop the pistol, and levering Jackson down, V shouted, "Down, Lieutenant, down!"

Half shielding Jackson with her body, V reached for the door ejection handle … A sudden jolt of the vehicle jerked it out of her grasp. Jackson was pushing, flailing, fighting to get free – V caught the drift of her thoughts. They were chaotic, homicidal, cannibalistic.

Damn! V pinned Jackson down. The woman had gone mad! She was possessed. And V felt it too, the invading darkness, pushing its way, a tsunami of evil flooding into her mind. She fought like a demon, pushing it away. It rolled back, foaming, angry, overpowering. It was a dark mental oceanic irresistible floodtide. *I have to ride this,* V gritted her teeth, *I have to ride this out, so I can escape it! Surf the evil! Straddle the maelstrom! Go with it! Master it!*

The vehicle in front of them swerved sideways, skidding off the road, disappearing in a huge column of flame. Coated in fire, it rocketed into the air – it looked like it had been hit by a huge punch from below – a giant invisible fist. It seemed to happen in slow motion – while still up in the air, the vehicle mushroomed into a ball of flame. The ball of flame came crashing down.

WHOOSH!

WHAM!

Reaching for the door, V shouted, "This is a force field of some kind! It's from inside, it's a …" She had no time to complete the idea. Their vehicle was tossed into the air.

V flailed, upside down, hanging from the safety straps.

She was tossed again. Now, they were right side up. Now, they were upside down. Jackson was a tangle of legs and arms, slick black bodysuit gleaming, legs and arms flashing, flames blowing in through the smashed door.

They came crashing down. One wall blew away, exploding outwards. The vehicle bounced, rolled over twice, and ended up upside down, a twisted hulk. Everything exploded.

The world dissolved in flames.

CHAPTER 3 – MUTANTS

Now we eat, now we eat!
Cosmos meat! Cosmos meat!
Is a treat! Is a treat!

Jingle Jangle
Tingle Tangle
What a treat
Raw flesh to eat
Stir the pot
And eat a lot
We are the woven web
Where Cosmos fear to tread

High stepping it, the mutants cavorted in a circle, with Nikki and Miranda at the center. The circle was shrinking, closing in, closer and closer, tighter and tighter.

From moment to moment, the chant became higher, deeper, howling, yodeling, singing – an incredible medley of tones and sounds, language and raw screeching.

Some mutants leaped into the air, others clanged pots and pans and bars of metal. Fire from the wreckage threw the mutants' shadows, huge capering shapes, onto the granite cliffs.

Nikki frowned. It was grotesque and total cacophony. The level of excitement and murderous hysteria was rising – approaching the breakout point. Most of the mutants seemed hesitant to approach any closer – the mystique of Cosmos perhaps holding them back. But Nikki knew that myths and mystique can only preserve a failing Empire for so long – and then ... suddenly, almost in a single instant, in a cascading series of failures, everything would collapse, not least the psychological barrier of fear and deference.

Miranda had imagined many things in her life, but never this. The mutants looked deadly. Maybe she and Nikki should fight their way out of the encirclement. She tightened her grip on her mother's hand.

One man-sized, toad-like creature suddenly broke away from the closing circle. With gluey, swamp-green, mottled, bulging bug eyes, he stared at Nikki. Drool spilled from the corners of his mouth. He stepped forward, his belly sagging, his large sexual organ – that's what it seemed to be – a sort of octopus or squid-like appendage – dangling – he faced Nikki.

"Well?" Nikki said; he was about two meters away.

"Grrrh," he said.

"Grrrh to you too," Nikki said, hazarding a smile.

In one bound, the toad man leaped, knocking Nikki down. He sprawled and crawled over her and pushed his long tongue, dripping and splashing saliva, against her mouth, while thrusting his sex – that enormous tentacular blob-like thing – against her groin.

Fast as a bolt of lightning, Nikki punched the creature in the face, side-chopped it on the neck, and as it reeled back, she leaped up and kicked it in the groin, "Piss off you fucking sod," she growled, "The next time I will bloody well kill you."

Miranda stared. It had happened so fast, she hardly realized what had happened. "Mother!"

The creature rolled in pain and howled, and gnashed its teeth, green phosphorescent saliva spraying in all directions.

"Mother, are you okay?

The other mutants stepped back, swaying in unison; it was almost as if they were moving, back and forth, to some invisible music.

"Fit as a fiddle, Miranda!" Nikki brushed herself off. She wiped the thick green foam of the creature's saliva from her face. She turned to the crowd. "Who is the boss here, or is anybody the boss?" she shouted, her voice ringing clear. She repeated the question in Spanish, "¿Donde está el jefe?"

"Boss not here," said the creature she had kicked. "I kill you. I kill you now and eat you, or I eat you and kill you."

"You bloody well try, my friend," said Nikki.

"You leave her alone," said Miranda.

The creature turned its gaze on Miranda; its eyes were bright green and bulged, and its mouth, which seemed to have no teeth, dripped more of that bright green saliva, "You? What you? Who you?"

"My name is Miranda."

"Miranda?" spittle flew, the eyes blinked.

"Yes," Miranda raised her chin and stared down at the creature, "And what is your name?"

By now many of the mutants had gathered closer around Nikki and Miranda, staring and sniffing at them. Part of the wreckage flamed up again. Miranda blinked. The scene was lit as if on stage or around an enormous bonfire. Grotesque shadows danced and cavorted on the rock face, on the stretches of pebbles and sand, on the bits of wreckage, on the scattered body parts, on the splashes of blood.

"Name?"

"Yes, what is your name, friend?" said Nikki, this time smiling.

"Friend?" the creature seemed puzzled; he blinked; his three-fingered hand scratched his chin. "Name is Scav …"

"Scav …"

"Scavenger," he said.

"Ah," said Nikki, "Well, Scav, my name is Nikki."

Scav burbled, "Hello Nikki, hello Miranda."

"Hello."

"Boss is coming," Scav said, "He will want eat."

"Boss! Boss! Boss!" all the other creatures murmured, chanting, and shuffled back and forth on their legs and paws, flippers, and hooves, some of them growled.

"Eat?"

"Eat you and Miranda, friend," said Scav, grinning and looking at Nikki and then at Miranda – well it did look like a grin, his long tongue slopping around in his mouth, and dripping green foam, "but cook first."

"I see," said Nikki.

"Yes, you see," said Scav, blinking at her.

"Awfully considerate of them to cook us before they eat us." Nikki pulled Miranda to her and stroked her hair.

"They may want a ransom," Miranda said, "I mean if they're pirates."

"No ransom, no more." Scav was sitting on his haunches, drooling and picking his nose. He looked up, his large, oval, protruding snot-green eyes fluttered flirtatiously. "New style born again religion – now sacrifice, not ransom."

"I see," said Nikki.

"Big Boss says any Cosmos is to be offered up in sacrifice to our one and only God, Dolly," said a small – three-foot-high – furry, vaguely humanoid creature, shuffling, looking down at its large widely spaced, four splayed toes, then looking up, blinking its slit red eyes through heavy lids and thick long eyelashes.

"Your God, Dolly," said Nikki.

"Yes, Dolly God, God Dolly, Most Holy, Most High," the small creature murmured and then crossed itself, "Demands sacrifice, in flames, on the cross, big cross, charred with fire of old times, all bad deeds redeemed, hallelujah, and all true Dolly People go to Dolly Heaven and Eternal Barbie Garden Among Innumerable Virgins. Amen."

"Sacrifice, and on the cross, well, that's even more promising," said Nikki with a bright smile, "It sounds more useful that way, as if one were contributing something, to society, I mean." She glanced at Miranda.

"I don't think this is a Cloud Game, mother. It's not a talk show."

"I do know that, Miranda, I am not entirely frivolous, nor an utter idiot. I do know that when one arrives at the difficult age, say about 13 or 14, that one does begin to consider that one's mother has the IQ of a marshmallow. And apropos of our present situation, there is something I must tell you, Miranda; I should have brought it up before. But I've been hesitating, you know, thinking how sensitive you are, and how dedicated to Cosmos you are, and how you love the President, our much-adored Leader, but now you are grown up, a little bit at least, you know what sex is, more or less, what with Kit instructing you and so on, and I think the time has come, well, to be a bit more forthright than I have been so far, I mean, on this present issue, what I mean to say is …" Nikki stopped and frowned and looked away and bit her lip, as if the subject was too delicate to be pursued.

Scav was scratching himself and gazing; all the others were watching.

Miranda stared at her mother. This was very strange. Usually, Nikki did not indulge in any circumlocution whatsoever. She was very direct; and, also, Nikki did not seem embarrassed by any subject – sex, or excrement, shit or piss or menstruation, girls making love to girls, guys making love to guys, men copulating with women, or vice versa, or the nature of cooking, or Pop Cult, or the Sexual Circus down in the Sin Zone, or Subs versus Cosmos … What could be so embarrassing that Nikki would get positively tangled up in her syntax; that Nikki could not bring herself to …?

Miranda's reflections were interrupted by a small striped black-and-white fuzz ball that came leaping through the air and landed on her T-shirt and stuck there. It crawled up to her shoulder where it perched. It had eyes, she noticed, and a mouth which was curled upwards.

"Lemur ball," said Scav.

"Lemur ball?"

"Friendly, won't bite, might lick," Scav grinned, drooling foamy green goo, "good for picking fleas, lice."

"Fleas? Lice? I am a Cosmos First Class! I don't have lice!" Under her tan, Miranda glowed crimson with outrage.

"You will," Scav grinned, slurped a curled tongue-full of green drool, and grinned some more.

"Let's talk about it all later, shall we," said Nikki, turning her bright smile on Miranda.

"Yes, okay, mother, but …" Miranda stopped. The Lemur Ball was tickling her and digging under her T-shirt and making a whiny sound. She tried to figure out which end she should pat or scratch – she didn't want to make a mistake. The creature might be very sensitive – this was clearly not a robot pet, and it did not come with encoded instructions – so she took a guess that just above the two big eyes might be a good place, and so she did begin to pat the Lemur Ball about two centimeters above its eyes. It sighed and flattened itself on her shoulder.

"Wants milk," said Scav, licking his lips and making fluttery green moon eyes at Miranda. "You are mammal, mammal give milk."

"Milk! I don't give milk!" Miranda blushed. This was more than outrageous! But the Lemur Ball had settled down and was quite cuddly. She stroked it. It shivered all over and made a purring sound.

The crowd had pushed in closer and began touching both of them – fingers poking, hands caressing, tongues protruding. One female – a humanoid piggish-like creature with an upward curving snout – seemed very interested in Nikki's jacket. "Neo-synthetic," said Nikki, adopting the intimate yet professorial tone of the Infomercials she did so often, "I had them design it this way, with the double lapel. Here, feel it." Nikki guided the female's seven-fingered hand.

The female felt the lapel and blinked its large, heavy-lidded, cloudy eyes at Nikki.

Miranda continued to pat the Lemur Ball and she said, "Mother, I think you should finish whatever you were saying. You wanted to tell me something really special and extremely important, it would perhaps be best to tell me, I mean, before we are served up as goulash, but –"

"Later, Miranda," Nikki said with a tight bright TV hostess smile, and turned her attention to the female who was fingering the jacket, "Here, try it on."

Miranda blinked. She had played many roles in Cloud Games and Cloud Simulators, but she had never expected to be in the middle of a desert in the Dead Lands, in the dead of night, with her mother putting on a fashion show and doing a partial strip-tease for a crowd of eager mutants. Well, this was certainly interesting! I would love to tell Kit about this – she might even be jealous – in fact, it would be great if Kit were here to share this adventure. She patted the Lemur Ball – it was licking her hand – and watched wide-eyed as Nikki slipped out of the jacket and gave it to the female, and then Nikki helped the female slip into it, tugged at the sleeves and at the hem a bit and patted the shoulders. "There. That's perfect!"

The females – about half the group consisted of females – moaned, "Oh, oh, oh …" They began to sway. Some linked hands and paws. "Stunning fit," said one voice. "It is perfect, Muffle," said another voice. The females all began to chant, "Oh, Oh, Oh … Nikki, Nikki, Nikki …!"

"Your mother is a witch," said Scav, sidling close to Miranda.

"She is not!"

But Miranda did begin to wonder if just maybe her mother was some sort of expert in psychological warfare; she must have played lots of virtual netwars when she was young or something. She had never seen this side of her mother before. Of course, she had never seen her mother outside of Elysium City before, so –

A shot rang out; it echoed and reverberated and then re-echoed down the narrow ravine, bouncing and ricocheting off cliffs and slopes and overhangs.

There was a long, yodeling, ululating yell; it seemed to come from the top of the cliff overlooking the ravine.

"Yooo … whooooo … doooo … loooo … doooo!"

It went up a few octaves and then down, and then up again, and after an interminable screaming yodel – it trailed off on a high note, "Yo – ooo, Yoho – Hooooo! Hooo! Hooo!"

They all turned to look

A young man was standing on the crest of the rock face; he was lit up by the burning fires of the wreckage of the presidential plane; the light rippled and glimmered on every millimeter of his deeply, tanned, oiled, muscular body – on his abs, his pectorals, his biceps, and his thighs.

Miranda opened her mouth to say something – but couldn't – so her mouth stayed open, her lips parted, round, as if she had been petrified, turned into a living statue, while uttering "O … h …"

The young man was naked except for a leopard skin loincloth. He held an ancient AK-47 up to the sky. – Miranda had seen the weapon's silhouette in Cloud Games – and looked it up in the Cloudpedia – and so immediately knew what it was: the classic assault rifle which used gas pressure from the exploded cartridge to reload and, if wanted, to fire the next cartridge, invented by the Russian patriot, Michael Kalashnikov in the late 1940s, just after the Great Patriotic War, as the Soviets used to call it. The young man also had a machete-like sword – or perhaps it was a scimitar – tucked into a leather holder that was slung across his shoulder and dangled lightly against his hip.

"Oh," whispered Miranda, "Oh."

Nikki shot her daughter a sharp sideways glance.

The young man was dark-skinned, had thick curly black hair, a smooth handsome open face, and a wide bright smile. The fire reflected on his teeth, big, square, healthy teeth, and on his oiled chest and legs, and on his flashing dark eyes.

On his head he wore at a rakish angle a pirate hat with a skull and cross-bones and on his feet were pointed black boots with floppy tops, just such boots as Long John Silver would have worn.

"Oh, oh, oh," Miranda's heart skipped a few beats. Here was her pirate!

"Oh, my God – Long John Tarzan of the Apes," muttered Nikki, "I do believe, darling Miranda." Nikki could feel that Miranda's heart was beating extra fast. "I do believe, Miranda, that you have finally found a real pirate."

He really did look like a pirate, a naked pirate.

"Surrender, Surrender in the name of the Skull-and-Cross-Bones! Put up your hands," he shouted. He swung the AK down, and pointing it at them, "Put up your hands, your paws, your flippers, all of you."

"A dream come true, Miranda," said Nikki, as she put up her hands.

"We surrender, oh Pirate," shouted Miranda, "We surrender!"

"He is Little Boss," whispered Scav, "Adopted Son of Big Boss. Little Boss

– is wanderer of the desert; Little Boss of the Dragon Tattoo, Little Boss of Origins Unknown."

Nikki glanced at Scav. "Dragon tattoo?"

Scav looked at her, opening his green eyes wide, "Yes, dragon tattoo."

"What's it like?"

"Green, red, scarlet; it comes and goes."

"Comes and goes?"

"Yes, Mistress Nikki, it comes and goes," Scav stared at Nikki and licked and slurped an extra-long spool of drool back into his mouth. "I fuck you soon. I fuck you good."

For a brief instant, Nikki looked even paler than usual.

Caliban gazed down upon the burning, brightly lit wreckage site. He grinned. Ah, what blazon of beauty and booty was this? What a joy it was to be alive, on such a night, on such a night as this!

Two women prisoners, fair demoiselles, Cosmos, undoubtedly Cosmos, undamaged, that was better than he had dared hope. Usually, all you got from such wreckage were bits of roasted flesh and useless pieces of burnt-out machinery – and mostly the surface mutants got there first and slurped up the most useful parts, but it was night and the surface mutants – who now feared the dark because of the newly arrived sulfur-smelling winged devils – were in hiding.

He leaped from the ridge and slid down the slope, pebbles cascading around his floppy black boots and tanned muscular legs; his ragged loincloth fluttered; his polished chest reflected ribbons of flame; his AK-47 was still pointed, vaguely, at the two female prisoners, his booty, two women, one with dark hair cut short and wearing a skirt and T-shirt, and the other was a girl, maybe 13 or 14, with tanned skin and blond hair and wearing skintight body-mold Cosmos teen wear.

He narrowed his eyes. These two were perfect – rich, valuable, First Class Cosmos undoubtedly, ideal sacrifices to be offered to Dolly. Oh, fairest of the fair, such favors as these two possessed were rare indeed! Dolly and all the auxiliary and ancillary gods and saints would exalt and grin from ear to ear; soon there would be feasting and dancing and much riotous mischief!

The fires from the wreckage flared up. The crowd pressed in on the two prisoners. The two Cosmos didn't look afraid. The female mutants seemed to be in some sort of a trance.

"Get out of the way, Scav," Caliban nodded the barrel of the AK at his old pal, Scav, who was drooling in utter lust over the white-skinned brunette. Scav had no impulse control, no control whatsoever.

Caliban half closed his eyes – the adult would be worth her weight in gold, he could see: She was expensive, really top-notch quality, a perfect Cosmos, even the clothes glowed like money, and she was beautiful … more than beautiful … Somehow just looking at her, just perceiving her, sent a dart of yearning pain through his heart. Her eyes gazed at him, intense, strange, dark eyes. Eyes you could drown in.

"She be mine," Scav's mouth hung open, bubbling green slime.

"Away, Scav! This high-class, first-class booty is not for you." He pushed Scav away. Scav pushed back. Caliban flashed his teeth. "Away, get thee gone, Scav, I tell you, man, these spoils are not for you!

Caliban looked the two women up and down. They appeared to be unscathed, untouched by the crash. This was passing strange. What magic was here? Neither the sages nor the magicians nor the shamans could do such a thing.

Staring at the one with the jet-black hair, and seeing her so proud, Caliban frowned. *I must test the mettle of this goddess!* He wagged the greasy barrel of the AK in her face, an inch from her lips, almost touching the tip of her nose.

He swallowed. *Her eyes probe deep into me, she seems fearless, and something more than fearless,* so *let us see her cringe,* "You are both my prisoners," he growled, "I am Caliban the Pirate and I also am Tarzan of the Mutant Apes and Other Such creatures and Miscellaneous, such as is preserved in the Ancient Comic Chronicles."

"Caliban?" she said.

"Yes, wench, 'Caliban' is my name; what of it? Dare you mock me, wench?"

"It just seems so … so right, so apt," the dark-haired one said, all the while the muzzle of the AK was quivering, an inch from the tip of her nose, but she didn't start back or look frightened; she didn't cringe at all. Her cool dark eyes smiled; they had strange deep lights in them.

"You are my prisoners!" Caliban snarled. He swallowed deep. The muzzle of the AK trembled. His finger itched – this chalk-white Cosmos goddess was somehow too close to him for comfort, this female was insinuating something, she knew something … Perhaps he should end it now. It would be easy – just pull the trigger, and splat – she would be gone.

"Of course we are," she said. Her teeth were bright, her lips glowed. She was an extraordinary beauty, an exceptional catch, "I absolutely agree, Master Caliban. We are most definitely your prisoners and yours alone."

"Yes, you are, you are my prisoners. You understand that. You belong to me now," he drew the rifle back, slung it low.

"Of course, we do! We belong to you." She reached out her hand, "This is my daughter, Miranda. And I am Nikki. Very pleased to meet you, Master Caliban." In spite of his best and most brutal intentions, Caliban shook her hand. "The pleasure is mine, prisoner," he said, bowing, and he swallowed. Her touch was like electricity. For some reason, he wanted this alien Cosmos woman – his arch-enemy – to like him, to really *like* him, perhaps to *love* him; he'd never felt this feeling – whatever it was – before.

"My daughter, Miranda," she said again, indicating the girl with her hand.

Caliban tore his eyes away from the brunette, and glanced, then, for the first time, really, at Miranda, focussing, yes, for the first time. His heart stopped beating. His lungs stopped pumping.

Miranda!

Her skin was gold, her eyes were amber, strange golden stars and nebulae burst like flashes of lightning in the iris and pupil, her hair was golden sunny blond, her teeth were perfect, not broken, crooked, and darkened like those of the females he knew; and her lips were full, precisely delineated, sculpted for kissing, shining bright. Her eyes – with all their stars – were radiant. Her mouth smiled, "Hello, Caliban," she said, fluttering her dark eyelashes, bright eye-stars bursting, and then she looked down, abashed. She blushed. And as she blushed, Caliban began to breathe. *She feels it too*, he thought, without even thinking.

Caliban's heart again began to beat, just barely. His jaw dropped. He almost let the AK fall. He wanted to say something, but he didn't know what he wanted to say.

He hesitated, and gulped. Nikki noticed his fine Adam's apple move up and down and the beautiful glow of his skin, the smooth way his muscles swelled, and how the tattoo just glimpsed on his shoulder and that ran down his back seemed to flair in excitement – her heart skipped a beat – and then the young man managed to say to Miranda, "Yes, I am Caliban," and, after a pause, he took Miranda's hand, which was awkward with the AK-47 wobbling at his side between them.

Miranda's grip was dry and smooth and firm, "Caliban! It is indeed a perfect name! Master Caliban!" she sighed, her eyes full of swirling stars, "You are a pirate!"

"I am a pirate." Caliban bowed, "Master Caliban, Pirate, and King of the Jungle – well, King of the desert seas of the Super Dust Bowl and Central Dead Lands, at your service."

"This is topsy-turvy," Scav bubbled, "this is upside down. There is no sense in this. Politeness is for dogs. Gallantry is obscene. Flirting and blushing are anathema. Fraternization is an abomination! We should sacrifice and eat them, Master, right away, tout de suite, I say, fricassee or broil or grill or roast or marinate or …"

"Shut up, Scav."

"I will eat the mother," Scav drooled, leaned towards Nikki, and fluttered his eyelids; the females pressed closer to Nikki and stared at Scav; he cringed and moved back.

"I told you to shut up, Scav," Caliban was still holding Miranda's hand. He took a deep, desperate breath. He must resume command. Such feelings as these – whatever they are – were dangerous. He risked losing himself to these two Cosmos. He must seize the tide and hoist sail. He must to himself be true!

He let go of Miranda's hand.

She smiled, inclined her head, and again gave him that look, this time from under her fluttering lashes. "Master Caliban," she whispered it, breathed it out.

"Yes, yes, Miranda," He bowed slightly, and then he spoke in a loud voice to all the assembly. "The hour hastens, demons lurk in the shadows and in the night skies," he glanced upwards, as if he could see those very demons sweeping down. "Come, friends, come, prisoners and slaves, let us go!" He pointed to the crest of the rocky ledge.

"Of course, Master Caliban," Nikki said, "Let us go." She gazed at his tattoo. As her gaze lingered, the tattoo flared up, spread over his back, a cool multicolored flame, it glowed. The tattooed dragon turned its head and its flaring eyes, to stare at her. "Let us go!"

And so, they went, up the granite slope, out of the ravine.

Caliban reached out to help Miranda over a rocky ledge.

Nikki was surrounded by admiring females. The female, Muffle, who was wearing Nikki's jacket, put out her seven-fingered hand, more like a claw than a hand. Nikki took it.

"I want to fuck music with you," said Scav, licking his droopy slobbery chops and gazing at Nikki, "You strum my strings! You are my melody tune."

"Later, Scav," Nikki said, "Later."

"Later! Later!" Scav launched into a jig; his arm-limbs raised in the air, twirling around, his bright green spittle spraying out in moon-lit rainbow colors. "Later, later, I tell you, alligator! In a while, crocodile! Whoopee!"

One of the females kicked him in the bum, just under his tail. Scav went sprawling face down in the sand and howled.

The sand was hard here, at the top of the ridge, but as they went up the slope, it became softer, more difficult to walk in, for this was the crest of a dune.

"I have never met true Elysium Cosmos First Class like you and your mother," said Caliban, "I think you are definitely True Cosmos, your mother seems like the most divine and highest version of Cosmos."

"Yes, she is, and, yes, we are," said Miranda, "We are True Cosmos, first-class, full Citizens, I am Leader of my Cosmos President's Youth Section. I have the President's medal. He gave it to me himself, handed it to me with his own hands, and pinned it, here, on my breast, and spoke to me. We live in Elysium."

"Rulers, the rulers of the world, that's what you think you are!"

"We don't *think* we are the rulers of the world, we *are* the rulers of the world!" Miranda stuck out her chin in defiance. Her eyes flashed. "Without Cosmos, utter chaos would be unleashed upon the universe! We are the only barrier between something and nothing. After Cosmos, comes the deluge!"

"So I have heard. Such is the Cosmos Doctrine and Religion. I read about it in an ancient sacred book called *Reader's Digest*, and another ancient holy text called *Gentleman's Quarterly*." Caliban helped Miranda up the last bit of the dune.

He stopped to give a hand to Nikki too, and when his hand touched Nikki's hand he felt something strange – a flood of warmth – it tickled his eyes and almost made water come.

"Thank you, Master Caliban, you are most gracious," Nikki said, her eyes gazing into his.

The gaze made Caliban afraid.

"You are welcome, Mistress Nikki," he said; he swallowed, realizing that his awe and admiration were mingled with terror.

When they got to the crest of the escarpment, a vast landscape of desert sands and low ridges spread out before them; it was black and white and bright silver in the moonlight. Everywhere above were pinpricks and spangles of light – *stars!*

Miranda gasped. She had never seen a real landscape before. Caliban stood beside her. For a moment, they said nothing, then ...

"You are Miranda, and I am Caliban," he said.

"Yes," Miranda looked up at him, "like in *The Tempest*."

"Yes," he said, "Like in *The Tempest*."

"Where did you learn about *The Tempest*?" Miranda's eyes widened. It was assumed by all right-thinking Cosmos that Dead Land mutants lived in a state of utter hard-scrabble illiterate barbarity, that they never read anything, and if they did read anything they wouldn't understand anything – she thought back on all those mutant jokes the kids used to tell in school.

"Reading," Caliban said, giving her a charmingly intense scowl, eyebrows arched and close together, eyes blazing, lips turned down; he pulled her close, so she was pressed against his chest, her face tilted up to his face. He stared into her eyes, "reading a book."

"A book, you have a real book, with paper and pages and a cover?" Miranda, breathing fast, was crushed against him – it was not at all unpleasant. She stared straight back into his eyes. She was more than surprised. Books were rare; it was such an ancient technology, though she and Nikki did have a very nice collection.

"Books are safe; they don't leave traces," Caliban said. He looked away. There was something horribly, exquisitely painful – terrifying – about looking into Miranda's eyes, "books aren't connected to anything, so books are safer."

"Ah," she said. She saw it clearly. The electronic world was totally connected and totally controlled; if you accessed anything, then they could find you; and, if you didn't want to be found ... well, ancient paper and a binding and two covers was a good idea.

When they reached the crest of the dune suddenly Miranda saw the true vast open moonlit desert; she had never seen anything like it before; she had never seen an open landscape before, it looked like the waves of a moonlit sea. "Awesome," she whispered, "awesome."

"Yes," said Caliban. For some reason, he had a lump in his throat.

"Sublime," said Nikki, hand in hand with her porcine mutant friend Muffle who was still wearing Nikki's fine jacket.

For many hours they tramped along, a long column of mutants with their two Cosmos prisoners.

Caliban kept glancing up at the sky.

"What are you watching for, Master Caliban?" Nikki looked up at the cloudless sky filled with a myriad of stars.

"Sky devils, they are new; they come at dusk."

"What are they like?" Nikki scanned the sky.

"Giant bats – vampire bat people, zombies, leathery with a broad wingspan, they are foul-smelling and deadly. We first saw them three nights ago."

"But tonight, there are none," Nikki glanced from Caliban to Miranda and back – they made a beautiful couple.

"Yes. Tonight, there are none. Dolly smiles upon us," Caliban's teeth shone in the moonlight.

The path led up over more dunes, and, here and there, Miranda began to see jagged bits of man-built material, machines, and towering pitheads from ancient mines. She realized, accessing her course on the history of technologies, that these things dated from the 20th and maybe even the 19th centuries, maybe early or mid-21st century; it was really ancient stuff. Once people and machines had worked here – and lived here. It was a frightening thought.

Then, after five hours march – Miranda checked with her wristwatch – they arrived at the foot of a looming pithead – a black twisted metal structure. It rose up like a giant stalactite, maybe ten stories tall, out of the sand.

Behind the pithead and cluster of old buildings and shattered machines and vehicles, a steep escarpment towered up; and, on a ledge on the escarpment, there was a huge metal door. It was half-hidden by sand, but Miranda saw it clearly, reflecting the light of the moon, it was like a plate of silver set in a wall of granite. They climbed up a winding path that led straight to the ledge and the giant silver door.

Caliban and his mutant creatures began to clear away the sand in front of the door. "We sweep, we sweep," sang Scav, "and yet it blows and blows."

Nikki saw two extra shovels. She took one and handed one to Miranda. "Let us earn our keep, Miranda!"

"Yes, mother, that is a fine idea," Miranda had been contemplating doing the same thing; but she had been shy; now she took the shovel and helped her mother and Caliban and the others. She was surprised – well not too surprised, after all, she and Nikki were Cosmos First Class – to see that she and her mother worked much faster than the best mutants; only Caliban could keep up to them, and he did it with ease.

Finally, the drift of sand was cleared away.

The giant door creaked open on its huge hinges.

When they had entered, the giant metal door clanged shut behind them. They were inside the entrance to what looked like a huge elevator shaft, with broad dark metal stairs curving downwards around the metal cage for the elevators.

Colossal wheels, and cables, and greasy columns of ancient metal towered up everywhere; the place was lit by burning torches and by the bright twinkly glow of what looked like phosphorescent mushrooms and luminous lichen. The walls and the dark greasy beams of metal reflected streaks of light. The place smelled of musk and metal and rust and engine grease and of sulfur.

Nikki took Miranda's hand, "Miranda, remember – this is not a game; it is quite serious."

"I know, mother," Miranda was puzzled. Nikki suddenly seemed *very* concerned for some reason.

"When things get tricky, and I ask you to do something, you must do it, without question and without hesitating – whatever it is, however strange or horrible it may seem – okay?"

Miranda stared at her mother, "Yes, mother, of course."

"You promise?"

"Definitely – I promise!"

"Swear upon the Cosmos ethos and the Leader-President!"

Miranda frowned. "Yes, I swear!"

Caliban said, "You two are plotting?" His teeth were very bright. His eyes sparkled. He seemed amused.

"Yes." Nikki gave him her most dazzling smile, "Yes, Master Caliban, of course, we are plotting."

"I thought so," he smiled at Nikki and then looked quickly away, towards Miranda, "Come, give me your hand, my prisoner, my slave, who shall be my Queen," he reached for Miranda's hand.

Miranda gave him her hand. His Queen – this was a new development!

Nikki's female friends were still clustered around and behind her, following her every step, mooning, stroking her skin and her skin-silk designer T-shirt.

One of the females, on all fours, was hopping from step to step and licking Nikki's skirt. Nikki patted the girl on the head, scratched her ears which were long like those of a rabbit or donkey.

"Tastes good," said the female donkey girl, "It's yummy, really yummy for the tummy!"

Scav, on his haunches, hopping down the stairs, a bit apart, picking his nose and drooling. "I fuck her; I fuck her soon."

"Right, Scav," said Nikki, flashing him a look. Her eyes emitted dark flames – pure focused fury.

Scav started back, crouched, put a paw in front of his eyes, and whimpered.

"Your mother would make a good desert pirate and warrior," said Caliban. "She has the stuff of heroes."

"Yes, she does. Yes, I think she would."

"She gives me a strange warm feeling I have never felt before."

"She does have that effect on people," said Miranda. She put her arm around Caliban's waist; he kissed her on the top of her head, breathing in the perfume, lemon and gold.

They began their way down the giant hollow iron staircase; the metal was ancient, greasy, rusted in places, with some of the steps torn out or twisted into weird shapes.

Their footsteps and talk echoed in the cavernous immensity; Miranda leaned over the railing – oh, but it was greasy, thick with filth! She tried to see to the bottom. She couldn't. It was lost in hazy darkness. It was clearly a very long way down. Dark obscurity rose around them. Twisted cables and beams, seared and half-melted, hung into the void.

Suddenly flames sprang up. Miranda shuddered; she tightened her hold on Caliban.

Then she realized – the flames were in her mind.

This place had been bombed, or perhaps there had been an industrial fire – an explosion. People had died.

She closed her eyes. She *felt* it and she *saw* it. People had died. She saw faces – a man in a yellow hardhat, screaming, tonsils stretched, gold glinting in his molars; a blond woman desperately clawing at a link fence, her nails broken and her fingers raw and dripping with blood; three people caught in a cage-like elevator as flames rushed up the elevator shaft; and she saw mere dark silhouettes, pillars of ash consumed in heat. She saw flames and faces – faces stretched, contorted in agony; and she saw, in slow motion, a billowing explosion of liquid fire racing up the mineshaft, racing up elevators, exploding out in the open air, a great whoosh of molten metal and giant sparks, a firestorm under the stars; she felt the pain, the horrendous pain! It seared into her heart and into her flesh, people dying, in agony, and also creatures who were not human, equally dying, equally in agony!

Ouch!

Why am I seeing such things?

Am I becoming psychic?

If only Kit were here!

She opened her eyes and blinked, suddenly seeing what was around her. Caliban had let go of her hand and was walking in front of them. Using an ancient flint lighter, he lit a torch. He held it high; it was bright and made a crackling sound; it was a real torch made of real flame, the flames flickered up, smoky and waxen, casting rippling shadows. It was magical. Miranda had never seen a torch with real flames, not in *real* reality. She supposed that the reason he was using a torch was that they were poor, and barbarians, and enemies of the State, so they would not have electricity, and in any case, electricity would be dangerous; electricity would be traceable. Caliban's back was tanned dark, it was shiny with light; the torch flames made ripples like dark cascading syrup on his muscles and smooth skin. The sinuous tattoo dragon, running down his back to his waist, danced, shimmered, and grew, until it covered all of his back, glowing, muscular, multicolored, and smooth. Miranda sighed. *Oh, he was scrumptious!*

"So, this is where you hide," she said, to make conversation.

"We don't *hide*!" Caliban quickly turned on her with a dark scowl – his mouth turned down, his eyes in shadows, his jet-black eyebrows in an angry knot.

Miranda almost giggled. His angry expression looked so comic, caught in the flickering light and shadow of the torch. It reminded her of one of the masks she had seen in a *commedia dell'arte* performance in the art archaeology course she had had implanted – she and Kit together – and how they tittered about it!

He was still scowling. "What do you mean *hide*? How dare you say *hide*! Caliban hides from no man! Caliban *hides* from nothing!"

"Oh, I'm so awfully sorry," Miranda gave him her best smile. "I just meant this is where you find shelter."

"Shelter, shelter, yes, shelter." He grinned. "Shelter is good. Shelter is an acceptable word. I shall not deny shelter. A mega-storm is coming, and there are wild winged fanatical demons abroad, so shelter is good."

"A mega-storm?" said Nikki.

"Yes, the gods are angry. They bring death."

"The gods," said Nikki, "You have gods? Yes, of course, Dolly!" Miranda glanced back at her mother.

Muffle, the pig-girl with the jacket, was clinging to Nikki as if she worshipped her; straggling behind them, in a motley procession, came the other creatures, Scav, and all the males and females.

"Our gods are mighty," Caliban scowled. "They are hungry too."

"Hungry?" Nikki smiled encouragingly.

"Hungry for Cosmos flesh," Caliban frowned, staring straight at Nikki – as if he had just thought of something very unpleasant.

So, they are cannibals, Caliban's gods! Miranda wondered if this beautiful boy, her perfect pirate, Caliban, was totally sane. Many non-Cosmos adults were reputed to be simple-minded because of the poisons they had absorbed as children during the wars and civil wars, and during the collapse of the old United States and the plagues. The very air outside the domed cities carried madness and disease, and the water, the experts said, was universally pestilential. And, then, too, folly was encoded in their very genes!

Was she falling in love with a naked madman? Science had progressed and there were genetic and chemical answers to almost all health problems, though, in theory, only Cosmos could afford them, or even know about them; though Miranda *had* discovered – through Kit – that Subs were quite ingenious at finding cures and solutions, and that among the Subs there was a huge black market it all sorts of goods reserved in theory exclusively for Cosmos.

But whether he was crazy or not, falling in love was an adventure, and this Caliban was very fine – like a glowing naked statue in some wonderful museum. She was pleased she was falling in love with him; it was just like in a book; but, then again, on mature reflection, she wasn't sure whether it was really such a good idea to have such strong amorous emotions. Emotions were messy, unpredictable, and they could get you in lots of trouble – that's what most of the stories warned of, in any case. Perhaps, since she was a true elite Cosmos, she should avoid emotion – and love – for a Cosmos must be a stoic, and proud, and detached, and lofty, and above all things.

Nikki had told her not to hurt people and she certainly didn't want to hurt Caliban – but was Caliban a person? One day when they were arguing about butterflies, Nikki had said that all creatures that were sentient – "sentient" was such a nice word, Miranda thought – that all creatures that were *sentient*, persons or not, were capable of suffering … so …

"We will have babies, lots of babies, oodles of babies," said Caliban, "you are a breeder. Females are breeders."

"I don't particularly feel like babies," said Miranda, "not yet, and I am still young, too young for babies."

"What does that mean?"

"I'm not ready, that's what it means, and I won't do it unless I want to do it." Miranda felt like stopping right there and stamping her feet and throwing an old-fashioned Cosmos youth tantrum, but she didn't. Nikki, she noticed, was smiling.

"You will do it if I make you do it. Prisoners and slaves even if they are beautiful and talented – and especially if they are Cosmos like you – do not ever do what they want to do; they do what I, Caliban, want them to do."

"Slaves and prisoners," said Miranda, "I suppose they don't do what they want to do; but I don't intend to be a slave or even a prisoner. I am very much my own person, everyone says so."

"You will be a breeder, my breeder," Caliban helped her down a particularly steep step where the iron was twisted, charred, and shattered; cables lay here and there, also, making it a regular obstacle course, "You will be producing babies, a baby a year I think would be good and …"

Caliban's words fell on deaf ears. Miranda was not really listening; she was thinking that she was not telling the whole unvarnished truth: *in fact, I almost never do what I want to do*: I've always felt there was another *me*, in another place, where things were really happening, so perhaps I'm not really who I want to be, and I'm not doing what I want to do; but then I really don't *know* what I want do to, and, to tell the truth, I've always studied, and I like to do that, and I've played soccer, and I like to do that, and I've swum and I like to do that, so I've *always* done what I wanted to do. But, what if life has built into me the desire to do things, so I would *think* I was doing what I wanted to do, but, in *reality*, I wasn't doing what I wanted to do, and so I would have to *discover* what I wanted to do, but unless I tried *new* things out, things I had never tried before, I wouldn't know what I wanted to do, so there must be some frontier here, that you would always have to push against, going further and further, trying out new things, until, by trying a gazillion things out, you discovered *what* you really wanted to do and *who* you really were. She sighed. One lifetime might not be enough for such an enterprise.

"I don't think I want to live in a mineshaft," she said, looking around, at the smoky arches, at the steel beams and braces and columns, at the greasy-looking rock faces. Her voice echoed against vaults and walls of stone, and frames of steel and iron and whatever those metals were.

"You will like it, besides, what a slave or a breeder or a female likes or doesn't like, doesn't matter in the slightest." Caliban looked straight at her, the whites of his eyes bright in the flicking light of the torch.

"I'm not sure I agree." Miranda gazed at him. His eyes were, oh, too, too, beautiful, dark, and liquid, and bright, and full of what for want of a better word she would call 'soul' – did mutants have souls? She was thinking, too, that she should humor him, as he was certainly crazy – his brains addled and frazzled – like everybody else out here in the Great Super Dust Bowl Dead Lands.

"We have food. We have water. You will have your own cave, for you and your mother, until your mother is sacrificed to All High Dolly."

"I will breed the mother," said Scav, who had caught up, and was hopping down from step to step. "Breed, breed, breed," he sang, turning it into a tune. "We begat, begat, begat!" He sneezed, "I begat; she begat; we begat!"

"Our own cave – how elegant," said Nikki. She gave Scav a lock.

"Breed, breed!" Scav chanted.

"Breed, breed!" Nikki said, "Forget it, Scav, no chance – not in a trillion years!"

Scav scuttled next to Nikki and gazed up at her with his bulging mottled swamp-green eyes, his tongue hanging out, wagging, luminous green drool dripping.

"Our own cave, that sounds cool," said Miranda, though sacrificing Nikki to Dolly Goddess What's Her Name didn't seem so cool. Miranda's mind was drifting. She was thinking that, several months ago, she had been a prisoner in a cave in *Gothic Wars* on Cyprus in *Dragon Country Version VII*. She smiled. "I'm sure, mother, that if we really must live underground, then having our own private cave will be more fun than being in the public dormitory."

They had almost reached the bottom of the stairs; strange noises drifted in from a vast nearby space, probably a huge cavern.

"You are prisoners. Now you must be tethered and shackled to look like prisoners," Caliban said, and he took two pairs of handcuffs from one of the furry humanoids who had been following close along behind Caliban and Miranda.

"Is this really necessary?" Nikki gazed at Caliban.

"They will not understand if they see you free," said Caliban, blushing.

"Well ..." Nikki frowned.

"Turn around," Caliban clicked open the old rusty handcuffs, and clicked them shut, around Nikki's wrists, pinioning Nikki's arms behind her back.

"You're really sure this is necessary?" Nikki glanced over her shoulder, "We're not going to run away."

"I am sorry, Oh, Beautiful Cosmos, I beg forgiveness," said Caliban, "But, unlike your beautiful daughter, who shall become my breeder, you are to be sacrificed."

"Sacrificed?" Nikki raised an eyebrow.

"Burned alive on the altar of the Goddess Dolly," Caliban blushed. He looked down. "I do beg forgiveness, oh, Divine Cosmos Nikki."

"Well, what must be, must be." Nikki rolled her eyes, and adjusted her wrists to make the handcuffs more comfortable. "And I certainly do forgive you, Caliban." Nikki smiled, but she did murmur, just under her breath, "Well, I never did much like religion." In fact, she thought that much that passed for religion was all rather bloodthirsty xenophobic tribal stuff, lurking under even the most benign surface, all about exalting a particular tribe, bestowing power on angry presumptuous old men or wild-eyed young fanatics, and fingering scapegoats, symbolic or real.

"You are *not* going to burn my mother! You wouldn't dare!"

"I am sorry." Caliban turned Miranda around, linked her wrists, and fitted the lock into place; he took his time doing it. His face turned red – Miranda couldn't see this, but she could sense it. His hands trembled as he finally clicked the cuffs shut.

"I don't like this," said Miranda, "And you are *not* going to sacrifice my mother. I forbid it!"

"I don't want to but, it's our religion and ..."

"Well, your religion is silly!"

"You mustn't criticize people's religion, Miranda," Nikki said, "They tend to get very upset and cranky and you never know what they will do."

"*People* ...?" Miranda fumed, "But, mother, are these creatures, *people* – are they really people? I mean, do they *count*?"

"Oh, Divine Cosmos, Nikki," Scav spurted green goo. "Down here everything is upside down and backward and topsy-turvy." He sidled up beside her. "They know not what they do, Divine Cosmos. They worship idols and they practice unending fornication and loll about all day eating mushrooms. They will burn you, most beauteous Cosmos, most beauteous Nikki, on the Cross of Dolly, and then eat of your flesh made sacred by the sacrifice."

"Fornication! Don't tell me, Scav, really! How horrible." Nikki recoiled as Scav's gooey foamy green saliva splashed on her shoulder and cheek. It was sticky stuff. It might not go away. And, now, handcuffed, arms pinioned tightly behind her back, she couldn't wipe it off.

"Yes, fornication, Cosmos," Scav bubbled over, dribbling everywhere, "I have seen it myself and I am eager to try it. There's always a first time, that's what I say! I shall take you on the very altar of sin, Cosmos, you and I, and we will become one, in the poetry of abandon."

"*The poetry of abandon*, really, what a phrase!" Nikki carefully stepped down one particularly difficult bit of burnt and contorted stair, "Scav, how poetic you are! Where do you get such ideas?"

"Oh, Cosmos, you have come from the skies, just for me, it is truly written in the Book, thus the Ending is in the Beginning."

They still had a little way to go on the Great Staircase. Nikki was treading carefully. The steps were high and greasy and made of grating where the high heels of her shoes could easily be caught. Taking a tumble would not be tactically wise. She glanced sideways at Scav who was slithering and hopping down the steps beside her. When waxing poetic, he spurted more green foam which, this time, spattered on the side of her face; as she couldn't wipe it off, it stayed, dripping; she could feel the drool hardening into the consistency of rubber – a mask of sputum; not very alluring. Luckily no paparazzi were in the neighborhood, though some art directors she knew would adore the splattered, gooey, defiled, mussed up effect.

"I dream the dream," Scav sprayed more of the green glue, "I dream the Flesh of Cosmos, and the Flesh of Dolly, united, then, I dream me, Oh, Cosmos, I dream me feasting on your bones, Cosmos, and I dance for you, and I will carry you in my dreams, for you are the predestined one, Cosmos, you are the spirit come to earth, the spirit of Dolly, and so you shall be consumed, your blood drunk, your flesh eaten, and your bones immortalized."

"You have an extensive vocabulary, Scav, and it seems to me that your syntax has improved. When we first met you could barely string two words together." Nikki wiggled and squirmed. Some of the green liquid was dripping down onto her shoulder and sneaking into her T-shirt's cleavage. A hot shower would be most welcome.

"I am inspired; I am possessed, Cosmos, possessed by love and desire, but this inspiration, this afflatus, this linguistic virtuosity, is temporary; it is due to your … your luminous, your liminal and divine, presence, Oh, Cosmos. Soon I will sink back to my own level, then I will be as dull and ungrammatical and mute as rancid dishwater, empty of spirit, just the old scrounging Scav, scuttling around, dropping onto all fours, begging, leaching, licking, slurping, farting, scrabbling for old cast-off snot colored marbles and leftover moldy crumbs of mushroom and lichen, leaving my signature tune, turds, behind me, everywhere, such I am, Oh Beauteous Cosmos. I saw you in the sacred text, I am sure I did!" Scav was so excited he let loose a whole cloud of goo that caught Nikki smack in the ear.

"And what was this sacred text, Oh, Scav?" Nikki asked, twisting, shimmying, her shoulders. A long, snake-like dribble of Scav fluid was crawling inch-by-inch down her backbone – as she stepped down, carefully, yet another rung, stretching her skirt to dangerous limits, and testing the resiliency of her high heels. They had probably gone down several hundred feet already; the goo that had nested between her breasts was now under her silk T-shirt, oozing down towards her belly. She wondered if it contained sperm. Scav was quite a mutant; he might reproduce by sneezing.

"*Vogue Italia* was the Text, the Word of Dolly, from the World before The Fall; it is kept sacred for all time, in the Holy Box, under the shrine to Dolly." Scav reached out one of his suction pads to steady Nikki.

"You keep copies of *Vogue Italia* in your shrine?"

"From the World before the Big Burp, before The Fall from Grace, hidden in caves, there were copies of *Vogue* – scrolls of *Vogue* – they show what life was like before the wicked Cosmos destroyed it."

Nikki wondered if she should enlighten Scav as to the reality of the world portrayed in *Vogue* – a world which, in any case, had perished many decades ago, in the Second Bubonic Plague and the Third Yellow Fever Influenza and also in the civil wars and General Ecological Collapse. But it was true she had modeled for *Vogue France* and *Vogue Italia* in the old days – so perhaps Scav had seen some of those Helmut Newton-style photographs she'd done for the Jean-Paul-Gaultier-type-*Story of O-Marquis de Sade* collection. But glossy high-fashion black-and-white bondage and S&M were not exactly typical of life in the early 21st century. Probably it was best not to disillusion Scav. She would let him dream the dream. If *Vogue* was part of their religion, so much the better; she was not going to criticize the Faith. She wanted to keep as many of the mutants on side as possible. The others, particularly the females, were following close by, murmuring, sighing, munching, their breath heavy and humid, a mass of shuffling, shadowy, malformed bodies, the product of suburban basement hobbyist bio-brick aspiring Thomas Edisons, of cutting-edge weaponry and bio-molecular research, of nano-technology married to bio-technology, of big drug company pharmaceutical speculation and underground experimentation, of solar radiation – due to the collapse of the ozone layer, which was due to global warming and high-reaching super-thunderheads – of nuclear radiation – due to a few accidents and spills and the great China-India-Pakistan War – products of industrial chemicals and toxic oil polluting the remaining aquifers, and of seafood transmission of genetic variants due to genetic transformations of plankton and krill and tuna and salmon due to ingurgitated broken-down plastic molecules, and due to …

And to think, Nikki bit her lip, that I am part of all that; in fact, I am at the origin of much of what has now happened, and …

And Miranda, of course, has no inkling of this.

Which reminds me; I must tell her about us, about the facts of life, about …

"Watch your step, Oh, Cosmos!" Scav sprayed a new shower of thick viscous goo, catching Nikki square in the forehead.

"Scav!"

"It is a sign of passion and pure love, Oh, Cosmos!"

"Well, I suppose that makes it all right then," murmured Nikki, flashing Scav an almost flirtatious smile and feeling the goo drip down one side of her nose and stick on her eyelashes. "How are you doing, Miranda?" she said over her shoulder, though, being extra sensitive as she was, Nikki knew that Miranda was absolutely fine.

"I'm hunky-dory, mother!"

As they went down there were pieces of machinery hanging from cables and ropes, and small flickering candles in front of the machinery, hubcaps, car radiators, an old internal combustion engine mounted on a statue of a horse, and a rusty kitchen blender which stood in front of a reproduction of a painting of the Virgin Mary – Nikki recognized it was a work by Jacopo Bellini cut out from some old book or magazine – and in front of the candles, some of which were burning, there were old coins, and brightly colored but faded bits of cloth, and three Barbie dolls were kneeling in front of a juice blender garlanded with dried mottled rattlesnake skins; two candles burned on either side.

Religion, thought Nikki, shrines of their religion.

"The manna will fall from the skies," Scav said, genuflecting towards an ancient bright red Sony Walkman and two half-crushed empty silver-and-red Diet Coke cans that sat on a small stone pillar, worshipped by two voodoo dolls with button eyes and that had been stuck full of pins, "The cargo will come down in balloons, parachutes, or wreckage."

"Miranda and I are, I imagine, cargo, or manna."

"Oh, yes, oh, yes, Oh Cosmos," Scav grinned. He began to chant in a warbling, high, falsetto voice, "Oh Cosmos to eat! What a feat!" He hopped down two steps to catch up with Nikki and Miranda, who had both stopped to listen to him.

Now, perhaps inspired by the sight of Nikki dripping his green goo, Scav let go with a full-throated falsetto ecclesiastical warble, "Our Mother who Art in Oblivion, bring us forth our daily pint, our mash, our bangers, let us in oblivion and unhappiness reside, let fear and trembling overshadow all our yearnings and cast sadness in our fallen hearts and sinful bodies, and sift the sands through the fingers of eternity, let all incorrigible wankers perish, Amen!"

"Golly," said Nikki.

Scav screamed a sacred scream, spraying green goo all over Nikki's neck, arms, and T-shirt, "Here's looking at you! Here's looking at you!"

"Here's Looking at you! Here's looking at you!" the crowd thundered back, "Here's Looking at you! Here's looking at you!"

And all the mutants shouted. They fell down on their knees, crying out, "Hallelujah! Hallelujah!"

"Well," said Nikki, "this is extremely interesting."

The crowd was still on the stairs, all lined up behind Scav and Nikki and Miranda and Caliban.

"Oh, beautiful Nikki, oh sublime Cosmos, cast a gander on the truly sacred and bow your proud Cosmos head in humility and abasement!" Scav pointed to a side niche where an altar was on display. He sputtered, spraying another wave of green sputum, splashing Nikki once again.

"That was the last Cosmos to come to ground as manna from the star-studded night here in the True Heart of Dead Land," said Caliban, pointing at a blackened and charred skeleton, hanging from a cross, nailed and wired to the cross, with snakeskins wrapped around its shanks and loins, like garlands and on its forehead was one snakeskin and the head of a rattlesnake poised at a rakish angle.

"Gosh," said Miranda. She had stopped on the same step as Nikki and they were shoulder to shoulder, arms pinioned back, staring at the crucified human – or "Cosmos" as the mutants called it. To Nikki, it looked like a man. Yes, definitely, from the bones and the skull, it was a male human, not that old either. Below, on the altar, just below the skeletal feet, two candles flickered, and there was a scorched navy-blue cap with gold braid and an eagle symbol. Gold letters spelled "Lufthansa."

"A pilot," said Nikki.

"Gosh," said Miranda, "He was young, too, about thirty years old, I think, and lived in Domed City Hamburg and had two children – a boy and a girl – he didn't want to die, but he was brave and very dignified, even unto the very end."

Nikki glanced at her daughter: from a few objects and from the charred bones, Miranda had read the man's past. Miranda's naturally rambunctious and all-encompassing empathy was becoming truly psychic; but, curious about everything, and with her attention directed outwards towards the world and other people, Miranda had not yet grasped what was happening to her; she didn't have an inkling of what was going on.

"That reminds me, Miranda," said Nikki, "There's something I really should tell you, and I think now's the time. What I mean to say is, you …"

"Silence, Cosmos!" said Caliban, raising his machete, "Silence, Cosmos Whore! Silence! Idolatress, Silence!"

"Yes, Master," said Nikki, "Yes, Master Caliban." She bowed her head and bit her lip. For several months now she had been thinking how to explain to Miranda the facts of life as they concerned, in particular, Miranda, but for some reason, given Miranda's education and attitudes, she found it exceedingly difficult to explain these specific facts of life to Miranda; and the more she rehearsed arguments and tried out phrases in her mind, the more contorted and inadequate they all seemed, the knottier the whole question became, which, as Nikki herself was aware, was most unlike Nikki, for she was rarely at a loss for words and she was embarrassed by virtually nothing, certainly not sex or other bodily functions, or money, filthy lucre, or illness, or weakness, or suffering, or death, or religion, for example; but, now, in fact, any excuse *not* to explain was welcome, because if she did tell Miranda, it would destroy Miranda. So this was a close call, and Caliban, *dear, dear Caliban*, however cruel he could be and was, he had saved the day. *Whew!* But then again, it was her duty to clarify matters, before it was too late, before …

They went down two more steps, and then through a huge, low, rusty metal arch – on which was written in massive letters of decaying iron, "*The Churn Halibut Mining Corporation.*"

Suddenly, they were at the bottom of the stairway.

"Oh! My God!" Miranda stared. It was a dream. It was a videogame. It was … a fairyland.

A giant vaulted cavern soared up, hundreds and hundreds of feet above them. Huge smoky torches burned here and there. Suspended walkways stretched along the sheer walls of stone and metal stairs zigzagged upward to the walkways. The shadowy mouths of what looked like caves were dotted everywhere. The vaulted ceiling, lost in mist and smoke, sparkled, as with a myriad of stars. The far end of the cavern was invisible, lost in the dusky air. The walls of stone shimmered and glowed, covered by a sort of phosphorescent lichen, and clusters of glowing fruit-like bulbs.

"The roof must be about 300 feet up," Nikki said, "Maybe more." She craned her neck and stared into the shadowy heights of the vast basilica-like space, where – lost in dimness – smoke curled, miniature clouds formed, and strange lights – they almost seemed like stars – twinkled. The walkways that festooned the high walls of the cavern were crowded with people – well, with mutants – and there were what looked like side-caves and tunnels, openings, carved into wall rock faces, opening onto all the walkways and hanging gangways.

Exotic-looking mutants – every variety – scurried everywhere, particularly down in a central sort of aisle, which seemed to be like a main street marketplace or bazaar. It thronged with creatures of all kinds, jostling against each other, bargaining, it seemed, for trinkets and food and booty. The market was lit by torches but also by the phosphorescence that shone from every wall and by huge grape-like formations of lichen and what looked like some kind of glowing fungus or mushrooms that rose on stalagmite-like formations, or hung, like enormous bunches of grapes from rocky outcroppings.

"No rain above, in the desert," Caliban, turned to Miranda and Nikki. His voice boomed, as if he were making a public speech, but sounded strangely hollow, resonating in the colossal greasy iron latticework and echoing against the cavernous walls of stone, lost in the steamy crowded colorful grandeur of the place, "but we do have water down here – in the Mutant Kingdom! We are the true inheritors of the earth!"

"Water!" the procession, still coming down the stairs, chanted, "Water!"

"Water!" spluttered Scav, staring at Nikki, "Water!" Nikki blinked; Scav had just landed three large green web-like gobs, she figured, right on her chin. Now I'll look like I have a beard! She was tempted to try to lick it away, but decided it would be more hygienic not to.

Spread out on the floor of the cavern were fountains of water – gray and silver geysers spurted into the smoky air – and there were fires in braziers and piles of machinery that probably once served to mine minerals or pump oil out of the ground, and there were tents and stands for merchants. Nearby, a huge Mack Truck lay on its side. A river ran down the middle of the cavern. Tent-like structures lined its banks, and creatures were tossing nets into the stream.

Huge winged shapes, like bulbous Chinese lanterns, flitted and fluttered through the glimmering smoke-filled air. They glowed. They throbbed, all the colors of the rainbow.

A purple and crimson Chinese lantern swooped down, paused, and fluttered its wings – perhaps a meter across each – just above Miranda's head; it made a little breeze.

Miranda tilted her face upwards. The air moved against her cheeks. She stared at the antennae, at the legs, at the many, many legs, and at the multi-faceted golden eyes, like a thousand golden beads, unblinking, which were tilted down, and staring back at her. The lantern hovered for a moment, its wings beating slowly, like a beating heart. Then gently, slowly, it lifted off and flew away, high up into the murky depths, and then off down the giant cavern, above the busy throng, until it was lost to sight.

"Fireflies," said Nikki, "Giant fireflies."

"Boy, oh, boy, they are beautiful!" Miranda was entranced.

"They're big," said Nikki, "two-meter wing-span, at least." Half her face was now coated in a thick, hard grunge of green, and a drippy mustache curled brightly around her mouth, making a rubber green beard.

"We really must clean you up, mother," said Miranda.

"Indeed, we must, Miranda, but shackled as we are," Nikki twisted her tightly pinioned shoulders, wiggling, "it will be difficult."

"Silence, Cosmos prisoners and slaves, and follow me!" Caliban gave the order briskly, in an imperious voice.

Immediately, beside him, appeared six large bear-like creatures, they were obviously police of some sort. They carried knives, machetes, lances, and truncheons, and they were wearing breastplates, and shoulder guards, and helmets with visors, and shin guards and boots. They had hands, Miranda noted, and not paws. Six pairs of brown eyes gazed upon Nikki and then upon Miranda – Miranda had the impression that they were not *entirely* hostile, but she wasn't one hundred percent sure.

Miranda glanced around. Everywhere were new versions of mutants. They had a fascinating variety of forms: One eye instead of two, no arms, tiny legs, or legs which were much too long. Some walked on all fours. Some crawled and wiggled or slithered and zigzagged. In many cases, it seemed, their DNA must have been mixed up, somehow, with animal DNA. Some perhaps had started as animals but had been gifted with something like human intelligence; some had started, perhaps, as humans, but had morphed into part-animal. Some had almost certainly been built from the ground up with DNA bio-bricks, almost totally original. Miranda had never seen so much variety before, not even in the Sin Zone, not even in the Religious Underground, not even in Vid Net Games. If only Kit were here to see all of this! She would certainly have some interesting theories.

The crowds of mutants were busy frenetically haggling with vendors in the little canvas stands. Some turned to gawk at the two Cosmos prisoners. One caught Miranda's eye, spat on the ground, stuck out its tongue, and turned away. Another blinked at Miranda and crossed itself. After a quick glance, most turned back to their haggling and bargaining.

It was like being in a Video Net Sensory Morph Game, except here the people – or *creatures* – Miranda still wasn't sure you could legally or morally or philosophically classify the mutants real "persons" – were trapped in their bodies. They couldn't just turn the game off, slip out of the furry coat or slimy scales, stretch, stand up, and become a Cosmos and Fully-Certified Human again, and go and make coffee, or dive into the pool, or go shopping on the shopping level.

Irreversible physicality made everything so real, so awful.

Caliban and two of the bears chased away Nikki's numerous female fan club – they went reluctantly, waving arms, flippers, and tentacles – and shooed away the rest of the procession – it went, squawking, clucking, squealing, and some of the females even called out:

"Goodbye, goodbye, goodbye …"

Scav objected to being chased away. He sputtered, "She's mine, the mother is mine, the mother is mine," and sprayed some more goo, but he was prodded by one of the lances wielded by a particularly determined bear and he skulked off, hissing and spraying goo left and right, as he disappeared slouching into the crowd.

Miranda's lemur ball which had been bouncing along beside her jumped on her shoulder and put its eating orifice next to her cheek and gave her what Miranda took to be a big soft dry kiss and then it patted Miranda's cheeks, and gently squeezed her nose, with two paws that appeared out of the ball. Then it purred, emitted a high-pitched squeak, and hopped off her shoulder onto the roof of a vendor's canvas stall, and disappeared – the vendor was selling something that looked like pumpkins but those pumpkins had legs and were trying to crawl away. The vendor, an immensely fat, spinach-green female character – it had what looked like breasts – with a scarlet topknot, grabbed the escaping pumpkins, slapped them, and plunked them back onto her overcrowded basket-tray. Other vendors, Miranda noticed, peeking through gaps in the crowd, sold what looked like spinach, and also fish and eels, but the fish and eels were all chalk-white and didn't seem to have any eyes.

Miranda and Nikki were hustled through the crowd, led up a swaying suspended metal staircase that zigzagged up one soaring wall of the cavern – the stairs creaked and groaned as they climbed upwards; finally, they reached a walkway that was maybe forty meters up and suspended from cables and held up by jutting support beams, and then they were hustled along the walkway to a cave which had iron bars for a door and which looked out over the cavern.

"Unshackle the Cosmos wenches!" Caliban turned to the bears. "I do not wish to soil my pure mutant hands with Cosmos infamy."

Two bears stepped up and unlocked the shackles.

They removed the handcuffs.

Nikki rubbed her wrists and then reached up to touch the goo on her face; it had hardened into a mask.

Miranda rubbed her wrists and glared at Caliban: *Cosmos wenches, Cosmos infamy* indeed! She would show him some Cosmos infamy!

Two bears stepped forward. Keys jangled from their belts. Delicately they unlocked and opened the barred gate.

"Here is your cave, Cosmos harlots," said Caliban, in a loud, declamatory voice. "This is your prison: this is your sty – wallow in it!"

"Our sty, how charming," from behind her half-goo mask Nikki gave Caliban a hard look; he blushed, looked down, looked up, and gave her a fierce look – of hatred or … or of something else … something undefinable …

The six bear-like creatures, all staring at Miranda and Nikki, stood impassively around Caliban. One of the bears cleared his throat. Two bears shifted their weight, clutched their lances tighter.

"Now," said Caliban, "you must divest yourselves of your Cosmos raiment and attire, everything, down to the most intimate items of apparel – and watches and jewelry too. Your nakedness must be total."

"What?" Miranda's eyes flared.

"Now, Master Caliban, what do you mean?" Nikki gave him her imperious look.

"Don't quibble, Cosmos! What I say is what I mean, it's quite clear, fair harlot Cosmos, Oh, Jezebel, Oh, Salomé, what I mean is: strip, undress, bare yourself, disrobe, divest yourself of your Cosmos frippery and idolatrous ornament, throw off all your clothes, all your vanity, you will not be naked long. Your prisoner garment – modest humble rough coarse apparel fitting your fallen and sinful Cosmos state – is lying there, inside the depths of your cage. And water too – there is a fountain – a cascade – where you can bathe and purify yourselves of Cosmos filth and Cosmos slime and prepare for what is to come. I must now go to the Great High Priest my father and tell him what booty we have brought."

With that, the bars swung shut and were bolted and locked.

"Now, hand us your clothes!"

"What do we do, mother?"

Caliban roared. "Now – hand us your clothes! Everything, every single rag and scrap, and morsel! If you don't, we shall come in and rip them off you, Cosmos swine!"

"We shall, Miranda, for the moment, do what dear Caliban asks us to –"

"*Dear Caliban!!!*" Miranda's eyes flared. "He didn't *ask* us, mother, he *ordered* us, and I will not for one instant stand for it, being ordered around by a man, a mutant, even if I love him and even if he is Tarzan and Long John Silver and the most impressive naked male I have ever seen, I will not stand for it and I'm going to –"

"Miranda," said Nikki, looking like a Jekyll and Hyde cartoon, with her monstrous frozen half-mask of grotesque goo, "Do calm down, get undressed, give them your clothes, and let's find whatever rags they've left for us and put them on. If we are going to fight, let us choose the best moment for a fight, which is definitely not now."

Miranda fumed.

She glanced at Caliban. Her horrible pirate was waiting outside the iron bars of their prison slapping his machete impatiently against his thigh. But he and the bears had had the decency to turn their backs.

"Well, okay, mother I shall divest myself of my Cosmos Humanity – naked like King Lear or poor Tom, or whatever he was, on the heath – but only if you take note of my most earnest and serious protest at our passively accepting the way we are being treated. Remember the Alamo, remember Valley Forge, Remember Waterloo, and the Blitz, and remember, blood, toil, tears, and sweat, and remember, never have so many owed so much to so few, and remember the sacred Cosmos Oath of Honor!"

"Your protest is duly noted, Miranda." Nikki had already slipped out of her T-shirt, and her skirt, and even her panties and shoes, and, glancing at Miranda, she handed them through the bars, "Here you are, Master Caliban," she said, and Caliban, shielding his eyes, and shuffling backward to be close to the bars, reached behind his back, groped, and found and took the bundle of clothes, shoes, stockings, two watches, and one necklace.

"Just a moment, please, Master Caliban, Miranda is about to give me hers."

Miranda stuck out her tongue, rolled her eyes, and slipped out of her T-shirt, her hot pants, and then her gym socks and neo-scamper shoes and she only hesitated for an instant before letting her panties drop around her ankles – with a little wiggle of her hips – and then she hesitated, sighed, rolled her eyes, gritted her teeth, and unstrapped her watch – it was an antique with a batty-looking yellow-faced cross-eyed mouse on the face – she handed the bundle to her mother who handed it through the bars to Caliban.

"I shall return," said Caliban, and then, in an instant, he was gone, and so were the bears.

"Well," said Nikki, gazing at her daughter.

"Well," said Miranda, staring at her mother. With her face a half-mask of green goo, with streaks of glowing crystallized rubbery sputum down her perfect chalk-white body, Nikki was an extraordinary sight. Miranda was used to seeing her mother naked since they both often swam naked in the terrace pool or just walked around the house without any clothes on; but, somehow, now, it seemed different: Nikki seemed *more* naked. *And I guess I am too. We have been despoiled, that is what has happened, we have been reduced to our elemental selves, whatever the heck that means.*

Miranda looked around, but didn't see the prisoner's garb – cast-off second-hand mutant rags – she supposed they were; the things that they were supposed to put on. The obscene, bloody things must be somewhere! Well, here we are! Prisoners! Miranda scowled. It was not exactly a pirate ship on the frothy, oxygen-drenched, fish-rich, bounding main!

She turned to look out of the cage – at freedom, at the huge cavern with its multitudinous echoing sounds of mutant life, at the flitting giant Chinese lantern fireflies – there were small ones too, sort of twinkle-fairies, blinking like little flying traffic lights – and at the spinach and crimson-colored hanging gardens, and the clusters of brightly glowing moss.

She wrapped her fingers tight around the prison bars – greasy with thick rust – and pushed her face against them, and peered out at the immense cavern – about 50 to 100 meters away, over on the other side, there were other walkways and she could see mutants walking up and down, and entering little side caves, and going about their mutant business – some of them tending to the hanging gardens – as if nothing extraordinary had happened, as if she and Nikki were not being treated in an absolutely atrocious fashion, as if …

"Let us explore, then," Nikki said, "and see about the fountain that Caliban talked about – and perhaps get ourselves some clothes – if there are any."

"Caliban doesn't love me."

"I'm sure he does, darling, he's just nervous – and here, among his people, he has to show that he is tough and loyal and not playing favorites. It's probably for your sake that he's being so gruff and cranky."

"*Cranky! Cranky!* I *hate* him!!" Miranda stuck out her lower lip; she was tempted to stage a gigantic pout. She tightened her grip on the greasy prison bars.

"Let's go, Miranda, I want to get rid of all traces of my friend Scav if I can." Nikki glanced into the shadowy depths of their prison. The cave tunneled away into the dank misty darkness; she thought she heard, vaguely, the sound of falling water; and, yes, she hoped they would find the "prison garb" Caliban had mentioned; it would be preferable for both of them, trapped in this place, to be clothed and not to remain stark naked.

"Yes, mother, of course, you are right, mother! I am being selfish as usual."

"Sometimes you are too hard on yourself, Miranda."

Miranda felt funny being naked and barefoot in this winding musty cavern with its mysterious wafts of sticky air, with its clayey fecund smells, and with the weird slippery stalactites and stalagmites, sticking up and hanging down on both sides, like some sort of weird petrified forest, and with the glowing lichen and big grape-like bulbous bunches of sparkling moss sending a silver light over everything. It was like walking naked in a magic forest in moonlight, all shimmery and ghostly and shivery, though with a blush of sweat and damp on her skin, and with her toes squishing in the inch-deep muddy warm softness. Nikki, who was in front of her, about three meters away, seemed to glow; she looked like a statue Miranda had seen in the Virtual Art Museum but with several squiggles of Scav's goo down her back like squirrely musical notations, a dribbled staccato perhaps, for a signature tune. The cave was like a tunnel; it turned a few corners, and went on for quite a way.

People – Cosmos and other prisoners – had scribbled messages on the walls. There were nooks and crannies, some supplied with thin mattresses, and there were what looked like little side caves to sleep in, and then, dim and far away, there was the rippling and tumbling sound of water.

"Where in the world would water come from here in this arid, drought-tortured desert?" Nikki said. "Come, let's have a look."

They turned a corner and – miracle! – There it was, a cascading waterfall, with a deep, bubbling pool, the water was steaming, mist rising up, and twirling around. Nikki took a deep breath. The water looked quite warm – it must come from very deep down, from some ancient aquifer that was surrounded by a stratum of hot rock. It looked promising, rather like a spa.

On a stone ledge beside the waterfall were buckets and bars of what looked like soap, and brushes and combs, and folded up, on another ledge, were two prisoner tunics.

Miranda lifted the tunics up.

They were rough pieces of cloth, armless, very wide neck opening, and very short, with a torn and ragged fringe. She turned them over; the material was coarse brown, something like burlap, but much thinner; on front and back, printed in glowing red – more *phosphorescence*, thought Miranda – was the letter 'P.'

"It means 'prisoner' I suppose," said Nikki.

"Not very elegant, not very fashionable," Miranda held the rags out at arm's length. She turned to Nikki with a comic grimace, a mask of dismay.

Nikki laughed, "Oh, I don't know, there once was a special edition of, I think, *Elle*, which talked about 'burlap fashion' and the minimalist, ragged, neo-scavenger look."

"Well, we would absolutely be in fashion then, decades ago, or centuries, or whenever it was," Miranda folded the two tunics carefully, put them down on the ledge, patted them down, and stood back, head tilted, stroking her chin thoughtfully, as if she had just laid them out in a luxury store window. "We can put them on later," she said and glanced at her mother.

Nikki's smile, contorted by the half-mask of goo, was tragedy and comedy all in one, but it was still the brightest, widest, most loving smile. "Yes, later – here, just you and I, Miranda, we don't need clothes. Let's enjoy this cave – it's like a spa, and this, Miranda, is a holiday."

Miranda blinked at her mother. It seemed that Nikki was not at all afraid; and for some reason, that meant that Miranda was not going to be afraid either, in fact – this was definitely going to be an *adventure*!

Nikki tested the water with her finger; then she put a toe in, carefully, and then she stepped into the pool and waded to the deeper part – which was up to her neck – and then she climbed up onto a ledge, and stood under the waterfall; Miranda followed. The water was warm and silky and *luscious*!

Miranda climbed out of the water and onto the ledge under the waterfall. She began to scrub Nikki's back and peel off bits and pieces of Scav Goo; Nikki carefully pried the half-mask of rubbery green off, and placed it on a ledge of stone, safely away from the water. Miranda used a brush to scrub the Scav scribbles off her mother's shoulder-blade and from the small of her back, "Stand still, mother, don't wiggle!"

"But it tickles!"

"It doesn't matter if it tickles!"

Finally, Nikki had been scrubbed and soaped quite clean. All mementos of Scav had been peeled away and placed in a little heap. Miranda was still soaping Nikki's back, slowly, down the spine, up and over the shoulder blades, then the nape of the neck, then down again, dribbles of foam flowing down the ivory skin; she loved being close to her mother, grooming her, pampering her. It evoked something primitive, like she was one of those chimpanzees she had read about, perched on a branch, picking fleas from her special friend, or a lioness, out on the savanna, licking her mother's whiskers and both of them purring contentment; it made her feel warm and protected, and, funnily enough, it made her feel protective of her mother, as if she, Miranda, were the adult, the shield, the warrior.

"Am I myself again?" Nikki looked over her shoulder.

"Yes, you're entirely yourself; but I'm enjoying this."

"Me too, Miranda, I like it when we're this close," Nikki wiggled. "There, there – right there, just above my right shoulder-blade. Oh, oh, oh … That is so, so nice!"

Together they slid deeper into the water.

The pool was a delight. The water cascaded down from a height of about twenty meters, and it was steamy and smoky blue, and the pool was maybe ten meters across and then the water tumbled away, through a crack, disappearing into the depths.

For a while, they just lazed, shoulder-deep, in warm bliss, not really thinking of much. The water was warm and suave with minerals and its very suaveness and warmth were sleep-inducing. Nikki's eyelids fluttered.

"I *hate* Caliban!" Miranda was up to her collarbone in warm, gently swirling water. She blew a soap bubble and whapped it dead with a backhand slap of her wrist.

"I don't think you do," said Nikki.

"He's a total, absolute monster!" Miranda mumbled. Her eyes fluttered. She was half-asleep. Her voice faded, "An absolute pig, so totally …"

"Maybe he isn't. Time will tell," Nikki slid closer to her daughter, put her arm around Miranda's shoulders, and Miranda resting her head on Nikki's shoulder, closed her eyes, nodded, collapsed against Nikki, and sank into the inchoate world of dreams.

"This thing rides pretty high on the thigh." Nikki tugged – unsuccessfully – at the fringe of her tunic.

"Might as well be naked," said Miranda.

"Well, a lot of the mutants go without clothes, so I suppose it doesn't really matter who or what catches what glimpses of what." Nikki glanced down at her own long white legs. She gave Miranda a sly, appraising look.

Miranda put her hand over her mouth and giggled; the tunic barely reached her own thighs which were tanned that permanent golden glow.

The next day, Miranda explored the side caves, sometimes alone, sometimes with Nikki, though Nikki insisted on inspecting everything first before Miranda was allowed to wander solo.

The graffiti on the walls spoke of prisoners and executions and sacrifice.

We've been here sixteen days.
My sister was sacrificed yesterday.
These mutants are devils.

Robert screamed. It was horrible to hear.
Kill them all! Kill each and every one of the vermin!
They burnt Karen, alive, two days ago.
Where are the Centurions? They should have saved us from these devils.

Miranda was in a little side cave. She put her hand up to one of the scrawls – *They burnt Karen alive, two days ago* – she got a strange tingling feeling and a rush of images, ghostly fluttering faces, skeletal hands pressed against stone, open, broken-toothed mouths, howling, chains and collars, and burning crosses, with people crucified, going up in flames – the flesh lighting up, glowing like molten glass, with dark streaming blood, and then flesh melting like wax, and …

She pulled her hand away. It felt like it had been scalded by a red-hot iron. She looked at the hand, at the palm of her hand and at the fingertips – no, nothing was burned, nothing was scarred or cut …

Suddenly, Nikki was there, standing behind her, a dark silhouette against the light from beyond the side niche. "Miranda, it's better not to dwell too much on the fate of those poor souls."

"Yes, you're right," Miranda gazed at her mother: *She knew what I was feeling, but how did she know?*

Miranda stepped back from the wall and rushed into Nikki's arms, thrusting her arms around Nikki and squeezing tight. She would never touch the writing again. Nikki was right. It was dangerous. The scrawled letters and drawings contained a sparkly mental energy of some kind, an energy she didn't like. It was painful, hurtful, and tragic. It was a frozen scream, just waiting to be released. She felt sorry for those who had suffered, but, now, after the fact, there was nothing she could do. To feel their suffering as it if were *her* suffering, well, that was just too much – and it served no purpose; and, as Cyril Bedford might have said in a seminar, in his cute pompous way, it was *counter-productive.*

Time passed.

Strictly speaking, it was not easy to reckon time so far underground, but Nikki and Miranda did have their well-tuned body clocks. The days went by slowly.

They were fed through the bars of their prison. They were brought a meal twice a day, by one of the bears, who would clang a metal cup against the bars and shout in a growling sort of way.

When this happened, Nikki and Miranda – who usually didn't bother with clothes – wiggled into their tunics and ran to receive the meal – thick smooth gruel which tasted like vanilla, chewy mushroom-like meat that came in hunks, something that seemed like tofu but wasn't, and various greens that were like spinach but weren't spinach. No utensils were provided; so, sitting cross-legged on a stone ledge, they ate with their hands and licked the wooden bowls clean.

"Yummy," said Nikki.

"Ugh," said Miranda.

"Delicious," said Nikki.

"You're an idiot," said Miranda.

"But a happy idiot," said Nikki.

"Yes, a happy idiot," sighed Miranda.

It was Nikki's duty to return the bowls, kneeling next to the bars, slipping the plates through the special slot, and setting them down on the metal walkway, where someone – probably one of the bears – would later pick them up.

Once, when Miranda went with Nikki to peer through the bars of their prison, Miranda's lemur ball came bounding through the bars and nestled next to her, and bounced up and kissed her, and then he – or she – was gone, bouncing back out of the cave, and down the gangway, until he or she was far away, and absolutely out of sight.

"True love," said Nikki.

Miranda frowned, "Yes, I guess so." It did feel like affection. But who could know what these weird mutant creatures were feeling or thinking?

It was a strange, isolated existence. Even pressing their faces against the greasy iron bars – and getting an imprint of flaky rust on their faces – they could not see the floor of the cavern; the angle was too steep, the gangway blocked their view, and the bottom was too far down.

From a great distance, they could hear the crowds milling about and occasionally there were songs and sometimes there were screams as if someone was being tortured; then it was just the hum of ordinary life again. There was no difference between night and day.

A small – three-foot-high – furry, vaguely humanoid creature, who shuffled along on its large widely spaced, three splayed toes, appeared at the bars of the cave and whistled a high sibilant whistle.

The creature, it turned out, was bearing books.

Nikki and Miranda, who were deep in the cave, just coming out from under the waterfall, slipped into their tunics and responded to the call, running out to the mouth of the cave, to the brighter light of the vast cavern, to their prison bars.

"Greetings," Nikki bowed.

"Hello," said Miranda, tilting her chin upwards and staring down at the creature.

"I am Fluff. I bear books, from Lord Caliban," he said, shyly, and then looked up, blinking his slit red eyes through his heavy lids and fluttering thick long eyelashes.

"Thank you, Master Fluff," Nikki accepted the books, "And, Master Fluff, may I ask? Where, then, *is* Lord Caliban?"

"Yes, where *is* Lord Caliban?" Miranda tugged at the skimpy burlap; she had been having *such* a good time with Nikki, playing together in their private spa, their private pool; but seeing Master Fluff brought back all her amorous anguish; she was feeling positively *insulted* by Caliban – or was she feeling *bereft* of him, or *lovelorn* for him, or was she just *furious* with him: it was a pickle, all very confusing. She wasn't entirely sure what she was feeling, but she did know that, suddenly, there was, once again, an empty, anguished, nausea-inducing, black void in the pit of her stomach and a dizzy whirl of dark morbid ideas – *he loves me, he loves me not, I love him, no, I hate him* – twirling in her head, whatever that meant. Did it mean love or hate, war or peace?

"Busy – Lord Caliban is busy. Said to send his most elaborate and heartfelt and diplomatic apologies! Revolt among females! Must be put down! Revolt has now been put down! Many females dead, alas, Dolly's will be done!"

"Oh," said Nikki.

"They will rise again," said Miranda.

"Maybe," said Master Fluff, "Doubtful. Dead do not walk, not usually." His eyes fluttered mightily, his long silky black lashes created a miniature breeze, and he looked down at his three-fingered toes, and curled one over the other, "Sorry, but must not talk politics; must leave now; good-bye."

And he was gone.

"Well," said Nikki, she was holding the books cradled in one hand, and trying to smooth the ragged fringe of the skimpy cotton-thin burlap down over her thighs with the other. Not having any underthings – not even panties – was positively inconvenient when one was meeting with strangers.

"Well," said Miranda, her fingers still gripping the thick greasy iron prison bars; she sighed.

"Let's see …What has he left us, then?" Nikki opened the first book. It had a greasy tatty dog-eared muddy cover and had obviously been heavily used. "Hmm, Emily Post – *Principles of Etiquette in Society, in Business, in Politics, and at Home.*"

Miranda sighed. She blew out her cheeks, "Poof!" Her full and quite exquisite, precisely sculpted lips were turned down in an exaggerated pout; she bit and twisted her lower lip, she ran her tongue along her lower lip; she rolled her eyes, and glanced heavenward – there was nothing, just a smoky vaulted, only partly visible, roof of stone. Again, she sighed. She rubbed her fingers up and down the prison bars, coating her hands with greasy, russet-colored rust.

"Well, Miranda, we have some light reading."

"I'm not interested," Miranda frowned, twisted her nose as if she smelled something utterly disgusting. She turned around and leaned back on the bars of the cage, the rough itchy parchment-thin burlap hitching itself up, on one side, high above her hip bone, marking her as effectively naked. *Too hell with that! Do I care if I'm naked!? No, I don't care! I don't care a fig!!!* She signed. "A wave of liverish splenetic suicidal black-bile melancholy has come upon me, mother. I want to mope. I am determined, in fact, to mope! I shall mope, in fact, until the cows come home!"

"Why, Miranda, what do we have here? Why, here we have: *The English Metaphysical Poets*, edited by …"

"Mother!!" it was a cry of anguish, "Oh, mother!!"

"And, now this is perfect, *The Leaves of Grass*, by Walt Whitman," Nikki said, cheerily, holding up the antique paperback, "one of my absolute favorites."

From under knotted eyebrows – misty tears sparkling in her eyes – Miranda was still leaning against the bars of their cage, the burlap hitched up with that askew, come-hither, curbside, I-am-a-fallen-woman look; she sniffled and wiped her nose with the back of her hand. Miranda had seen instructive examples of the come-hither stance down in the Sin Zone when slumming with Kit and she thought *I too shall become a fallen woman; I shall ply my trade next to the underground gutters and smoky malodorous runnels of the world.* She sniffled, wiped away her tears, and gazed at her mother. "Thank you, mother, thank you for trying."

"You're welcome, dear afflicted Miranda. As you are, I am sure, aware, the Bard said, 'Lovers and madmen …'" Nikki was beginning to realize just how serious Miranda's crush was. The girl definitely needed to be distracted from her morbid yearning for and speculations about Master Caliban. Nikki knew quite well that even the most brilliant of girls is perfectly capable of consuming all her mental energy and turning herself into a sheer idiot merely by worrying about what some callow insignificant and totally mediocre boy is thinking, or doing, or – God forbid – feeling! A feeling boy, that was almost an oxymoron! And, in Nikki's experience, callow boys never thought about much at all, except maybe baseball scores and surfing and horsepower, or possibly, if slightly more mature, how to get into the girl's pants, or in rare nerdish cases, about nuclear and sub-atomic physics, cosmology, and engineering, or, God truly forbid, theology. No boy was worthy of such obsessive thought – waste of brain-power and brain-time – on the part of a girl as brilliant as Miranda – not even if the callow boy – well, young man – happened to be the superbly equipped, muscular, wild young man, their very own Master Caliban, for whom Nikki nursed a special and very particular ...

"We should escape," said Miranda.

"Where?"

"Well, we could cut through the bars of the cage."

"Yes, and then ..."

Miranda frowned, "We could tunnel through the rock."

"It is rock, Miranda, solid rock, and we are at least two or three hundred meters underground, maybe much more. And we don't have tools. In any case, I think our moment will come, when they are all distracted, and we are outside this cage."

"Okay," Miranda pouted, "Okay, mother, but still I think we should definitely raise the flag of Cosmos revolt. After all, we are Cosmos, warriors one and all, and, under our Glorious President, we are the Masters of the Universe."

"Let's raise the flag of Cosmos revolt later, Miranda, but right now let us enjoy this place. It is an adventure and it is in fact rather like being in our very own spa, don't you think?"

Miranda looked at her mother, sighed, and then had to smile – However dire the situation, Nikki always took the half-empty glass and made it seem half-full – and full of champagne!

Miranda pushed herself away from the prison bars. "Let us go then, Nikki, my dear incorrigible mother, and let us bathe in the bubbly waters of Lethe and let us read the poets and sing of lost love, hopeless love, of love forlorn ..."

And, so, they did.

The phosphorescent glow of the walls covered everything in a glamorous gelatinous clayey sheen. They sat in the water reading poetry, or bits from Emily Post, and thick bubbles formed gently around them. Nikki's skin glowed like wet ivory; water trickled from her hair; she ducked her head under the cascade; or she stood there, letting the water course over her, like a silver rippling veil.

Miranda's skin glowed like burnished gold, smooth splendor, when she stepped out of the water, or when she stood next to her mother, both closing their eyes, just letting the water cascade, shower down, sparkling and warm, over their bodies, touching, illuminating every millimeter of skin.

"I wonder if they spoke the way they wrote," With both hands, Miranda ran wet fingers through her hair, "those 17th century poets – the English ones. I mean, some of them were Puritans, and fought in the English Civil War."

"Probably like most men they were more forthcoming in poetry than in life," Nikki let the water splash over her forehead, "at least many people are less afraid of a blank page – though that can be terrifying – than they are of another person, a real person, present in flesh and blood, particularly another person they … desire … or love. Love and desire are fearful things."

"Yes," Miranda sighed. "Nikki, was I really foolish to fall in love with Caliban?"

"No, you weren't, Miranda. We all need to love and be loved," Nikki pulled her daughter close, the two wet bodies, skin-on-skin, rivulets of water snaking down between them. Miranda leaned her head against Nikki's shoulder, snuggling towards Nikki's breast. Nikki stroked Miranda's hair. The drenched blond strands, some of them straggling, fanned out, flattened, and clung to Nikki's wet ivory skin, making an art nouveau floral arabesque, so it seemed to Nikki. Inwardly, she sighed, *Oh, my child, oh my dear adorable child, what a difficult road lies ahead.*

A trumpet sounded.

It was clearly audible even above the rush of water.

"What was that?" Nikki turned, one hand still stroking Miranda's hair, the other around Miranda's waist.

Miranda lifted her head, "I think it's … a warning … a warning of some danger."

More trumpets sounded, a ripple of alarm. Drums began to beat, deep threatening, three-beat sound, ominous, like an advancing army, frightening echoes, even in the depths of their cave spa.

"Let's go!"

"Yes, let's see!"

Nikki and Miranda stepped out of the water; still dripping wet, they pulled on the tunics, smoothed the coarse fiber, and ran – feet squishing and splashing in the mud – to the bars of their cave and looked out.

The vast cavern echoed with trumpets of alarm.

From far below, came cries, shouts, squawks, bellowing, neighing, and the beating of drums, a rhythmic urgent thunderous beating, as if calling up the troops, or as if marching off to war.

On the opposite wall of the cavern, on the hanging runways and gangways and suspended walkways, people – creatures – were running, shouting, crying. Females – mothers probably – were gathering the smaller creatures, children probably, and herding them into side caves.

"They're afraid," said Nikki, "but of what, I wonder?"

More trumpets echoed, a mournful alarming blare; sirens wailed. More drums were beating, far away. On one of the walkways opposite, several of the big bear-like creatures were carrying small creatures, presumably infants or children, delivering them to the females.

"Something horrible is out there in the night," Miranda said, closing her eyes, her fingers wrapped tight around the iron bars, "It's outside the cave, not inside; it's …" Her eyes still shut tight, Miranda shuddered; her fingers were white, clinging to the bars.

"What is it? Can you see it?"

"It's vague – I'm getting fluttering sort of images – like bits of a half-remembered nightmare – but whatever it is, it flies on wings, big wings, and it is horrible!" Miranda shuddered in disgust, "it is something new, and the mutants do not know what to think – or what to do."

"Well, there is nothing we can do here, not now, so let's go back to the pool. What do you say?"

"The monster flying things themselves seem confused, whatever they are."

Nikki put her hand on Miranda's shoulder. "Let's go, Miranda, back to the pool."

Miranda opened her eyes; her eyelids fluttered; for a second, only the whites of her eyes were showing. She blinked and her eyes were normal – except the golden stars and nebulae were really doing their dance, spiraling into hijinks and fireworks. "Yes, mother, you're right – let's go back and jump right into the pool and read John Donne!"

No Man is an Island
No man is an island entire of itself; every man
is a piece of the continent, a part of the main;
if a clod be washed away by the sea, Europe
is the less, as well as if a promontory were, as
well as any manner of thy friends or of thine
own were; any man's death diminishes me,
because I am involved in mankind.
And therefore never send to know for whom
the bell tolls; it tolls for thee.

Miranda recited it well.

Nikki did not want Miranda to probe any deeper into the monstrosities that flew in the night; she did not want Miranda to see things which were horrible. She did not want Miranda to plunge too deeply into her own mind. There would be time enough for that. The horror – the total horror – would come soon enough. And so …

They bathed in the pool and stood under the waterfall and they read the poets and Emily Post,

Miranda declaimed, "Etiquette is the science of living; it embraces everything; it is ethics; it is honor."

"That is wise," said Nikki.

Miranda considered for a moment. "Yes, I suppose it is. I guess how you behave defines who you are. When you add up everything you've done – and some things you have left undone – then, in the end, that's who and what you are."

Nikki just nodded, played with a small lump of clay, and looked up at her ferociously precocious daughter. Miranda was far away, deep in thought.

The phosphorescent glow, particularly beside the fountain and pool, was bright enough to read by. Miranda also felt that just perhaps her night-vision was really getting quite good, excellent in fact – maybe this was part of growing up.

Nikki was full of stories and anecdotes and made Miranda laugh and forget, for a moment, the horrible things she had seen, and even forget, for a moment or two, her great love – and the truly unique tragedy of Caliban's betrayal – the likes of which had never before been experienced by anyone anywhere anytime ever in all of human history – the tragedy of her abandonment by that fickle desert pirate, Caliban. "But he will liberate us, mother, he will save us, I know he will!"

"I don't know, Miranda; their religion, if I understand it correctly, requires that Cosmos be sacrificed ... and ..."

"But Caliban will save us, he will ..."

"You are expecting a great deal of Caliban, Miranda. This is religion we are talking about; this is religion, and with people's religion one does not tamper or tinker lightly ..."

"But are the mutants really people, mother? That is the question ... I mean do we consider them ..."

"That is an interesting question, Miranda, but not exactly relevant, because if their religion is important to *them*, then it doesn't matter *what* they are or, more precisely, it doesn't matter what *we* think they are."

"Hmm," Miranda frowned, "What I think is this ..."

Caliban appeared weary, even to himself. He climbed up the metal stairs and along the suspended walkway to the mouth of the cave where the two Cosmos women were prisoners. He stood for a moment, hesitating. He was half-inclined to retrace his steps and forget about it; he didn't really need to tell them; they would find out soon enough. But he steeled himself and he whistled.

Nothing! Where were the prisoners?

He whistled again.

He looked around, nervously.

He whistled again.

He shouted, "Miranda! Nikki!"

Miranda and Nikki were far away, at the deep end of the cave, splashing in the fountain and at first did not hear him; then, they did.

"What's that?"

"Whistling – somebody is whistling for us."

"Caliban!" Miranda's eyes lit up, spools and sparkles of gold unwinding. "Come on, my dear daughter! Let's go!"

Laughing, they scrambled through the water on hands and knees, and leaped out of the pool. Still soaked and running with water, they shimmied into their scanty shifts and ran to the mouth of the cave and to the iron bars to greet their jailer, their master.

Caliban stared.

Trickles of water streamed over Miranda's face. Her blond hair, curled and soaked, straggled down her cheeks in interwoven twines of bright and dark gold; her cheeks shone, flushed with excitement; her eyes sparkled, spinning stars and galaxies of gold; her skin was golden too, burnished, luminous, and flawless; her prisoner's tunic, with the large 'P' glowing like a scarlet stigma, was scanty, ragged and torn, hitched up over one thigh and hanging low off one shoulder, the burlap drenched to near-transparency; her legs, Caliban suddenly realized, were long legs – golden, elegant legs, legs made for running, swift of chase and swift to flee, fine-boned, high-born, exquisitely well-bred legs, legs of wealth and privilege – Cosmos legs. She glared at him and scowled – her lips turned down in a pout, which made him unaccountably but dreadfully nervous. Then – Oh, the gods! She smiled! It was a wide-open loving, joyous smile, like the sun rising, like infinite forgiveness. Stars and nebulae of gold shone, exploded, imploded in her eyes, and drifted, putting on fireworks, a show the likes of which the world had never seen. A sense of horrible radiant excitement and disarray flooded over him. *Who am I? What am I? What am I doing?* What will I be without this divine creature, this Cosmos? Caliban gulped and thought of words he had once read but never understood – not until now.

A sweet disorder in the dress
Kindles in clothes a wantonness:
A lawn about the shoulders thrown
Into a fine distraction:
An erring lace, which here and there
Enthrals the crimson stomacher:
A cuff neglectful, and thereby
Ribbands to flow confusedly:
A winning wave, deserving note,
In the tempestuous petticoat:
A careless shoe-string, in whose tie
I see a wild civility:
Do more bewitch me than when art
Is too precise in every part.

Now, by Dolly, I do understand!

But it got worse: Nikki came up behind her daughter and put her hand on Miranda's shoulder – and Caliban held his breath – more different two women could not be. Yet both were Cosmos, and both were beautiful. Nikki's dark eyes glowed like fluttering doves, bright flashes in dark moonlight; her jet-black hair sparkled with points of watery silver, stars twinkling adrift in the deepest of nights; her chalk-white skin, flawless as the purest marble, was beaded with water, like pearls of milk; the thin, soaked burlap pressed against her, as if it were a mere transparent nothing, just a pattern impressed upon her skin. "Master Caliban, greetings," she said, her smile bright, and just for him, "We have missed you."

"Grave affairs of state," he said, and blushed.

"Of course," said Nikki.

"Oh, poor Master Caliban, how boring for you," said Miranda.

"Not boring, not exactly," Caliban could not stand it; he looked away, "You see, Miranda, you see, Nikki, I've been trying to get a stay ..."

"A stay ...?" Nikki raised her eyebrows; a shadow appeared on her cheekbones; her skin turned paler – a sterner, chalkier ivory.

"A stay of ... of execution, of sacrifice," Caliban steeled himself and turned to look at the two Cosmos.

"And ...?"

"I cannot, l did not, and I was not able to ... The Great High Priest would not accept my arguments; we fought, I ..." somehow Caliban managed to keep his gaze steady, trying to encompass two sets of eyes – Miranda's and Nikki's, darkness and light. Miranda looked quizzical, as if she were a stern schoolmarm deciding whether she should scold him – or not. Nikki's smile had tightened.

"What does that mean, Caliban?"

"It means tonight you are to be sacrificed."

"Sacrificed?"

"Tonight?"

"Yes."

"Sacrificed?"

"Yes, anointed, consecrated, and then – sacrificed to Dolly."

"I see, and ..."

"Both of you ..." Caliban looked hard at Miranda, and then he looked away, "both of you are to die."

Nikki said nothing; she just stared at the profile of this young man; she had just gotten to know him; a few days ago, she had no idea he existed; and now, now she knew … him … and … she knew he lived, and she …

Miranda bit her lip. She was tempted to say, "I thought you loved me, my dear pirate, my dear Tarzan, my naked tattooed desert hero, I thought I was to be your queen, I seem even to remember your saying – correct me if I'm wrong – that we were going to have babies, oodles of babies, but now it seems that you …" But she said nothing, not a word, not a syllable. Betrayal was a horrible thing, and betrayal of fresh innocent love was worse, it caused a bitter emptiness and darkness in the soul. She felt water rise in her eyes – and anger. Strangely, she was not afraid of dying, though she thought it would be horribly unpleasant, undignified, and even humiliating; but she did not want to lose Nikki; and she did not want Nikki to die; somehow she believed that Nikki couldn't die, it was not possible; it was inconceivable …

"When is this to occur, Master Caliban?" Nikki smiled at him, as if she understood, understood and forgave – in advance – everything.

"Tonight, as I said, in about five hours, I'm sorry, I …"

"Don't be sorry, Caliban. I'm sure you did all you could."

"Mother, what are you saying? *All he could!!* This is … this is …" Miranda stopped. If she tried to say one more word, she would choke.

"May I have a word with you, dear, dear Caliban," Nikki smiled, and the smile also seemed to be in her voice. He couldn't believe it: She was being ironic; she must hate him; she must … Caliban turned to her, expecting to be spat upon, expecting to be derided, expecting … an insult, a vicious, spitting, cat-like assault of rage. Instead, Nikki's smile was steady – it even seemed real.

Caliban blushed, "The Great High Priest, he insisted. I fought, and I fought, and I fought, but … He will sacrifice hundreds – including children – if you are not sacrificed, for he is sore afraid."

"And of what is the Great High Priest sore afraid? Is he afraid of these new-fangled demons that fly in the night?" Nikki said, glancing at Miranda. Miranda blinked. The half-seen images returned, flashing before her mind, squawks and cries of rage, souls and spirits in torment, hatred and fear boiling up, a bubbling up of horror, and inside the flying, winged bodies and minds was pain, utter unstoppable irredeemable pain. Yes, she thought, I have seen them. Ill omens and evil forces are gathering around us, forces that will destroy everybody, including the mutants here in their underground nest. Miranda sighed. This was far from the Domed City of Elysium and beyond

the reach of the Cosmos Centurions – and, then, to be betrayed by this …
this … this …!

"I shall now take private counsel with Master Caliban, if you don't mind,
Miranda." Nikki turned to Miranda. She put her hand on Miranda's shoulder
and kissed her on the forehead, "Perhaps you could wait for me by the pool."

"Mother, what can you have to say to this … this … this poltroon, this
coward, this scaredy-cat, this … this Brutus, this whey-faced, chicken-livered
… this moral pipsqueak, this tattooed naked traitor, this … this … Ugh!" Miranda turned towards Caliban, her eyes flashed – pure blue ice, utter scorn,
unspeakable contempt, withering irony, unending disdain, and etcetera,
etcetera. Caliban tried to hold her stare – but he couldn't; he turned away.

"Miranda …!" Nikki's eyes tightened and flashed darkly.

"Okay, okay, mother knows best, I guess." Miranda rolled her eyes, and
displayed her most magnificent pout. This was disgusting! Now we shall die,
though I don't really believe in death, not really, and maybe nobody does.
She put her arms around Nikki and held her for a long, lingering instant, and
she kissed her mother carefully, very carefully, very deliberately, very visibly,
a slow, careful, voluptuous kiss, on the cheek – *There, you see, you see, Caliban, you see how I am capable of love and how loving I am, you see what you
have betrayed, you see what you have lost* – and she turned away, without
even a glance towards young Caliban, and, her back turned, the nape of her
swan-like neck held high, and her golden legs flashing, she ran away, deep
into the cave, leaving her mother to say whatever she was going to say to the
fallen idol, that creep, that total jerk, Caliban. As big a jerk as Kit's Sniggy
Propane, he was! Even worse! Ugh!

"So, what did you say to him, mother?" Miranda had discovered a bottle of
Lemon Ecstasy Shampoo sitting in a niche near the fountain and, her shift
cast carelessly aside and hanging from small, pointed stalagmite, she was sitting on the scalloped rim of the pool, naked, giving herself a very vigorous
shampooing. With both hands she was massaging her scalp; bubbly suds
were dribbling down over her ears and onto her forehead and into both eyes.

"Oh, I just wanted a few details about our execution. It's important to get
things exactly right in these important ceremonial events."

"Oh."

"Yes."

"And …?"

"Well, we are to be shackled again, handcuffed, collared, and led barefoot and in chains down to the main cavern floor," Nikki lifted off her shift, folded it neatly on a stone ledge, and stepped into the water, lowering herself down next to her daughter.

"Oh, is that all?" Miranda pushed the soapy dribbles away from her eyes, "I don't like that."

"Neither do I. Then we are to be paraded as captive helpless Cosmos booty through the jeering crowd to the cathedral."

"What cathedral? They have a cathedral?"

"Yes, it's in a side-cavern and apparently quite large."

"Oh."

"There we lose or are divested of our raiment and –"

"You mean, we're going to be stripped naked?"

"Yes, it seems so, Miranda, but –"

"These mutants are disgusting!"

"And then we are given a purifying sanctifying bath."

"We are already clean, squeaky clean. And as for being sanctified, we are Cosmos, First Class, we have no need of sanctification, and we are –"

"Yes, but for the mutants, all of this is rich in symbolism, Miranda, so …"

"I don't care a fig for their symbolism."

"And then we are anointed with sacred oil – lubrication is the term they use, or so Caliban told me."

"Lubrication! We're not bicycles!"

"And then we are put on the cross, bound to the cross I believe; Caliban said that they don't use nails; they use bonds or bands of metal."

"Hmmm …" Miranda put her hand on her mother's shoulder, slid off the ledge and into the water, waded over to the waterfall and stuck her head under the cascade of warm water, then popped out, blinking, "And then?"

"And then," Nikki, stood up, dripping, out of the water, and hesitated before answering, "And then they light the match."

"Ah … and then we die …"

"Well, perhaps we do, and perhaps we don't, Miranda."

Miranda just looked at her mother. Nikki picked up a towel, beckoned, and when Miranda came to her, Nikki began to towel down her very own fresh frisky young Cosmos beauty, gently, gently.

And so, the fatal night came – though one could not really tell the time very easily – 300 or 400 meters underground. Up above, the sun had gone down, the sands slowly cooled, but not by much, as the temperature remained just above 100 degrees Fahrenheit. All normal living creatures had gone to ground, for there were horrors flying through the night, monsters, mysterious and freshly hatched, thirsty and hungry.

The moon rose and shone with clear silver light on sand and escarpment, on broken gleaming bits of metal and towering blackened and abandoned pitheads, on rusting oil derricks, on dunes of drifting sand and on thousand-mile stretches of silted highways, blocks of pavement buckled and fractured, on gravel paths that once were country roads, on broken patches of melted asphalt, on one abandoned half-dead bio-teddy-bear who kept crying "mummy," on skeletal ghostly remains of cities, tower blocks and condos and malls, and on silos and farm buildings, on all the phantom-like places where once human beings had built and destroyed, loved and hated, raised families and grown old, where screen doors had slammed shut on summer nights, where voices had cried out in the firefly twilight, "Come on in now! It's bedtime! It's bedtime, you hear!"

But now there were no voices – only a chattering and cawing and whirring of vast wings in the night.

The moon, where once, over a hundred years ago, humans had set foot, shone down, indifferent and silver and full, on what had once been the "Promised Land."

Far away, it seemed so far away …

The first thing they heard was the clash of cymbals. Then the distant beat of drums, then a hooting of horns, and then cries went up: "Cosmos! Cosmos! Cosmos!"

Somewhere, deep horns were bellowing, and then there was chanting, deep, deep chanting, *basso profundo* – it sounded to Nikki like an ancient Russian male chorus.

Miranda looked at her mother, "The time has come, mother." She held out her hand. Nikki squeezed it. "Don't worry, Miranda, this will end well, and all's well that ends well."

"Really?"

"Yes, really."

Miranda raised an eyebrow – and tried to smile.

Caliban came for them with his Praetorian Guard of ten large bear-like creatures who were wearing their leather breastplates, and leather skirts, and who were armed to the teeth, with sabers and swords, and lances and short-handled machetes. At his hip, in addition to his scimitar, AK-47, and machete, Caliban had a coiled leather whip with a woven leather handle.

The barred gate was unlocked. And Nikki and Miranda stepped out.

"Good evening, Master Caliban," Nikki said; and turning to the furry guards, she said, "Good evening, gentlemen."

Two of the bears looked her in the eye, and bowed.

"Cosmos Whore," Caliban said curtly, a stern fixed look on his lips and a hard, unforgiving light in his eyes, "Turn around, Cosmos Whore!" Nikki bent her head and obeyed.

"Put your wrists tight together behind your back, Cosmos!" Caliban put his hand roughly on Nikki's shoulder, "Tight, I said, tight, damn you!!"

"Yes, Master Caliban," Nikki, head bowed, pressed her wrists together, palms of her hands pointing outwards. "Is that satisfactory, Lord Caliban?" she asked.

"Silence! Speak only when spoken to!" Caliban snapped thick handcuff-restraints on Nikki's wrists and forearms; he zipped the leather casing up, squeezing her arms tight together, and clicked the lock shut, the handcuffs twisted Nikki's arms, bending her spine, forcing her shoulders back, breasts forward, stretching the fabric of the thin tunic.

"Turn!"

Nikki turned to face him, her head still bowed, eyelids lowered; it seemed she dared not look at him. Caliban considered the result. His hands on his hips, he smiled.

"Ah, Cosmos whore, this is the way you were meant to be – a slave!" He lifted Nikki's chin between forefinger and thumb, forcing her to look at him; there was utter disdain in his eyes, metallic disdain, as if he were appraising an animal in a country fair.

Miranda was appalled, itching to attack; but for the moment she dared not say a word – she remembered her mother's injunction – obey me in every-thing! But her muscles were tensing, she was about to leap, she was ... *outraged!*

One of the bears handed Caliban a thick iron and rubber collar. With a shiver, Nikki saw that it had two large iron rings, and two chains. Caliban played for a moment with one of the rings, and he weighed one of the chains, bouncing it slightly in his hand, and smiling.

"Cosmos whore!" He leaned towards Nikki, and slowly, seemingly taking great pleasure in it, he placed the thick high collar around her neck and closed it. It clicked shut, automatically locking. "Cosmos Idolatress," he whispered, close to her face, his breathing on her, his lips an inch from her lips, "you shall wear this collar as a mark of your Cosmos shame."

Nikki didn't blink.

Caliban attached one of the chains behind Nikki's back, to the handcuff-restraint, tightening it, twisting Nikki's shoulders farther back; she winced, but didn't say a word. "There," he said, "You are done." He clicked the chain's lock shut, "You are marked forever, Cosmos."

The other chain, which was about six feet long and served as a sort of leash, he handed to one of the bears. The bear took it in his great hand-like paw, and tested it by tugging, pulling Nikki forward, closer to him; she looked up at him; he blinked, and said, in a gruff, throaty voice, "Cosmos," and inclined his head. Still staring into his eyes, Nikki bowed her head, and said, "Yes, Hans," which was the name carved on the bear's breastplate. The bear shuffled, looked down, and cleared his throat, relaxed his hold on the chain.

"This is outrageous," Miranda's hands were on her hips, legs slightly apart, knees and muscles tensed, readying herself to leap, her eyes blazing, and Nikki sensed that, if one more second passed, Miranda would leap on Caliban and scratch his eyes out. If Miranda went on a rampage, it might well be unstoppable and there was no telling what would happen – the consequences could be horrific.

"Miranda!! Miranda!!"

"Mother! This is grotesque; this is horrible!"

"Do not resist, Miranda, do not protest!"

"Mother!"

"Miranda! I order you!"

"Okay, alright, I surrender; but I protest!"

And, so, Miranda too was shackled, her arms pinioned behind her back, a thick collar snapped around her neck, and she was attached to a leash to be led by one of the bear-warriors.

"Caliban just wants to humiliate us, mother."

"Be patient, Miranda, our moment will come."

Miranda glanced at her mother.

"Silence Cosmos!" Caliban shouted. "Now we go. Now you confront the justice of the people and the wrath of the gods and of Goddess Dolly."

They marched along the suspended iron walkway, Caliban in front, Nikki and Miranda, shackled and chained, led by their bear-warrior guardians, and the other bear-warriors forming a sort of Praetorian Guard, beside and behind the two prisoners.

A roar of approval rose from below – cheering, catcalls, whistles, squeals, clapping, stamping, jeers …

Miranda glanced down through the rusty metal grate of the walkway – which was hard and hot and greasy under her bare feet – and she hazarded a quick look through the railing. Down below, at least fifty meters down, a huge crowd of mutants had gathered, milling around, many were staring upwards. The little river that ran down the center of the cavern looked like a silver snake, glittering, meandering. Mist rose off the water; the banks were crowded with mutants, hardly a single foot of ground could be seen, there were so many.

"Oh," as the procession began to move, a hushed cry went through the crowd. All the faces looked up.

"Cosmos! Cosmos!" a huge cry erupted. Faces turned upwards, weird grotesque faces, some beautiful, some ugly, all frightening. Creatures began to jump up and down and wave. A scream of joy and rage and triumph and hatred swept through the multitude. It reverberated, echoed, thundered against the walls and vaulting of the vast smoky cavern. The deafening sound washed over Miranda. It drenched her, covering her in the acid of their hatred and joy – seeing her humiliated, almost naked, despoiled – and about to die.

"Cosmos!"

"Kill, kill, kill the Cosmos!"

"Cosmos!"

"Kill, kill, kill the Cosmos!"

"Mother, they hate us, they really hate us."

"They may have their reasons, Miranda."

"Silence, Cosmos!" Caliban cracked the whip, scowled; he cracked it again, it uncoiled and snapped with an explosive *whap* right next to Miranda's shoulder; she felt the hot airburst burn against her skin; a strand of hair blew across her eye. Instinctively, she tried to brush it away – but her arms were pinioned, tight behind her back; she blew at the strand of hair, wiggled her shoulders desperately, and glared at Caliban and mouthed, "Oh, I hate you, I hate you!"

He held her gaze and even smiled; he prodded her with the handle of the whip – as if she were a cow or a mule!! "Down, slave," he said, "Calm yourself, you have a long journey before you!"

Her blood boiled. Her gaze hardened. She swore utter total unending vengeance.

An extra-large multicolored Venetian Lantern firefly fluttered close and hovered next to Miranda, only a few feet away. It followed along the gangway, the rhythmic waft and beating of its wings tickled her bare shoulders and stirred strands of her hair, clearing that one annoying strand from her eye. The firefly, accompanied by a raft of colorful little fireflies, continued to fly along beside her. When they came to the metal stairs, and began to go down it to the floor of the cavern, the firefly was still there, next to her, its giant wings gently beating.

"Hello, friend," she whispered. The firefly hovered closer. Miranda felt it really was a friend. Its many-faceted eyes gleamed. Its colors turned into a rainbow of iridescence. It came so close, it actually touched her, caressing her cheek, and then, slowly, it rose in the air and wafted away.

As Miranda and Nikki were led through the clamoring, mutinous, shouting crowd, their heads were bowed, their neck-collars attached to the chain leashes, each leash held by one of the bears; and there were two bears in front and three on each side; Miranda and Nikki, shackled, tugged this way and that, shuffled, and stumbled forward, humiliated, the chief attractions, in the middle of the procession.

About two meters in front, Lord Caliban pushed ahead, the leather whip in his hand, the smoky lights reflecting in dark satin ripples on his amber and gold back and on his muscular legs, his shoulder-to-waist tattoo brilliantly flashing, his white loincloth fluttering, his AK hanging neatly from his shoulder, and the dark blood-stained machete dangling at his side. Mutants clapped and acclaimed him. They fell away before him. It was clear that Caliban was a true hero, the young idol, the crown prince, of the mutant kingdom.

"Caliban! Caliban! Caliban!" The cry went up.

Caliban raised his arms in triumph.

When he passed, the crowd pushed in. They wanted to reach the two Cosmos prisoners. The bears, each more than six-foot-tall, pushed the crowd back, trying to protect the prisoners. It was not easy.

"Back, back, you rabble."

"Back, get back I tell you!"

"These prisoners are sacred! They are not to be defiled!"

"Back, you devils, back!"

"This devilish rabble must be taught a lesson." One of the bears flailed out with his truncheon, forcing a few members of the crowd back, but only for an instant.

Somehow Master Fluff managed to wiggle through the barrier of furry warrior bears; Miranda noticed that the bears knew he had pushed in and that they tolerated him. He stood there, for an instant, in front of Nikki and Miranda, looking at his toes, which curled up nervously, as they always seemed to do. Then he glanced up, fluttered his eyelashes, flashed a timid glance, and said, "I'm sorry!"

"Thank you, Master Fluff," said Miranda.

"I shall remember you in my dreams, Master Fluff," said Nikki, straining against her leash.

"Those females, friends of yours, who are not dead but in prison, send greetings." Fluff fluttered his eyelashes, turned a bright shade of crimson, and scuttled back between two bears who seemed quite inclined to let him go, and even seemed to appreciate what he had done. One of the bears caught Nikki's eye. He nodded. She inclined her head slightly and nodded back, and the bear did the same, and then turned his attention once more to the crowd, shouting in his deep guttural voice, "Back you rabble, get back!"

The clamor and screaming and shouting and pushing and shoving and whistling and howling were deafening. Miranda wanted to put her hands over her ears, but, of course, she couldn't.

Flakes like ticker tape confetti began to rain down – but they were smidgens of black ash, and sticky like tar, not a celebration of victory, but a badge of shame.

"Shame, Cosmos, shame!!"

"Shame, Cosmos, shame!!"

"It's just one thing after another," Nikki murmured, as the falling stuff thickened and stuck to her shoulders and arms; she looked around: everybody was getting covered in the stuff.

"Shame, Cosmos, shame!!"

"Shame, Cosmos, shame!!"

Miranda blinked against the blizzard of flecks of tar. It was in her hair; it was on her legs; it was everywhere; and – even worse – her tunic was hitching itself up, higher and higher, and it had just fallen off both shoulders, and was about to expose one breast; she wiggled to try and bring it back up, but, pinioned, she could do nothing about it – in fact, she just made the situation worse. She was naked, really naked. She felt all the strange mutant eyes eagerly feasting upon her, and all those mutant eyes, filled with derision and hate, could see every bit of her, every inch of skin, every inch of shame; she shivered as if it were cold, but it was not cold; it was hot, steamy heat and haze rising all around them, coating her skin, like the flakes of tar, and her feet were bare, and underneath the soles of her feet, the very stones and earth seemed to be gazing upon her, touching her, tentacular, like the eyes that stared, eager to fondle her, violate her, and kill her.

The rain of tar-flakes ceased.

Now stones and chunks of muddy clay showered down from the high suspended walkways; gobs of slime came arching out of the crowd. A thick slab of half-liquid clay splashed down on Nikki's shoulder, dribbled down her breast and inside her tunic.

"Shame, Cosmos, shame!!"

"Shame, Cosmos, shame!!"

A stone about the size of a fist hit Nikki on the head, and bounced off, almost hitting one of the bears. Nikki ducked – too late of course – and then she looked up at the place on one of the cliff-side gangways from which the stone had been thrown: an angry rooster like creature – humanoid but covered with feathers and with a yellow beak and a tall floppy fleshy crimson comb or crest above its small yellow eyes – was leaping up and down, and in its claws, it held another rock and its companions were urging it on. Nikki shot the rooster one of her dark flame-like glances. It recoiled in confusion, ruffled its feathers, and turned away. The others jeered, one took the stone and threw it, but missed, the stone whammed down just next to Nikki's feet, shards of stone slashing at her legs.

A hairy creature – yes, female, a sort of curvaceous ape woman – her lineage, Miranda guessed, had probably originally been designed as made-to-order sex toys and playmates – pushed out of the crowd, curled up her crimson lips, and spat a huge gob of smoky white phlegm straight at Miranda; the gob, trailing mucus like a terrestrial comet, smacked into Miranda's cheek and began to dribble down; Miranda shook her head as much as the collar would let her, trying to flick it away, but the gob clung like glue, spreading like varnish; it flowed down towards the corner of her mouth; the woman laughed and jeered at Miranda – "Cosmos whore!" she shouted – and then she was pushed away. The guards desperately tried to push the crowd back. "Back you idiots, back!"

It looked like the bears would not be able to contain the crowd, "Back, get back, back, get back!" Hands and claws were clasping, grasping, reaching, feet were kicking the bears, trying to force them to open a way to the hated Cosmos witches, witches that deserved to be burned – burned alive, soaked in precious petrol, and set alight.

"Cosmos – you brought the sky demons, now you will pay!"

"Kill the Cosmos!"

"Kill! Kill! Kill!"

"Kill the Cosmos!"

Miranda was amazed at the anger and hatred. Why do they hate me so – just for what I am? I never did anything to them! Mother never did anything to them! In a strange way, it was extra-horrible, being hated merely for what she *was*, not for anything she had *done* or even anything she *thought*! They didn't want to kill her beliefs or her actions; they wanted to kill *her*. Somehow, under the fear, Miranda thought it must be all some terrible misunderstanding; somehow she wanted the creatures who were throwing mud and stones and spitting, she wanted them to like her, to love her, to accept her, and to love and accept Nikki. How could anyone not love Nikki? Nikki was so cool and yet so kind, so gracious, so … Miranda glanced at Nikki. Nikki's tunic was splattered with tar-ash and mud and part of the tunic had been ripped away, halfway down Nikki's back. And Miranda was aware that her own ragged burlap tunic, off both shoulders and hitched up high above one hip, now torn to rags in several places, and baring one breast, seemed more transparent than ever: no protection at all, really. Yes, now she really was a naked prisoner of pirates, but this was not a video game.

Miranda glanced fearfully at the crowd. How strange to be at their mercy! *Me*, a Cosmos Full Citizen First-Class! Small creatures, miniatures with very large teeth, were jumping up and down between the bear's big furry legs, fangs bared, cheering and jeering. They reminded Miranda of gremlins; they looked deadly, with those razor-sharp teeth and sharp little claws. If they come at me, they'll tear me apart; I won't be able to defend myself, Miranda wiggled her pinioned arms.

She looked up. Farther away in the crowd, on a balcony, was a woman who was tall and totally white, white as snow, and covered – body and head – in white hair and who had a beautiful long mournful face with large oval eyes that made Miranda think of a painting by Modigliani, and she could see that in that face – the woman was holding up a baby – there was sadness and recognition. *Oh, no, that creature is feeling pity, pity for me, pity for Miranda Hughes!* Pity was almost more horrible than hate. Then Miranda saw that what the woman was feeling was something richer. It was identification – *the creature was thinking: that might easily be me* – she was feeling compassion … Miranda blinked at the woman; the woman blinked back, and nodded – it was just an instant, and, luckily, nobody saw it.

"They know not what they do, Miranda," Nikki said, clearly, over her shoulder. One of the bears, busy pushing back the furious crowd, glanced at Miranda.

Caliban cracked his whip. "No talking, vile Cosmos! Hateful witches!"

"I love you, mother."

Caliban turned back and cracked the whip. It created a thunderous bang, and an airburst, just over Nikki's shoulder. He glared and shouted, "You are slaves, Cosmos, you are animals! No talking!"

"And I love you, Miranda," Nikki stumbled, but managed to shout, "Remember, Miranda, you swore to obey me, no matter what – you do remember?"

"I remember."

"Swear again, Miranda."

"Silence Cosmos whore!"

How vile Caliban was – a total traitor! Miranda was doubtful about obeying her mother. She was afraid for Nikki. Nikki was going to sacrifice herself. Miranda was about to object, and say, "No, I will not, I cannot," but, when Nikki twisted around to face her, pulling on her leash – but her bear jailer stopped, and turned, and let his prisoner do what she was going to do – the dark flashing look in her mother's eyes told Miranda that she absolutely must obey. Nikki would brook no refusal.

"I swear, I will obey you, mother, I swear," Miranda swallowed. She had an awful feeling about this, a terrible feeling, she had a vision – her mother perishing in a wall of flame, her mother crucified naked on a cross, her mother dying, alone, abandoned, and dying, her mother …

"Good, thank you, Miranda. I will always love you, no matter what happens, no matter what separates us."

"And I will always love you mother, I will always, always love you, Nikki."

There was a huge shout, "Hurrah!"

The crowd was again acclaiming Lord Caliban.

"Caliban, Caliban, Caliban!"

"Caliban, Caliban, Caliban!"

It changed to a chant, "Now, now, now!"

"Death, now, now, now!"

They had arrived.

The procession halted.

"Right Turn!"

The procession turned right. A hush fell over the milling, pressing, scream-ing crowd. Banners and flags surged up. Some of the fluttering flags bore skull and crossbones insignia. Miranda did not find this reassuring. Others bore images of crucified skeletons. Or animal totems – images of sheep, goats, lions, buffalo, and dogs …

In front of them was a giant side cave. This, clearly, was the cathedral. The stone walls soared up, arching inward, meeting in a point, like an ogive in a medieval gothic church, like Notre Dame de Paris, or like Chartres.

Miranda blinked. Giant torches flared, pyres of incense smoldered, huge sta-lagmites soared up, giant stalactites hung down. Cables dangled from walkways along the side of the Cathedral. Giant, glowing, multi-colored mural paintings, shaped like Gothic stained glass windows, portrayed mutants in various poses of devotion; a monkey man crossing himself, what looked like a human alliga-tor on its knees, a giant beaver was giving out alms to small rat-like children. The smoke and steam were denser, the air mistier, the smells smellier, the colors dimmer, the mold moldier; the voices deeper, the screaming, once again, more acute, intolerably high-pitched. At the far end of the cathedral, towards the altar, a huge, vague, horrendous shape loomed up, but Miranda couldn't make it out. It was lost in a thick, drifting fog of smoke, incense, and steam. Festooning the soot-darkened walls, bleached skeletons dangled in cages or hung from crosses.

Staring down at Miranda from the wall, right at the entrance to the cath-edral, was a delicate, gaunt, eyeless skull; strands of long blond hair – one held together with a faded pink clasp in the form of a butterfly – skimpily straggled over the bony dome; the empty eye sockets stared down. It was – it had been – a young woman. Miranda swallowed; her lips were dry and chalky; her tongue was heavy; she swallowed again.

The blond martyr's arms – mere bones – were chained, crisscrossed, above its head, its skeletal legs, crossed at the ankles, were nailed and tied to the central beam. Below this grotesque, five small skeletons were lined up on a wall shelf, like a miniature choir, skeletal hands held high, bolted to the stone.

"Children," whispered Miranda.

"Yes, children." Nikki nodded.

On both sides of the soaring walls, there were skeletons crucified on crosses, illuminated by flicking light. Torches lit up everything. The phosphorescent lichen and clusters of grape-like, glowing mosses cast a wet glamorous look over the soaring stone walls, over the paving stones, over the steps which led up to the altar at the far end of the chapel, and over the altar itself, a vast stage of stone, and above the altar was an enormous cross and on the cross …

Bulbous bunches of what looked like giant luminous grapes hung like chandeliers, casting the cathedral in a dim sacred light.

There were pointed, vertical, flame-like smudges on the walls, between the glowing murals, where votive offerings – humans – had been burned – alive or dead.

The procession surged into the Cathedral, everywhere mutants were pushing and shoving and stumbling. The bears fought to clear a way for the two Cosmos prisoners.

Caliban snapped his whip. "Make way, Make way!"

Thick clouds of incense rolled over the procession and the worshippers; it was syrupy sweet, too sweet.

Slowly, out of the thick swirling mist, things became visible, gradually revealing themselves. Priests were lined up standing on a sort of stage. Well, to Miranda they looked like priests because they were wearing long gowns and some of them had miters and straw boaters and top hats and a medley of other ecclesiastical-looking appurtenances. It took her back to the religious underground – she suddenly wished that Kit were here; perhaps the three of them – she and Kit and Nikki – could fight their way out of this mess.

The procession, pushing and shoving and yelling and hollering, was moving deep into the Cathedral.

Suddenly, Nikki and Miranda were thrust forward, the mutants made way, a void opened up – and Nikki and Miranda, were standing, both of them, alone, and shackled, before the stage-like altar.

At one end of the line of priests, stood a little girl in a tunic, with a belt and sandals. The little girl, who was, from what Miranda could see, very pretty and who was smiling, had two thick curved horns on her head. She stood next to a shower – a single pipe going up and an old-fashioned showerhead with a chain of the sort you pulled to make the water come – and, yes, there was a water tank … and under the showerhead there was a bathtub.

Then, oh, horror, there was a blackened and scarred metal cross, next to the bathtub, and the cross had metal bands – to attach ankles and neck and wrists – this was the cross upon which she and Nikki were to be crucified – and burned alive.

Underneath the metal cross, the stone steps were dark. Black, slippery, waxen, carbonized body fat had obviously soaked into the porous stone of the altar, a thick dark stain that spread onto the floor below the altar, fat that had dripped off burning bodies. Clearly, it was here that most Cosmos were burned – alive.

"Now, Cosmos, behold!" Caliban pointed upwards with his machete.

A vague form emerged out of the smoke and incense, above the altar, and at the very end of the cathedral. It was an enormous crucifix. It soared towards the ceiling – almost reaching the roof of the cathedral, and on the enormous crucifix was an enormous statue, hanging out over the crowd.

It was a sheep, its head and muzzle and great sheep eyes projecting forward, and its legs sprawled out on the giant two-armed cross. In huge, deep, rough-hewn words, the text "Goddess Dolly" stood out on a board hanging above the sheep.

Around the central altar, and just under the crucifix, Barbie dolls were lined up in shrines and a few teddy bears too. Under each Barbie doll burned a flame of worship, or remembrance.

"It's a sheep," said Miranda, "A lamb."

"Yes, a sheep," Nikki, "Dolly the Sheep."

"The first cloned mammal," said Miranda, remembering her DNA Design Course 101 implant, the beginning of generic re-design and –

"Silence!" A huge mutant surged up. He looked to be over seven feet tall and was very bumpy and slimy and resembled a large toad, or perhaps a frog, with his bulbous outward slanting eyes very close together and a very low ski-slope forehead, "Prisoners, no talk, no Cosmos talk which is most vile and poisonous and a thing unwanted, unacceptable, unwished-for by Dolly."

"Certainly, by all means," said Nikki.

"Down, down on your knees, Cosmos!" Caliban unsheathed his scimitar and pointed it at Nikki's breast.

The crowd howled, "Kill! Kill! Kill the Cosmos!"

Miranda glanced at Nikki; Nikki nodded: *Yes, Miranda, get down on your knees!*

Miranda gritted her teeth. She growled. Somehow, she would get her revenge! They both sank to their knees, awkwardly, unsteadily, arms tightly pinioned behind their backs, bowing their heads. Caliban stepped forward and stood over them.

"Gaze upon the Goddess and worship!"

Nikki and Miranda turned their faces up and gazed at the Goddess. It was not easy, kneeling, with their arms pinioned behind their backs and the thick high collars around their necks.

Through the incense-filled and smoke-laden air, the great sheep head stared down at them with huge compassionate blind eyes, painted eyes, the color of charcoal.

A priest stepped forward. His long wispy robes swished around him. He intoned in a high-pitched warbling voice, "We worship our Queen, she is the Queen, and Our Forbearer, and all is owed to her for with her everything began, Oh, Dolly our Queen, the Sheep of all Eternity, the Lamb that sacrificed, so that we could come into the world!"

The other priests intoned, in deep basso profundo voices, a true choir as if it had come from the deepest ancient reaches of the Russian Orthodox Church, "Dolly, Dolly, who came into the world so that a greater one could follow, Dolly, Dolly, Pathfinder, Dolly, Dolly, Pioneer, so that the True Greatness could be Born, so that the Origin could out of Nothing be Created, so that generation upon generation could follow, Dolly of Origins, Dolly the Sacrificed One, Dolly, Dolly, Oh, Dolly ..."

"Dolly!" the massed congregation, now pressing up against the holy space where Nikki and Miranda were kneeling, waiting for whatever destiny fate would bestow upon them, Nikki and Miranda, with Caliban standing over them, his scimitar raised as if he were about to decapitate both women in one fell swoop, Nikki and Miranda, heads lowered, eyes raised, looking up at the charred, empty, waiting cross of sacrifice, and up at the monstrous head of Dolly, and looking up too at the priests, all arrayed in splendor, and looking up too at the smiling little girl in the purple tunic, her two curved and polished horns gleaming, and who stood ready next to the bathtub and showerhead, waiting, waiting to fulfill her role in the ceremony which would soon, inevitably, begin. The fever was rising. The crowd was turbulent – edging towards utter hysteria. Banners, effigies, and idols bounced and bobbed above the heads of the worshippers.

"Dolly!" All screamed. The females fell on their knees; the males fell on their knees. "Dolly!"

"Yes, Dolly," said Scav, who had pushed his way to the front of the crowd, "The first Lamb, the Holy Lamb ..." He splattered some green go. A blob of the stuff, somehow reached Nikki, splashed in her hair, down one cheek, and a separate gob, hit her shoulder, dribbled down her back.

The public screamed. "Let the ceremony begin!"

"Eat, eat, soon we will eat," shouted Scav, standing in front of the first row of the multitude; he danced up and down, a floppy, fluid jig, spraying glowing green goo.

"Everyone please rise!" intoned, in a booming fog-horn voice the tall frog-like priest; somehow his voice easily carried above the clamor, "Everyone please rise!"

"Eat, eat, soon we will eat!" The crowd stood up. Everyone took up the cry and began to sway and jump in rhythm.

The temperature was soaring; the great cavern was getting positively steamy. Smoke rose from the great torches.

"Prepare the sacrifices, prepare the flesh of Cosmos!" The tall priest cried, "Prepare the flesh of Cosmos!"

"Prepare the flesh!"

"Prepare the flesh!"

"Prepare the flesh!"

"Stand, Oh, Cosmos, stand, and look upon the hour of your death, anticipate the hour of absorption, when you become one with Dolly, when your flesh becomes our flesh, when you are honored in the feast and cease forever and forever to be ..."

Nikki and Miranda, struggling, still pinioned, stood up, awkwardly, which was extra humiliating.

When she stood up, Miranda's tunic slipped further. She blushed.

"It doesn't matter, Miranda," Nikki whispered, "It doesn't matter in the least."

The guardian bears, who had been standing back while still holding the two leashes, stepped forward, and unlocked the restraining handcuffs, and opened the collars and took them off.

Miranda felt the sweat evaporate from where the collar had been.

Nikki rubbed her wrists and smiled.

"Back, down on your knees, Cosmos whores," the two bears said in unison.

Miranda and Nikki knelt. Miranda felt all this kneeling and standing up, and all this noise and shouting, was making her dizzy. She was being warmed up, she realized, she was being stunned, prepared for sacrifice.

"Eat, eat – soon we eat!" the crowd screamed. The mob was exciting itself, driving itself up to a hysterical fever pitch. The mutants chanted, danced, swaying all together, slapping their thighs. Banners, Idols, fluttering flags bounced, jostled, in a frenzy of excitement.

"Oh, the Great High Priest!" the crowd exploded with renewed hysteria.

"Oh, the Great High Priest!"

Nikki turned to look. The Great High Priest had appeared, far off, close to the huge Cross of Dolly. He was standing on a sort of dais. He had the face of a goat, a wispy goatee, a high, narrow forehead, peaked hairy ears, and two horns. The beautiful little girl, waiting patiently by the bathtub, was probably, Nikki thought, a distant relative.

The Great High Priest turned towards the assistant priests. "Begin preparations," he declaimed. The crowd exploded into full jubilation mode.

"Eat, eat – soon we eat!"

"Eat, eat – soon we eat!"

Priests approached the two kneeling half-naked Cosmos women.

Scimitar raised, Caliban stood ready. He glanced at Nikki and raised an eyebrow: *Now?*

Nikki nodded: *Yes, now!*

Caliban grabbed Miranda by the waist and, in one swift movement, he threw her over his shoulder – bouncing, like a sack of potatoes.

"What! What! Let me down!" Miranda's eyes flamed; but dazed and caught up in a confusion of mixed feelings and untoward sensations, she didn't think to fight the steel-like grip of the Pirate-Tarzan. "How dare you!!" She flopped down his back, arms dangling.

"Let me down, you monster, you traitor! Let me down!" Her fists hammered weakly against his backside.

Caliban leaped off the altar stage, he leaped to the high hanging walkway that ran along the right side of the cathedral, he skirted the dangling sacrificial skeletons, one of them rattled and inclined its head in recognition as Caliban and Miranda whizzed by. He zigzagged past a giant, broad-shouldered warrior bear, who had jumped onto the walkway, and was standing there, confused, his hand on the hilt of his undrawn sword.

The congregation at first did not understand what was happening. Then they all looked upward.

"Lord Caliban!"

"He's going to chop off the head of that Cosmos!"

"He's going to throw her into the fire!"

"No, he's going to impale her on the sacred stalagmite!"

"He's going to carve her up, debone her, hang her bones as a skeleton, and throw the flesh down for us to eat!"

The cry went up. Lord Caliban was preparing for them a particularly spectacular and bloody form of sacrifice; surely, she deserved it – this Cosmos, too beautiful by far, and privileged, and spoiled, and rich!

"Hang her bones!"

"Hang her bones!"

"Hang her bones!"

"Throw the bits to us!"

"Throw the bits to us!"

"Throw the bits to us!"

Caliban bounded to the end of the walkway, he grabbed a dangling loop of cable, and, with Miranda still flung over his shoulder, he jumped into the void, and the cable swung in a great arc above the crowd, carrying Caliban and Miranda to the very entry of the Cathedral, to the peak of the great glowing sacred Saint Barbie-Blondie stalagmite. Twirling like a dervish, he swiveled around the sacred Saint Barbie-Blondie stalagmite, almost slipping on the greasy pointed peak, with Miranda bouncing against his back, her waist firmly grasped and pressing on his shoulder, and, still moving, without a pause, Caliban leaped to the next walkway, seven feet away, and shimmied to the next level, 25 feet up, the middle walkway, which led into the main cavern, and he raced along the wall, and towards the entrance, the great sacred staircase and elevator shaft that led up to the surface of the planet, to the desert, to the sky with all its unknown and known new and old terrors.

"Let me down, you traitor!"

"Oh, Lord Caliban!" The crowd was suddenly uncertain. What was Lord Caliban, the hero of heroes, the adopted and favorite of the Great High Priest, doing? Where was he taking the luscious prize?

Darts began to fly; arrows whizzed, but as Caliban raced and leaped and weaved and zigzagged – his captive blonde bouncing on his shoulder – all the arrows and darts missed.

Suddenly, it was clear; suddenly, it dawned on some of them, and then, by that sort of instantaneous communication in the moods of mobs and crowds, he was taking her away! Lord Caliban was escaping with the prize; he was racing towards the Great Sacred Stairway, then upwards, and away – Lord

Caliban was a thief and a traitor! He was going to keep the prize for himself!

Now there was a roar of rage – screams, twitters, squeaks, growls, roars, and even words – from the multitudinous throng.

Then there was the thunder – of hooves, claws, paws, and feet – as the mutants galloped, ran, scurried and leaped in pursuit of Caliban – the traitor, the miscreant, the apostate – and in pursuit of the delicious sacrifice, the divine young blond Cosmos, an image of edible perfection, Miranda, whom many of them had been looking forward to munching on, dreaming of licking her bones until they glowed, as if lacquered.

Nikki turned to follow the action and caught a glimpse of Caliban, his shoulders gleaming with oil and sweat, with Miranda tossed over his shoulder, her blond hair and wild eyes and golden arms and kicking legs, high in the air, on the iron walkway.

Then Nikki caught a last glimpse of Caliban's boots – with their floppy pirate style tops – zipping up the broad metal steps of the walkway, she saw a flash his shoulder, brown skin, and flashing tattoo, and Miranda's blond hair and flailing arms; they disappeared around a corner – and that was that.

They were gone.

A thunderous pursuit, bear-warriors and every creature imaginable followed them, and cries and sirens and drums beating.

Nikki swallowed, and licked her lips.

Now it was coming.

The fury was palpable. The congregation was chanting.

"This one we eat."

"Yes, this one we eat."

"This one remains."

"You become of us – Cosmos!"

"We ingest, we digest – you become one of us – Cosmos!"

The crowd surged towards the altar, where Nikki was now kneeling, alone, in the ragged remains of her tunic, splattered with mud and bespeckled with feathery tar; she was now the single destined sacrifice.

She was the *only* sacrifice.

The six bear-warriors formed a line to protect her and to force the howling, furious, heaving congregation back.

The Great High Priest had at first stood still, high on his isolated dais confused by what was happening, and then when it was explained to him and when he understood what had happened, he let out a bellowing roar of anguish and rage. "Caliban! Caliban, my Son, what have you done?"

In the confusion, Scav somehow slipped past the bear warriors and he sidled up the Nikki – opened his mouth wide – "I want you, Cosmos, you are mine, it is true love, Cosmos" – and he tried to kiss her and then, just as he was approaching her, about to leap and land a big fat Scav kiss on her cheek, and as she was recoiling away, he sneezed, spraying her with green goo.

A bear grabbed Scav by the scruff of his neck, held him up, and kicked him like a football. Scav soared off into the heights. The bear muttered *harrumph* and glanced at Nikki, almost as if he were looking for approval.

Blinking away a veil of quick-drying goo, Nikki nodded at the bear and watched, awestruck, as Scav, screaming bloody murder, made an arc through the misty air, green phosphorescent spittle flying out like sparks behind him, like the tail of an unholy terrestrial comet. He just missed the wings of a giant blinking and lumbering aquamarine firefly that was flapping its way lazily over the crowd, he soared past the stalagmites, past the soaring frescos, past the dangling skeletons and luminous stalactites and then he disappeared, smashing down somewhere in the middle of the mob.

"Oh, poor Scav," Nikki murmured.

A giant Chinese lantern firefly fluttered in close, hovered just over her. She looked up into its multitudinous eyes, each facet a universe. She saw tiny images of herself, in each little octagonal lens, as if she were captured in a myriad of universes, the different universes being separated, and she knew this was in reality truly the case, by only the thinnest of membranes, and so, being part of such a multiple-dimensioned immensity, it didn't really matter if she lived, or if she died. *What would be; would be.* The insect's wings beat slowly. Time stopped. Nikki was alone in eternity with the strange creature. Along the crested edges of its body, lights blinked and sparkled; its eyes were iridescent with a rainbow of colors; it was, she knew, a friend, and whatever happened, it would be a friendly witness to … what would soon happen, to the sacrifice. Slowly, as if with regret, it lifted away; it rose up, towards the smoke-darkened ceiling, and then it hovered there, looking down. Nikki shook herself, suddenly aware of the shouting, the shoving, the tumultuous chaos.

"Crucify the Cosmos!"
"Crucify her!"

"Seize her!"

"Take her!"

"Burn her!"

"Consume her!"

Actions followed the words. The crowd overwhelmed the bear warriors and rushed onto the altar stage. Hands and claws were laid upon Nikki's shoulders, legs, breasts, and face. "Here, grab her! Grab her!"

"We eat her!"

"She is ripe for sacrifice!"

The High Priest intoned over the chaos, his voice ringing out, now in a tremolo goatish falsetto, "Oh, Dolly, blessed art thou, Oh, Dolly. We consume the flesh of Cosmos in thy name, Oh Dolly."

The crowd was on the point of ripping Nikki apart.

"Let us through, you rabble, out of the way, get out of the way, unhand the sacrifice, let her go!" Helped by the bears, the priestly assistants fought their way through the crowd to where Nikki was being pushed and shoved, clawed, grabbed, scratched, bitten.

"We must strip her naked!" shouted Brother Rat.

"We must pluck her from the rabble!" screamed Brother Toad.

"We must cleanse her before the sacrifice!" Brother Rat, biting and pushing, waded through the crowd, "She has been defiled!"

"Yes, and Scav must be punished for he has profaned the sacrifice; see the seed of Scav smeared upon the sacrifice! Scav has profaned the Cosmos!" shouted Brother Toad, catching a glimpse of the gobs of green glowing Scav saliva splashed on Nikki's hair and face and shoulders.

"Oh, abomination!" the Brothers chorused.

"Oh, shameful crime!" the Brothers echoed.

"Oh, profanation!" shouted somebody in the crowd.

The Brothers got to Nikki. They seized her by the shoulders and pulled her out of the mob.

Some of the female mutants, meanwhile, none of whom seemed to know how to speak in sentences of any ordinary terrestrial language, were squeaking, screaming, ululating, and trying to defend Nikki from the clawing and scratching and from the fangs, but in vain …

"Don't worry," Nikki managed to declare to the closest females, "Don't worry!"

The females whimpered. There were tears in their eyes. Their hands and arms and flippers and tentacles reached out towards Nikki as the Brothers seized her and she was torn away from the hostile and friendly throng.

The Brothers wielded swords and torches and pushed the crowd of wailing females back.

The giant bears formed a phalanx, the light of the torches bright on their angry eyes, bared teeth, and ruffled fur.

The priests, fighting all the way, hauled Nikki toward the steel framework, hight on the towering stage, near the altar where a great fire burned.

Weird little lizard-like creatures, about two feet high, were dancing around the fire. Their shadows, magnified and grotesque, streamed up the walls of the cave, cavorting, capering, leaping, arms up, arms out, squatting, and running.

The Cross of Sacrifice soared up. It was made of dark, charred metal. It was about ten feet tall and stood on a platform next to the giant Dolly Crucifix.

The Brothers lowered the Cross of Sacrifice and pushed Nikki towards it – and then she was there, out on the exposed sacred space, above the crowd.

Nikki stood alone, curious, looking around, not resisting – seemingly accepting everything. She appeared to be entirely passive, following everything that was happening around her – and happening to her – with strangely calm, detached, intelligent eyes. One of the Brothers stumbled. Nikki bent down and helped him up.

He was Brother Toad. He stared at her. She smiled at him. He blinked. He turned to the Chief Assistant Priest.

"Chief Assistant Priest, should we do this? This woman is …"

"Yes, Brother Toad, she is perfection; therefore, it is written that we must do this: the better she is, the more beautiful she is, the more we are impelled to sacrifice her; she is Cosmos Perfection – she is Evil Incarnate – she is an ideal sacrifice to Dolly!"

The priests led Nikki up onto a stone platform on the altar where the rusty white metal bathtub stood on its scruffy chipped lion-paw feet with a shower-head, on a crooked stand, hovering over it

The beautiful little girl in her tan-colored, belted sheath – she looked perfectly human except for the two curved horns rising out of her forehead – held the chain which, presumably, released water from the large tank which loomed over the showerhead and had "Drink Pepsi" scrawled on it in faded, once stylish letters.

The little girl was dark-skinned and remarkably pretty, with bright intelligent eyes; her features were exquisitely human. She was quite different, in fact, from the Great High Priest, who was obviously a goat-human synthesis; she was probably the descendent, Nikki decided, on closer inspection, of some genetics-modifier body artist – the Gen-Body-Art Movement of the late 2080s had been keen on designer babies, and on genetically and surgically redesigned children: some glowed in the dark, others had claws or horns or patterned fur or built-in phosphorescent tattoo patterns that blinked, or …

Inwardly, Nikki trembled; but she kept her outer calm.

It was hot near the altar's giant fire.

"Disrobe, Cosmos, or we shall tear thy raiment from thee!"

"Right, then, I shall disrobe," Nikki said, thinking there was not much to disrobe, just the tatty and ripped tunic; and not much of it was left.

"Do not tarry, do not delay, Oh, Cosmos!" called out a priest who had a rat-like muzzle, with a wet black nose, twitching whiskers, and beady eyes set far too close together for the breadth of his face. Nikki glanced at him. He bared his teeth and licked his incisors. Nikki shivered. He was eager to see the Cosmos naked.

"Take it off!" the crowd screamed, "Take it off!"

"Take it off, Cosmos! Take it off!" The screaming was higher and higher.

The priests and brothers nodded, their faces – one looked like a goat, one like a fox, one like a toad, one like a rat – bobbed up and down, rhythmically, as if some puppet-master were pulling a single string, controlling them all.

"Yes, Cosmos," said Brother Toad, gently, "You must be naked: take it off, take it off!"

"Okay," said Nikki. She lifted the rag over her head, and shimmying out of it, she handed it to the young girl.

"Oh, Cosmos," The crowd screamed, swelling with passion; some of the younger priestly creatures, dressed in cheap, white, lacy, badly stained nightgowns, had to push the worshippers back.

The bear-warriors struggled, desperately trying to discipline the mass, pressing forward, threatening to overwhelm the younger priests, threatening to overwhelm everything.

Finally, the bears and priests prevailed.

There was a moment of awestruck silence.

Nikki stood patiently, naked, exposed, on the platform, visible to all, waiting for the next step. She rather wished she were an anthropologist. The whole event was, among other things, extremely interesting.

"Oh, Cosmos!" the crowd bellowed, "Oh, Cosmos!"

"We shall consume thee, Oh, Cosmos!"

"We shall consume thee, Oh, Cosmos!"

"Thy soul shall be ours!"

"Thy soul shall be ours!"

The priests took ragged sacred cloths and mushroom sponges and began to carefully wash away from the body of the sacrifice all traces of Scav. The seed and sputum of Scav was profanation and blasphemy; it had to be eliminated. Nikki patiently turned around, lifted her arms, spread her legs, so the mutant priests could complete their part of the sacred ablutions. Close by, the little girl with the curved horns stood patiently, waiting to play her role in the sacrifice of the Cosmos. She smiled at Nikki. Nikki smiled back.

And so, it came to pass that Nikki Hughes, ultra-privileged citizen of Elysium City, Cosmos First Class, actress, graphic designer, and fashion model, was naked, cleansed, and now, in a few moments, she was to be offered up for sacrifice to the Goddess.

Nikki Hughes squared her shoulders; she was ready for the sacrifice.

She was indeed the truest of Cosmos.

CHAPTER 4 – CLOWN

How much time had passed?

It was hard to tell.

Maybe it was a couple of seconds, maybe minutes, maybe …

Damn! V shook her head. She was stunned, sitting on the ground, not far from the overturned, burning wreck of the Armored Desert Bug, her back propped against a low ledge of rough limestone; the belt that had strapped her into the armored seat was dangling from her waist; her wraparounds and lips were smeared with something. It smelled like blood.

She reached up with one gloved hand. Yes, it was blood – blood and gore, thick, clotted. A gooey sheen, and drops, dripping from her face.

Lieutenant Jackson, who had been sitting opposite her, must be dead.

WHAM!

Explosions rang inside V's head, echoing, muted explosions, as if from far away, as if heard underwater.

WHAM!

She was deaf, dazed, sealed off from reality. Things drifted in the air, slow-motion, dream-like. Chunks of metal careened lazily through the evening glow, bright bits of burning flesh and fabric floated slowly by, a silent storm of bright festive tinsel. Dust rose, white veils, in a silent, slow-motion, surreal, hieratic dance – a fresco painted on some ancient wall. She was separated from the scene, from her own sensations, by a wall of sound-proof, bullet-proof glass.

She tried to get up. "Ouch!" A burning sensation – a sharp pain – a lightening bolt, flashed in her belly. *Oh, no, damn it!* Wet sticky warm fluid flooded her crotch. Her life was leaking away.

"Damnation!"

She shook her head. Everything drifted in a buzzing, blood-smeared, slow-motion silence, echoing, like the ringing of a bell underwater. She must have been wounded, badly wounded, in the explosion.

"Damnation!"

She steeled herself and looked down. A triangular piece of glittery metal stuck out from her side. *This was bad! Damn it!* She glanced around – no one was looking. Maybe no one was alive to look. Anyway, it didn't matter. Look if you want to! Look!

She pulled the metal out – one quick jerk.

Ouch!

The wound began to close even as the point of the metal came away from her skin. Still, this little accident could make her weaker and more vulnerable. Every wound, every healing had a price.

She didn't see or feel any other damage. She drew her machine pistol from its holster. Cautiously, she tried to move her legs. Yes, no problem. She levered herself up, carefully, slowly, getting into a crouching position. She flipped up the blood-smeared wraparounds and squinted into the flaming smoky darkness.

About five meters away, Lieutenant K M Jackson lay sprawled on her back next to a small jagged outcropping of rock, lit up by the lowering sun.

V stood up slowly, glanced around, and walked over to her.

Jackson's wraparounds had been blown up over her forehead. They seemed undamaged. The woman's eyes were open – blank like glass. She looked intact. But – No, she wasn't. Her stomach had been pierced; the torso section of her body armor had been pulverized. But her chest was rising and falling. The girl was alive.

Around Lieutenant Jackson, were charred bits of metal and pieces of smoking meat. An instant before the explosions, those slabs and strings of smoking meat had been elite warriors defending Cosmos Civilization – the young Centurions.

Now they were nothing.

The Centurions who had been in V's vehicle lay all around her – smears of blood and slabs of flesh. Some of the bodies smoldered, as if the blood were turning to steam; a few were burning, little red and yellow flames, charred detritus of cloth, skin, bone, brain, flesh.

V walked up the line of the destroyed convoy.

V didn't see – or sense – any other survivors.

The other seven vehicles were flaming wrecks.

The empty vehicle, the one probably designated for hybrid prisoners or SINs was smashed, lying on its side.

She heard a buzzing, a rustling sound; she swiveled around, her machine pistol at the ready. Would she have to defend herself from whatever it was that had done this?

A bio-nano drone, buzzing lazily, fluttered, came close and sniffed at her, hovering. She was about to question the drone. "What …?" It burst into flame, and dropped like a stone. She looked down. It was dead, a tiny curl of smoke drifting upwards.

Bio-nano drones were independent of their immediate command vehicles, so whatever had done this – or was doing it – had infected the drones too.

She began to hear things – the stunned silence, the echoing sensation, was fading. The soundscape returned, and with it, reality.

Smoke rose everywhere. The scene was silent, except for flames, cracking metal, and sputtering explosions, like a battlefield, a field of blood, after the firing has ceased. Then, ammunition belts detonated, modest ripples of bang-bang, like a string of firecrackers. Fuel reserves went up, here and there, flaring with a deadly whoosh!

V walked back to Lieutenant Jackson. She might have to put the lieutenant out of her misery – a quick shot to the temple would do it; or, perhaps, more usefully, she could drink the lieutenant's blood, replenish her own energy – kill two birds with one stone. The young woman clearly had excellent DNA, and first-class blood.

Jackson was still breathing. Her guts hung out, coils of intestine. With one hand – fingers spread – she was trying to hold them in.

Yes, that was excellent, could be useful. The lieutenant was alive; her blood was drinkable, still good.

She crouched down close, looked into the lieutenant's eyes.

Lieutenant Jackson blinked.

She sees me, she's still conscious, still rational.

"Lieutenant," she gazed into her eyes. To drink her dry, or not to drink her dry – that was the question.

"Major – who's hurt, who's hurt?"

"Everybody's dead, Lieutenant. You and I are the only ones left."

"Shit!" Lieutenant Jackson coughed. Blood spurted from her lips.

"Easy, Lieutenant. Take it easy." She put her gloved hand on the girl's shoulder.

"Major, I'm hurt bad." Jackson coughed, licked her lips, "You'd better leave me."

"I don't think so, Lieutenant," V had a decision to make. She slipped down her wraparounds, so they covered her eyes. All InfoFlows and ComFlows were dead. Still, the wraparounds' independent sensors could be useful.

She stood up and looked around. The convoy was strewn out in front of her, a smoking ruin – crackling, small explosions, here and there.

Her aroused hybrid senses – with the added infrared and Gestalt sensors of the wraparounds – did not register any approaching danger. No human-oid life forms, no land or air drones, and no incoming missiles. And all the bio-nano drones must be dead, wounded, or dormant.

"Let me have a look, Lieutenant," V knelt. She peeled away the girl's shred-ded armor. The midriff of Jackson's armored bodysuit was reduced to bloody shreds. There was a raw, deep, open wound, slashed across her stomach, all the muscles ripped away. A bulging edge of large intestine was pressing out, held in by the girl's fingers. It would extrude – meters of it – if V didn't do something, and fast.

She hesitated. The others were dead. She and Jackson were alone. All com-munication streams were cut. With the Web Nerve Center broken or severed, the interconnected world had been shattered, fragmented. Snail's pace time and space would once again be real.

If she drank the girl dry, no one would ever know.

Yummy!

An extra burst of energy – of blood fuel – would be excellent!

Whatever lay ahead, it was going to be difficult, dangerous, strenuous.

Without the vehicles, a mile would be a mile, a kilometer would be a kilo-meter. The horizon would be a long way away – her target was God only knew where.

Progress – unless V could salvage a vehicle from the wrecked convoy – would be one painful step at a time. And they were in the heart of the bad-lands, on the edge of the Super Dust Bowl.

V had many powers, but she couldn't, so far as she knew, fly. They would be down to walking speed. She and Jackson were alone, as if tossed onto an alien planet.

"Okay, Lieutenant, let's see what we've got," V probed at the lips of the wound. Jackson was really a woman. But V thought of her as a girl, a young-ster. Even if the girl was a killer, she was somebody to be protected, nurtured.

She was a female – a breeder, valuable, the future of the race. Men, like sperm, were dispensable. "Lieutenant, I can help, but you are going to have to trust me, and I am going to have to trust you."

"Yes, Major, do what you have to do. If you must leave me, or shoot me here, I understand."

"I'm not going to shoot you, Lieutenant. Close your eyes. By the way, what's your name, what does the K stand for?"

"Kat, Kat's my name."

"Kat," V blinked, "like in meow?"

"Yes, except with a *k*." The bright teeth shone against the dark lips, almost a smile, the facial skin was already numb, the lustrous milk chocolate was fading to gray, the eyes glazed, filming over; she was going. "A hard *k*, a very hard *k*," Kat murmured. Her voice lapsed into silence. She blinked and closed her eyes. Blood and spittle bubbled at her lips. Nearby, in the silence, hot metal snapped; fires crackled.

"Okay, Kat, now, I'm going to try to fix you up." V glanced around. The healing process took concentration. While she was concentrating, she was vulnerable – any assault could be fatal.

She focussed her hybrid powers, scanned the area: no sign of attackers, no sign of dangerous drones, no bio-forms except a few small animals, a burrowing rat, two or three snakes in their nest-like refuges, and a couple of small reptiles, and none of them close or threatening.

Crouching over Kat, V laid her hands on the girl's shattered belly, and concentrated. "You will probably lose consciousness, Kat."

"Whatever, Major, whatever …" Kat's voice faded; her eyes opened and rolled up and Lieutenant Kat Jackson was gone.

V explored the shattered Centurion Convoy, more in depth this time. There were no survivors, of that she was now sure. She stepped through the debris – twisted metal, burnt plastics and synthetics, and broken smoldering bodies, and found what she was looking for.

Colonel Edwards was lying on his back, face up. His body had been cut in two. There was nothing left from the belt down. He was not wearing a wraparound and his helmet – he obviously hadn't had time to put it on – was clutched in one hand, bright, unscathed.

V crouched next to the torso. The colonel's face was strangely untroubled, pure, seemingly untouched. He was a handsome man, V thought, not for the first time. His eyes were open, crystal clear, only slightly filmed over. And, all things considered, he was a good man, a good man by his own lights, by the Cosmos warrior ethic he served, a warrior from ancient pre-Columbian times, remade for modern times. She laid her hands on his forehead and pressed the eyelids down. It looked like he was asleep.

She poked in his flak jacket. Yes, here it was. The mission instructions. Stored in a Mission Stick around his neck. She unhooked the chain, and pulled it slowly away, only lifting the colonel's head slightly, to make it easy. The chain was attached to the Mission or Mega Stick. Mega sticks were supposed to be utterly independent, isolated from the World Mind and Net, and only receiving periodic, one-way, micro-burst, communications. She hoped it still worked and that it had not been infected by whatever had infected everything else.

She slipped the stick out of its armored casing.

It certainly looked okay – but …

She held it for a minute, concentrating, absorbing information, and then she uttered the code – the "open sesame."

And then – she held her breath.

Oh, God!

Oh, God – where am I?

Kat blinked, trying to remember. Where was she? What had happened? And, at first, *who* was she?

Pull the pieces back together, girl!

She shook her head. She was sitting with her back propped against the wall of a stone ledge, her legs straight out in front of her, tips of her boots pointing up.

Looking down at them, her legs looked weird, as if they didn't belong to her, as if they were alien, inanimate objects. Dare I test them? She moved one booted foot, and then the other – no problem. Her legs worked. Strange! It seemed they were still attached to her body and to her mind. She bent one knee upward. Yes, perfect – it worked.

Still, she felt unreal, scattered, broken into little pieces, as if there was no center, no gathering point, no self.

She looked down. Her uniform was shredded. The skintight armored material was shattered, strings of flesh and blood – and she knew it was *her* flesh and blood – were smeared on the black glossy synthetic surface, down to her crotch, and dribbled down both thighs.

Her belly was exposed, naked. It seemed unmarked. She ran her fingers over her stomach muscles: the skin was smooth, muscles tight and sculpted from all that tough training, perfect abs, no scar, no wound, no nothing.

What the hell?

How could that be? She'd been shredded, she remembered …

She noticed that her sidearm and machine gun had been taken away and were leaning against the rock face, almost within grasp, but not quite. She flexed her legs again – no pain. She flexed her arms. No pain and no difficulty.

What the hell had happened?

She had been wounded, mortally wounded, her guts bursting out. And somehow, now, a few minutes later – she glanced at her watch – now, less than fifteen minutes later, she was okay, just as before, except for the uniform – even the metal belt was chipped and singed … At her midriff, the armored catsuit was a peeled, tattered rag.

Kat narrowed her eyes.

The major was about ten meters away, peering over a ridge of rock, limestone, Kat noticed. The major was using a small pair of binoculars. She'd taken off her helmet and slid her wraparounds up over her hair and she'd pushed the close-fitting beret to the side, at a jaunty but unorthodox angle. The setting sun just caught the edge of the beret, tingeing it dark gold. The major, Kat noted, had pale white skin, almost chalk-white, and jet-black hair, cut short, a rather stylish cut. From this angle the major was good-looking, too good-looking.

The major was concentrating.

It was getting dark; the sun was far down; part of the sky above was a deep smoky red – the dust of the dead lands desert – it was cooler; it must be only about 98-100 degrees Fahrenheit.

Kat watched as the major carefully put the binoculars into the pocket case and turned and walked back and crouched in front of her.

With the dark wraparound up over her hair, the major looked different – slender and fragile. She had dark eyes, so dark Kat could see no reflection in them, and the bright white skin was perfect, again, the major was too perfect, and the very even teeth, perfect teeth, too perfect; her beauty was unearthly.

"How do you feel, Kat?"

"I feel good. I feel too good."

"Right," the major frowned. "You trusted me, and I cured you. Is that right, Kat?"

"Yes, Major." Kat shifted her shoulders; she had an uneasy feeling about this.

"I salvaged a small radio. There's nothing, not on medium, not on short, not on long wave. Primitive old-fashioned technologies usually keep going when there's a general breakdown. Not this time. There may be some sort of black-out over this area." The major was still staring at Kat, dark eyes gazing into dark eyes. "Our own communications are still down – no Cloud, no Mind, and no GPS – nothing, in fact."

Kat said nothing. The major was still looking straight into her eyes, as if waiting for something. In Kat's experience, it was impossible for communications to be fully down, there were so many back-up systems, extra-circuits, though recently things had begun to collapse everywhere – many satellites were out of action, from budget cuts, inexplicable accidents, new-fangled untameable net and electro viruses, and rebel and mutant sabotage, and … People whispered that civilization was coming to an end; all systems, they said, would soon collapse.

So maybe it was true.

"All the others are dead, Kat. While you were unconscious – only a few minutes – I went over the ground. I double-checked. Then I checked again. I was thorough. Nobody's left."

Kat blinked. She'd been with the team ten years, since she was thirteen years old; this was her family; these were her friends. She had no other family. She felt sick to her stomach – she went into free fall – it was as if she had been dropped. She was plunging, flailing and alone, into a deep black hole, infinitely deep, with nothing at the end.

The major reached out, put her gloved hand on Kat's knee. "I know; they were your family; they were everything."

Kat felt she might start to cry, but demonstrations of emotion were strictly forbidden in the Centurion Corps. She blinked at the major, such a serious, compassionate expression. Kat could fall in love with the woman, but …

"You want to know how I fixed you up," said the major, her hand still on Kat's knee.

"Yes, Major, I do want to know." Kat swallowed. She steeled herself. She stared straight into the major's eyes.

"Hybrids are not just killers, Kat," the major's gaze was steady.

Kat held her breath. She didn't want to hear what was coming next. Kat had been trained to hate hybrids from the moment she had lost her parents, aged 12. That was when she became a hunter.

She had gone through the aptitude tests, preliminary training, and induction. And she'd learned: Hybrids were the greatest most fearsome enemies; hybrids were invaders, aliens from another planet, they were obscene shape-changers, they mated with humans, they were filth, they lived in excrement, in the sewers. Under a mask of beauty, they were hideously ugly, they drank human blood, they were out to contaminate the blood purity of the human race; they were … And she'd killed two hybrids – strange, beautiful creatures, already paralyzed and helpless – it was something she would never forget.

"I know you hunted – and killed – hybrids, Kat."

"Yes, yes, I did," Kat said, evenly holding the major's gaze.

"Well, that was your task – then."

"Yes, it was."

"Okay, I'd better explain, Kat. Hybrids have certain powers; and one of the powers is to heal."

"You are a hybrid, Major," Kat struggled to keep her gaze steady. "You are telling me you are a hybrid?"

The Major smiled. "Don't try to kill me, Kat. I'd have to stop you."

"You *are* a hybrid!"

"Yes, Kat, my name is V by the way."

Kat did feel like reaching for her gun, or for her knife, which was still in her belt, or for the machine gun, but instead she just blinked and repeated, stupidly, "Your name is V?"

"Yes, V."

Kat kept her voice low, almost a whisper. She felt she'd been plunged into a history book, an ancient tale of myth and sorcery, of dragons and fearless warriors, a tale that might have been told, or whispered, by bards sitting around campfires in olden times. "You are the mythical one, the source, the Mother Monster, the original alien, the invader from space, the source of pollution, the Devil …"

V favoured Kat with a thin smile. "That's very flattering and exaggerated, Kat. I know, yes, that's what they call me. But, as you can see, the reality is much more prosaic. I'm really just me – what you see – though I do have a few other shapes, yes."

Kat took a deep breath, tensed, readying herself to spring into action. "What are you going to do – with me?"

Night had fallen – it was swift: one minute, there was light; then, there was darkness. But the land was still lit up, vaguely, by the burning wreckage of the Centurion column, sparks, and flashes, here and there.

V was sitting, her back resting against the rock face, when she noticed, out of the corner of her eye, that the clown-preacher was back. So, he had not died or evaporated; he had not returned to Hell; or perhaps he had gone to Hell, but now he had come back.

He floated just above a big round boulder that resembled a six-foot-tall granite melon. He looked like an untethered balloon. "Hello, ladies," he said, "I see we have some survivors."

"What is that goddamn thing, really," whispered Kat, and, turning towards the apparition, she said, out loud, "What the hell are you?"

"I am merely a figment, my dear Kat, a humble lowly trickster figment, an emanation of higher powers, of ghostly presences, an intimation and gentle hint of the Apocalypse, sent for your instruction and delectation. I am a low-level belch of divinity!"

"Ignore him. Let's see if we can salvage something," V stood up, hooked her thumbs into her belt, and looked around. "Maybe there's a bike left."

"What, the hybrid can't fly?" Kat shot V a sardonic glance.

V gave Kat the once over. Kat was extremely attractive, even more so with the midriff of her armor torn away, her flat black stomach streaked with dry blood, its muscles glowing with sweat.

Kat stood up, her hands on her hips, looking defiant and mistrustful. Even if V, the mythical hybrid, had saved her life, Kat was damned well not going to cower or kowtow.

"Very funny," V said, "No, this hybrid can't fly. Glide, maybe; fly, no."

"Ha!"

"Yes, as you say – *ha!*"

"Well then, Major, we'd better get wheels." Kat gave V a narrow smile and looked around – ruins, dead bodies, and smoking fragments vehicles.

"The major finds you very attractive, Lieutenant," said the clown, floating in close and licking his lips, "You'd better watch out! She is a seductress, this hybrid. She'll jump into your pants, lickety-split, hippity-hop!"

"Jesus," V said.

"Ignore him."

"Right," V sighed, "I save your life and you start giving me lessons."

"Right."

"Now ladies, let us not quarrel, let us not squabble!" The clown glowed and flickered and wavered. "Here beginneth the first lesson. Our text is taken from Jeremiah the Misanthrope. Oh, woe, oh, woe, woe is me! The end is nigh, sackcloth and ashes for all of you! Line up for your sackcloth and ashes! Hear ye! Hear ye!"

"Let's go," V said.

"Yes, let's." Kat glanced at the clown. He shimmered and bowed a deep reverential bow. "Oh fair demoiselle, oh, fair Kat, thy breasts art as comely as a conical pile of ripe dark dates gleaming in the sunlight on market day in the old quarter of Bethlehem, thy breasts are as the shimmering heights of Kilimanjaro, thy belly is as taut as a rippling moonlit sea, thou art fresh as a sparkling fountain sprinkling its delights high in the hills above the Jordan, thou art light and lofty and carefree as the clouds, as the proudest drifting cirrus and cumulus, thou art smooth as the smoothest ebony or anthracite, thou art cool and lithe as the shifting shades in the mountains of the moon, thou art …"

"God almighty," Kat rolled her eyes.

"Ignore him."

"Right," Kat shot V a narrow-eyed look.

The clown-priest followed them as they walked up the hillside. He floated beside them as they scanned and searched the valley where the column had been ambushed. The drones were all dead, lying on the ground. Bodies and steel frames were scattered everywhere.

"You know, Major, this is weird. I don't see any traces of the strikes. I mean, there are no signs of the shells or weapons that destroyed the column."

"That's right." V crouched down and picked up a piece of metal. She sniffed it. "Whatever destroyed the column and killed everybody is not conventional weaponry. It was from within that the column was destroyed"

"It was the madness, that killed the column," said the clown, "folly and hysterics and short-circuits."

"The madness?" Kat looked up at the clown. He was seated cross-legged, floating about six feet above the ground, like a levitating fakir, his half-crushed top hat tilted at an impossible angle. "What are you talking about? What madness?"

"I set upon them myself and I made them mad – the machines and the men and women too. But the machines were so quick, the men – and women – didn't have time to go truly mad. It was all over."

"I see," V said, "you drove them mad and they started to short-circuit and then ..."

"... and the machines turned all the automatic systems inwards, so they would destroy them all – destroy you all, I mean to say."

"And how come we were not killed," Kat stared at the clown, "If you drove everybody mad?"

"V here, your demon friend, your foul hybrid pal, is immune, and her presence, her aura, protected you, alas. And then this hybrid-demon – she really is very wicked – patched you up and made you whole. So now I have two survivors and my mission is a failure, an abject failure, since two of you made it out of the Inferno, and none were supposed to survive. Thus, I am condemned to linger here as a shade and haunt you two refugees who survived my trickery."

"Let's go. I think I see something interesting," V said, "Follow us and tell us more, clown, if you will."

"Oh, I will! Delighted, absolutely delighted! I love to talk! It is my whole raison d'être I might say, my whole reason for coming into being."

"Chatterbox," said Kat.

"Exactly, Lieutenant, I'm a chatterbox, as you so neatly put it, an echo chamber, a loudspeaker, a ..." The clown drifted just behind them. He flowed like jelly over the ground, floating, skimming, dipping, rising. "I am like John the Baptist; I come before He who comes after."

"That's a frightening idea," murmured V.

At the end of the column, the self-propelled robot-driven trailer was on its side, but intact; it contained the light mobile guns, stored drones, and several scout motorbikes.

They approached the overturned trailer with their weapons drawn, because, with their Info flow sensors not receiving any bio-nano drone input, they were vulnerable. Even V felt she could be taken by surprise. Her sensory capacities, though exceptionally good, were not infallible.

Yes, the trailer had been turned on its side; but it had not exploded from within; the vehicle was undamaged, except for the engine and main computer, which were both shattered.

One two-person motorbike had been thrown off the trailer and had landed on a big drift of sand, so perhaps it was in working order.

Kat climbed onto the drift of sand and looked down. The two-person Desert Warrior Bike was half-buried in sand. The fuel tank was intact, and an extra fuel tank was attached to it, though it had come loose.

"This looks like just the thing," V said.

"Yes," said Kat, glancing sideways at the hybrid.

V and Kat pulled the bike from the sand and stood it upright. They attached the fuel tank with the extra reserve straps. They rolled the bike down to level ground. In theory, the tiny reactor and its fuel would allow them to go for hundreds, even thousands, of miles.

"Now that we can go – where do we go?"

"We continue the mission," said V.

"But we don't know what it is."

"Yes, we do."

"All we knew was that it was Camp Terminus, and hybrids, but the colonel didn't give us the coordinates, the details, so ..."

"The details are here." V lifted the chain with the Mission Stick from around her neck where she had tucked it inside the armored bodysuit. She spoke the open sesame, "Casablanca-42." The hologram appeared, shimmering between them, about a meter in height. It looked like a mine – an ancient pithead, a monstrous dark tangle of beams and crossbars and struts, and huge wheels, a second giant pithead, and then a map, and a satellite shot, and coordinates, GPS coordinates.

"That's our final objective." V pointed at the map.

"Which is ...?"

"It's a mine, an ancient mine. That's what Camp Terminus is."

"What's there?"

"Well, apparently," V hesitated, fury rising inside her, "The colonel told us – remember? Camp Terminus is where very valuable bio-resources are kept, very valuable resources which the President – our Glorious Leader – does not want to fall into the hands of ... of whatever is coming at us from the west."

"Bio-resources? Oh, yes – hybrids! Bio-resources!"

"Yes. DNA, alien DNA in various combinations."

"I don't know. I'm not sure I –"

"Here, Kat: read it for yourself. If you flip to text, it will give you the details. While you were unconscious, I retrieved it from the colonel's body." V handed Kat the Mission Stick. The text flashed in space; a virtual document.

Ultra-Secret flashed on the cover.

"May I?" Kat glanced at the hybrid.

"You might as well, Kat. I broke the code; it won't blow up in your face or disintegrate in your hands. You are alone here, with a hybrid. You are the sole representative of humanity. This is a joint command."

"And with a clown," the clown said, "Don't forget me! I'm here too!"

Kat read the briefing. She glanced at the major. This was a hybrid. This was the archetypal enemy. The hybrid must have an ulterior motive.

"You have your own agenda, Major."

"Yes, I do."

"Do you mind speaking it out loud, sharing it with me?"

V hesitated and then said, "As I said, I think that Camp Terminus is where they buried the bodies of the hybrids and the SINs."

"So – you want to see for yourself."

"Yes, I want to see for myself. And there's an outside chance that the hybrids are alive, not just frozen corpses or vials of DNA."

Kat walked around in a circle, thinking; then she turned back to V, "And you'll want to liberate them."

"Yes, I'll want to liberate them."

"And I should try to stop you."

"Yes, if you wish to do so, you can try to stop me. I'm going anyway."

"We both have our work cut out for us, then."

"Yes, we do, Kat, we do."

Now that V and Kat were independent of – well, cut off from – all Cloud In-feeds of energy, information, and navigation systems, they would have to guide the bike manually – which was best. It would make them independent of any virus in the Cloud or World Mind. Their only possible contact to the outside was the Mission Stick, snuggled under V's bodysuit. V had switched the Mission Stick to passive and local mode – ready to receive messages, but not to accept programs or programming changes; and only accept local messages, not universal or satellite messages. But of course, there were, for the moment, no messages from anywhere.

"So, we are on our own, Major," Kat said, "just you and me – and our friend here."

"Yes." V hooked her backpack, next to Kat's, on the open pack carrier at the back of the bike.

"Okay?"

"Okay."

V slid onto the bike and revved the motor. It worked perfectly, smooth, ultra-powerful, a fine example of Cosmos engineering. It was a pleasure, riding it, with all that slick smooth throbbing Cosmos power clenched between her thighs.

Kat climbed on behind V, adjusted the seat, and then wrapped her arms around V's waist and leaned against V's back. "I'm ready, Major."

The hours went by; the sun rose; the desert landscape barely changed.

There were ruins here and there, and stretches of abandoned highways and superhighways.

The clown drifted along beside the bike as it raced over the dunes, up and down the valleys and ravines; sometimes he was close, sometimes far away.

V knew that he was an emanation of whatever had attacked them – that in fact, he was, as he said, a key part of what had destroyed the column – but she didn't feel any hostility. It was comforting somehow, having this Cloud figment float close to them, following them.

Soon they began to find bodies.

Something had come through the desert like a wave of darkness and killed everything in its path.

V brought the bike to a stop overlooking a shallow ravine.

The clown drifted behind them, perhaps thirty meters away.

V and Kat got off the bike. They wiped the dust from their wraparounds.

Kat walked to the edge of the cliff, overlooking the ravine. V followed. They looked down.

V glanced back at the clown and nodded.

The clown drifted closer, until he floated next to them.

Bodies were scattered among the pebbles and boulders and drifts of sand on the bottom of the ravine.

Once it had been a river.

"Jesus," said Kat.

"Not pretty," V wiped the dust from her face; shook herself to get it out from under her black skintight bodysuit. The dust made everything so damned itchy – even for a hybrid! "They were killed here, I think, right here."

The bodies lay scattered, face-down, face-up, or curled, fetus-like, on their sides, whole, or torn into pieces. They had roasted in the sun, sizzled and baked and seared in the twanging ultraviolet air – the ozone layer in many places gone, half-destroyed, frittered away – like so much else.

V scanned the valley floor with her binoculars. The bodies would have drifted down the rivers, carried by the torrents, if there'd been rivers.

But out here, there were no rivers, only dry gullies, strands of sand and pebble and cactus, and gulches, a few ruined farm buildings, and ancient gas stations, or ghosts of small towns, where nobody had lived for decades.

"Woe to the righteous, for they shall perish from the earth." The clown drifted to the very edge of the ravine, as if to get a closer look.

In the simmering silence, vultures circled, fluttering down next to the bodies, or onto them, perching hungrily on a leg or an arm or a chest.

"Those are naughty birds," said the clown, "I do not like them. They feast on carrion. It is unseemly, unclean."

There were splashes of dried blood on the bone-white pebbles, rivulets of dried blood between the pebbles. Many of the bodies had been ripped open, many had had their faces ripped off. Faces …

Yes, whatever it was, it didn't like to look upon … the human face.

"Paradise lost is a horrible thing," said the clown.

V looked up: a brittle, high blue sky without a cloud, without ozone, or hardly any at all. It looked like a perfect world. But, of course, largely, increasingly, it was a dead world.

"Jesus," said Kat, pointing at one cluster of bodies, twisted, and torn into shreds.

"Definitely not pretty," V said.

"I've killed hybrids," Kat said, as if seeing the dead humans made for some reason a confession necessary.

"She knows, you know; and you know she knows you know she knows; and she's already told you she knows, and yet she loves you still," said the clown, "The demon knows, and the demon turns the other cheek."

"Yes, I know. You know I know, Kat. I told you already that I knew," V said; she put her gloved hand on Kat's shoulder; Kat didn't shake it off.

"Hybrids didn't do this," Kat said.

"No, hybrids definitely did not do this," V's hand was still on Kat's shoulder.

"True, most true! Hybrids, who are truly angels, had no hand or claw in this, the work of the Devil," the clown drifted closer, so the three of them were standing together, looking down on the floor of the ravine, "Why, oh, why do people refuse salvation?"

The clothes the bodies had been wearing had been ripped to ribbons, at least, if they had clothes. Most of them, in the last agony, eyeless and stark raving mad, it seemed they'd torn off their clothes, bared their flesh, just as they stripped off what little was left of their humanity.

"What did this?"

"I don't know, Kat, I don't know."

"I know, I think I know, but I shall not tell," the clown put the thumbs of his big white cartoon-like gloves into his vest; his stovepipe hat was tilted forward, sagely, over his eyes.

V thought that, yes, the people had gone mad. But something greater – deadlier than madness – had torn them apart. Something horrible and indefinable. She focused, extended her mental antennae, tried to visualize what thing had done this; all she got was a fluttering darkness, an over-powering stench, and then nothing. She looked up. Whatever it was, it came out of the sky.

And now the vultures ate what remained.

There were two large Desert-Bugs, abandoned, wrecked, doors open, win-dows smashed, axels snapped, engines uncovered.

"Colonists, settlers," said Kat, "trying to …"

"Yes, trying to reclaim what was lost."

"Yes."

"They were running, trying to run, from whatever it was," V said.

"But they couldn't run fast enough," Kat turned to look at V.

"Seen enough?" V took her hand off Kat's shoulder.

"Yes, Major, I've seen enough."

"I drive?"

"You drive."

They got back on the bike and drove on.

The sun was low on the horizon. Dusk would be brief. Night would come suddenly. From light to darkness, in an instant.

V stopped the bike. They got off and glanced around: nothing. The clown was gone. They were alone in the vast dead silence.

"Shall we make camp here, Major?" said Kat, her hands on her hips, staring at the setting sun. It reflected darkly in her wraparounds, a smeared, elon-gated, flattened, red ball.

"Yes, Lieutenant, let's camp here."

The backpacks contained fold-out ultra-thin sleeping skins. V laid out the sleeping skins while Kat collected some dried twigs from a stand of dead willows and lit a fire. Ancient habits die hard; out here, in a hostile land, a fire gave a sort of atavistic comfort …

Yes, fire gave comfort, even if the temperature was 102 degrees.

The sun was gone. They sat staring at the fire. Kat ate from a food pouch. V ate nothing; she did drink some coffee concentrate that Kat had triggered into liquid form over the flames.

"So, Hybrid," Kat said, "good night."

"Good night, Kat."

They slipped into their sleeping skins.

"Sleep tight, ladies, I shall watch over you," the clown said, suddenly back, materializing out of thin air. He hovered near the fire and rubbed his hands as if he wanted to warm them.

The temperature dropped, perhaps to 95 degrees. The air was sharp, bone-dry. The sky deepened to a stark dark blue. Then it was black, filled with stars.

V never knew whether she slept or not – it seemed to her that she lay awake all night, thinking.

But, then, suddenly …

"Rise and shine, ladies," the clown floated close, "rise and shine!"

"Okay," V said, "Keep your britches on!"

"God Almighty," Kat whispered, shifting on her side, hands clasped making a pillow under her cheek, blinking, sleep still in her eyes.

They got up and drank some coffee.

Dawn came gently – a yellow-green line, threading along the horizon, then an aquamarine streak, and then the blue, the burgeoning, brightening, deepening blue of a full, long, cloudless, sizzling hot day.

They rode through the morning. Again, there were bones. All the bodies along this stretch had been picked clean.

The bodies were merely bones, sparkling white, bleached, immaculate, as if they had been dead for centuries.

And yet, V thought, it has only been days, perhaps hours.

On that second day, by midday, Kat developed a fever.

They stopped on a hilly drift of sand.

The sun was high in the sky.

"Can't tell the angel from the devil," said the clown, "Our theology nowadays is topsy-turvy, all values are turned upside down, black is white, and white is black, or is everything all relative, just one big gray indistinguishable foggy smudge? I forget which is which."

He hovered a few feet away from Kat. She glanced up and stared.

"Don't look at it," V said.

"You don't believe, do you," the clown said, turning to V, "You don't believe in the force of Evil."

"No, I don't," V glanced at the clown, "Not with a capital 'E.' I don't even like the word."

"Man's belief is a fine and beautiful thing," the clown said; it was now talking to Kat, grinning at her. It had put its white-gloved hands, thumbs hooked under the lapels of its jacket, where the large brass or copper buttons gleamed. "You want to believe, young lady, you must believe; you do not want to throw in your lot with a heathen demon, a pagan throwback to primitive idolatrous times of long ago. Our hybrid friend here is a goddess from the benighted time before the True God revealed himself and engineered a hostile takeover of all that was sacred! Ms. V here comes from a bloody pitiless world, a world that accepted human sacrifice, blood sacrifice, and child sacrifice. She is an abomination, that's the word for it."

"Ignore it," V said.

"I can't. It speaks the truth."

"That gibberish is not the truth, not the whole truth anyway."

V could see the clown was getting inside Kat's head. Worse, V could see that her handsome girl companion – V did have a crush – was ill, truly ill. Kat had a high fever. She was burning up.

"Let's go over here, Lieutenant; you can sit down by that rock and I'll have a look at you."

As they walked towards the rock, Kat stumbled, righted herself, and took off her wraparounds. She turned towards V. Her eyes rolled up, with only the whites showing, blank slick white, the blind white of a hard-boiled egg. Thick foam bubbled between her teeth. She kept walking, blindly walking.

"Kat?"

There was no answer. Just a spurt of foam, it dribbled thickly, the consistency of whipped cream, down her chin, splashed on her shattered body armor, spurted down onto her belly and thighs.

Kat turned her blind face to V and snarled.

The clown hovered close. "You see, demon, you can't count on anything in this brave old world, this is the end, you know, you pagan, you old-time goddess, you alien fetish, you ..."

"Shut the fuck up, my friend," V said, evenly, over her shoulder. She concentrated on Kat. "Kat?"

Kat growled, spurted a splash of foam that caught V straight in the eyes. Kat leaped at V, teeth bared, grabbing for V's neck, trying to bite it.

"Kat, Kat," V swiveled aside.

Kat stumbled blindly.

V grabbed her arms, got a lock on her wrists, spun her around, and forced her against the wall of rock and then down onto the ground.

"Oh, fabulous one, oh sublime demon, thou art carrying out the Lord's work."

"Whose side are you on, Clown?"

Kat was far gone. The madness that had been part of what had killed the others whose bodies were scattered everywhere was upon her. V was sure it was the same. How was this madness transmitted? V glanced at the clown.

"It wasn't me, sister, it was not me. I did not infect her. I love you both. I truly do. I pray for you, evening and night!" He belched.

"You do, eh?"

"I do! I truly do!"

V frowned. He was telling the truth; the infection was in the air; it must have hovered over the dead bodies they had passed, or perhaps the Spirit of Evil – that bloody awful abstract Platonic word again – was sending out an emanation – a contagion of madness and murderous folly. Could this sort of plague be transmitted through hyperspace, skipping sideways from one universe to another? Could it slip into bodies though the very air – even in the desert?

"Your friend is about to become a mad dog – or a zombie, or something worse, much worse," the clown hovered closer, leaning down, like a doctor examining a patient.

"Thank you for telling me." There was only one thing to do. But V hesitated. She had to do it just right. Any mistake and she would create a monster. If she did that she would have to kill Kat or Kat would kill her.

"For a devil, thou art a foolish devil."

"Yes, Clown, perhaps I am." V hesitated for just an instant; one part of V wanted to kill the haunting floating ghost figment, but another part of her rather liked him. He had broken loose from whatever had created him, from whatever Force had destroyed and devoured the human spirit of all those dead lying in the desert.

Kat was breathing faster now, bubbles of foam rising to her lips, spittle flying. V licked her lips. "I cannot hesitate. Kat must live, or she must die."

"Do it," the clown whispered, "Risk it. Otherwise, she dies."

"Yes," V said, glancing up at him; perhaps now, yes, it was true: he was on her side.

"The passage is narrow, the window is closing. You must be quick."

"Yes."

"This is the true death dance! Look, I do it easy. Look ma, no hands!" The figment was floating next to V, doing a vaudeville soft-shoe routine while peering over her shoulder.

V turned to him; he was too flippant, "Oh, shove off now! Just for a minute, please! Let me concentrate!"

"Oh, mistress mine, you break my heart, you truly do!"

"Button up!"

"I come a-courting and you toss me away like an empty bag of cold greasy old popcorn! How can you be so cruel, oh demon mine?"

"Get lost, just for a moment – please!" V stroked Kat's forehead; the girl was unconscious, thick white foam dribbling from her mouth.

The clown flickered for a few minutes, then he moved away a few meters and glowed brighter and sang, "Hi diddle, diddle, the cat and the fiddle!"

"Shut up!"

"I shall not cease to speak!"

"Damn you!"

"I am the cat's meow."

V didn't want to do it, but she could not wait any longer. Kat was feverish, and she was foaming at the mouth and groaning, only half-conscious. The forces of darkness were gathering within Kat and around them. V glanced up. The clown looked down at her, a benign grin on his bulbous crimson lips. He glowed – emanating a whole ribbon of waving iridescent colors; it was quite a display. "You are a naughty demon," he said.

"You think so?"

"I know so."

V felt something. I was just an impression, a dream-like darkness, filling her mind, making her hesitate. Then it was a sharp vision. A fluttering, leathery, feathery evil was coming out of the darkness. Somewhere humans were being transformed into venomous bats, with giant wingspans, and skeletal hungry furry bodies, ravenous, dangerous, fetid, clawed and fanged creatures.

What in the world are these things?

"Oh, the horror," said the clown, glowing bright and subsiding, "Oh, I have seen what I have seen. Take heed mistress mine! You stand on the edge of the abyss into which you have just glimpsed."

What in the world are those things?

A fluttering leathery evil …

"Take heed!" cried the clown, "Take heed, oh foolish girl, the passage is narrow, oh demon mine, the passage is narrow, and the moment is brief. There is a tide in the affairs of man and of demons …"

"I know, the stakes are high and time is short," V said, thinking: I have to do this; I can save one person at least: the human race was dying; it was divided into sects bent on destroying each other; it had laid waste to most of the world and obliterated most of the creatures in it, and now nature, and something else, was taking its revenge. Some final struggle was about to take place. We had to be ready – now!

"Okay, let's go!" V morphed into vampire form – pointed fangs pushing back her blood-red lips, skin chalk-white, blue veins pulsating, ears slightly pointed.

"Oh, the Heavens preserve us!" The clown crossed himself and hiccupped, "I have seen wonders, wonders indeed, out beyond the farthest reaches of Orion, among the Pleiades, demons and angels, and right here, right now! Oh, what I have seen! Oh, Lordie! Oh, Lordie me!"

V bit Kat, her fangs sinking into Kat's neck, delicately piercing the jugular.

She drank a sip, then another, Oh, it was good. She was tempted to continue – to drink Kat dry.

"The girl's a milkshake, and champagne and fizzy cream soda! Oh, how delicious!" said the clown, hovering, smiling, benign, thumbs hooked under his sparkling mauve vest.

V, still drinking, looked up, and narrowed her eyes. Energy surged into her. But, then, carefully, she stopped drinking – her lips now smeared with blood – and from her fangs she injected the DNA fluid, like poison, but life-giving, life-transforming, and sealing the wound.

"Oh, oh, oh," said the clown, hovering close, "Now you've done it, demon, now you've really done it!"

"Yes, I have." V drew back; the fangs disappeared. She was herself again.

Kat jerked like a puppet whose strings had been yanked upwards. Her arms and legs kicked, flailed. She trembled. She bounced, kicked, kicked again, and then again, knees, elbows thrashing. Suddenly, she lay still – unconscious, a broken thing, hardly breathing, her naked, blood-streaked, gleaming abs barely twitching, the fractured armored chest plate hardly rising and falling at all – a ripple of quick shallow short breaths.

The clown hovered over V and Kat. V looked up at him. She wiped her mouth with the back of her gloved hand: blood.

"You missed a cute splotch, on the end of your nose," said the clown, gaily, "And a smudge – Charlie Chaplin or Adolf Hitler style – right under it."

V wiped at her nose and licked at her lips. "Did I get them?"

"Perfect, impeccable, immaculate – like the conception … Innocence is restored, virginity re-established! Hallelujah!" His nose glowed; his clerical collar was undone and flapping loose. Under his unbuttoned Jesuitical jacket, he was naked and semi-transparent, a ribcage of virtual bones.

Kat jerked again. Then she fell quiet, not moving, hardly breathing, beads of sweat covered her face; she groaned, a trace of silver saliva ran from her mouth, down the side of her chin. V wiped it away.

"Oh, you have killed her, mistress mine. You have killed the beautiful innocent dark one."

"I have not killed her, you idiot, and you know it."

"If you say so, now it depends on how you define 'death,' doesn't it? I mean, dear scaly demon, does life-in-death or death-in-life count as death or as life? I for one have consulted Saint Thomas and luminaries beyond number and found no answer. It depends on your accounting principles, I suppose."

V just looked at him.

"You are sullen, demon."

"I'm not sullen – I'm waiting, and I'm thinking about what you said."

Kat opened her eyes, blinked blindly. The light reflected off the glutinous surface of her eyes, just sightless light. She focused, pupil and iris narrowing, suddenly defined. She was back, "What happened?"

"You had a fever; you were unconscious."

"Tell her, Hybrid, tell her what you did! Tell her what you have done – that which cannot be undone," The clown was fading now. "Oh, Lordie, that I should live to see the days, and good girls turned, and virginity lost, the very heart of the flower de-flowered, and virtue tossed buck-naked out the window and sinfulness flaming up everywhere, all tricks turned, humanity undone, and, woe is me, all is lost, all is vanity, puffed up feathery peacock vanity, the knots and nooses are undone, all is ashes and dust, the center cannot hold, I assure you, I truly assure you!"

"What is he talking about?"

"Nonsense, Kat, he's talking nonsense."

"Fie, fie on thee, evil Devil, sulfurous female up from the nether regions of hell, cloven of hoof, and forked of tongue, skin of scales and eyes of snake."

"I do not have cloven hooves!" V turned to him. "I am beginning to lose patience with you, my friend. Shut up now!"

"You do have a forked tongue, ah, ah! I got you there, long and slender and forked and makes you hiss when you reveal your true colors which are scaly turquoise and blue and gold and green! And I love thou just as thou art. I would not have thee different, not by an iota, not for the world!" He launched into a little jig, three feet off the ground.

If V could have blasted him with a laser gun, she would have. But the laser gun would have no effect whatsoever. Nothing Colonel Edwards had tried had worked. These static-riddled mind-mirages were artifacts of Cloud disintegration and virus propagation. Of course, they often generated independent but ephemeral virtual personalities with minds of their own, true minds, subsystems gone mad. In his own way, the clown was real.

"It's not the Cloud I represent," he said.

"No?"

"It's the Boy, El Niño, the Prophet ..."

"Yes?"

"But now I am unanchored; I am my own man, truly – all on my lonesome, just me and my shadow, hurrah! You see, demon, I am me – purely me!"

"You are absolutely annoying, you know!" V understood. Their clown-preacher friend had been kidnapped from the Cloud and morphed into a spy, and now, for whatever reason, he had been cut loose.

"If you two would stop fighting, Major, I damned well want to know what happened and why I feel so funny and what you did to me!" Kat was regaining her energy, in fact, her skin glowed, her eyes were fierce; at any moment she would spring up and try to throttle V; she was beautiful – even more beautiful than before – a sublime example of her species – and it pained V that she had had to ruin Kat's pure Cosmos humanity by ..."

"Speak up, Major! What did you do to me?"

"I had a choice, Kat," V said, still kneeling beside her.

"You had a choice, what choice?" Kat licked her lips. "What did you do to me? I feel strange. I feel …"

"I bit you."

"You bit me. What does that mean?"

"It means I injected fluid into you; I changed your DNA, added to it; I changed you."

"You changed me?"

"Yes."

"You changed me into what?"

"Oh, tell her demon, tell her, Oh, that I should live to see the day! Glory, glory, hallelujah!"

"Kat, you are a hybrid now, like me."

"What?"

"You heard me."

"You heard her, sister. Now fall on your knees and repent. You have been turned monster. Soon you will sprout horns, hooves, and a flicking pointed tail, and you will thirst for blood, you will drink virgins dry, you will …"

"Shut the hell up!" V snarled at him, baring her teeth.

"Oh, my God," Kat's eyes opened wide. She raised her hands and stared at them. They were normal hands, not claws; her skin was the same beautiful dark chocolate, with perhaps an extra bit of glow. Outwardly, she had not changed at all, except the fever and the madness were gone.

"You can't tell a sauce by its package."

"Shut up, Clown!"

Kat looked up at V. "Why?"

"You were possessed, Kat, you were infected, you were going mad; you were going to try to kill me and you were turning into something monstrous, I'm not sure what it was, or what it would have been. But it was bad, very bad."

"Oh, my child, my innocent, fallen child, the Evil Holy Ghost had possessed you, and this devil here undid it, she chased out the ghost, exorcised it! You had to choose between one hell and another." The clown was hovering close to Kat; he was almost completely transparent now.

"I doubt very much that it was the Holy Ghost," V said, turning to the clown.

"No matter, my dear demon," he replied, "It was the Spirit of Evil, the Dark Force, and it's on-coming like a super-fast freight train from olden times, headed straight for you; it is the dark force entering through a rupture in time and space, the Dark Force from another universe, all-consuming, and which takes many forms, often disguising itself as things most holy, such as the Boy, el Niño, or the Prophet as he loves to be known. Many seemingly holy men and women have done its bidding, have served this force, the dark force, the evil force – it has existed always, and it always will. So, demon, I hate to admit it – but you did a good deed, turning this beautiful girl into a scaly snake-eyed monster. The other thing she would have become is worse, much worse!"

"What are you two talking about?" Kat struggled to her feet; she stood up, placing her legs slightly apart, an aggressive stance, with one hand on the holster of her laser gun, looking down at V still crouched in front of her – and at the clown floating a few feet away.

"I am a figment of the Cloud gone mad." The clown grinned, "I am Mini-Cloud, a mini-monster, I must admit, an evil emanation, but modest, hardly worth noticing." The clown's grin, ghastly, its broken and blackened teeth fading between the bulbous crimson lips, and the thick King James Bible he now clasped to his breast was wavering, becoming fainter and fainter. V glimpsed a fragment from Ecclesiastes withering to curled ash.

"He's fading," said Kat, looking at him, her dark eyes glowing, full of life; yes, V thought, Kat is beautiful, even more so now.

"I am an artifact," the clown bowed, "I am divine-mind-static of the kind mystics so enjoy. I am one with all; everything is me! I am stardust gone astray and a bubbling *space*-blister that needs a plaster. I am a cyber pimple, about to pop! I am a wanderer, far from my home."

"You are fading," V said, echoing Kat.

"Yes, my two lovely female friends, I am dying, you see. I'm a figment, a fragment projected from the Cloud, the Mind, an outpouring of dying neurons and synapses. I am the conscience of the world, a bit of Zeitgeist incarnate. But I was kidnapped by the Dark Force, by the Boy, and used to drive you and all your machines mad. And now I am free and shall soon fizzle out. You are doomed, doomed; all humans are doomed."

"Well, friend," V said, "we are not human – not entirely."

The clown grinned. "Then you will be alright, then. You will be hunky-dory, peachy cream, the cat's meow, you will be a straw boater worn jauntily, circa 1920 on the head of an apprentice banker with greased-down slicked-back hair, you are lawn-bowling under bright artificial lights at midnight in October 1929, you are Tin Pan Alley, you are barbershop quartets singing 'Shine on

Harvest Moon,' and an old couple gossiping in rocking chairs on moonlit ver-
andahs, and you are vanilla ice cream and roast beef and gravy and turkey at
Thanksgiving and all the good things of the olden times when everything was
Great in the Great Republic that long ago perished; but I must tell you – and I
am truly sorry to do so – that all that you love will perish from the face of the
earth, the floods will flood the land and the dust will rise and fill the skies and
the locust, human locust, transformed into man-eating vultures, fierce and
pitiless, will sweep the earth and all before them, the sun will burn it all to a
crisp, and even worse, much worse, the air will fill with noxious fluid, a true
plague, man-made, unleashed by a madman under the influence, and the
ripe smooth beautiful pampered unblemished skin will burst in volcanic pustules and bodies will melt into universal pus. It is written; it has been decreed."

"How do you know all this?" V frowned: Were these prophecies in some
way real, or were they the mere crazy ramblings of a disintegrating mind?

"Look, Major, if you like to gossip with a ghost …" Kat stood there, defi-
antly, legs straight, thumbs hooked in her belt, every inch the ideal Cosmos
Centurion warrior.

The clown turned to Kat with an enormous benign avuncular smile, "Now,
now, my dear, the major, as you so fetchingly call her, has your own interests
at heart; she is trying to see clear in the darkness. You see, I am a clue, a
collection of clues, a relic, a spattering of things done and not done, an echo.
And V here is playing Sherlock and you are Doctor Watson. You see, all force
fields have memories; energy is eternal and from its signatures, you can learn
– particularly you hybrids who are so cute and so intuitive – what has been
and what shall be forevermore, and perchance what shall come, amen."

"Really, Clown, I'm not so sure. I …" Kat now had her hands on her hips;
she was frowning, overflowing with energy, eager to *do* something.

V had seen this in neophyte hybrids before – energy was bursting out and
new unknown and unprecedented thoughts were racing through Kat's brain;
shortly she would either go crazy for a time – which would be very inconvenient, since they really *must* get going – or she would become frivolous, or she
would focus, her energy might find a target, and … She might try to kill V …

"Kat," V turned to face Kat straight on, "You were being turned into something like a zombie; whatever it was, whatever it is, it is spreading. I couldn't
let you be changed. Hybrid DNA protects against almost everything. So, I
bit you, so you wouldn't turn into some sort of vampire-zombie or ghoul – I
don't know what it was, but it was bad."

"Vampire zombie, ghoul, Oh, come on, Major, I know there are mutants, and I know you are a hybrid, but zombie vampires, oh, come on!" Her hand was nervously tapping the butt of the laser pistol; one booted foot was tapping the ground. Energy sparkled like stars off her ebony-dark skin.

"Dear Lieutenant Jackson, the good demon lady, whom you so kindly refer to as major, is truly your friend – indeed she is somewhat in love with you – and she truly speaks the truth, oh beautiful Lieutenant, you were foaming at the mouth, you were growling and snarling, your eyes had become hardboiled eggs, all white and slippery and rolling around your eye sockets, your sublime silken chocolate skin had lost its sheen and was turning a deadly ashen gray and in a few seconds you would have grown fangs and leathery three-meter-wide-span wings and you would have –"

"Wings, grown wings? Jesus Christ!" Kat licked her lips; her teeth were very white; very bright. Her eyes widened. She almost looked frightened.

"I wasn't sure about the wings." V frowned. This was not good. If people were being turned into monsters that could fly, then whatever the contagion was, it would spread much faster: a virus with a body with wings as a vector ...

"Well, I assure you," said the clown, "These new devils – mere instruments in the hands of the Evil One, who styles himself "The Boy" or "el Niño," come equipped with wings, poor things, and hatred, they hate and devour all they see. They hate the most the human face; it reminds them of what once they were. I never tell a fib, cross my heart and hope to die."

"I had a choice, Kat," V said, "I could kill you or I could bite you; so, I bit you."

"Damn," said Kat, hands now on hips, eyes narrowing, considering her options, "Damn you, Major! I am a Cosmos, First Class Cosmos, Full Citizen, and a Centurion, damn you, you damned hybrid!"

"Sticks and stones will break my bones, but nasty names will never hurt me!" the clown drifted up and down, his button eyes brightening and then fading, "Now, my dear Lieutenant, my dear Kat, you are a chrysalis out of which a new being will be born, you are a mere husk, dear Lieutenant Jackson, a shell! The worm is in the bud; the curled up amorous worm which will consume you from within, Kat, it will eat your life away. When you burst out you will no longer be you but another thing – isn't that cute!"

"It's horrible!"

"It's not so bad!"

"It's horrible!"

"We have to go," V said.

"Yes, go then," the clown wavered. "The forces of darkness are gathering. You know, the Boy converted me; he captured me; he spoke from inside me. But I have broken loose now. I am fading fast, so my friends … I must bid you adieu."

"This is nonsense," said Kat.

"I'm not so sure."

"He is Evil Incarnate," said the clown, "He poses as the Saviour."

"Who is he, the one you speak of?"

"He is the one who is coming."

"Who is coming?"

"The False One, verily, and I cross my heart!"

"The False One," V said, "I don't want to appear stupid, my friend, but …"

"The False Messiah, my dear scaly demon idiot. Your IQ must have plunged these recent decades. You are slow as mud, dull as dishwater. It is He who ushers in the Kingdom of Evil on Earth, the end of days, the prelude to the final hours of human life on this planet; it is He who preaches The Rapture; you have already met his manifestations before – you went far into the future to fight him; you fought him in the past, you fought him in the Vatican, you fought him in the desert, in North Africa, you fought him in a slimy muddy cave, when He was a giant serpent, you fought him when He was a shuffling elf-like gnome; it is He who comes in the robes of …"

"Thank you," V said, "That's enough."

"You're welcome." The shriveling clown bowed deep.

"Let's go," V said, turning to Kat.

"I should kill you, Major."

V stood up. "Alright, Kat, do it!"

Kat stared at V and then she circled around, just a few feet away, looking V up and down, as if inspecting V for a vulnerable spot. V did not move. She felt the killer tension pouring off Kat.

But it was clear, too, that Kat did not know what to think or how to react. Pure energy, such electrifying dizzying energy as she had never known, coursed through her veins. She was changing – inwardly changing. V could see it happening. Kat stalked around V several times, ever closer, as if con- templating the best way to execute the hybrid.

Then she stopped in front of V, facing her. "You're right, Major," she said, "It's time to go."

"You'll thank me one day, Kat."

"I will follow you, now, Major. Later I will kill you."

"Fine, that sounds good, Kat, it's a deal. Now, let's go, let's leave our friend here. I think he has no heart or strength to follow us."

"Adieu my friends, adieu, I leave you now perhaps for all eternity as I fade away and soon, I shall be no more!"

And in fact, he did flicker and go out – like a flame gutted by the breeze; he was there; then he was gone.

"Adieu, friend," V felt strangely bereft.

"Weird," said Kat.

"Yes, weird." V slipped down her wraparound and so did Kat.

The wraparounds had not been receiving any outside information since the systems had failed three days about, but now …

In the same instant they both said, "There's a signal".

The signal was a tiny flashing red dot and a beeping sound, activated as soon as they slipped the wraparounds on. Inside the wraparound, the tiny red dot was blinking furiously; it was giving longitude, latitude, coordinates – it was a call for help, a ghost from the dead electronic world, from the dead Cloud and World Mind, or perhaps, just from an independent emergency frequency … That would explain why it was alive.

"It's local," V said, "It has to be local. I think it's …"

"It's a distress signal – a plane, a plane crash …"

"It has coordinates," V hesitated, "It must have locked onto the last coordinates before the Cloud failed."

"Or maybe it's still in touch with the Cloud."

"Maybe, but I don't think so. I think … The coordinates are close to those the colonel was using; so …"

"It's from a plane."

The mini distress signal file was now unpacking its information – that for some reason had been stored on the wraparounds, but not released until now: it was giving the nature of the signal, the object of the signal, time and date of the crash, terrestrial coordinates …

"Right, a plane …"

"Yes, a plane …"

"A presidential bloody superliner …" V breathed, "A bloody … presidential superliner …"

"This is from three days ago." Kat instinctively put her gloved hand on V's arm, "I mean, if the president …"

"Three days ago …" V absorbed the idea: a presidential aircraft … used only for cabinet members, top brass, and for … the president …

Kat and V turned towards each other, wraparound reflecting wraparound, lips moving …

"No, he couldn't be!"

"He might be; but then …"

They both nodded. They would follow the signal and see what it led to – if it led to anything, the crash site, a decoy, an illusion – whatever.

"We go to the signal," said Kat.

"And then we go to Camp Terminus," said V.

"And to your hybrids," said Kat.

"To *our* hybrids, Kat," said V.

Kat bared her teeth in a grin, "I should kill you now, hybrid."

"Later, Kat, kill me later. Right now, let's see how long this will take us and whether we're still on the right track."

V and Kat did have a problem. Since their GPS connection and navigational systems had failed, they would have to use dead-reckoning to find the crash site and Camp Terminus, calculating their probable position by recording how fast they were going, and judging the direction they were going by the sun and the stars and the old-fashioned magnetic compass, if it worked.

"Like the explorers of old," said Kat.

"Exactly," said V.

"You were alive then, weren't you," Kat had read – in the confidential file – that the woman standing beside her, the semi-mythical hybrid V, had lived for centuries, millennia – if any of it was true, and not pure myth.

"Yes, I was, but that doesn't help much." V pulled a foldout plasticized military map out of her backpack.

"So where are we now, exactly?" Shoulder to shoulder, they did the calculations. Yes, the crash site was probably about four or five hours away; they could guide themselves by the sun and by the old-fashioned magnetic compass on the bike – it was primitive – but it might just take them where they wanted to go. In these days of chaos, primitive was better than newfangled and sophisticated.

"Okay, let's go!"

V got on the bike and glanced back at Kat. Kat stood defiant for a moment, nursing murderous thoughts; then she hopped on behind V.

"Ready?"

"Yes, I'm ready."

They sped off into the desert.

V frowned. The clown was not following them. He was truly gone. His work was done – he had destroyed the column and then he had hovered, watching over V and Kat, the two survivors, the two who had cheated death, and turned his mission into a failure. Being without him was strange.

V thought that many of these figments, like brief flames in the night, had souls – quantum energy figments – which were just as real as the souls of so many creatures who had lived and suffered and loved and fought and died through the 4.5 or 4 billion odd years of life on earth.

"Funny not to have that idiot tagging along," Kat shouted into the wind, "It almost makes me feel lonely."

"Yes," V shouted, "Me too."

Kat clung close to V, shifting her weight to help V turn corners, angle up outcroppings, and, though she certainly hated V and feared V and though she wished to kill V and perhaps would try, the movement of the bike and the rush of the hot wind and the feel of her arms around V's waist gradually lulled Kat into an almost hypnotic state and she forgot about the horrible trans-formation she had undergone – that she was a hybrid – the implications of which she had not really started to imagine, and she forgot, for a time, about her desire – and duty – to eliminate V from the planet earth.

After five hours, they came into a shallow ravine, and for about three minutes rode just below the top of the crest alongside the ravine. V slowed the bike down. "I think we're close to the crash site."

Kat looked up, and peered through her wraparounds. "Getting dark."

"Yes, it will be night soon." V glanced up at the sky. The sun was low on the horizon; in a half an hour the world would plunge into darkness. "Let's have a look."

V gunned the bike up to the top of the crest, so they could overlook the rav-ine – she felt Kat's approval: It was better to not go down into a ravine where they would be vulnerable; up here, on the high ground, it was safer, unless, of course, the attack came from the sky; but V didn't feel the presence of any drones, aircraft, or hostile bio-creatures. The sun was low. Already, on the ridge, they were in shadow; but, up above, in the pale blue, a few strands of high cloud, a few wispy herringbone strands of cirrus, were shaded pink by the setting sun.

Near a high outcropping, V skidded to a stop, and the bike kicked up a plume of dust.

"So, this is it: where the signal came from," V said.

"Yes," Kat got off the bike.

They stretched their legs – V wiggling her shoulders. Ouch! Even hybrids get cramps. They walked, then crawled on hands and knees, to the very edge of the ridge overlooking the valley and lay down side-by-side on their stomachs, where the cliff fell away. Better to be careful. There was no knowing what they would find down there. In their wraparounds, the little red light continued to blink: *help, help, help!* About seventy meters below, in the dusky depths of the valley, lay the scattered wreckage.

"God," said Kat, "what a smash up."

"Yes."

"It really is one of the Leader's jets. See the presidential insignia."

"Yes," V scanned the wreckage; the idea of the Leader, the Glorious President, aroused very mixed feelings; she was about to …

"He wasn't on it, I'm sure." Kat turned to V. "Otherwise, there'd be … a swarm of …"

"I agree," V breathed a sigh of relief, "He wasn't on it."

"It happened three days ago …"

"Yes." V used her pocket binoculars to scan the ravine, which, farther on, broadened out into a valley. The skid marks in the sand had not yet been obscured by wind and sand drift; they were as sharp as if they had been made yesterday. Some of the wreckage was still smoldering. "So, three days ago …"

"It happened when our communications went down."

"Could be – maybe the plane was a victim of the same …"

"Phenomenon …" Kat bit her lip.

"Yes, phenomenon …" V turned and smiled at Kat. If you don't know what a thing is, at least give it a name: "phenomenon" was a good non-committal word: it meant "something" but it didn't mean anything; it was an empty box, a question mark – something to be mapped and explored.

They scanned the ravine – using the wraparounds infrared and visual spectrum analysis. There were bodies – but no sign of life. And there was the source of the signal; the small battery-powered box transmitting the automatic distress signal. The whole floor of the ravine and of the small valley that opened up beyond the ravine was strewn with wreckage.

They looked at each other, nodded, and stood up. "Let's go and see," V said.

"Right, Major, let's go and see," Kat even smiled – teeth bright in the twilight.

They got on the bike, found a gentler bit of slope and rode down into the valley. V stopped the bike, kicked the stand into place, and they got off and looked around.

The fuselage was broken into five parts. It was one of the President Leader's Super-Liner X-47s, designed specifically to carry VIP passengers. The central luxury compartment was largely intact, but one wall had exploded – it looked like the safety pods had been ejected. V and Kat circled around.

They climbed into the central luxury compartment. Yes, the two safety pods had been ejected. V put her hand on the ejection mechanism. It was still in order. It had ejected the pods.

V stood there for a moment, thinking: there was a feeling of something, something familiar. Kat walked out of the compartment. V lingered, trying to identify the familiar feeling, the echo. It was a memory trace of something or somebody she knew.

"Safety pods, over here!" Kat shouted.

V stepped out of the compartment looked up at the sky. Soon it would be dark. V felt something impending, some evil force, some …

She walked over to where Kat was standing, next to the two pods that stood upright on the sand. The pod doors were open, but still on their hinges, and undamaged, apparently undamaged.

"They look in good shape," V said.

"Both opened from the inside." Kat checked the locks.

"Yes, if both safety pods are intact," V said, "Whoever was inside, they got out alive."

"Two women got out of these pods. Two women were here," Kat said.

"Oh," V glanced at Kat. Kat looked down.

"And …?"

"And … then they …" Kat began to walk the ground. She came to a body – a woman with a deep wound, a body reduced to a charred statue. "One of them tried to save this woman, a stewardess … And the other walked into the flames, here, and tried to cut this man loose from his seat, but she couldn't …"

"They sound very brave, these two women," V said.

"Yes, but …" Kat stopped, she bit her lip; she lifted up her wraparounds and looked at V almost sheepishly. "This is part of it, isn't it? I mean this intuition – this *vision* – of what happened, this … I feel their suffering as if it were mine. This is part of it; this is part of being …"

"Yes, it's part of it."

Kat leaned against the rock face. She covered her eyes. She was crying, totally unlike a Centurion, totally unlike herself, but part perhaps of the first emotional vertigo of becoming a hybrid, "They were sad. They couldn't save anybody. Everybody else was dead. But ..." She opened her eyes and stared at V.

"Yes?" V smiled encouragingly.

Kat frowned, "This is strange. They weren't hurt. I can't see it clearly. I just feel it. They both walked into the flames, and reached into the flames, right into the flames and neither was hurt. A girl and a woman, mother and daughter and yet not mother and daughter."

"What?" Now V was interested. V concentrated. She sent out her mental tentacles, her antennae.

"Why didn't you tell me it is like this?"

"Like what?"

"Like this – this feeling of everything – I feel their suffering, I feel the pain of the man who died, I feel the last minutes of the stewardess – I even know some things about her – I can smell all sorts of things. The stewardess had a mother who died in an automobile accident; she was thinking about her when she died ... I think I'm going to burst; I'm feeling and seeing so much; this is some sort of overload, I don't know if I can ..."

"You can," V smiled. "Besides, it's intermittent; it's not always like this."

"And then, and then," Kat said, walking along the rock face, her hand on the places where there were smudges of smoke and flame, "and then things came; and ..."

"Things ...?"

"Mutants ... a herd of mutants ... and they took the two women ..."

V concentrated and focused and saw ... in sketchy form ... she saw what had happened and who the two women were.

V's heart leaped; then it sank.

"Their names, the two women were called ..." Kat's hands were splayed open against the cliff, as if she wanted to push her way into the rock, "Their names were ..."

"Nikki and Miranda," V said.

"Yes! How did you ...?" She turned to me, her eyes wide, "Of course, how silly, how silly of me, I didn't think."

"Let's go," V said, "I think we should go."

PART TWO – DEADLAND

CHAPTER 5 – FUGITIVE

Miranda's heart beat super-fast.

When Caliban grabbed her, she hammered her fists against his back and squirmed, suddenly dizzy, suddenly upside down, her hair hanging over her face, her tunic hitched up – probably – over her waist – she kicked and squirmed and pounded her fists on his beautiful smooth skin, on his shining bright dragon tattoo, and shouted, "Let me down, you beast, you monster, you traitor, you jerk!" And she heard, in the whirl of all this, the mob shouting, "Kill, Kill, Yes, Prince Caliban, dash her upon the rocks, throw her from the heights, Prince Caliban, kill, kill, kill," and the screams of joy and excitement as Caliban – with her wiggling and struggling on his shoulder – leaped up to the first balustrade and then to the hanging walkway, and all the faces, she could see through the tangle of her hair, all the faces, staring up, shouting, gleeful, and the chorus of "Kill, Kill, Kill!" and then, she saw, just for an instant, Nikki, and Nikki's face too was turned up, and Nikki was smiling, and Miranda heard Nikki's voice, clear as a bell, though whether it was inside her head or outside, she didn't know – and now Caliban leaped through the air, it was a breathless sensation and it seemed to happen in slow-motion – they were both flying through the air – and then, she felt it more than she saw it – Caliban grabbed a dangling looped cable – like Tarzan seizing a vine in the jungle and, yodeling, swinging from tree-to-tree – and then Caliban swept them up, and gravity seemed for a moment suspended, as if the two of them were weightless, floating in the air, and he landed, gently, somehow, on the outer walkway, the steel resonating under his feet – twenty meters up in the main cave, and while all this was happening, and she was still hammering on his back and kicking – but more weakly now –she was feeling breathless from the very sweep and movement of the thing, and Nikki's words were echoing in her mind, *"Caliban is saving you, Miranda! Help Him!"* and she heard too that the screams of joy from the mutants had changed to screams of hatred and betrayal, "Stop him! Stop him! The traitor! He's taking her away! He's taking the prize away! Stop him!" – she stopped struggling and lay still, bouncing over his shoulder, her arms dangling down his back, trying to absorb this weird turn of events, and she heard Nikki again – how did Nikki do that, projecting her voice straight into Miranda's mind? – Was it an illusion? – Nikki was saying, "And, Miranda, don't worry about me! I shall be perfectly alright! Just save yourself and help save Caliban!" *Help save Caliban? What did Nikki mean? What was that about?*

Caliban stormed along the main cavern's suspended walkway and Miranda glimpsed the mutants chasing behind, some were trying to climb up to the walkway, and a couple of the bear-warriors were already on the walkway, running as fast as they could to catch up to Caliban.

But Caliban was faster and now ... There was a last flash from Nikki, "*I love you, Miranda!*"

So – Caliban and Nikki had cooked this up together!

So, Caliban was her Prince, after all!

And now, his legs pumping like greased lightning, Caliban raced up the main staircase, towards the Exit, the Great Door that led out of the Mutant Kingdom.

A herd of angry mutants galloped and leaped up the stairs behind them, hot on Caliban's heels. Miranda was still slung over Caliban's shoulder. This was more exciting than even the best Cloud Game. It was so much more tactile and smelly and dynamic – and, most unusual, it was really real!

"They're gaining on us! Run, Caliban, run!"

The stakes were real – the stakes were high!

"Run, my Prince, run!"

To be burned at the stake or not to be burned at the stake – that was the question. To be eaten, or not to be eaten – that was the question! To be drunk dry or not to be drunk dry!

Behind her, as she and Caliban raced up the stairs, a big bear-like warrior – like her usual bear guards but this one – his name badge said Yorick – she didn't know him – he was really bear-like, covered in curly brown fur and displaying really impressive incisors and he had a gleaming breastplate and brass leg coverings – had almost caught up to them. Miranda could feel his steamy carnivorous breath against her face.

With her adrenaline pumping, Miranda suddenly heard the Big Bear's thoughts, bouncing around, right inside her head – *"Hmm, she'll be delicious to eat!"*

"Fat chance!" without thinking, she shot her own thought back at him like an arrow and, to make sure he got the point, she stuck out her tongue and transmitted: *"You're a big sissy!"*

What!

What!

The bear went into a rage. It made him so mad he stopped to growl and pound his chest – like a gorilla making a strong proprietary patriarchal statement in a jungle. And – throwing a regular temper-tantrum – he slammed his paw-hands against the railing of the staircase – WHAM!!

This caused a *Holy Virgin Barbie Doll Shrine* to explode and, sending out a spray of flaming hot red wax, all the votive candles flip-flopped onto the stairs and the Barbie Dolls catapulted, somersaulting, and bouncing down the steps, terrorizing all the other mutants who had surged up right behind the bear.

The bear roared, "This Cosmos girl has driven me mad!"

The bear came to himself – looking for a split second abashed. How horrible! He had for a second let go of his phlegmatic sangfroid of which he as a bear-warrior and hunter was quite proud. *This Cosmos girl has driven me out of my wits!* He roared a humungous roar and rocketed up the stairs.

Miranda knew that she could jump off Caliban's shoulders and run up the staircase herself – she was a champion runner and had won the Elysium City Teenage Cosmos Marathon – three times in a row – the President – *the Leader, oh, the Dear, Dear Great and Glorious Leader* – himself had hung the medallion around her neck and had paused to talk to her for a second time – looking her straight in the eye – and he had talked for longer than he had with any of the other girls – so she could certainly sprint up these wicked stairs: no problem!

Hail, Hail, All Hail!

Hail, Hail, All Hail!

But she rather liked being slung over Caliban's strong broad shoulder, with his strong smooth arm and hand pinning her thighs to his chest; she was rather partial to being bounced on his broad smooth muscles, which were right under her midriff, with her legs kicking above his chest; she was rather pleased by all this tactile, epidermal, and muscular contact, which was giving rise to unique new and extremely pleasant sensations; which, she was quite sure, Kit Candy would be absolutely interested in and totally able to elucidate in the finest detail.

"You're just a furry old bear," she transmitted the thought at the racing ursine giant, "And you really don't want to eat me! You prefer porridge, which is definitely baby food"

The Bear-Warrior was truly mad now. He was certainly not going to accept any ambiguously snide diplomatic namby-pamby nursery rhyme olive branch trial-balloon drivel being offered by the golden-skinned blond female Cosmos whose eyes were flashing at him, and who, somehow – and this really made him furious – had gotten *inside* his brain where she was talking to him just like his wife did – in a scolding, hectoring, scornful, ironic, and definitely schoolmarm tone. *He couldn't stand it! He really couldn't stand it!* He was going to catch this impertinent Cosmos!

In any case, he couldn't stop pursuing her even if he wanted to. Pressing behind him – meowing, caterwauling, screeching, clucking, shouting, oinking – came a whole enraged posse of mutants, pig people, bird people, dog people; they were desperate to seize the sacred sacrifice – the divine Miranda Hughes, Cosmos First Class and Elysium Cosmos skipping-rope virtuoso and champion five years in a row – who would, when cooked and devoured, bring prosperity and peace and the blessings of Dolly to all mutants everywhere for all time. Her blood would be elixir! Her flesh would be manna for all! But this Miranda creature, hoisted over Caliban's shoulder, was escaping from their clutches.

It was Prince Caliban, the traitor, who was the true villain. In truth, Caliban had always seemed to the Bear to be suspiciously human. He even looked like those half-naked male Cosmos glimpsed in the pages of the Sacred Scrolls, *Gentlemen's Quarterly*, or GQ, which meant that, perhaps, Caliban was not really a mutant, after all, perhaps he had always been human, a Cosmos Spy! He had, after all, appeared as a baby stark naked in the desert in the midst of a terrible sandstorm and just after a Cosmos train crash.

Oh, for the Bear, this thought was too horrible to bear!

Why he had once thought of Caliban as his best friend!

He and Caliban had hunted by the light of the moon.

He and Caliban had fished for mutant fish in the most distant underground lakes and rivers. They had slept side-by-side on the same ground. They had talked of the nature of Dolly and of the beginning and end of Time. They had argued over the ancient archaic texts known as *Playboy* and the Prophet Hugh and the Bunny Mutant Acolytes who had those special ears and little furry round tails.

Now, thinking of friendship and brotherhood lost, the Bear's heart ached: it was the fault of this female Cosmos; it was all the fault of Miranda and her Evil Mother Nikki, an archetypical Cosmos if there ever was one. They had brought Sex into the World, and with it they brought Betrayal!

The mutants thundered up the giant metal stairs, past the *Divine Shrine to the Refrigerator*, past the *Hub Cap Chapel*, past the *iPad Sacred Fountain*, with its muddy water dribbling from two statuesque iPads held up by Neo-African Barbies, past the *Make-Up-Mascara-First-Blush-Spa Plinth*, past the …

The mutants were getting closer. Soon they would overwhelm Prince Caliban, that miscreant apostate, and his Babylon Cosmos whore, and throw them both to the ground, the traitor and spy, and the beautiful young hussy of Cosmos Elysium Babylon, and Long John Tarzan the warrior and the fallen prince – Oh, traitor, traitor Caliban!

Miranda heard their thoughts – this was really *weird* the way she was hearing everybody's thoughts – in fact, it was positively *annoying* – and she saw that they were closing in: she was not sure she liked being classified as – as she automatically translated the less polite phrases – as a "Sex Worker in Babylon," even if it was as an exotic and sacred and sacrificial "sex worker." These mutants considered her something between a Quick Snack and a Divine Temple Priestess. By drinking my blood and consuming my flesh, they think they will acquire some of my "virtues"! *Where did they get that idea? Whatever are they thinking?* She quickly referenced a number of classic anthropological texts dealing with sacred scapegoats, redemption, and the transfer of virtues, including Sir James George Fraser's *The Golden Bough* and Saint Paul's *First Epistle to the Corinthians.* All of which was extraordinarily interesting, but in the meantime …

In the meantime …

She had to *do* something, not just dangle bouncing deliciously upside down over Caliban's shoulder.

Just as she had this thought and and just as she was wracking her brain to figure out what precisely she could do to slow the multitude, Caliban whipped around a corner in the giant staircase and – lo and behold – Miranda saw her chance.

There it was, glittering like a mirage: *Pepsi & Cola.*

The Pepsi & Cola shrine …

She stretched, plunged, reached out, and grabbed one of the thin metal struts that supported the Giant pyramid-shaped *Most Holy Shrine to Holy*

Pepsi and to Sacred Cola, the two ancient *Diet Divinities;* she gave the strut a quick yank – zip and tug! Just like that!

The strut rocketed out across the stair, twanging like a pole-vaulter's pole, and it spun, round and round, down the staircase where it threatened to spear and fricassee three frog-like, bug-eyed mutants.

To Miranda, the *Shrine to Pepsi & Cola* seemed to be collapsing in slow motion. She realized that her mind was now going very fast, and the adrenaline-driven acceleration seemed to decelerate time; the faster the mind, the slower the time, she concluded, thinking: this could be the subject of a thesis for an extra Ph.D. There was an inverse relationship between …

In slow motion, the Shrine was undergoing an implosion-explosion cataclysm – fascinating dynamics.

One Pepsi can popped out, then another Pepsi can popped out, then a Cola can, then five more, then twenty-five, and within 0.75 seconds thousands of full antique Pepsi & Cola cans, were bouncing and rolling down the stairs. Lots of empties were bouncing too.

Oh, boy! Miranda could see what was about to come.

The Bear, suddenly, was running hard just to stay in place, like a lumberjack on a rolling log, turning over and over in the water, except these were rolling Pepsis and rolling Colas.

The Bear was struggling desperately not to fall, his big bear foot paws running, running, running, and his big bear paw-hands swimming, swimming, swimming, grasping at the empty smoky air, as the Niagara of Pepsi and Cola cans bounced down the stairs under him.

Miranda, disappearing upwards, giggled, and then transmitted "*Sorry, Mr. Bear, that was naughty of me!*"

She heard the Bear transmit "Little Lady, I shall huff and puff and blow your house down and then I shall pick you up and put you on a rotating spit and I shall roast you and eat you, little girl! I shall pick my teeth with your bones!"

Miranda transmitted a thought to the Bear which surprised her and the full meaning of which she did not really understand and would not begin to appreciate until twilight of two days hence came and much more time had passed; and that thought was: "*You really have no idea who you are dealing with here, my dear Mr. Bear friend! I might be the one to eat you!*"

The Bear roared, almost tumbled but, arms outstretched, regained his balance, like an acrobat on a high wire, and disappeared, his legs high-knee pumping like a wild water-log-jogger lumberjack.

The other mutants, caught in a cascading avalanche of Pepsi and Cola cans, were bouncing, tumbling, and falling, sprawling down the stairs, and disappearing in an ocean of Pepsi and Cola.

Just before she was whipped around another corner, Miranda caught a glimpse of a fat duck-like creature – quacking madly – as it fell flat on its fat feathery backside. It tried to get up but then was hit by more Pepsi & Cola cans and was carried away in a cascade of bouncing aluminum cylinders.

Miranda was carried top speed by Caliban around the bend in the stairs and the chaotic scene was lost though she could still hear exploding Pepsi & Cola cans, rattling Pepsi & Cola cans, sloshing Pepsi & Cola cans, clanging Pepsi & Cola cans. And she could still hear – almost *see* – the tumbling screaming squawking multitude.

Above the chaos, she could hear the roar of the Bear who was roaring something like, "I shall take my revenge. I shall devour every last shred of flesh of that wicked blond Cosmos girlie!"

"Girlie?" thought Miranda. Who does that Bear fellow think he is?

"Good work, Cosmos, you are a true pirate's mate and worthy of Tarzan and Long John Silver and Roy Rogers and Tonto and the Lone Ranger and all the saints themselves that dwell in the ether and the past forever as long as electromagnetic waves propagate," shouted Caliban over his shoulder as he raced up the stairs.

Miranda, hanging upside down, hair over her eyes, arms dangling freely, blushed.

She began to think that, though the experience was very enjoyable – titillating, ticklish, and sensual – and though it corresponded precisely, image by image, to some of her favorite exotic Cloud games and Exotic Jungle Girl and Pirate Girl Comic Cloud dreams, but, but …

But, in reality, perhaps, being slung half-naked – no, almost wholly bare-assed naked – over the shoulder of a young but quite muscular and almost entirely naked wild savage but strangely erudite and literate land pirate or jungle boy, was perhaps not entirely compatible with her sense of dignity as a fully liberated, highly educated, 22nd century, young female Cosmos from Elysium City, top Cosmos Scout and Recipient of the President's Special Cosmos Badge for Extraordinary Achievement.

After all, she was one of the Elite of the Universe, a status of which – and she now for some reason blushed to admit it – she was inordinately, even arrogantly, proud, yes, proud. *Why even the President has shaken my hand – more than once!*

Hail, Hail, All Hail!

Hail, Hail, All Hail!

Her heart raced.

Her blood churned.

Oh, Elysium!

When she thought of Elysium City, and the beautiful translucent dome, and the soaring ethereal towers, and the layers upon layers of buildings and platforms, and the perfection, and the rushing electro-trains and the intercontinental airships delicately landing, and, when she thought of the ceremonies, of the tens of thousands of beautiful boys and girls all lined up, in identical spotless uniforms, in perfect geometric patterns, surrounded by pillars of light and by marching music, all to honor the Leader, the President, when she thought of all this, her heart sailed upward in pride and delight and even a sacred sense of awe; and when she put her hand on her heart and sang the anthem and thought of the President – his image floating above them in the sky – tears of pride – and, yes, tears of love – came to her eyes. *Cosmos, forever Cosmos!* The anthem echoed in her mind. She had even thought – sometimes – that she would volunteer for the Centurion Corps, the elite of the elite, and go and fight on the frontier.

To that little dream, Nikki had put her foot down, saying, "No, definitely not, over my dead body, Miranda Hughes!"

Nikki – maybe at that very moment Nikki was being burned alive at the stake! No, that was impossible – it could not be!

Nikki was a survivor; Nikki would survive; besides, Nikki had ordered her to submit to Caliban – and to save him!

This was a true adventure!

Being swept away by wild savage Caliban was just so … so yummy!

She could hardly wait to tell Kit Candy!

And she would tell Nikki too!

"You can let me down now," she shouted. For some reason she felt like tickling his backside, or his underarms, or maybe undoing the knot that held his loincloth in place – the knot was nicely placed right over his right hip-bone, just next to his bouncing scimitar – she could easily reach it – and seeing his loincloth fluttering down the stairs like a wayward handkerchief, leaving him buck-naked and at her mercy, was indeed a tickling, pleasurable – though slightly vague – thought. This, though, she decided, was neither the time nor the place for such puerile sophomoric pranks. "You can let me down now!" she repeated.

"Just a minute," he said – and she noticed he was huffing and puffing, just a bit. His heart was beating like mad; she could feel it: it was delicious; it was warm; it was throbbing; it was pumping blood – it was pumping warm rich delicious blood, the stuff of life! Blood! Sweet blood! Delicious Fragrant Blood! Caliban paused, gulped air, and gasped, "We are almost there!"

Again, he set off, up the steep incline. His legs pumped and pumped; they were fine and muscular, Miranda thought, looking down at them as she bounced up and down just over his backside; the legs gleamed in the smoky light of the phosphorescent spores and moss and lichen. Up and up and up they went. The rusty greasy iron steps disappeared, one after the other, flashing and flickering and clattering off into the gloom. From far away – and muted by distance – came the sound of cans bouncing and rattling and screams and roars and curses and quacks.

They came to a platform – loops and ropes and cables hung down; a giant cobweb obscured part of the metalwork.

Caliban set Miranda down on her feet and, for just a second, she felt dizzy, the stairs and metal spinning gently around; but almost immediately the sensation passed.

Caliban's legs were spread heroically, and his arms were outstretched, his back muscles and his biceps, bulging and neatly delineated; he was straining every muscle to turn the giant metal wheel set in the giant metal door. Then he lifted a bar of metal.

The giant metal door slid sideways. "This was all made by the ancients, before the Fall," said Caliban, "Our whole city was made by the ancients."

"A mine," said Miranda.

"Yes, it was something called a mine."

A sign, Miranda noted, said, "Welcome to Churn Halibut Corp: Eternal Greed by Divine Right!"

They stepped through the door and out into the above-ground world. The giant circular door swung shut behind them.

The door to the underworld had been built on a ledge, up about twenty meters from the foot of the escarpment; below the entrance, on the plain, were scattered tools and machines and ruins of buildings from before the Fall. The sky was a pale, milky, fading blue with a pink glow.

"Wow," said Miranda, thinking that many days must have passed – possibly five or six – or more – time was fluid and uncertain in the flickering underworld, and so much had been happening, she had not really kept track.

The sun was setting. Night was near. Soon it would be almost as dark as the shadowy underworld, probably darker, though, other than the night of the crash, Miranda had never experienced real night. In Elysium, lights were always shining, and the dome kept out the night, the real night.

"Yes," said Caliban, "Time has passed."

"It's beautiful," Miranda took a deep breath. The sun was fleeing the sky, out west, heading down below the horizon. Dusk shimmered.

"They will not follow us here," Caliban said, "My fellow mutants, I mean."

"Good, Prince Caliban, that's good," said Miranda.

"Well, Princess," he said, glancing at her, suddenly shy.

"Thank you for saving me, my Prince, my pirate master. But – why won't they follow us here?" She shielded her eyes from the low sun. It seemed, and this was strange, to be swelling and bloating as it approached the horizon. Miranda gazed, wide-eyed, at this strange new world.

It was like an unfamiliar planet. She suddenly realized how strange it was. She had never in her life set foot outside the Dome of Elysium City with its hanging gardens, ethereal towers, passageways, and electro-cars, and perfumed air, and layer upon layer of hygienic and purified heights and depths.

And after the crash, it had been night, and she had not had time, really, with the dead and dying all around, the burning wreckage, and then with the mutants and with Scav and the Lemur Ball and the females, all gathered around Nikki, and then with Caliban, Divine Prince Caliban, no, she had not had time, really, to appreciate the landscape.

Besides, it had been dark – nothing much to see except cliffs of stone, reaches of sand, and the stars – the glorious stars – in the sky above.

Stretching before her, beyond the ruins of the mine, was a flat, lifeless, darkening landscape, with dunes of sand and outcroppings of rock and almost no vegetation, just a few lowly scrubs crawling along the ground and dark lichen on some of the rocks. It was magnificent – like some giant sculpture, stretching to the horizon. The world, Miranda decided, was a work of art.

"What is that?" she pointed to a yellow-black smudge rising on the horizon; it was beginning to devour the sun.

"A sandstorm," said Caliban, his hands on his hips, squinting towards the rising cloud, and suddenly looking weary, almost adult.

"A sandstorm," Miranda frowned. "Is it dangerous?"

"Very," said Caliban.

The sandstorm appeared to be a cauldron of swirly powdery gold, branded with ribbons of black. In the western sky, it stood, a dark brown and gold wall-like cloud, through which, dimly now, the dying, disintegrating sun glowed like a dying ember.

"Why won't they follow us here, the mutants?"

"Out here, with darkness comes fear," said Caliban.

The setting sun and vast cloud of sand turned the landscape – and Caliban, his pectorals and abs glowing – into a warm sensuous amber; though there was also the hint of a silky, yellow, jaundiced tincture, quickly spreading through the air, that seemed to Miranda distinctly unhealthy – for some reason it made her think of malaria and of the plague.

"Really?" said Miranda and, with a toss of her head, she flipped her hair back from her eyes, "What kind of fear?"

"A new kind of fear: it is recent, these last two weeks only. It comes from the sky." Caliban looked upwards, and then, blinking his eyes dazzled by the sinking sun, he glanced at the distant wall of dust rapidly coming on from the west, "That sandstorm is coming fast. They are evil spirits, they have wings, they ..."

"Evil spirits?" said Miranda, thinking: this sounds really interesting. It was like that Cloud Game – The Ghoul-Godzilla War IV – she and Kit Candy had played only two weeks ago ...

Gosh, only two weeks! Yet it seemed like an eternity, it seemed like another world, it seemed like a dream: she wondered: Was Kit still alive, did Elysium City still exist, was Nikki's drawing board – with Nikki's charcoal sketch of that cute mouse holding a flower and plucking the petals – still pinned up in the kitchen? Was Miranda's collection of antique books still lined up on its shelves? Was all her former life real, or was it just a dream, wrapped about with a bearded mystic's or poet's sleepy snooze, and lost in the deep dark inexistent backward abyss of time – or some such dreamy metaphysical matrix-like thing?

Somehow, she didn't think her life had been a dream.

Elysium was real; Kit was real.

But now she, Miranda, was most definitely in a different place.

"You said *evil spirits*?" She blinked at Caliban.

"Evil spirits – they were once humans – Subs, I think, or Burb refugees, maybe religious pioneers, utopian colonists, from out west, True Believers of some sort, I think. But they have been possessed by a Spirit of Evil and they have morphed – or been morphed – into something horrible; and now they fly, human-sized vultures or bats, and they kill everything living, mutants above all. They have these really big wings." Caliban stretched out his arms, "Big like this! And they smell foul as a blocked sewer or and leathery as an old rotten carcass."

"Oh." Miranda considered this, "And I suppose they bite."

"Yes," said Caliban, frowning, "They have fangs and they bite, and they have claws and they swoop down and tear mutants and animals apart with their claws and beaks and fangs – and humans and Cosmos too, I suppose, if they found any."

"You will protect me, though, won't you, Caliban! You are so brave, my pirate, my Prince, my Caliban, my exquisite jailer, my new-found-land, my shining knight, my Tarzan," Miranda was about three inches shorter than Caliban – she leaned up, on tiptoes, and kissed him, full on the lips, lingering for just an instant.

His eyes went wide. He gazed at her.

She grinned, didn't look away, and pushed back a straight strand of blond hair from one eye. "I love you," she said, thinking that such were the words one was supposed to utter in such a romantic circumstance – all the literature she had absorbed indicated as much – and she truly wondered what was happening to her. She had never before said those words – not with this heavy freight of tremulous and titillating meaning in them – not even to Kit Candy had she uttered such words, even though Kit did, just by being Kit, give her a tickly little yearning in the pit of her stomach, an intense, almost nostalgic tremulous desire to touch and be touched, like when she saw Kit bite her lip and give Miranda that sly sideways look, or like when Kit casually slung her arm around Miranda's shoulders and pulled her close, or like when Kit looked straight into Miranda's eyes and laughed that special way that Kit could laugh, her head tilted to one side, her lips curled up at the corners, which was so, oh, so, so, so; or like when Kit …

"Ah, Cosmos, my Princess, my prisoner, my blond, blue-eyed, golden-eyed, golden-skinned girl, my goddess, ah, ah, my …" Caliban was visibly struggling to come up with some long-winded romantic, amorous flattering speech.

Miranda could see the wheels grinding painfully in his head – *crunch, crunch, crunch* – her mind-reading powers seemed to be getting more acute by the moment. It was fun, but disconcerting. People's heads were becoming transparent. She wasn't sure this was a good thing.

This much was clear: Caliban was normally the strong-silent-jungle pirate Tarzan type. Amorous chitchat for him was a real challenge; he was more comfortable tossing a girl over his shoulder – though until now he had never done such a thing in his whole life – or he was really comfortable yodeling to a crowd of mutants to gather them for the hunt or for the kill or maybe going hunting and fishing with one of his Bear friends.

Putting together a romantic speech for an ultra-sophisticated visiting Cosmos teenager from Elysium City even if she was his captive and his slave – and she could see he was still uncertain about what precisely he wanted to do with her – captive, lover, princess, mistress, or breeder of bambini – was stretching the poor fellow's rhetorical abilities to the limits.

"I know you love me, Caliban," she said. She leaned up again – and kissed him again – on the lips, deeper this time, her tongue reaching out, doing a bit of teasing and tickling.

"I …" His tan darkened; his eyes sparkled; his lips trembled.

"We love each other. Such is our destiny," Miranda's eyes spun wheels of gold.

"I …" Caliban looked around desperately. How could a man deeply wish something and be utterly terrified of it at the same time? "That sandstorm is getting closer, and it is getting dark. We'd better climb down from this ledge and look for a place to take shelter."

Miranda smiled. "Yes, my master, of course."

They climbed down the winding path that led from the Great Door on the ledge to the plain and the ruins of the mining town below.

"So, here we are," said Miranda, smoothing down her rebellious tunic – it kept crawling up her thighs. She put her hands on her hips and surveyed the desolate landscape – just a few caves in the escarpment rock face, a few ruins, and bits of machinery, and smashed and twisted old trailers on blocks of cement, and no hint that a vast underground mutant city lay under their feet. "So, what do we do now, my dearest and most adorable pirate and master?"

Caliban cleared his throat. This was more solid terrain; he knew how to do this; taking command and going into action is something a man definitely knows how to do. "We find shelter from the Evil ones and from the sandstorm and then I will go back and try to save your mother."

"Yes, my mother," Miranda felt they should be afraid for Nikki, but somehow she wasn't; Nikki had seemed so self-assured; it was as if Nikki knew something that nobody else, not even Miranda, knew; it was as if Nikki were invulnerable or invincible; or, perhaps, Nikki just didn't care whether she lived or died, though Miranda shrank away from the latter thought, because she loved her mother, loved her with a fierce passionate love that somehow, she thought, went beyond love. She took a deep breath. She could not conceive of life without Nikki!

The sun disappeared into the rising tide of distant yellow dust. The dust storm was perhaps 40 or 50 kilometers away. It was hard to tell. Miranda had had no experience judging distances outside Elysium's Dome.

The air turned dark; the shadows faded and disappeared.

A round sand-darkened moon appeared – fascinating!

"They come out at night," said Caliban, "The evil ones."

"Oh," said Miranda; she shivered – though the temperature was still something like 102 Fahrenheit – and she detected, too, on some vague newly discovered wavelength of sensibility, that there were, nearby, indeed very close, stirrings of desire, stirrings of hunger, evil stirrings, stirring of some immense and evil thought that … Dark shifting things, things filled with self-hatred, slaves to some Evil Immensity, they were restless, they were waking up, they were getting ready to take flight, and when they did … "You are right," she said, "We must find shelter."

They began to search the abandoned old mining camp, the half-ruined buildings, the rusty overturned ore wagons, the tangled bits of machinery, and farther on, the slagheaps, vast piles that were pointed like dead volcanoes. Everything was half-buried in drifts of sand.

"They first appeared eight nights ago," Caliban was saying, repeating what he had first said, mulling it over.

"They are something new," said Miranda, looking at an overturned Desert Bug. No, it would afford no shelter; all its windows and armor were shattered.

"Yes, they are something new."

Miranda could feel the stirrings of these creatures – Evil Creatures – all around them. Where were they?

She looked up at the escarpment. Ah, yes, the caves; if they came out at night, if they didn't like the light, probably they slept in caves, far from the sun, perhaps hanging upside down like bats. That would be interesting to see. If they didn't like the light of day, they would love the mutant's cave. That was a scary idea, what if … She let the thought trail off. She glanced away, shielding her eyes.

To the west, the wall of dust was higher now, blocking out the darkening sky; one star appeared in the pale blue just above the advancing wall of sand; soon other stars would appear.

Seeing the sky – and the way its appearance shifted continuously – was an experience. In Elysium City, under the Dome, Miranda had never seen the sky; now it almost gave her vertigo – the depths, the emptiness, and the subtle and changing gradations of light, the clouds and fragments of cloud. And, now, came the darkness, which, if it weren't for the oncoming dust storm, would be full of stars.

And then it happened.

"Look!" Miranda pointed.

Caliban looked up. On the face of the escarpment, about two kilometers from the Great Door to the Mutant Kingdom, out of caves on the side of the great stone wall, came dark shapes, grotesque blotches on the pale, moon-lit rampart; they spread their wings and took flight – and they were headed for Caliban and Miranda – screeching, cawing, roaring.

"Let's go," said Caliban.

"Yes, boss," said Miranda, "but where?"

The winged creatures zoomed downwards. Boy, they were big! Miranda stared, then she and Caliban ran, sand spurting up under their heels.

"There's an old drainage pipe I think it must have been. I think it's too narrow for them – their wings make it impossible ..."

"Right!" Miranda's blood was racing now. This was exciting. She could hardly wait to tell Nikki and Kit about her adventures!

The evil winged creatures – whatever they were – came flapping down through the darkening sultry air. They zoomed in close. Miranda felt the beat of wings just above her head, the fetid downdraft, rotten putrid breath, the alien thump of strange inhuman hearts, the razor-sharp talons sweeping through the air, just a few inches away, brushing past her blond hair which was whipped by the foul downdraft of evil.

"Oh, boy!"

One of the giants swooped down just in front of them; they swerved to miss it; Miranda caught a glimpse of its long, fanged face and its eyes – its eyes radiating an abyss of pure hatred. She zigzagged, and swerved again, her heels spurting sand. Two more of the things swooped down; the stench was horrible; one of the evil monsters lunged – Miranda leaped out of the way, just in time.

Caliban and Miranda ran and ran, skidding in the sand, swerving, ducking, leaping, and finally, they got to the opening of the drainage pipe Caliban had spoken about, and Miranda thought, yes, that looks like an old drainage pipe, probably used to pump out the mine. She'd seen such things when she and Kit had explored downwards, deep in the depths of Elysium City, near the Religion Bazaar.

"Go, go, go!" shouted Caliban. Miranda dropped to all fours, crawled, and shimmied down onto her belly, and using her elbows, she swiveled around and wiggled backward, bare legs and feet first, into the pipe.

She'd read that poisonous snakes sometimes hid in such things as old drainage pipes, but there was no time to think of that now!

Caliban was just behind her, backing his way into the pipe. She grabbed his ankles to pull him in. He was in the pipe up to his waist; then he screamed, "No! Get off me! Be gone!"

She heard the slash of his scimitar thudding against metal, then against alien evil flesh, and she felt – her mind now totally attuned to his – his horror. In close-up, she saw the winged monster, its foaming fangs and claws, and she felt its wings as they smashed into Caliban's flesh. His sword struck one of its wings; she heard – in her mind and in her ears – the beast scream, and she felt that, yes, oh, the gods! – It had once been human! She was pulling on Caliban, trying to desperately drag him into safety.

But, with one sudden jerk, Caliban was heaved from her grasp – his ankles were slippery with oil and sweat – and he was gone.

Caliban was gone!

A fluttering of wings, and suddenly silence.

Caliban was gone!

A void opened.

The end of the pipe, darkening silver-gray, was empty.

Miranda's heart beat like crazy. She took a deep breath and crawled and wiggled half out of the pipe.

She looked around. She pulled herself all the way out of the pipe and stood up. There was nothing. Nobody. It was dark. The air was hot, close, and clammy. A thick coppery smell of blood hung in the air. She sniffed, her nostrils quivering. *It was not Caliban's blood.* A piece of lead pipe lay half-buried in the sand; she picked it up and glanced around. Darkness – and no hint of a thought, no hint of Caliban's presence.

"Caliban!" she shouted, "Caliban!"

Suddenly the air was moving, and she heard a hissing sound, a sibilant rattling rush. It was the sandstorm.

In an instant, it was upon her, sand whirling around, making it impossible to see, impossible to breathe.

She shimmied back into the drainpipe and crouched down on her elbows, watching the darkness; she held the length of iron pipe ready. She pushed herself a bit further back into the drainage pipe, in case the vultures returned.

She had lost everything – her mother, Caliban, everything, everything.

But a Cosmos can overcome; a Cosmos must overcome. A Cosmos defies the odds; a Cosmos never gives up! Victory or Death!

Cosmos! Hail! Hail!
Cosmos! All Hail!

CHAPTER 6 – ZOMBIE BATS

"Ready?"

"Ready!"

V flicked on the headlights and gunned the motor and the bike roared down the sandy gulf that was the bottom of the valley and came out onto the plain as the valley opened up and was lost in flat immensity.

V felt Kat's arms tighten around her waist. In the west, the sky darkened as if there were a great cloud on the horizon. But it was not a cloud – not exactly.

It was something evil – and it was coming their way.

"I think we'd better go back," V said; she wheeled the bike around, skidding in the soft sand, and almost throwing both of them off. It shuddered to a halt. In the sudden silence, they looked up.

"What are those things?" Kat had sensed them too.

"I don't know."

"I sense them – they're not mutants. They're …"

"No, you're right, they're something worse. Something the clown spoke about, something …"

"They're zombies," said Kat, almost laughing, "Flying Zombies! And I didn't take him seriously – I didn't believe – I didn't take either of you seriously! Now I'm crazy too!"

V gunned the bike. The attack would come from the air. They needed shelter. The only thing V could think of was the large piece of fuselage; it was open only at one end. If they got inside the fuselage, they could make their stand; when they fought, they would only have to face one way.

The creatures wheeled overhead screaming, darkening the night sky, hiding the moon, blocking out the stars. Orion disappeared, and Sagittarius was masked by dark flapping wings.

"They're not like vultures," said Kat, "they're like bats."

"Right," V shouted, "Bats, vultures, vampires … Whatever they are, they are not good news."

The sum of all our nightmares!

Yes, Kat's thought echoed back, the sum of all our nightmares!

Wham!

The Zombie Bats attacked, swooping down. V pushed the bike to its utmost limits. The engine screamed.

The creatures came smashing down with a great flapping of wings, one brushed V shoulder.

V gunned the bike; she zigzagged, using the heel of her boot to spin the bike around, dodging, turning, turning again, spurting up waves of sand, and then gunning again. She could feel Kat, sitting behind her, with one hand locked around V's belt, swiveling around and unsheathing her automatic, and letting off spurts of laser fire – splat, splat, splat …

Kat hit some of them. They fluttered, wheeled, cart-wheeled, and fell smashing to the ground, twirling away, lost behind the racing bike, others were overhead, circling, heading towards the hurdling Cosmos Bike, but now they were more cautious – keeping their distance, screeching their anger.

"We are going to have to stop and stand and fight," V shouted over her shoulder. "We don't have enough ammunition, and they are going to just tip the bike over and swarm us."

"Not even a hybrid can resist?"

"No, not even a hybrid can fight such numbers!"

V raced the bike down into the narrow valley and up into the ravine. There, in front of them, was the wreckage of the Super Liner X-47, strewn over the floor of the valley, dark hulks of metal, fragments of a dying civilization.

The bike bounded and bounced over rocks and ribbons of stone and sand. V forced it to the maximum, racing up the sandy bottom of the ravine, bits and pieces of wreckage standing out like inky shadows, jagged stalagmites, in the silver moonlight.

One large cross-section of the fuselage, lying on its side, was like a fortress, a shelter.

"Hold on!" V shouted, and she aimed the bike straight at the big round opening of the fuselage cross-section.

The bike bounced into the broken aircraft and screeched to a halt in a shower of sand and pebbles.

This was to be their metal shelter – V just hoped it would work!

For a moment the bottom of the ravine – flat sand and bits and pieces of wreckage and one or two bodies – looked peaceful, sculpted in bright silver moonlight.

"That was close," Kat sighed, still aiming her automatic at the oval cross-section of sky, "and now …"

"Yes, and now they will come," V said.

"So, hybrids are not invincible," said Kat.

"No, we aren't," V said.

"Too bad," Kat gave V a charming grin.

"Yes, it is." V smiled back.

"I'd really like to be invincible."

"Me too," V shook her head; Kat was becoming a sister, maybe even a friend.

"Look at that!" Kat pointed.

A dark fluttering came out of the night. It landed next to one of the bodies – the dead stewardess – and began to tear at it ripping off bits of flesh.

"Oh, my God," whispered Kat.

"Vultures," I said, "Human vultures – or bats …"

Suddenly, a whole flock of human bats – or Zombies – they were six feet tall, five feet tall – fluttered at the entrance to the fuselage.

Two tried to enter, Kat blasted them to pieces.

"These are humans," V said, "they've been transformed somehow, but I don't know how …"

"Who or what could do such a thing?"

"I don't know. But, Kat, we need to be ready to fight with all we've got. So, I warn you: I'm going to morph."

"Morph?"

"Yes." V unzipped and unpeeled her uniform, like a sleek second skin, the black armor slid off. She folded it carefully.

"What are you doing?"

"I'm going to show you the other side of me, Kat."

"Oh boy," said Kat.

V wondered for an instant if Kat would turn the gun on her – when she saw what and who V was … and what Kat would one day openly become … Inside the chrysalis that was Kat this other being was being born.

And just at that moment, another of the giant bats lurched for Kat; it was male, and it was more than six feet tall. The fluttering wingspan blocked out the moonlight.

Kat fired off a burst of fire into the large male bat. He had the remnants of a pastor's collar around his thick muscular neck – the collar had burst open and was stuck in his fur.

"You've seen pictures of hybrids, I guess, Kat."

"Yes," Kat was using a piece of metal to shove the cadaver – she'd blown the top of its head off – out of the fuselage. The clerical bat was not quite dead; it reached out with its claws and grabbed Kat by the ankle.

Kat was so surprised she dropped the machine pistol. She kicked, and she shouted, "Major, this damned thing is still alive!"

Behind her, Kat felt a sort of whirr. "What's happening?" Kat pulled the machete from her belt and raised it.

Above her – Kat had been dragged halfway out of the fuselage section now – and over her loomed another human bat, fluttering down, its wing spread blocking the moon, and, damnation! Its face – all enormous fangs with tiny eyes and the ghost of a face – was horrifying.

Kat could see that once this creature had been a woman, even beautiful – a twisted mask of a face, waxy white with russet freckles and a fringe of blond hair, like a halo, around its face and enormous fanged mouth, and long dripping tongue, and Kat couldn't decide where to strike.

Just an instant of hesitation and indecision could mean death. She hung back. She couldn't decide whether to hack off the arm of the half-dead former priest that was dragging her out into the open or to slash at the female's yawning jaws – it was a huge beak-like jaw with yellow fangs – and a black tongue and black, dripping gums – that were about to gouge her neck and her face.

There was a flash of turquoise and gold and – WHAM – the giant female bat was swept aside, slashed into floating bits of fur, rags of a wing, one twitching arm; a clawed foot spun into the air and the threatening beak was gone.

Kat blinked, and, pulling herself up to a half-sitting position, she brought the machete down on the priest's arm – and chopped it off.

The priest's claw, still locked into her boot, quivered, and then opened; it let go. Kat kicked the thing away; she staggered to her feet and swung around, conscious out of the side of her eye of something that had come whirring in beside her.

Kat raised the machete ready to strike – and saw beside her a reptilian female, glowing in the moonlight, turquoise and gold, its breasts and belly and arms streaked with black.

"This is bat's blood," said the reptile woman, pointing to it. "This black stuff is human bat's blood."

The reptile's claws were dripping, black stuff, like tar, making a little black puddle that shone in the moonlight. "These things are like zombies," the reptile girl said.

Fluttering above them were other bats, and they plunged.

"It's you, the hybrid." Kat felt stupid just saying it.

"Yep, oh, the horror, oh, the horror, as our preacher-clown friend used to say," said the female demon who seemed to have risen from some exotic hell; she flashed a reptile grin.

"Will I look like you?"

The bats swooped downwards.

"Not necessarily."

It was difficult to believe that this glittering fanged creature and Major Emily Rodriguez were one and the same.

Wham!

Kat was hit by the sweep of a bat's wing. She lifted the machine pistol and let go a short sizzling burst – blood, fur, bone, gristle splattered …

Kat found it difficult to remember exactly the sequence of events after that. It was one long endless battle. The major – rather, V – the demon hybrid – moved like lightning. The zombie-bats were terrified of her.

Kat stood beside V, slashing cut with the machete, sometimes using the machine pistol.

Bodies, hideous faces, wings, claws, arms, breasts, thighs, appeared and disappeared, loomed up, and shrank back, grinned like the very incarnation of evil, and then exploded in a cloud of gristle, fur, teeth, and that black sticky blood, and bones.

Behind all this, the moon moved across the sky.

The constellations – Orion and Cassiopeia and the Great Bear – wheeled around slowly.

In front of the fuselage section, a heap of dead bodies piled up – some were still twitching, quivering, spasms, as if they were still alive.

The sky got lighter. The sun was rising.

The valley was still in the shade.

The bats screamed and circled and screamed.

A few of the higher bats were hit by the sun's rays. They exploded – or seemed to explode – puffs of smoke and splotches of blood and then a dead smoking rocket of flesh dropped straight down with a last hideous scream – crashing into the ground, where some lay still and others twitched and squirmed for a moment and then were still.

The other bats flew off, squealing, keeping low in the valley, hugging the shadow side, as far from the rising sunlight as they could get, and then the sun rose fully; its rays reached the bottom of the valley; now the sand, boulders, ridges of pebbles, and the whole ravine seemed quiet.

Kat wiped her brow. She looked down. She was smeared with bat blood, treacle-like, it was sticky and thick and tar-black; it ate the light. She brushed at it, the stuff stuck on her glove. It truly was like tar.

V the reptile was equally covered. She was standing out in the ravine, claws on hips, looking down at one of the human-bat bodies.

Kat joined her.

"We could both use a shower," said the hybrid, turning and giving Kat the once over. Mouth curved upward, the hybrid blinked her big yellow serpent eyes.

"There is no water," Kat felt she was walking and talking and thinking like a zombie; she also felt, inside, a surge of power and energy as if all her nerves and muscles were electric. There was a disconnect between her mind and body.

"Look at that!" V pointed. One of the bats, a male, was lying face up; its fanged jaws were wide open, frozen in a last scream, its arms spread-eagled, as if it had been crucified, in its breast was a gaping hole left by Kat's machine pistol. As Kat watched, the face twitched, the features melted, the gaping jaw closed, the face swirled as if seen through a wavering glass or shimmering trembling air over the desert and then – poof – it was a human face, a handsome strong-jawed face, tanned, a blond guy, maybe 35-years-old, blue eyes wide open, staring at her, and Kat realized, suddenly, with horror, *she could see herself through his eyes.*

Oh, my God!

There she was, Lieutenant Kat M. Jackson, standing over him, a fierce black Amazon warrior, a Cosmos Centurion, in a black armored somewhat tattered and battered Centurion catsuit with a machine pistol in one gloved hand, and streaked with tar-like drying blood, her wraparounds tilted back up over her forehead, and she could feel – hear – yes, she could *hear* his thoughts:

"What have they done to me? Why have you done this to me? What have

I become? Where is my daughter? Tell me, where is my daughter? What has become of my daughter?"

Kat turned to V: "He's alive! He's ..."

V shook her head. "No, Kat, he's dead."

"But I can hear his thoughts; he's looking at me."

"It's just the after-image, the echo, the electric energy, something like that. It happens all the time. It's one of the things about being a ..." V hesitated.

"One of the things about being a ..." Kat echoed, griping the machine pistol tighter, staring at the slender reptile woman, the gold and turquoise scales shimmering through the midnight-black streaks of blood.

V nodded. "Do you want me to spell it out in more detail? You're beginning to see how it works."

"Yes, spell it out." Kat's heart fluttered. But at the same time, she felt incredibly calm and strong; she could smell and see and feel and touch and understand an infinite number of things, things she had never before felt or understood – the doors of perception were opening. It was terrifying. "Yes, spell it out."

"One of the things about being a hybrid is you can sometimes read minds, and sometimes, when people die, you feel or hear their thoughts, only sometimes. If the death is violent and if the passions are strong, you even see with their eyes; for a moment or two, maybe longer, you *become* them."

"Oh, boy," Kat shook her head, "I don't know if I can stand this."

"You can stand it and you'll get used to it, Kat," V said, and glancing around, she pointed. "Look! When they die, they revert to something like what they were when they were ... human."

"This is horrible," Kat whispered.

"Yes." The golden reptilian eyes blinked at her. "It is."

The zombie-bat bodies writhed and melted and reformed: they were becoming the people they had been before they became – well, before they became whatever they were. And then, when the rays of the sun touched them directly, the bodies began to smoke, and then to burn.

Soon nothing was left but bits of crisp fried flesh; then smoking ashes, and the wind began to carry those away.

"Ashes to ashes," V said.

"Dust to dust," Kat echoed.

The sun was by now high in the sky; the sky was blue, pure blue, untroubled by clouds or aircraft contrails.

Kat looked up. The wind had risen; dust devils moved across the crash site; the pitiless, liberating, life-giving, life-destroying sun shone down.

The huge engines of the presidential aircraft lay, broken, shattered, already half-buried in sand; the wings were farther away, one had been sliced in half, the other lay on its side, intact except for the engine which had been ripped off.

On one tail fin was the Logo, and Eagle, "The Imperial Cosmos United States of ..." The rest of the words were broken away.

On the far edge of the ravine, several hundred yards downstream, small creatures appeared. They ignored the two-legged creatures, the human and the hybrid.

"We have visitors," said Kat.

"Yes," V turned to look at them. The sunlight glittered on her scales and rippled darkly on the splotched, tar-like splashes of zombie blood.

The newcomers were small humanoids, some of them. Most of the others ran on all fours. They were scavenging in the wreckage. One of the big motors seemed to be of particular interest. They had tools. They began to rip off bolts and to rip up textiles and pick up and examine objects.

"Mutants," said V.

"Yes, mutants," Kat watched them. They seemed harmless enough; as a Centurion she had hunted mutants; most were innocuous, incapable, really, of defending themselves. She thought back two days, or was it three, to the mutant-massacre near that schoolyard. It suddenly made her feel very unhappy, almost queasy. She saw the beautiful albino mutant, protecting her child, and then both of them consumed in a pillar of flame.

"Let's have a look," V said.

Kat glanced at her hybrid partner – *damn I keep forgetting I'm a hybrid* – and she nodded. "Okay, yes, let's go have a look."

Kat lagged behind as V approached one of the creatures; it looked like a large beaver, about three-and-a-half feet tall. It was busy unbolting a seat from the cockpit and crew section of the aircraft, a section that had been ripped open; the five seats stood neatly in a row, some of them stained with blood.

"Excuse me," said V.

"Fuck off. No time, no talk!" The Beaver-like creature did not turn around.

"The people who were in this plane," V said; she laid a claw on the Beaver's thick shoulder, "where did they go?"

The Beaver looked over his shoulder, blinked, and looked up. "What are you? Who made you? I never saw such a thing as you. Are you dangerous?"

"Yes, I am dangerous," V scowled, "very dangerous."

"Fuck you. I fear no danger." He stared, his large brown eyes blinking up at her. His two front teeth were very large, made – once upon a time – for hacking down trees.

"I asked you a civil question," said V, smiling her fanged smile, widening her serpent eyes.

"*Civil*, what is *civil?*"

"Polite, it means polite," V flicked her tongue, allowed her eyes to flare – bright fiery gold.

"*Polite* – what is *polite*?"

"It means being nice to other creatures." V's tongue flicked impatiently. She pawed the ground, "Not to piss them off. Not to put them into a rage."

"Ah, I learn every day; more words, more power, thank you." The Beaver blinked at her. "Two humans survived – two female Cosmos, First Class and Top Quality Merchandise – they were captured, taken prisoner, and transported, over the ridge, towards the south, to the mutant pirate mine. They feast; they celebrate; they sacrifice the Cosmos."

"Sacrifice the Cosmos?"

"Two women – they are Cosmos: rich, famous – beautiful as all Cosmos are rich, beautiful, and famous, star quality Cosmos, excellent young vintage, and from Elysium, center of Cosmos East Coast Empire."

"I see," V flicked her tongue.

"Yes, you see. Burn Cosmos alive naked and oiled on Old Wooden or Iron Cross, then eat roasted Cosmos. Drink hot blood. All happy and dance, Hallelujah and Great Offering to Mutant God Dolly and so forth and so on. Such things are called religion, I am told."

"They went that way?" V pointed with one claw.

"It will be a party. They all dance and bubble on fermented mushrooms and roots of open sesame that widens horizons and puts one outside the box."

"They were taken beyond the ridge?"

"Yes, I come to top of ridge. I show you," said the Beaver, leaving his work and brushing his paws and wiping them against his sides like a motor mechanic on his overalls. The other mutants had followed the dialogue for an instant; then they had gone back to their work; one creature – it looked like a weasel – had come close to Kat, circled around, stood up on two legs, sniffed at her uniform, licked its lips, blinked and then brushed its mustaches while staring at Kat out of sleepy, blinking eyes. "And who are you?" said Kat.

The weasel grinned, "None of your fucking business – mate!"

"Jesus!"

"I learned that: Old Antipodes Parlezvous Palaver videos from transcontinental super-train wreck and pirated down-streams. How was I?" The weasel grinned again, wagged its tail and licked its lips, "Oscar good I reckon!"

"Good, great, perfect." Kat figured that's what you said to a creature auditioning for something, aspiring actors and wannabes were everywhere and very sensitive, thin-skinned. "The accent was divine, worth two Oscars," she smiled at him.

"Ha, ha, I knew it!" the weasel grinned again, said, "Thanks, mate – Ta!" It skittered away.

Kat gazed around. Incredible! Life had headed off in a thousand different directions once bio blocks had escaped into the general population. Evolution had accelerated exponentially – and gone wild. It was no longer evolution, it was a revolution – a permanent unstoppable revolution. Evolution, and the survival of the fittest, the best adapted to whatever environments the world offered, would have to catch up – and it probably would, quite soon, and then the great sorting and culling would begin.

Kat was still musing on this thought as she followed V and the beaver as they headed up to the top of the ridge.

Kat caught up with them and turned to V, "I never realized …"

"That it had gone so far – mutation … You've lived a protected life, Kat," V laid a reptilian claw on the young soldier's shoulder. "You Centurions live in barracks, among the purest of the pure. And, when you go outside the domain of Cosmos, it is only to kill."

"I guess in some ways, yes, I have lived a protected life," Kat sighed. She had fought many battles – mostly in the burbs or in coastal wastelands or in distant anarchic countries – but she had never been out here in the heart of the Dead Land, in the heart of the desert, alone or almost alone. And she'd never had a conversation with a mutant. *And here I am, in the desert, and my partner is a hybrid.*

"This is very kind of you," said V, turning to the beaver who was huffing and puffing, laboring his way up the steep crumbly slope.

"You taught a new word, very useful, thank you."

"You are very welcome."

The beaver stared for a moment. "Welcome, ah, yes, new word meaning. Yes. Thank you!"

They got to the top of the ridge. The beaver stood, huffing, puffing, catching his breath, and pointed out over the vast undulating dusty desert plain. "There. That way! It is an hour travel perhaps – or two – on your two-wheeled monster. After sunset come the new dark wings, huge leathery dusty things with long beaks. Be not here."

"No, we won't be here."

"Be not under the sky."

"No, we won't be under the sky," said V, glancing at Kat who raised an eyebrow: where the hell would they be at sunset? Out there on the desert, it did not look like much shelter was available.

In silence, the three of them walked back down to the crash site. The sky was now a deep high pure blue. The sun blazed down.

"Goodbye, my friend, and thank you."

"Goodbye, then, and thank you."

The beaver watched the speaking reptile female humanoid and the human female walk down the ravine. The human female looked like she was some sort of Cosmos warrior, too beautiful for words. They both had those tools called weapons which were frightful things. He wondered if the reptile was a type of human or something else from somewhere else – he had heard there were other countries with unbelievably strange beings – or perhaps she was an intelligent machine the Cosmos had made or perhaps she was a reptile or snake that had been morphed by the Cosmos into something else; the humans and the Cosmos had made a horrible mash-up of everything, combining everything with everything else, everybody knew that; it was the talk of the natural world. The humans – who were undoubtedly geniuses – in particular the Cosmos who were the World Rulers and the most intelligent and dangerous and beautiful of all creatures alive – had interfered so much with the natural order of things that now there was no natural order of things.

He waddled quickly back to the wreckage. He could salvage something, perhaps, before the dangers came. Danger took many forms – but the worst, now, was the winged human bats or vultures or whatever they were – well, they had once, it seemed, been human – that had first appeared six sunsets ago.

The things came, so far, only at night, but you had to be underground when they came, otherwise they swept you up and gobbled you up and dropped your bones – and bits of flesh – down on the desert sands and rocky outcroppings …

He waddled and waddled and waddled …

The weasel was waiting for him, holding a bit of machinery. "I undid this for you, mate! It's bloody-well ready to go."

"Yes, we'd better hurry," said the Beaver.

"You hit the nail right there, bloody square on the noggin, mate!"

The sun had reached its high point and soon it would once again be getting low in the sky.

The beaver glanced over his shoulder. Down the ravine, the two humanoids were standing beside their infernal machine. They were preparing to leave. Well, that was good, though the beaver would have liked to know more about them. They had things to teach. Learning was always good.

CHAPTER 7 – DESERT GIRL

Midnight – the witching hour.

Maybe Miranda had fallen asleep. She was not sure. She was half-buried in sand, just inside the mouth of the drainage pipe. Sharp white moonlight lit up the narrow, curved opening, and the sharp edge of the sand drift. Miranda began to push the sand away. She had to get out. She had to find Caliban. She had to …

Then the wind came again.

Then more sand.

The moonlight was lost. A dark wall of sand, whistling, rustling, hissing sand blocked the mouth of the pipe.

Everything was dark.

Miranda waited. She yawned. Her eyes fluttered, her cheek settled onto a pillow of sand, the hissing sand made a musical sound, like a basket of serpents. Miranda shook herself, tried to stay awake – then she was asleep.

Afterward, she thought that perhaps she dreamed; she wasn't sure.

Hours later, the sandstorm must have subsided.

Miranda stretched, twisted, bursting with energy, but filled with anguish. She must wait – wait until the end of night.

Perhaps she could sleep a bit more.

No, it turned out she couldn't.

More sleepless hours passed; dawn came; the sun rose over the desert. The drainpipe entrance was half under sand now and Miranda dug, and pushed and crawled and wiggled her way out.

Still on hands and knees, she shook herself; she was covered in sand, itchy sand under her rough prisoner's tunic, itchy hot sand everywhere. She shook herself again, stood up, ran her fingers through her hair, sticky with sweat and clogged with sand. She looked around.

There was no sign of Caliban, and no sign of the zombie bats or whatever they were. No sign of anything.

Miranda wondered what she should do.

Well, a Cosmos First Class never hesitates.

"Life is Action," said the President Leader, "Action is Life."

"Decision is Action," said the President Leader, "Action is Decision!"

So, Miranda would act, and act now!

Several hours later Miranda was far out in the desert – in search of Caliban. It really was desert – where farms had been, and where grain and cotton once grew, there was now sand and dust and dunes and naked rock. Some instinct told her this was the way to go.

Miranda crouched down and picked up a handful of dust and let the sand – fine grains of absolutely dry sand – stream between her fingers. She saw in her mind how it had happened: after decades of drought, the soil had dried up, and, with no water to glue it together, it had crumbled into dust, and the wind had carried the dusty soil away; the plants didn't grow, so there were no roots to hold the soil down; the animals that fed on the plants died; and the humans who depended on the animals had left.

At nightfall, the zombie-bats would come hunting – and probably for her – she was sure of it. She had an instinct as to where she should go: she felt she was headed in the right direction.

Was Caliban still alive or had he been torn apart by those squawking jabbering furies?

She could not have fallen in love, just to lose her lover, her ideal, Prince Caliban, her pirate and jungle hero! No, she could not believe that such a thing could happen. It was just not possible!

She climbed over a ten-foot-high ripple of sand. In the desert landscape, there would really be nowhere to hide, unless she got to an abandoned farmstead of the kind she had seen in video histories and in e-books and real books. As she walked she saw ruined basements of buildings, and hulking silos and the collapsed remains of barns. But they might shelter zombie-bats too. Miranda knew she could run pretty fast, but she didn't think it would be fast enough – after all these things could fly!

She walked on and on and on.

The wind rose and the dust swirled. Miranda narrowed her eyes; dust and sand were tangling in her eyelashes and eyebrows and getting into her hair. It was uncomfortable, but it was an advantage. The mutants and the zombie-bats didn't have instruments to find her in the dust storm.

She came to what looked like something humans had made. Its rounded angularity surged up in the swirling windy ribbons of sand. Head down, pushing against the sandpaper wind, she climbed over a low dune to investigate.

It was a tractor, turned over on its side, the skeleton of a tractor; it had been cannibalized for parts. The motor was almost entirely gone.

In faded writing, it said, "John Deere."

Not much was left of the chassis and body of the tractor; but – if her course on "Ancient Agricultural Technologies" was anything to go by – the presence of a tractor – even a long-dead tractor – would mean a farm or a town or *something* was nearby.

Soon afterward, she came upon what looked like a highway, or at least a road: a long stretch of asphalt, broken up by heat. Some of the tar had melted and flowed away and most of what remained was covered with ribbons or banks of drifting sand.

She stood very still. Should she follow the road or stay away from it? It might lead somewhere. But any hostile life forms – mutants, zombie bats, or whatever else there might be out here on this strange, hostile planet – might follow the road too.

She was glad she'd read a lot about the Dead Lands and she'd watched lots of documentaries, because otherwise, this place would be utterly unfamiliar and like Mars, but with much worse dust storms. In Domed Elysium City even asphalt and gravel and sand were foreign concepts.

She coughed and then she sneezed.

The sand had turned to dust and it was fine and stuck to her skin, a golden layer of sticky powder on her golden skin.

She was covered too in a lather of sweat – again, sweat, real sweat, was something unfamiliar, except after sport, and then the sport was always in an air-conditioned well-lit place and she would have a shower right after, and then everything would be cool again, really cool.

It must be a 115 Fahrenheit – 46 Celsius – or more, even with the sun invisible and the dust swirling everywhere. It was like being in a furnace. The dust was on her like a crust. When she licked her lips, her tongue felt thick and gritty.

I'm being baked alive, she thought. I'm a pie, a baked pie, she thought, grinning, wishing there was somebody she could share the joke with, a baked pie with a crust of dust, I'm a poet and I don't know it!

I'm delirious.

No, not really. If I can think the thought, "I'm delirious," then I'm not really delirious, not totally, not yet. Or am I just deluding myself with this puerile bit of sophistry?

She frowned.

What a forbidding alien place this was!

She had read – on an outlawed Cloud samizdat site published apparently somewhere in the Independent Russo-Chinese Republic of Siberia – that there was a danger the atmosphere might spin out of control and that earth would become something like Venus, where the atmosphere was 97 percent carbon dioxide and the average temperature at the surface was 467 Celsius or 872 Fahrenheit, and the place was covered in clouds of sulfur dioxide and probably no life forms that humans or Cosmos would recognize as such existed – or maybe no life forms of any kind at all. No probe to Venus had ever survived long enough to find life there, if there was any, and, aside from that triple hydrogen bomb explosion on Mars, set off ten years ago by the Independent Islamic Popular Republic of Baluchistan, space programs had pretty much dried up in the last few decades. There was no money for such frivolities. So, no recent probes had been sent anywhere.

Maybe the sulfurous Venus creatures just don't want us to know!

She blinked against the sand and walked onto the fractured asphalt road. The dark parts burned her feet.

The sandstorm was really thick now. She could see about five or six feet in front of her she figured, maybe two or three meters, maximum.

Okay, she had no bearings other than the road; in this soup, she might end up going around in circles; the only thing to do was to follow the road – in spite of the dangers.

She walked, and she walked, and she walked.

The asphalt became hotter and stickier. She was getting a layer of tar on the soles of her feet. She shifted to walking along the side of the road.

She came upon some bones sticking out of the sand and one human skeleton picked clean and lying face down, glued into the asphalt. The sand drifted around the backbone and drifted in small ripples inside the ribcage.

Only a few feet further on were other bones – these were small and looked like the bones of a child. Miranda crouched down. Yes, it certainly looked human; and it was small and delicate, probably a child.

Picked clean …

Miranda stood up; a sudden sandblast slammed into her; it whipped at her hair and pinned the ragged prisoner tunic to her stomach and thighs. The sand sifted inside the tunic too. Ugh! She shivered. It was like being bombarded by little tiny boulders or pepper spray. A peculiar emptiness – something like fear – opened in her chest – her heart disappeared, and lower down too, her belly had somehow been hollowed out. Without Nikki and without Caliban, she was lost. Her mind was empty – no echoes, no echoes at all …

So, this is love …

It's like pain …

An empty pit in the stomach …

It's like being hungry but …

Now, Miranda Hughes, you are a Cosmos First Class; seize hold of yourself, my girl! It was Kit Candy's voice, loud as a bell, right inside her head.

You're right, Kit. Okay, I've got to take stock of my situation. Where am I? What am I doing? Where am I going?

She concentrated.

Right now she was on a road in the middle of nowhere, half-blind from the glare – the sandstorm must not be very high. Light was still getting through the dust cloud. Blinking her eyes against the blowing fine dust that coated and stuck like glue to her eyelashes, she looked up. She could see bits and suggestions of blue sky. She looked down. She was barefoot, sand blowing under the thin, fluttering, tattered prisoner tunic.

I really need a map.

"Hello! What's that?" Miranda squinted. A rodent, a sort of desert gopher of some kind, was scurrying along the side of the road. How the heck had it survived? Well, it was something living – something that even looked natural!

She said, "Hey, I won't hurt you," and transmitted the thought, sending it out as gently and as powerfully as she could.

The rodent stopped, turned, and stood up on its hind legs and blinked at her.

"You are really scary," was its thought, "you are big and scary but I can run faster than you can," the thought was clear in its bright alert eyes, in its muscles ready to spring and run, in its whiskers that twitched.

"I know I'm scary," Miranda added a little funny face-smile to the thought she sent, thinking maybe visual icons are clearer than word-packaged thoughts, and to the funny face she added the message, "But I'm not going to hurt you."

The rodent pawed carefully at its whiskers, grooming, thinking, blinking against the dust.

Miranda sent the thought, "It's been nice meeting you," and she continued to walk, climbing up over a narrow rippling dune that crossed the road, and down the other side, to show that she was not going to chase the rodent.

An ancient telephone pole soared out of the blowing sand – it was leaning hard to one side, a tangle of wires hanging down, rattling and snapping in the wind.

Just farther on there was an old mailbox.

Miranda walked across the road to look at it; she'd seen such things in ancient movies and paintings and cartoons. Yes, it was the thing called "*mailbox.*" It said, "Fred and Mabel Henning." The letters had been gouged into the dull silver metal; otherwise, they would have been worn away by the blowing sand.

The rodent followed her. It came up to the mailbox and stood up on its hind legs.

The mailbox swung in the sand-filled wind and made a creaking sound. Miranda listened. There were other sounds: the rattling of the tangled telephone wires, the whistling of the wind, the rustling sound of sand on sand, sand sifting, sand hissing, sand blowing, and sand streaking across the bits of bumpy boiled asphalt, sand piling up, yellow sand, golden yellow sand. Miranda bit her lip. Fred and Mabel would have had a farmhouse.

She tried to see where the farm lane might have been – nothing, just blowing sand. Usually, a lane went at right angles to the road, she remembered, from movies and photographs. In flat land, with no obstacles to twist the road around, a right angle would be logical, so she started to walk straight, at a right angle, away from the road.

The rodent followed. Miranda looked back. She didn't want to get lost in a directionless world of blowing sand and nothing else. Soon the road was invisible, buried in sand, lost in a wall of scurrying drifting sand.

Miranda stopped, looked back, keeping one foot with the toes pointed straight ahead, so she would still have a sense of direction. She could no longer see the mailbox or any trace of the road, or anything, the sand swirled around her.

Well, the glow in the sky in the sand cloud was brighter in front of her, so she was heading, she figured towards the sun, roughly south, probably, depending on what time of day it was. The sun, she figured was pretty high, towards its zenith, so it should be close to noon, so the sun would be south.

The rodent was in front of her, about four feet away; it stopped, raised one paw, and its tail went back and forth. *Oh, oh, it senses something, something it doesn't like.*

The rodent turned, rose on its hind legs, and snarled and hissed at her; it was not hissing and snarling *against* her; it was warning her, warning her of something.

Of course, I'm an idiot, she thought, if there is a farmhouse out here, it will be dangerous; any ruin will be occupied by smugglers or mutants or those zombie bats, or maybe something even worse. But I need food and out here there is nothing to eat, just a few scrubs, and I need water. She had sucked the moisture out of roots, and she had chewed, carefully chewed, a few spiny leaves, but that was not enough.

"*What is it?*" she asked the rodent, thinking, I really am straining the semantic limits here.

"*Hulks,*" came the image, rather than the word, and it was a silhouette, dark, shadowy, and merely a silhouette, that the rodent transmitted, with an aura of fear, even terror; the silhouette was something like her, like Miranda, *something like me, upright, on two legs, humanoid, and, of course dangerous, worse even than me!*

The most dangerous animal in the world, Miranda had read somewhere in an old book, was the human being. She could believe it. She'd never really seen any other dangerous animals, except in simulations, and except – now – those winged things, the zombie-bats, that came through the night, and the Bear-Warriors, and …

Well, the list of dangerous creatures was suddenly becoming quite long – maybe it was endlessly long. Living in Elysium City had given her a false sense of security. The most dangerous and horrifying thing she'd ever heard of was the *hybrid* – but they were probably all extinct; and, in any case, maybe they were just a story made up to frighten kids. It made her feel shivery just to think of them – Ugh, *hybrids* …

These hulks the rodent had seen, could it be they are *hybrids* hiding out here in the middle of nowhere?

She felt a wave of fear, then …

She straightened her shoulders. In her mind's eye, she saw the image of the President-Leader: Cosmos Honor and Cosmos Courage were at stake here! *Hail, Hail, All hail!*

Oh, well, whatever it is up there, if there is a farmhouse, let's go and see what it contains!

One effect of her privileged upbringing – and Miranda was quite aware of this – and of playing virtual Cloud Games – and she was aware of that influence too – was that she didn't know fear, or, if she knew fear, she felt she would always be able to win, always be able to slip out of whatever catastrophe she had gotten herself into. Whatever danger presented itself, Miranda Hughes, Cosmos First Class, knew she would triumph.

"Okay, my friend, I am going to see what is there, I am going to see these 'hulks' of yours, but you don't have to come with me."

The rodent got down on all fours and looked left and right and sniffed the ground. It looked up at her, its eyes shifting back and forth, and it flicked its tail; it disapproved. *"This will end your period of living,"* it said, *"They will eat you."*

Miranda saw the image of the death of Miranda Hughes in her mind: Two hulks, wings folded, squatting on their haunches, and her own body, dismembered, being devoured, and one of the hulks chewing on what looked like a calf, a foot, an ankle.

The rodent, still plugged into her mind, growled.

"Oh, my friend," Miranda sat down cross-legged. Sand drifted – in a tickling cascade – over her ankles. She smiled at the rodent. He showed his teeth, in friendly fashion, flicked his tail back and forth, and looked around, scanning the blowing sand – a guardian, on the alert. He can hear things I can't hear, Miranda thought, all the ultra-sound vibrations, much higher frequency than human hearing, higher than me too I bet, though I seem to have a larger range than most humans, and I can switch my extra range off, or shut it out. The sand hissing must be really painful; I wonder how he stands it; animals must have selective switch-off attention too, she thought, and a capacity to focus only on what is, in any particular moment, relevant, otherwise, they'd collapse in confusion from sensory overload.

"Okay, I'm going in," said Miranda. She stood up. "I'm pretty impulsive," she said, without thinking, to the rodent.

He looked at her, puzzled, his gaze concentrated, his ears twitching nervously.

"Sorry," she said, frowning, "But I really am too curious about what I might find!"

The rodent grinned and repeated, "Don't go! I like you!"

Miranda bent down, "I like you too! You stay safe. I'll go. I'll come back." She bit her lip. "I think I'll come back."

The rodent did the equivalent of a rodent shrug. "I will watch for you," he said, wiggling his mustaches.

"Thank you," said Miranda.

And then he was gone – high-tailing it back towards the road and the antique mailbox where – and she somehow understood this – he was going to wait and stand guard.

Now she was alone.

She didn't particularly want to be alone: she thought of Nikki, and of Caliban, and of Kit.

Now, yes, her past life did seem like a dream – the luxury apartment, high in the artificial clouds of Dome City, with their very own swimming pool floating out on the deck, the Jacuzzi, the sauna, the wall-to-wall soft white-cream self-cleaning carpets, and the exercise room, and the invisible computers everywhere that did virtually everything, their soft voices asking what you wanted, what they could do to please you, and Nikki's studio with its computers and brushes and pencils and pens and drawing boards, and, outside the windows the other towers and spires rising up, majestic, in the soft filtered air light. She wondered where Kit was now. And where was her mother – where was Nikki …?

Was she alive?

There had been something so self-assured about the way Nikki reacted to the mutants and to Caliban and to the mutant kingdom; maybe Nikki had a card up her sleeve. Nikki was certainly more than she seemed.

Nikki and Kit and Elysium and the Mutant Kingdom and even Caliban – it did all seem like a dream here in this empty lost world of drifting sand.

Miranda again started up the old farm lane, or at least what she suspected was the old farm lane, buried under drifting sand, leaving her rodent friend behind. She glanced back. He had stopped and was standing watching her; he was almost invisible in the blowing sandstorm; she could just see him; he was standing upright, looking in her direction.

He raised a paw.

She raised her hand in salute, and then she turned and continued her way towards the invisible farmhouse she was sure she would find.

It emerged slowly from the dust. It was a wooden frame clapboard house like those she had seen in ancient paintings and photographs and movies; it reminded her of a painting, "American Gothic" except this house was taller and thinner, and it looked like it had a porch or veranda that ran all the way around the ground floor.

The house was ramshackle. Some of the clapboard had been torn away, windows panes were broken, part of the roof was gone, and the whole thing leaned drunkenly to one side, and behind the open verandah it looked like most of the windows were broken – but not all of them.

There were no lights, or any sign of electricity, and Miranda thought maybe there was no food either or water. I am being foolish, she mumbled, but if there are "hulks" or humanoids or zombie-bats there must be food and water. Besides I'm curious. I'm a Cosmos Scout Explorer. I have to see what these creatures are like, up close; and she thought too that she was in danger-ous territory, that she was a long way from Elysium Dome City where she had lived her whole life.

Still, if there is no danger, there is no heroism!

Cosmos forever!

Hail, Hail, All Hail!

Old machines, just heaps of junk metal, were stacked around the house – an ancient automobile, some sort of farm machinery; one heap of scrap metal looked like a harvester, another had once been a tractor.

There was a plow too, half leaning into the earth. Miranda walked over to it and felt the blades which were still sharp and smooth and shone darkly in the dim, ghoulish-yellow light of the pattering sandstorm.

"Once you turned the earth," Miranda whispered, running her hand along the sharp blade and having, at first, no idea, really, what she was talking about. She was mourning something. The overturned plow was a monument to something lost – it was a memorial, a gravestone.

"Real earth, real soil," She knelt down and lifted up a handful of dry dust. "Yes, what is gone is real earth you could walk on, real earth you could clutch with your toes, lift up and crush in the palm of your hand, sniff and taste and smell, real dark damp earth with earthworms and centipedes and beetles and seeds and roots and … real earth full of life …"

She let the dust run out between her fingers. She stood up and turned to the farmhouse. *Okay, be brave, Miranda Hughes!* On the steeply slanted roof were what looked like shattered 21st or early 22nd century solar pan-els; one twisted panel hung sideways off the roof; it rattled and banged in the blistering gusts of sand. There was no sign of life. Somewhere a shutter banged, and then banged again – a spooky, scary sound.

"No matter," Miranda steeled herself, "I'm going in!"

The rickety house loomed above her; there was definitely something eerie about it – it was an ideal nest for psychos and serial killers and zombie-bats and monsters from other dimensions. It was the sort of place into which a young lady, even a Cosmos Scout Gold Medal Winner, should not perhaps venture alone.

Yes, it was clearly an ideal trap.

"To hell with it," Miranda headed towards the veranda. She placed her foot on the first step.

The boards creaked under her toes; she glanced upward. The blank windows were like eyes staring at her. For just a moment, she thought she caught a glimpse of something, a fleeting white face – a monstrous face – a skull with bulbous eyes and dripping fangs – behind one of the dirty window panes.

"Well, Miranda, Cosmos Scout," she clenched her fists, "*Hail! All Hail!* Now or never – forward!"

CHAPTER 8 – AMERICAN GOTHIC

Caliban crawled out of the overturned oil barrel. He was bruised and with cuts here and there which stung; but none, he thought, were serious.

He stood up, rubbed the sore parts, and felt his chest and arms and face. Yes, everything was still there: the loincloth, the machete, and the AK-47, safe in their slings. The scimitar lay a few feet away. He picked it up. It was streaked with blood and crusted with sand.

He wiped dried blood off his face and forearm. It was not his blood.

The tussle the night before had been a close call, a deadly fight, but he, Caliban, Prince of the Mutants, Pirate of the Desert, had triumphed. While being carried up into the sky, he had managed to unsheathe the AK and he had shot the zombie-bat in the wing. The thing let out a god-awful screech, but it didn't let go. Together, they went spinning down.

They landed in a foul-smelling tangle on a sandbank – which was lucky. The zombie-bat was still alive. Snarling and growling, flailing desperately, the bat had tried to slash him with its talons and blind him with its claws.

Caliban had jumped this way and that, rolled here and there, somersaulted once, and just managed to miss being impaled, having his face torn off, or blinded.

But other zombies-bats were closing in. So he took refuge where he could, in a lucky find – an overturned oil barrel. He did have some bad cuts – one slash across his chest, another across one leg – and bruises, but he was okay, and all of that was nothing and soon vanished. All night the zombie-bats scrabbled and raged around him. By morning they were gone.

In the morning, he found his way, as fast as he could, back to the drainage pipe. Miranda had disappeared.

Had the zombie-bats gotten her?

Surely not! He had a feeling, a strange intuition, that she would have headed towards the light of the sun. He went into one of the abandoned mining buildings, he came to an old set of lockers – where the workers of years of yore must have stored their accoutrements and equipment – and he unlocked the old combination lock – and he pulled out a backpack which he had stored away and which held lots of ammunition for the AK and a few packs of dried lichen food. He left the building, looked around, and hitched the backpack onto his back. Now he was ready. He would find his Princess and save her.

In the early afternoon a sandstorm came up. Caliban kept going, trying to navigate in the blistering and blowing sand. He could only see about ten feet. The air was thick, hot, sweaty, and filled with a yellow, sickly, jaundiced light. The gluey air-borne sand stuck to him. It seemed to drain his energy. He thought that, without that strange new creature, Miranda, that beautiful Cosmos, he would not be able to live. What was this yearning, this empty feeling, this weakness, this sinking feeling in his stomach and in his heart? He had never felt anything like it before. It made him ache – it lifted him up and it tossed him down.

Was this that thing the Sacred Texts called *love*?

It was twilight when he came to an old paved country road. The asphalt had boiled up and was coated in sand but soft and sticky underfoot; he decided he would follow the road; perhaps Miranda had discovered the same road and, somehow, he knew that if she came to the road, she would have followed it. He walked along the edge of the road, in the ditch or just beyond it, so his feet would not sink into the soft tar. He looked for footprints or signs, but the sandstorm would have blown any remnant of Miranda's presence away.

He looked up.

The sun had gone below the horizon. The sandstorm dropped off and the air was suddenly clear. The first stars appeared.

There was a slow heavy ominous beating of wings.

Caliban took the AK out of its sling, checked the magazine – even with his supply in the backpack, these bullets were rare and precious things.

He looked up towards the sky.

He saw dark forms, their wings spread, flying high – looking for prey, he hurried. He must find shelter. If they found him out in the open, not even a first-class pirate with a Kalashnikov 47 would stand much chance …

Yes, they were coming. Where to hide? Where to fight?

"Hello!" Miranda shouted. Her voice echoed in the empty space. Waves and ribbons of dust wrapped themselves like mist around the spooky tall thin farmhouse; sand drifted across the veranda which did seem to go all the way around the building. The wind was rising, blustering gusts of rasping sand slapped and whipped around her. Miranda blinked, covered her nose. "Hello!"

Nothing ...

"Hello!"

She stepped up onto the veranda and glanced around: warped floorboards, a veranda railing supported by scrolls of elaborate ironwork, two hooks in the veranda roof from which maybe, once, a rocker had been suspended, three broken light fixtures, and graceful pillars of wrought-iron that held up the veranda roof. The place was a time warp; it had popped up, dilapidated but almost intact, out of the distant past, or so it seemed.

She took a deep breath, hesitated, then knocked on the door. There was no answer, just the hollow echo of her knock. The sandstorm blustered and squealed; yellow waves skittered across the floorboards. Her tunic snapped against her and was ripped from her shoulder. She pulled it back.

Shielding her eyes from the yellow glare radiating from the incoming waves of sand, she peered through the narrow window next to the door; it was streaked with dirt, but, strangely, it had not been broken; it was difficult to see through; it was frosted with dust and dirt and some sort of sticky guck. Compared to the ghastly light of the storm, the inside of the farmhouse was plunged in thick gray darkness. She could only make out dim shadows and eerie, ghostly reflections.

But, as she stared, blinking against the beating sand, her eyes got used to the darkness: a shadowy interior: a thin hallway, a narrow stairway leading upwards, with its banister broken in places, and, beside the staircase, there was a latched door, probably leading to a basement.

And there was no sign of a ghostly skull-like face.

She stepped away from the window and considered what she should do next. She was thirsty and hungry. The heat was withering – or should be – for someone like her who had lived all her life in the perfectly controlled atmospheric bubble of Elysium City, but she realized, now, with a slight sense of wonder, that the sweat had evaporated, and that, in fact, she was really not suffering from the heat at all. She rubbed her forehead. I am odder and odder; I am becoming really weird!

Maybe this is all an illusion.

Maybe I really am dead.

Maybe Nikki and I did die in that plane crash!

Well, whatever – I'm here now, in the dream.

She turned the round brass doorknob and gently pushed the heavy wooden door. It fought back. It didn't want to be opened. She pushed again, harder.

The door opened, slowly, grudgingly, with a creaking, grinding and crunching. She gave it a final push, and peeked around the edge. A pile of something lay behind the door – bones.

"Oh," she whispered.

It looked like they were dry old bones, picked clean.

"Gosh."

She slipped sideways through the door, ripping a new hole in the repulsive prisoner tunic. She fingered the ragged slash – which was at least five inches long and just below her left breast. She looked around.

Seeing nothing threatening, she crouched down over the pile of bones – a tibia, a ribcage, and a hipbone, human or humanoid. That anatomy implant course AE-346 – courtesy of New Elysium University – was turning out useful.

She looked up.

Above the bones a red ribbon had been pinned to the wall; it was tattered and faded but you could still see that it had been red. A jingle bell was attached to the ribbon; and somebody, perhaps a child, had drawn or scribbled in charcoal a face, and, over the face, a cross.

Miranda sniffed, searching for smells, tell-tale odors. Nothing registered; nothing in particular, but there was a lingering musty musky smell.

It was something like sex, the smell of sex, but faint, very faint.

The dust-dry bones had been there a long time. There were no traces of death, no stains in the floorboards that she could see. With the palm of her hand, she cleared away a thin layer of sand. It looked as if the bones had been brought here and left – maybe it was a shrine, a memorial, or some sort of ritual place.

An image jumped into her mind – a weird, chalk-white skeletal creature, on all fours, kneeling, and clumsily trying to draw the cross with a thick piece of charcoal; the creature's fingers – which for an instant became Miranda's – were long translucent and pointed, with long nails, like claws.

Miranda was flooded with a sense of mourning and of yearning and frustration: it was really hard, almost impossible, to draw the cross, but it had to be done. The urging was mysterious, but overpowering – a thirst, a need, a blind lust pressing down on the piece of charcoal … to express … what?

The image was gone. It popped like a bubble. Miranda stared at the charcoal cross. Maybe *the cross* was really an *X*. Maybe it was not worship but obliteration, not reverence, but dominance; not "I worship here" but "I have canceled you, crossed you out!" Hmm! What did it all mean?

And why had she been invaded by the image of the weird creature and even by its thoughts? She felt she had been inside the creature's mind, slipped into its body; or it was as if its body had slithered into hers. *I became it, and it became me!*

Crouching over the bones, Miranda hugged herself. In the withering heat, she shivered – an inner chill.

Outside the storm rose and fell, whispered and whistled, grains of sand pattered against the windows, whispered under the door.

Still crouching, still hugging herself, Miranda glanced around. She sensed life – something alive was close by. The yellowing gray dimness of the spectral room wrapped itself around her, clinging, clammy, like a damp shroud. It was a flood, an invading fluid. It was not pleasant.

She shook herself and stood up. "Hello!"

Nothing.

"Hello!"

Nothing.

The only sound was the wind and the sliding, slithering, rustling sand, sifting and drifting in everywhere; the door creaked gently, back and forth, on its squeaky hinges, scraping the bent warped floorboards. Dim light filtered through the windows, tinting everything in a livid yellow sheen.

"Hello! Is there anybody here?"

Steeling herself, Miranda stepped into the room to the left of the hallway. It was an almost square space, with high windows on two sides. The dimming sand-driven air glowed through the filthy panes, with sharp-angled, brighter splashes of light, where the glass had been shattered.

In one corner of the room, a wooden rocking-chair stood under the skeleton of what must once have been a reading lamp. And there was a table with an oil-lamp – an oil-lamp! Electric power had probably failed and then even the solar power units would have failed when no replacement panels were available, and no money or technicians – so people reverted to oil-lamps, and candles, and wood fires; but of course there would have been no wood, probably not for dozens or hundreds of miles; and then even the oil and the candles would run out.

On the small round table that stood beside the rocking chair was an old-fashioned photograph with a frame. The glass had been shattered. Miranda picked up the photograph. It showed a handsome middle-aged couple with a young man, probably their teenage son. It must be the family that once lived here, Miranda frowned. What had happened to them?

A thick book lay beside the smashed picture: it was the Bible. The leather cover was warped and scratched. Miranda opened it.

She was surprised to see it was the King James Version. The paper was rippled and yellowed with age and use. The book fell open at *Revelations 16*. The page was marked with the same clumsy cross – or "X" – that had been scrawled in the hallway over the pile of bones and the skull.

Miranda read:

"And I heard a great voice out of the temple saying to the seven angels, Go your ways, and pour out the vials of the wrath of God upon the earth."

"The vials of wrath ..." Miranda whispered the words; she glanced over the different verses and their prophecies: the oceans would die and be poisoned; the rivers would dry up; blood would replace water; the sun would scorch the earth and people until they flared up like torches; darkness – maybe sandstorms, super-tornadoes, and giant hurricanes – would cover the land; people would be monstrously disfigured and die from plagues.

Miranda ran her finger along the lines:

"And I saw three unclean spirits like frogs coming out of the mouth of the dragon, out of the mouth of the beast, and out of the mouth of the false prophet."

"For they are spirits of demons, performing signs, which go out to the kings of the earth and of the whole world, to gather them to the battle of that great day of God Almighty."

Unclean spirits, demons, and *beasts!* The words sounded like they referred to mutants and those other creations of biotechnology, those evil and monstrous *Synthetic Individuals* – she could hardly bear to think of the SINs – false and deceptive simulacra of real people – and maybe even those half-mythical monsters, the very worst of all things under the sun and the moon, *hybrids!* How horrible!!

Miranda shivered in disgust.

Why had the book fallen open at that particular page? Somebody had been reading, or *trying to read,* those words, over and over and over. And that somebody, or something, had drawn the cross, or tried to, on the pages, or, yes, maybe it was an "X."

Or maybe it was a cross.

Was it a sign of hope or of hopelessness?

Was it a sign of assent and agreement or of dissent and condemnation?

Was the author of the "X" a believer or a non-believer?

She put the Bible down carefully, exactly where it had been, and patted it gently. Somebody was afraid, somebody was really afraid. Or somebody was sick, really sick. Or both.

She walked out of the ghostly sitting room where the feathery light from the storm rippled like sunlight deep under a cloudy and troubled sea, and went back into the gloomy dusky hall where everything seemed much more still and funereal. She peeked into the room on the other side of the corridor. It was empty. One window was broken. A cobweb-like curtain drifted up and down, in and out; sand had swept in, creating a sand dune – four or five feet tall – which covered most of the floor. Leaning against the far wall, just beyond the dune, was an old-fashioned broom, its hard, straw brush worn and darkened and twisted from use.

Somebody had been obsessively clean and hard-working, long ago.

She went back to the hallway, glanced at the staircase that went up to the second floor; she went down the hall to the back of the house and came to the kitchen. There was an ancient hand-powered water pump.

She tried the handle; it moved up and down; it creaked and groaned; but of course, no water came, but, just to be stubborn, she kept pumping and she did think she smelt water – smelling water!

That was another new sensation!

She pumped and pumped and pumped!

Suddenly water gushed up, rusty water, and she splashed it over her face and neck and shoulders; it dribbled down inside the tunic, soaking the burlap; the trickles of water tickled.

She was tempted but she decided that drinking the water would definitely not be a good idea. Who knew from what foul depths it came? She sniffed – Yes, dead things and poisons were down there, seeping and creeping through the earth and rock strata, the whole world had become poisonous! "Yes, indeed," she sighed, shaking herself, "this water is poison." The rust-colored water dribbled from her hair, streamed between her breasts, down her belly, and ran in rivulets down her legs.

"And I saw three unclean spirits like frogs coming out of the mouth of the dragon, out of the mouth of the beast, and out of the mouth of the false prophet."

Something thumped on the floor directly above her.

Miranda's heart flip-flopped.

She stopped pumping, looked up, and stood absolutely still. There it was – another thump!

Without daring to move, she looked around. Darkness was falling; in a few minutes, it would be night. She breathed slowly, deliberately: Was it safer to stay in here? Or better to go out into the open, into the night? Outside, those rabid bat-like zombie things might be on the loose, in spite of the sandstorm; and in fact, as she looked out the broken window that was next to the pump, she saw that the sandstorm was abating. Without the sandstorm, the zombies would almost certainly take flight, and they would hunt her down; it was better to stay inside.

"Okay, I stay here."

But if I stay here, I have to find out what's making the banging noise. She ran her fingers through her hair, wet and sticky and clogged with sand. She squared her shoulders, took a deep breath, and walked quietly back to the front of the house. She stared up the narrow shadowy staircase, took another deep breath, and began to climb the stairs. She thought of the President-Leader, so handsome, so brave, so gallant.

Hail, All Hail!

Hail, All Hail!

A Cosmos Warrior never hesitates and never flinches!

A Cosmos Warrior heads straight into the heart of danger!

When she got to the top, she quickly went through the rooms. They were bare, just a few bleached bones here and there, human and animal, and a few pieces of broken furniture, a rocking chair with one rocker missing, a dresser reduced to a skeleton without drawers, a pinned-up child's drawing, it looked like a toy house and two people, and the sun shining, almost faded to nothing. In one room there was a crib – the baby's room.

Miranda tried to envisage living in such a bare and desolate place with nothing but the wind for company.

Then she saw that the crib was on rockers and that when the wind touched it, it rocked back and forth – bang, bang, bang, thump, thump, thump – so that explained the banging.

There was a trap door in the ceiling of the baby's room and even a ladder, pale blue paint flaking from its wooden rungs, leading up the attic. She wondered if she should try to get into the attic but decided not to.

She went back downstairs, noticing that her wet footprints were already fading. Then she saw it – the door leading down to the basement was open. It was only slightly ajar. Before it had been closed, she was sure of it, and the latch had been bolted. She took a deep breath. A musty moldy mushroom smell came up from below: cooler air, damp, fecund, clayey and somehow smoky – and turbulent with silent suggestions of flesh – of life.

It was not normal human flesh …

She pulled the basement door open slightly; narrow unpainted wooden steps led down into inky darkness, thicker now with smells, with those alluring and subtle odors of flesh.

Inky darkness spilled upwards.

The fleshy smell was stronger.

Certainly, it was not Cosmos flesh …

It was not hygienic, purified, perfumed Cosmos flesh, no …

She sniffed. Her nostrils – finely chiseled perfectly human nostrils – seemed to be literally quivering in eagerness, hungry for the smells.

She clenched her fists, feeling a surge of energy. The sensation almost made her dizzy. *What in the world is happening?* She leaned against the doorframe and steadied herself.

Maybe I really am dead!

Yes, this is all a dream!

If it is all a dream, well, then, there is nothing to be afraid of!

She pulled the cellar door open and took a first cautious step down into the dark dank cellar. A breeze rippled, tickling her skin. She sniffed again; she could smell them, something, something was living down here – they were more than one, whatever they were.

This is crazy. I'm going to get myself killed. This is exactly what you don't do if you are in a Haunted House or Gothic Castle in a Horror Game in the Cloud. You do *not* go down all alone into the dangerous dark hidden places. A cellar or a dungeon can become a tomb. Behind her, the cellar door creaked and swayed, opening and shutting, the dying light rhythmically brightening and fading, brightening and fading …

Idiot, she clenched her teeth, *I really am an idiot!* She took two farther steps into the darkness. She could never resist a dare; that was true. Cyril Bedford just had to say, "You wouldn't dare!" And she would do it, whatever it was, and however foolish or stupid it was. Goosebumps rose; her skin felt all prickly. Darkness flooded up like liquid tar – it was up to her thighs – It was going to consume her, darken her spirit, and make her invisible; it was coating her, like a living rubbery fluid, cloaking her, suffocating her. She shuddered: I should go back.

Hail, all Hail!

But no … As she went down, the darkness parted, and there was light; the thick, fecund, clinging air cleared. She could see, faintly at first, but she could see, and her vision got clearer by the instant. Just as she realized this, and just as she reached the bottom of the stairs and was standing with her feet on the cool bare earth floor, she heard a bouncing sound behind her; she turned.

A ball was bouncing down the stairs.

Bounce, bounce, bounce …

She froze.

It looked like a tennis ball.

It rolled across the dirt floor and came to rest at her feet.

She knelt and picked it up. Yes, it was a filthy tennis ball. She threw it, underhand, up the stairs, neatly tossing it through the half-open basement door. She caught a flicker of a shadow up there; there was definitely something or somebody up there.

She waited.

The ball came bouncing back down the stairs. It rolled to her feet. Somebody had tossed it; there was no doubt about it. She knelt down again, and picked up the ball and held it. The ball was dark with deeply ingrained dirt.

She turned it around in her hard. Okay, she thought, if this is a game, I will play. She tossed it back up the stairs.

The ball flew up and disappeared through the door. The little daylight that remained was fading quickly now, but Miranda could see, better than ever. Her eyes, it seemed, were getting used to the darkness.

The fleshy mushroom-like smell was stronger. Miranda felt movement behind her.

Just as she was about to turn around and investigate the shuffling and clicking movement from behind her, the ball came bouncing down the stairs again.

Miranda caught the ball, tossed it back, neatly looping it through the half-open door, hearing it land, and bounce, bounce, bounce.

She swirled around. Part of the wall of the basement – it was really an ancient piece of warped plywood leaning against the wall – was scraping against the rough dirt floor. Somebody or something was pushing it outward.

A damp feathery breeze tickled Miranda's skin; the sheet of plywood must hide an entry to a cave system. She suddenly had the intuition – almost a vision – of an underground labyrinth, narrow tunnels and caverns, stretching off every which way, a drafty underground kingdom.

So, this old farmhouse was a gateway, but a gateway to what? Her vision suggested – but did not show her – that weird life forms were swarming everywhere in that underground world, and that the underworld went on, and on, and on.

From around the edge of the plywood, a white claw-like hand appeared. It pushed the plywood farther away from the wall. Yes, behind the plywood was the mouth of a cave, and some of the inhabitants were coming out.

Miranda bit her lip and exhaled a puff of air. Stand firm, Miranda, stand firm! You are one of the elite. You are a Cosmos, *and, yea, though you walk through the valley of death you shall fear no evil, for you are among the chosen.* The Cosmos are the Masters of the Universe – no damned doubt about it! We Cosmos have conquered everything and we can face anything. Cosmos are unique in courage and steadfastness. She thought of her mother, of how cool Nikki was, and how unfaltering, an exemplary Citizen and First-Class Cosmos: Nikki was never ruffled, never panicked, and Nikki, like the President-Leader, was ready to look even Death straight in the eye. *Yes, Cosmos Forever!* She would not let her mother down. And besides, Miranda, you've confronted almost every conceivable scenario in the Cloud Games.

So, buck up!

Stand High Young Cosmos!

The honor of Cosmos is at stake!

The honor of the President!

Hail, Hail, All Hail!

Hail, Hail, All Hail!

Out of the cave, from behind the rotting plywood, came, with shuffling hesitant gait, a naked chalk-white, glowing, hairless, gangly, human-shaped thing. Its teeth were long and thin and pointed, like true fangs; its eyes were chalk-white, droopy, and oblong; its feet, with five spread out, pointed toes, were like foot-claws. Its slithery white tongue hung out, perhaps four inches; its body was muscular, with knobby knees and elbows, and the thing was naked, except for a long straggly white beard. It was male – definitely male.

Oh, boy, thought Miranda, this looks like a nocturnal afraid-of-the-light bug-eating monster out of *Ghouls Versus Dragons on Venus, version 34-B*.

The ghoul-like thing stood up stiffly, bent over a bit, as if it had arthritis or crotchety, badly-oiled joints; its baleful, empty – iris and pupil were barely visible – oblong eyes gazed in her direction.

Behind the male was a female. It shuffled forward, moving in a sideways sidling half-crouch, waddling out of the dark cave that had been hidden by the plywood; it looked up, doddered forward, and stood up. The female was naked too, with heavy, pointed, pendant breasts that hung down below her waist; and, like the male, she had long fangs and a tongue that dripped white saliva, making thick little pools that sparkled and glowed.

Miranda stared. Oh, boy, day-glow saliva!

These creatures looked like mutants, definitely mutants; not the evil winged ones that came out of the sky, but humanoid mutants that for some reason had regressed or evolved to some non-human state. Was it a virus, an experiment, radiation, or a witch's curse, or legal condemnation to being morphed into ghouls?

They had the aura and odor of death upon them, not quite a glow – but more like a fleshy and musty cannibalistic perfume. They were killers and cannibals; that was clear enough. Miranda sensed, somehow, that they killed and ate people – when they could find people, which was rare. She somehow sniffed it out of them, sensed it in their bodies, saw it in those blank oblong eyes.

Miranda frowned. What, exactly, does the *Girl Scout Cosmos Code of Honor* require in such a situation?

Well, definitely, it was helpful to make a comparison with past experience, even if it was virtual experience. Yes, these creatures were straight out of *Ghouls Versus Dragons on Venus, version 34-B*. They were hyper-real, neatly delineated in every luminous detail, like the lips, the heavy lids of the oblong eyes, the faded, almost inexistent pupil and iris. Whoever or whatever created these things really knew what they were doing! Boy! Of course, maybe they were the result of some bio-bomb or mutating weapon that changed people into non-people, into things, monsters, the living dead …

The ghouls – she had decided they were *ghouls* – yes, "ghouls" was a good name for them – stood there for a moment, arms dangling at their sides, tongues hanging out dripping glowing spools of that thick white glowing saliva. They stared at Miranda.

Bump, bump, bump, bump …

The ball bounced down the stairs and somehow – without even turning to look – and this surprised her – Miranda caught it. She weighed it for an instant in the palm of her hand, lightly bouncing it, and then tossed it towards the two mutants – or ghouls – who'd just come out of the wall.

"Here, catch!"

The male ghoul caught the ball and looked down it and then his blind-looking mournful eyes looked up, at her.

"Good catch, amigo," Miranda said. At least she had broken the ice.

"Grrhh," he growled, spittle splashing from his flickering tongue; the growl was deep in the ghoul's throat. Miranda decided to call him "Deep."

"Do you speak English?"

"Grrhh."

"Mooooo," the female said; or at least it sounded like "Mooooo" to Miranda.

"Mooooo," the female repeated, gazing at Miranda.

Okay, that did it; she'd call this one "Daisy," after some charming cow she'd read about somewhere.

"Grrrhhh."

"Maybe you don't speak English, huh. Well, that's cool. ¿Habla español? Parlez-vous Français? Do you speak Mandarin? Russian? Portuguese? Japanese?" Miranda ran though her Cosmos training and Cosmos language implants.

"Grrrhhh." The male ghoul – Mr. Deep – tossed the ball back.

"I guess you don't speak anything," Miranda caught the ball, bounced it in the palm of her hand. "Come on, guys," she said – adopting the leadership role that came naturally to a First-Class Cosmos Presidential Storm Trooper Girl Scout – and she turned and started up the stairs – and then stopped.

The door at the top of the stairs swung open.

There, standing at the top of the stairs, was another of the ghouls, a male ghoul, very male to judge by the state of his erection, which Miranda figured, must be quite outstanding in the erection field, though, in truth, she had so far seen very few erections in her time, not even very many virtual erections; but she did look forward, if she survived the present situation, to studying the subject in detail. Kit had given her a few pointers; but they were purely theoretical.

She wasn't sure what the purpose or aim of this particular erection was. Perhaps a diversion was in order, so …

Miranda tossed the ball. He caught it. She kept coming up the stairs, deliberately, step-by-step, wondering whether they would try to trap her, try to rush her. She wasn't too worried; she was a black belt two-time world champion in reality, and also virtually, in *Ghouls versus Dragons*.

And at least four times she had whipped Chris Barton – who was twice her size – in the Black Belt completion, flipped him over her shoulder and pinned him down and kept him there – wiggling and swearing.

The ghoul at the top of the stairs growled and snarled.

"Tough bananas," Miranda muttered and she kept coming, and, when she got close, she gave him the "*Cosmos* stare" – the fixed arrogant down-the-nose-who-the-hell-are-you look which she had learned was one of the best weapons of the upper Cosmos Class – that and the upper crust Mid-Oceanic Cosmos accent – when dealing with inferior species.

He snarled again, but he gave way, and moved aside.

"Grrhh," he said as she passed, drool spooling down. It did glow; it definitely glowed, even up here. She decided she would call him – the male ghoul with the super erection – "Bouncer" since he was the one who kept bouncing the ball. In fact, it was amazingly bouncy for a tennis ball.

Bounce's erection, she noted, was intact.

He didn't grab for her or try to trap her. They let her pass and then they trooped behind her.

Bouncer – the hulk – the ghouls were sort of like hulks but not as big or threatening as hulks, they were human size, not larger – at the head of the stairs, came right behind her, still dripping saliva.

She would tell her rodent friend about this if she ever happened on him again; but she supposed for a creature his size, these ghouls would be very scary and dangerous too – they probably ate rodents and rattlesnakes as well as people.

Miranda wondered what the formula was that caused the drool to glow: would it be DNA design *Firefly 75* or *Firefly 34*?

Or maybe it was something else entirely. Could it be radioactive? Maybe some Dead Lands humans or colonists had been morphed into ghouls by radioactivity from that Chinese experimental bio-satellite, with the nuclear engine and all the genetic bio-experimental material on board that had crashed just outside Dallas, Texas, in the year 2101, poisoning some 350 square miles, or from the Texas nuclear missile base that had exploded – probably not far from here, wherever "here" was – in the year 2142. Or from the overflow of super-gen-bio-fertilizer that had sucked up and transformed all life forms, mostly in the 2130s, turning corn and wheat and hay into vicious and aggressive and inedible lichen. It could be any number of things.

She led the three ghouls into the sitting room, with the rocking chair, the old lamp, the little table with the big old leather-bound dog-eared King James Bible, and the shattered family photograph.

Mr. Deep – the elder male ghoul – went to the Bible. He picked it up, clutched it to his chest and groaned. He rocked back and forth and groaned deep in his throat.

It was obvious he retained some atavistic trace of being human.

"I'm sorry," Miranda said, not really knowing what she was sorry for, but then thinking that these creatures had definitely once been human, that they remembered being human, that they could no longer talk or read or perhaps really think like humans; they were mourning their loss. They had lost their humanity; they had lost their souls; they had been abandoned by their God, or they had been forced to abandon Him. They were in Hell, the equivalent of Hell, far from the Vision of their Divinity. It must be awful. "I'm sorry," Miranda repeated, "I really am sorry."

Miranda then realized that in an oblique and very sketchy way she recognized them; they were the three people in the smashed photograph: father, mother, and son!

"Moo," the female shuffled close. She sniffed at Miranda – sniff, sniff, sniff, along Miranda's arm. Miranda wondered if Daisy was going to try to take a bite out of the inside of her forearm which, she had to admit contemplating it in the fading dim yellow sandstorm light, which now had a ghostly lunar quality, looked pretty tender and perhaps delicious for a cannibal-type ex-human being. If the ghouls were the people in the photograph then definitely they had once been human.

So something horrible had happened.

Or maybe a whole lot of horrible things had happened.

Daisy looked up at Miranda and then sniffed and sniffed at Miranda's forearm and her long tongue came out and licked at Miranda's skin – lick, lick, and slurp. For some reason, Miranda was not afraid, nor even disgusted; for some reason, she really did think she could overcome these creatures if, as it were, push came to shove, and they engaged in a full battle.

Daisy stopped licking Miranda's arm, started back on the balls of her feet, and gazed up at Miranda, her gluey white blank eyes widening.

Suddenly, Daisy squealed, fell to her hands and knees, and banged her forehead on the floor, over and over, and so hard that a cloud of dust rose around her and the floorboards rattled and bounced.

"Whatever are you doing?"

Daisy began to kiss Miranda's feet; it tickled; Daisy's long gooey tongue slithered over Miranda's toes, which was spooky, the big sloppy kisses cleaning off the crust of dust.

"Hey, what in the world are you doing?"

The other two ghouls, Mr. Deep and Mr. Bounce, stared at Miranda for just an instant, then fell on their hands and knees and banged their foreheads against the floorboards – thump, thump, thump. It looked like they were not going to stop.

"Hey, guys, what in the world are you doing?"

What was going on? Miranda then remembered that she had begun to develop the capacity, with a little effort, to read thoughts. The problem was: Did these creatures have thoughts?

Well, I guess if I can communicate with a rodent, I can communicate with them. So, she sent out her newly discovered mental tentacles, probing, questioning, while Daisy continued to slobber over her feet.

Miranda concentrated and concentrated: and out of the mists came an image. It shimmered, it glowed, and then she saw it clearly.

She, Miranda, was a sort of goddess. She was shining and luminous, benign like an image of the Madonna in an old painting, and bright like a brightly lit Russian icon; and that she was dressed in … *what was that?*

Wow!

The goddess Miranda was dressed in glittering *sequins*. Boy, what a fabulous dress, it was just amazing! It made her look like a mermaid. It would be a stupendous thing to wear to the President's Spring Equinox Ball! It was like she was a Cloud Film Star, appearing on a stage, all glittering gold for some Media Award.

It was very flattering but somehow, it was really scary. It was idolatrous, for one thing, and, though Miranda was not religious, she did believe in the dangers of hubris. Cosmos warrior pride was one thing – and totally useful and functional – but Icarus flying-to-the-sun or Faustian God-envy was something entirely different, and the President-Leader had warned against such things and would certainly not approve. On the occasions, very few indeed, when Miranda had overstepped the bounds, Nikki had said, "Keep your feet on the ground, Miranda, and your head on your shoulders!" Right now, with the ghouls banging their heads on the floor, Miranda had a feeling of vertigo, as if she were disappearing, being swept upward, or withering, transforming, becoming something else entirely – some monster, perhaps a ghoul-goddess.

No! Help!

She looked down at herself. No, she was still just Miranda, dressed in the ragged and torn remains of the prison tunic – hardly anything left of it, actually – and her arms and legs were just the golden tanned Cosmos arms and legs they had always been, her hands were hands; her feet were feet; even the clear nail polish from her last day in Elysium was still there.

The mutants were now on all fours were looking up at her, as if awaiting orders, as if ... And then one of them – Mr. Deep it was – apparently the paterfamilias – scuttled away towards the back of the house.

Then, after a few minutes during which there was a clattering and banging sound in the back of the house, Mr. Deep came back, and, kneeling in front of Miranda, he lifted up something – it looked like gray flesh.

What? They want to turn me, Miranda Hughes Cosmos First Class, into a cannibal!

Miranda sniffed at the gray lump: *yes, it was flesh!*

But it was the flesh of a *mushroom*, thick flesh, with pearls of what looked like *water*, silver pearls – that were very tempting – because, really, Miranda was extremely hungry – and thirsty, really thirsty!

Mr. Deep held up the chunk of flesh. "Grrrhhh," he said, and his eyes seemed to be absolutely begging her to eat.

"Well, Mr. Deep, I do suppose I should be polite," said Miranda, "since I am your guest and all."

"Grrrhhh."

"I mean, after all, I *am* your guest, aren't I?"

"Grrrhhh," they all said in unison, bobbing their heads and staring with those weird blank glutinous eyes. Moonlight shone through the shattered windows, making bright patterns on the floor. So, the sandstorm was definitely over. It was night. The sky was clear.

"Well, thank you, then," said Miranda; and, having convinced herself, she took a bite of the mushroom. Oh, it was delicious; it had a bold bouquet, a velvety texture, and a multi-faceted multi-colored taste – and aftertaste – which caressed her taste buds and caused her saliva to gush and so she took another bite, and she had the impression that the mushroom was full of magic pure spring water, splashing up from somewhere deep and sacred and pristine, infinitely cool and good.

"*No, no, no – don't please don't!*"

Into her mind flashed an image of her friend the rodent standing on its hind legs by the mailbox and shaking its head in dismay – "*No, no, no,*" Its mustaches twitched; its eyes glowed.

"*No, no, no – please don't do it!*"

"*No, no, no – you will become one of them!*"

The ghouls were crouched worshipfully around her and taking big bites of the mushroom. They moaned and swayed on their haunches, their fangs dripped white liquid in drools, as they too ate of the sacred mushroom.

Well, it is delicious, thought Miranda, and I'm sure it's not dangerous!

The rodent shook his head and faded slowly away.

The ghouls took large munches, chewing deliberately, with flakes and droppings spilling over. Sometimes they caught these droppings with their tongues which flicked out of their mouths in a really amusing fashion, or so Miranda thought.

She pointed at their flicking tongues – which now seemed positively enormous – and giggled. But the ghouls didn't seem to mind. They were slobbering and munching happily, and one of them even waved a claw at her and – had she seen right? Its right eye winked!

Miranda's world suddenly spun around – two full rotations, like a merry-go-round, and then it turned upside down – though Miranda was also quite aware she was still sitting in her tatty prison shift, solid flesh and cross-legged, on the floor of the Farmhouse Gateway to the Underworld – at some point, which she couldn't quite remember, she must have sat down – the floorboards and grains and lumps of sand were rather tough, she thought, on her backside – and she was slowly chewing and deeply savoring a large piece of mushroom – but, though the world had righted itself, and stopped spinning, the house, while still swaying, had now also taken on a distinctly tipping or slanting appearance, as if it were an antique ocean liner slowly capsizing, like that ancient mythical luxury liner the *Titanic*, with the slanting decks – deckchairs tumbling, people losing their grip, sailors toppling over into the icy waters, and the members of the band, gamely bracing their legs to avoid plummeting into the icy dark waters, gaily playing "Near My God to Thee."

Miranda was now sitting cross-legged on the ceiling.

The law of gravity had been suspended.

This *was* rather strange.

Then the world was right side up again.

Miranda thought this was a truly interesting and entirely new perceptual experience. She was seeing certain details for the first time, like the fine way the ghouls' thin lips were etched and delineated, as if in watery white marble, fluid and petrified; then there was the translucent and even transparent quality of their skin and even their flesh; it was as if you could see right clear through it; and then there was the way their ears stood out, and up, like those of a donkey, and how sharply those ears were pointed; and then there were the long distinguished-looking nostrils that reminded her, ever so slightly, of a horse's nostrils; and then there were their long dirty claw-like nails at the end of slender, filthy, and surprisingly delicate-looking fingers.

"You will become one of them!" The voice echoed in her head, *"You will become one of them!"* The little prairie dog was looking at her with infinite disapproval. She giggled. He was such a *cute* little gopher!

While seeing the details of everything with a limpid clarity which was almost frightening, Miranda also realized that *everything* in the universe was *connected* to everything else, and that each grain of sand contained the whole *meaning* of every single object and ensemble of objects in the whole of everything – from a freshly painted wooden kitchen chair to a slowly rotating spiral galaxy such as Andromeda with its 200 billion stars – and each object, however humble, also contained the meaning of every event, too, past, present, and future; and that this universe, too, was but a grain of sand in a multiplicity of bubble-like universes, popping in and out of existence, which were infinite and unending in number and extent, and that there were adjacent universes, even now, merely a thin membrane of sensibility away from our universe, just a hair's breath away from this universe, but disguised behind the fragile thin vaporous veil of the present, hidden behind the buzzing manifold of reality, behind the luminous presence of the old house, the desert, and behind that illusory object called Miranda Hughes, and that, with the right attitude, with a total abandonment of the self, with a casting away of that fragile being that was called Miranda Hughes, with a disappearance of the filmy diaphanous ephemeral intermittent thing called *self*, all would become clear and she would slip easily to the other side, one of the many other sides, and be in an alternative universe, just a quantum leap away, in the small, itsy-bitsy tiny sense of the word "quantum," below the level of sub-atomic particles where it all became a slippery, porous latticework through which one could easily slip or fall. She felt herself getting very, very small, small enough to slip through the very fabric of being itself; and she felt herself getting very, very large, so that she saw all things, past, present, and future, with a single glance. She sat on Olympus. She strode the world like a colossus, seeing Elysium City, the soaring Dome the ethereal towers, the tailor-made atmosphere, the different status layers, one stacked upon the other, and then she saw it before it was Elysium City, but a place called Manhattan, with soaring steel and glass and stone towers, and traffic jams, and hot dog stands, and tickertape parades, and men in gray flannel suits, and a garment district, and Soho, with artists and beats and deadbeats, and then, suddenly, the island was as it had been before Europeans came, with woods and swamps and wetlands marsh grass, a few small Indian camps, smoke rising from campfires, a flight of ducks taking off, and two big rivers, and multiple little streams, and stony outcroppings, she saw an eagle circling around in a blue-blue sky, men in a canoe paddling down the Hudson River, and then, as she zoomed back in time, fifteen thousand years earlier, it was all right at the edge of a mile-high block of ice, the wind howled and the snow blew on the giant walls of ice, over a mile high that faced directly upon the ocean, and that weighed down the continent. Suddenly, she was somewhere else: she saw armies on the march, snow blistering around their wagons and horses and men with tall fur hats leaning into the icy blizzard – Was it Napoleon, retreating from Moscow, galloping desperately back to Paris? And she saw scenes from the Bubonic Plague IV – bodies lying in the streets and pustules turning black and bursting, as bodies, even the most beautiful of bodies, became masses of sores, whirling pestiferous maelstroms of blood and pus, and Nikki was standing, looking down at the bodies and saying, "This will happen again, but much, much worse," and then Miranda was alone, standing on a sandy beach, all alone, wearing a light cotton dress with horizontal blue and white stripes like a Russian sailor's T-shirt, which the breeze pressed against her body, and the sun was low in the sky, and the ocean looked calm and pure, with crisp little waves and ...

Come back! Come back! Oh, you are lost! Oh, she is lost!

... and she stepped out of that thin light dress and out of her underthings and barefoot and naked, she walked into the water, thinking, Oh, how warm from the dying sun the sand is, and how warm and pleasant and clear the water is, and she looked down and saw a flat sandy rough-edged lozenge of a thing floating flat on the sandy bottom, nibbling at her toes, and she realized it was a sole, a fish that had once been considered a very fine thing to eat, the nibbling was pleasantly ticklish, and she sighed in pleasure and looked up, towards the darkening setting sun, and out of the water, perhaps 10 or 20 meters from where she stood, huge tentacles, with giant suckers on them, rose up, and curled and coiled, and uncoiled, gleaming and dripping, in the sinking light of the sun, and she was not afraid for she knew that nothing, but nothing, could do her any harm ...

Come back! Come back! Oh, you are lost! Oh, she is lost!

She realized that she was standing not in the room in the farmhouse, but out on the veranda. *How did I get out here?*

The ghouls were also out on the veranda.

She had somehow taken off her prisoner's tunic; she was standing – she looked down at herself – naked, like a statue of silver, in the moonlight.

Come back! Come back! Oh, you are lost! Oh, she is lost!

The cool – it was still near 100 degrees Fahrenheit – the cool white light of the moon spilled over her shoulders, touching her arms and belly and breasts and legs, a caress like that of a cosmic lover from whom she had no secrets.

Oh, yearning!

Oh, Caliban!

She saw too that, on the floor of the porch, about three meters away, as she stood like a statue or an idol, above them, Mr. Deep and Ms. Moo were locked in an embrace, growling, whimpering, making love, on the silver-striped veranda floorboards – they were humping and drooling and thumping and growling, the female's bottom banging on the floor.

Bounce was crouched close by, drooling; he still had that rather large – well, "gigantic" was the word that occurred to Miranda – he had – he *still* had – that rather large erection; it looked like an over-sized glittering moon-lit chalk-white asparagus, sticking up between his crouching thighs; he was drooling – two continuous bubbly white ribbons cascading from the corners of his mouth; and he was rhythmically bobbing up and down, and growling in a low, sing-song, self-satisfied kind of way. He glanced at her, his pale blank eyes definitely taking her in, and he grinned, while still drooling, and continued bobbing up and down, with the two other mutants now entwined so closely it was difficult in the bright moonlight to tell their slick white hairless limbs apart or to know who was who or what was what. It was like an abstract sculpture in wet white marble.

Miranda thought that this was all very interesting and perhaps, aside from just sex, it was maybe some sort of religious ritual; and that she, just perhaps, was part of the ritual – it would have been useful to consult Kit Candy about this since Kit was an expert, certainly, on sex, and, with all her visits to the Religion Bazaar, she was almost certainly an expert on religion too. Feeling a sudden whirligig of vertigo, and a tingling sensation all over her skin, every single inch of it, she took a deep breath and – worrying that perhaps she had been transformed into a *ghoul* or a chimpanzee or some kind of Cloud Game reptile – she again looked down at herself.

"Come back! Come back! Oh, you are lost! Oh, she is lost!" cried the little Prairie Dog.

Nikki looked up from her drawing board, "Tread softly, Miranda, tread carefully!"

Oh, gosh! Miranda looked down at herself …

Whew, yes, she was still human.' Her golden skin – that mysterious permanent tan – certainly looked rather sculptural and white in the moonlight; but otherwise, she was recognizably herself, recognizably human: truly, an upper-class Cosmos, naked as the day she was hatched, of course, and lost out among the ghoul mutants in the Super Dust Bowl heart of the Dead Lands, what an adventure!

Feeling just a bit goddess-like, and rather prophetic, Miranda began to speak:

"So, you see, Bounce, I mean, maybe life is all a dream, like, you understand what I mean, that life is all a dream, and rounded by a sleep. You see what I mean, right?"

She looked over at Bounce; he was still bouncing, he seemed lost in a trance, but he glanced sideways at her. His fist went up and down, pumping. He was working hard. His erection glistened silver in the moonlight.

"Things are either very big or very small, Bounce, I hope you are listening, Bounce, I hope you understand, for I think I am conveying to you some very profound and unique thoughts, here, dear Bounce, thoughts about the universe, Bounce, and about our place in it."

Miranda sighed. True insight lay far beyond the capacity of language to express what one needed and yearned to express. Words were inadequate; words were merely little puffs of sound, lost on the wind, or inert marks on paper, or ephemeral bits on a screen or in the aether of the Cloud, nothing, really, and not connected to anything really, not connected for instance to these grains of sand. "And, as for people, if you peel a person like an onion, what do you get, Bounce? There's really nothing at the center, Bounce. Do people ever say what they truly mean, Bounce? *Can* they really say what they mean? Do people have a *center*, Bounce, or are they merely things you can peel – one layer off at a time – like an onion – without ever finding a core? Perhaps self-knowledge is like an endless striptease, with nothing to show for it all, in the end. Oh, Bounce, all of this is so hopeless!"

She frowned. The really annoying thing about these inexpressible epiphany things is – they are made to be shared; they are like love, they cannot exist alone; they yearn to be shared; they *demand* to be shared, but they *cannot* be shared; this was extremely frustrating – it created a yearning like love, like desire, like ... a sort of mystical horniness ... hmm ...

"Epiphanies are private, Bounce; they are prisoners in the dungeon of the self, Bounce. The Soul is a cage, Bounce; but ecstasy is infinite, Bounce. I hope you see what I'm getting at here, Bounce."

Bounce groaned and worked even harder, pumping with his fist. Drool splashed from his lips.

"Reality is unreal. Right now, in this present moment, we – you and I – are also thousands or millions of years ago, Bounce. Look at those stars, Bounce! They are light-years away! That star there, *Sirius*, and that one there, *Betelgeuse* is its name, why the images we have of them, now, left those stars 8.6 light-years and 640 light-years ago, so when we look at the sky, we are looking at *time*, we are looking at the *past*. That's Sirius 8.6 years ago; and that's Betelgeuse 640 years ago, when Europeans had just discovered America and the printing press was less than 100 years old. Just think of that! That's what those little lights are, Bounce: they are the past, the distant past."

"Grrrhhh."

"We are here, in this our local present time, Bounce, but we are also with the stars, dozens, hundreds, and thousands of years ago, or we are with the Andromeda galaxy 2.5 million light-years away, a smudge in the sky, as it was 2,500,000 years ago, from the time before humans were human."

"Grrrhhh," Bounce's closed drool-soaked fist was going up and down, up and down, faster and faster; his blank oblong eyes stared at the stars.

"Yes, with the more distant stars and galaxies, it's the really ancient past. We are gazing back towards the beginning of time. I mean, like, it's *awesome*!"

"Grrrhhh," Bounce drooled; his eyes rolled.

"And we are all part of it, Bounce, I mean you and I and Mr. Deep and Ms. Daisy, we are part of this vast togetherness which is this universe of ours, every pebble and galaxy and supernova, every quark and molecule and blossoming flower and wiggly earthworm and stumbling bumblebee, every minuscule fragment of DNA, all the same thing, all part of the vastness, the unfolding ground of Being, of Absolute Being." Miranda sighed at the beauty of it all. Her thoughts were traveling on wings – faster than light.

"Grrrhhh," Bounce glanced sideways, amorously, his pale oblong ghoul eyes rolling, his dripping tongue hanging out, and he kept at it, bounce, bounce, and bounce.

Part of Miranda's mind was still as clear as a crystal and that part of her mind was asking itself whether Bounce ever actually *came* and had a real orgasm with ejaculation and the whole messy shebang or whether he just continued to exist in an eternal ecstasy of anticipation and desire and yearning, forever approaching the goalposts but never getting there, perhaps a mystical consummation devoutly to be desired, though, in her experience, it would be, she suspected, truly frustrating. On the other hand, such eternal or prolonged excitement was a bit like the exaltation of the ego – and of control – in the mystical exercise of Tantric Sex – Kit had lent Miranda a text on the subject – or transcendence and the abolition of the ego, in pure pre-orgasmic concentration and …

While part of her mind was focussed on wondering what *being Bounce* as he was presently constituted would *feel* like, another part of her mind was focussed like a laser beam on a grain of sand: she was staring single-mindedly at that particular grain of sand, sparkling in the moonlight; it seemed to contain all things bright and beautiful, and even all things grotesque and hideous, that grain of sand. Indeed, for an instant, it *was* the universe, every single bit of the universe and all eternity in a grain of sand. So it was and the poet had said it:

To see a world in a grain of sand,
And Heaven in a wildflower,
Hold infinity in the palm of your hand,
And eternity in an hour.

"The atoms of which we are made, Bounce," Miranda was sitting on the porch steps now – though she didn't remember how she got there or when she sat down. She wrapped her arms around her shins, laid her chin on her knees, and stared at the endless, undulating desert of sand, a frozen ocean, crystal clear under the moon and stars. "Why those very atoms were born in the stars, the helium, the oxygen, and the carbon, and the iron and zinc! You and I are starlight, Bounce, that's what we are! We are made of atoms forged in the furnace of stars and supernovae! We are brothers and sisters in starlight, Bounce!" Miranda sighed. It was all so beautiful!

"Grrrhhh!" Bounce, who was sitting on the steps beside her – she didn't remember him sitting down either – and he was growling and slurping. He was still working hard on his eternal erection.

Miranda looked around. Daisy and Deep were still on the veranda and still thumping, thumping, thumping! What love! What an image of domestic bliss! They seemed tireless, locked together, two sides of the same coin, their glossy white hairless pelts gleaming, the two-backed beast – was that a phrase from Ancient Elizabethan Times? Oh, yes, that particular image and perception went back at least to the 16th century! *The beast of two backs!* Oh, it was divine, the vital force that drove every seed and every tubular growth, every probing tentacular phallic bud searching for sunlight, every root pushing aside the earth, and every poetic thought of desire hatched in utterly stoned, drunk, and feverish, or totally sublime, and stone-cold sober brains! There were so many roads to paradise!

"Grrrhhh," Bounce drooled, dreamily, coils of white creamy goo. He rolled his eyes. He was totally concentrated, busy tending to his erection.

Miranda, arms wrapped around her shins, thought the erection looked interesting; she wondered what it felt like. If only she could ask Bounce, she might learn so many things about ghoulish and masculine sensibilities and inner feelings as embodied in the erect ...

She looked up ... Something, somebody was coming ...

"Hey!"

Bang! Bang!

Wham!

"Hey, hey, there!"

Bang, bang, bang, rat-tat-tat!

She heard shouts. At least it seemed like shouts, and a ripple of gunfire. The voice was familiar: *Caliban!*

Daisy and Deep were still humping blissfully, groaning and growling and slobbering, oblivious of any new developments. But Bounce looked up.

Miranda jumped to her feet and, followed by Bounce, she ran to the bend in the veranda, at the corner of the house, just in time to see someone – a human-like shape – vertical and on two legs, running towards the farmhouse.

It was Caliban!

Wow!

Her heart leaped. She shouted, "Caliban! Here, over here!"

Bounce was standing beside her. He danced up and down, his erection bopping back and forth like a high-stemmed daffodil in a whiplash desert wind, which was interesting, Miranda thought. He growled happily. He seemed elated, in a sort of celebratory mood. Maybe life was usually boring for these ghouls, with no thoughts to keep them amused, except remorse and loss and yearning, staring at a Bible they could no longer read or understand and at a photograph that reminded them – perhaps – of what and who they once were – and sex, she supposed, which must be, in their state, a godsend. She caught a flashing mental glimpse of Bounce crouched on his haunches, munching on somebody's tibia. Yes, they were cannibals too, alas. She had forgotten that. She chased the image and thought away.

Caliban came running, galloping, swerving, jumping. He swung his AK around towards the ghoul and Miranda, instantly reading his intentions, shouted, "No!"

And she stepped in front of Bounce.

Caliban threw the AK up over his shoulder and came zipping up to the porch, and skidded to a stop, throwing up a small wave of sand.

"You escaped!" Miranda couldn't resist. She threw her arms around him; oh, he smelled so good, so sweaty and dusty and sunburnt and manly!

"I shot the evil pirate zombie buzzard with this," he held out the AK, "and the cursèd aerial corsair blew apart into flecks of blood and flesh and zombie innards, and tidbits of ripped canvas sail from its leathery wings and dropped me like a stone – from not too high up which was good – and I landed on a bank of sand, which knocked the wind out of me, and I was attacked again – claws and fangs and flapping wings every which way – I scrambled in the dark over the sand, fighting them off, and finally I hid in a greasy old oil barrel, I think it was, anyway some rotund rusty old metal artifact from the old times of smoking chimneys and liquid fire, and the other zombie air pirates, who had begun to fight among themselves, didn't see me, so they just circled around cawing and squawking in that odd obscene offshore lingo they have, and then they perched and waited, and, I crouched in the oil drum, and I waited until daylight – then they were gone – and then I went in search of you, my Princess, but I found the drainage pipe empty and saw where you had clawed and dug your way out and I saw a few traces and clues – I am an expert desert tracker after all, Princess – this sand is my bounding main – and I followed the ruins of the old southern Imperial US road hoping you'd be here. The old melted asphalt track guided you. I knew it would."

Bounce crouched at Caliban's feet and sniffed at him.

"Did he harm you?" Caliban looked down at the naked ghoul, and prodded Bounce with the muzzle of the AK.

"No, he didn't touch me."

"And your tunic – what happened to your prisoner's tunic? You look like you have been cast up, naked, a golden mermaid, slathered in silver moonlight, orphaned, bereft, helpless, on the dry sands of the bounding main."

Miranda blinked at him, fluttered her eyelashes. Oh, how he spoke, when inspiration struck him! Like a true Renaissance Pirate and King of the Jungle!

Caliban swallowed. "Yes, I mean, what happened to your sailor's tunic? I mean, your prison shift, your slave rags. You are naked, Princess."

"Yes, I am naked," Miranda blushed, looked down, upon her nakedness, and upon Caliban's loincloth, then she looked up, into his eyes, and grinned.

Caliban looked pleased in a weird way – his eyes flicked back and forth over her body. His eyes were very bright – but it was clear he was, like, embarrassed, or so it seemed to Miranda; it was, like, you know, like, he didn't know where to look, like, his big dark eyes were zipping here, like, and then zipping there, then zipping back again, finally, like, coming to rest on her eyes in which golden stars and galaxies were exploding, roiling in infinite depths. He cleared his throat, and managed, "What happened?"

"I divested myself of my humanity. I rid myself of obstacles. I tore off all vestiges of Civilization. I tossed them away; it was more comfortable – freer, like I had returned to paradise."

Caliban stared, eyebrows raised, puzzled – trying to understand

Miranda put the palm of her hand, comforting, reassuring, up to the side of his face. "You see, Prince Caliban, I ate a mushroom. I partook of the sacred bubbly flesh of the transcendent carnal night. And then, suddenly, I was having mystical visions and talking philosophy, metaphysics and mysticism I do believe, with Bounce here. I wanted to remove all obstacles between myself, my body, my mind, and Absolute Being – and the grain of sand, and the farthest smudge of distant galaxies, of course."

"You ate a mushroom?"

"Yes."

"You mean you ate the sacred schizophrenic glowing watery mushroom that only the Great High Priest is allowed to eat? And you discussed philosophy and metaphysics with this ghoul?"

Gazing at Caliban, her hand still pressed against his cheek, Miranda bit her lip. She looked down. "I guess so. I mean, I don't know. It was more mysticism than philosophy. I mean, I didn't go into any conceptual depths. I mean, we didn't discuss Plato or Aristotle's categories or Kant and the categorical imperative or Wittgenstein and showing the fly how to get out of the bottle or Karl Marx, or Karl Popper and the falsifiability criterion, or Isaac Newton, or anything like that."

Caliban rolled his eyes.

Miranda swallowed, looked up, blinked as submissively as she could, "I hope I didn't break any taboos."

"By the Spirit of Dolly," Caliban whispered, he moved his hand along Miranda's shoulder, ran it up to her slender neck; he stroked the fine muscles, the vulnerable jugular, "Thou art a Princess!"

"Remember, dear, dear Master Caliban – I'm not from around here, I'm suffering, I guess, from culture shock or culture disorientation – or something. I probably need counseling."

"Counseling – what is that, dear Princess, dear Slave?"

Miranda put her hand on Caliban's, "I mean, being cast upon an alien foreign shore, among dashing pirates and jungle apes, and pagan priests and ghoul-like mutants with erections. It's confusing. I was hungry and thirsty. Those mushroom things are very juicy! And they do glow! Boy, do they glow!" Her eyes shone even brighter – more golden stars exploded, if such a thing were possible. It was as if her eyes were a gateway to something vast and immeasurable – a whole universe. She licked her lips. "Besides, I think this experience, with the mushrooms I mean, gave me some very useful mystical insights into the basic structure of the universe, down to the sub-quantum level, quarks and dark matter, and so on, and up to the ultimate frontiers of time and space, curving space, and straight-out, flattened space, backward and forwards spacetime, expanding, accelerating, or infinite and standing still spacetime, and I obtained sideways or lateral insights, too, definitely outside the usual perceptual-conceptual toolbox, insights into the multiverse of which our universe is but a small, insignificant, and perhaps imaginary figment."

Caliban smiled. His teeth sparkled, "This is not pirate, or mermaid or princess or slave-girl talk, Miranda. I don't understand a word you are saying," he gently pushed her tousled blond-platinum hair away from her eyes, looked into the cool blue-green depths, imploding still with stars, and pressed his lips against hers.

"Well, it's ..."

"It's not Tarzan talk either." Caliban drew back and looked quite stern; he was clearly not at home in metaphysical flights of fancy; it gave Miranda a definite thrill to see his thick dark arched eyebrows so angry and perplexed, his god-like tanned cheeks, with just a shadow of five o'clock, flushed with, hmm, with anger, with desire, with ...

"It's difficult to explain," she gave him a quick peck and her brightest smile, "For a while there I soared far beyond the limits of human – or mutant – understanding, including, clearly, my own."

"Hmmm, so the Princess admits to some limits."

"Indeed, she does, dear, dear Master, dear Prince: That which cannot be said, had best remain in silence or unsaid. I believe some philosopher said as much once."

"And a wise philosopher he was too."

"I wonder if he ate mushrooms. Some people say William Shakespeare ate mushrooms or smoked hashish. I really have not made up my mind on that question."

Caliban leaned over and kissed her again, sealing her lips, for just an instant's reprieve from girlish philosophic chatter. He too was fascinated by the Bard, but now was not the time for such alluring dissertations. In love and lust, silence is golden. They were silent, for a moment, eye-to-eye. Looking into Miranda's eyes, Caliban felt he was verily looking into the gates of eternity, into green pastures and sunny uplands, slowly rotating golden galaxies, a sensual apotheosis, physical and spiritual unity, male and female together, blissful possibilities he had never imagined, entry into a whole new life – Cosmos, Imperial, American, bucolic, paradisiacal life, a soaring speculative life – of which he knew nothing. His heart flew skywards.

For that long moment, for just a few seconds, before all hell broke loose, their lips locked them together, in lofty, erotic, philosophic silence.

Miranda, remembering the story of Heloise and Abelard, nibbled just a bit, then she let the tip of her tongue explore; this was fine, very fine, even better than talking. She was extra glad she had taken those intense kissing lessons from Kit.

Bounce, still crouching, hopped up and down.

"Mmmm," said Miranda, as the kiss lasted.

"Mmmm," said Caliban.

"So, now – what do we do," said Miranda, drawing away and running her hands down Caliban's smooth muscular chest – great pectorals, great abs, she was thinking, Boy, what a Tarzan! Boy, she could really show him off in the 68th-floor gym in the Sublime Seventh Tower – Gillian Ho would turn green with envy and Katherine Hong would have a fit! (What an uncharitable thought, Miranda Hughes – you should be ashamed of yourself!) "By the way, there are two other ghouls at the other end of the veranda, performing a sacred rite."

"A sacred rite?" said Caliban, putting one hand on his hip, just above the jaunty knot of his loincloth.

"Sex," Miranda breathed, moving close, closer, closest to Caliban, "Endless iterated copulation, over and over and over … They can't seem to stop."

"Oh," Caliban looked embarrassed. He couldn't help looking down at Miranda's breasts, pressed against him; she drew back, giving him a better look, and evaluating him – *her* man.

"Oh," Caliban said again. Miranda's body, tanned, slender, full-breasted, supple and elastic, seemed, indeed, *was* a thing of perfection – beyond dreaming.

"Yes, anthropologically speaking it is very interesting," Miranda said, reining in a rising tide of desire, and sobering up, briefly, "They have lost almost all their human qualities but they still have, I think, a deep religious sense. So, they are doing their duty, under the full moon, full copulation, classic missionary position, lots of grunting and groaning and drooling. They still have a full libido – in fact, their libido overflows. It is a veritable cornucopia. I think once they were very religious – there is a family photo of them when they were human. I'm almost 100 percent certain it is them. And they yearn after soulfulness. There is a King James Bible inside – marked at Revelation 16."

"*The vials of wrath,*" said Caliban. The right corner of his loincloth was slung particularly low on his hip, "If they worship the Bible and if they are making love as a sacred rite, then, I think – my dearest Princess Slave – that maybe they've confused religions, though I don't know much about ancient sacred beliefs."

"Yes, you're right. They may be indulging in an excessively ecumenical or syncretic approach, which, ah, might not be approved by the respective ecclesiastical or rabbinical authorities, or the mullahs, or ah …"

Miranda suddenly frowned. She sensed something – it was something dangerous, and it was coming towards them, through the air. "Caliban, my Prince," she said, "I think …"

"Yes, they are coming," said Caliban. He motioned at the cloudless night sky. The moon was full. The stars were brilliant. The Milky Way sprawled across the midriff of the heavens like a sparkling royal road, and up above, the constellations Orion and Taurus and Aries brightly shone, unblinking, upon the earth, a scattering of lights from infinitely differing epochs.

"The zombie-bats – they're coming, again?"

"Yes, the zombie-bats are coming," Caliban said.

Bounce squealed.

A giant black bat-like creature zoomed out of the clear starry night sky. It slammed into the veranda railing, just two feet from Caliban. It turned and looked up with its wicked luminous eyes, its giant wings beating up a cloud of dust and sand. It lunged over the railing.

Caliban and Miranda and Bounce were already running. They zipped around the corner of the veranda, Miranda, as she whizzed by, shouting, "Get up! Get up! Run! Run!" to the copulating pair; Mr. Deep and Ms. Daisy were a white smudge, a mingled blur, in the moonlight

Another Zombie Bat slammed down on the veranda just where the front door led to safety. Miranda and Caliban and Bounce vaulted the railing, leaping off the veranda. They swerved around this new cannibal bat, as it swirled towards them. Its frothing, fang-toothed jaws and claws slashed at them, clumsily, its wings entangled with the columns of the porch.

The foul and odious thing screeched. Foam flew from its snout. It lunged for Daisy and Deep. They were disentangling themselves and rolling over and over in a spray of glowing spittle and bodily fluids. With the giant jaws taking stabs just behind them, whamming into the floorboards, the two ghouls crawled and scrambled on all fours, stumbling out of the creature's reach – just in time.

With Caliban and Miranda in the lead, they all raced around the next corner of the house. Miranda shouted, "If we get inside, there is a cave entrance in the basement!" She skidded in the sand. Another Bat came thundering down. The beating of its wings blinded her, darkening the starlit sky. Its eyes stared straight into her eyes. Its wings enclosed her, wrapping her in a fetid leathery, tomb-like, dusty stench. She was held in the embrace of death. It was about to hurl her down to Hell, its huge poisonous jaws headed straight for her face, as, trapped by its wings, she kicked, swerved, ducked, dodged, fell backward, freed herself, and crawled, desperately crawled, fingernails grasping the warped and cracked floorboards. There was an explosion. She turned. The bat's face flew apart into a myriad splatter of bone, gristle, blood.

Miranda tore herself free from the flailing, winged cadaver, as it flopped down on top of her. She jumped up. She ran and kept running – whipping around another corner of the house. Caliban was sprinting beside her, the ancient AK, its barrel smoking, in his hand.

"Thank you, my Prince! You saved me!"

Miranda glanced back. Right behind them came Bounce and Daisy and Mr. Deep. But Mr. Deep was in trouble. He was stiff in the joints. Caliban, sensing what Miranda was thinking, swung around and just as a giant bat silhouette swooped down on the staggering bearded old ghoul, who was scrambling desperately on hands and knees …

Wham, wham, wham! The AK spurted fire.

The Winged zombie-bat exploded just above Mr. Deep, its gristle and guts flying in a dark spray, splashing the veranda and the side of the house.

Caliban, still running, turned, pulled the trigger again and another bat silhouette exploded in dark fragments – spraying out in the sky, against the stars, bits and pieces fluttering over the moon like a quick-flying flock of blackbirds.

Mr. Deep squealed and staggered forward.

"They are too many of them, Princess," Caliban shouted, "but if we can get inside, then maybe, maybe …"

Then as they leaped back onto the veranda and came around the corner of the house they were greeted by more wheeling screeching bats. The night sky was dark with flailing wings, extended claws, gleaming yellow eyes. Some of them had already landed on the porch. The way to the door and windows was blocked.

"Oh, gosh and golly," Miranda skidded to a stop. They were trapped. They were pinned against the wall of the house – there was nowhere to go!

The bats zoomed in. They were clearly working together. One bat on each side, they landed on the veranda, spread their wings, and other bats clustering outside, fluttering over the sand, just beyond the veranda railing.

Miranda backed against the wall – right in front of her was an opening in the veranda railing, and steps leading down to the sand. She felt strong, but paralyzed. Maybe she could tear these bats apart. As the Leader-President said, "You never know what you can do until you try!"

Yes, you are a Cosmos, Miranda! You are one of the Elite, Masters of the Universe – act, and act now! *Offense is the best defense*, so said the President-Leader.

Hail, hail, all hail!

The closest was a Man-Bat; his evil snout was really long; the monstrous thing shuffled forward towards Miranda, its jaws, splashing rabid foam, opening and shutting, clack, clack, clack …

Miranda glanced at Caliban. He was jamming a new magazine into the AK. The ghouls were cowering between her and Caliban.

If only I had a sword or a machete, Miranda thought, I could slash and fight, but I've only got my bare hands. She looked at her hands – dirty but still well-manicured, highly civilized Cosmos human hands.

This was not a Cloud Game.

Hail, hail, all hail!

Hail, hail, all hail!

This was not home. This was not Elysium. Miranda could not just flick a switch or sigh and get up and run down the hall to Nikki in her studio and receive wisdom and comfort, a kiss and a caress and a bright loving smile, and maybe a cup of tea and a long earnest and funny "chat." No, this was …

The giant bat plunged through the opening in the railing.

Miranda ducked, bent double, gritted her teeth – *A Cosmos never hesitates! You fight now or never* – and charged headlong, wham, butting into the Bat's belly, a soft gooey place that smelt like a sewer and made her want to vomit; the bat staggered back and fell off the veranda, getting all tangled up in its wings.

But there were two more giants behind it. This was never going to end!

Miranda was on hands and knees on the sand now. A huge bat took a swipe at her; the claws slashed whirring though the air, just missing her face. The glance was of pure hatred. She understood: It wanted to rip her face off!

No way, José! Miranda ducked, weaved, grabbed for the Bat's foot claws, seized its ankles, and heaved with all her strength. The Bat toppled over, staggered back, and righted itself, its claws sweeping down again – Miranda was trapped between two bats, talons and fangs swooping down on her – *slash, slash, and slash!* She kicked, squirmed, and crawled on hands and knees, galloping, zipping under them – they were clumsy bloody things! They took sweeping razor-sharp swipes at her face and back.

"This thing is jammed," she heard Caliban cry out, and she glimpsed that he was slashing now with the machete. "Damn, the AK never jams!"

The battle could not last long. Miranda glanced around. Could they smash their way through the wall of the house and gallop down into the caves. The cave entrance would be too narrow for the zombie-bats. She managed to kick away the two bats that were clawing at her. She leaped free and back onto the veranda. The three ghouls cowered against the clapboard wall, shaking and trembling, their blank droopy eyes wide in terror.

"Don't worry, guys," she said, "Everything will be okay!" But she knew it was a lie.

Caliban was slashing with his scimitar – longer, easier, and more deadly. He handed his machete to Miranda. And she began slashing, stabbing, dodging …

Evil eyes, foaming fangs, and flapping wings and foul-smelling bodies, as if risen uncleansed from the grave, were all around, closing in.

There were just too many of them.

We are trapped, Miranda realized, and we are going to die! Was such a thing possible? Even for a Cosmos, even for her? Death, eternal death?

CHAPTER 9 – THE RISING SUN

V turned her face to the rising sun.

The sandstorm was over. The days seemed brief. Soon the sun would sink down in the sky; in a few hours it would touch the flat golden horizon; night would come, and with it the creatures of the night – the winged messengers of death.

The endless desert beckoned. Somewhere, out there, amid the dunes and stony outcroppings, were the two survivors of the plane crash, Nikki and Miranda Hughes, then, farther on, was the ultimate objective, the graveyard of the hybrids – Camp Terminus.

The wreckage of Presidential Super Liner 47 – with its crowd of mutants – and the friendly beaver – had been left far behind.

Kat drove the bike. V, who had returned to her human incarnation, leaned against Kat's back and clung to her waist. Kat had noticed that when V changed from reptile back to human – an instantaneous morph – a ripple of white fire zipping along V's body – the morph had burnt off the zombie-bat blood. When the human version of V emerged, naked, from the luminous blur, she was cleansed, and entirely without the streaks of treacle-like blood.

"Where did the blood go?" Kat had asked.

"I think the energy of the change operates at a quantum level," V was slipping into her skintight armored black catsuit, "It disintegrates material that is too close and expulses it; otherwise the body, when it re-composes, might absorb alien material. I think that's how it works anyway." V pulled on her boots. The buckles automatically closed and locked, "And that's why I strip – if I have time – when I morph. Otherwise, the clothes are evaporated – being a quick-change hybrid is hard on a girl's wardrobe."

"Right," Kat flashed a grim smile. The wardrobe problems of a hybrid! Damn! Soon those would be her problems!

Now, hours later, they were headed toward night – toward danger.

Kat gunned the bike, the wheels spun in the dust. Then they were rocketing over the rough stony ground, bouncing, leaping, almost capsizing, righting themselves. They raced onwards, ever onwards, swirling up to the top of dunes and small hills, then down into ancient gullies and ravines. Decades of drought had stripped the land of cover and of life, and revealed its skeleton – sand dunes, and ribs and escarpments of rock.

Towards dusk, another sandstorm overtook them, an onrushing dark yellow and gold tsunami of dust. Kat stopped the bike, and both of them got off; Kat turned to V. "That looks ugly. What now?"

"We'd better find shelter. Otherwise, when night comes we may find ourselves out in the open when we're faced with another attack by the zombie-bats."

"I heard lots of religious thoughts when they were dying," said Kat.

"Yes," V said, pushing up her wraparounds. "Me too."

Kat stared at V. V looked worried. If V was worried, Kat figured she should be worried. Then V smiled. Kat – thinking, *whew!* – smiled back.

The sand whipped and stormed around them, but visibility was not yet zero.

"Should we find shelter now?"

"Yes, shelter – absolutely – good idea."

Kat got back on the bike. V slid on behind her and Kat gunned the bike and braving the sand blizzard they bounced across what had once been fields.

Kat maneuvered through the whirling maelstrom of sand, wondering at her own ability to sense unseen obstacles and shifts in the slope and shape of the land.

For an hour they went on, blindly.

Then, suddenly, just as the sandstorm was dropping down, and as the sun was about to set, and the air was clearing, a high stretch of thick coiled barbed wire surged up in front of them, blocking their way – it was half-buried in sand, but at least six feet high, and twisted and broken, a dangerous obstacle. Kat swerved and skidded to a stop, spewing up sand.

"I'll cut a way through," V jumped off, pulled the laser gun out of her backpack. She fired. The wires flared up in sparks and curled away. Rivulets of sand skittered between V's boots. She fired again and again, and the laser sliced through the wire. The path was clear.

"It'll soon be dusk. I'm going to morph," said V, beginning to strip; she folded her catsuit neatly, and slid it into her backpack.

"The better to fight those things?" Kat was sitting astride the bike, still the very image of the impeccable, consummate Centurion warrior.

"Yes, the better to fight those things." V dissolved into a shimmering blur. The human V was gone. The hybrid stood there, an alien creature, blinking at Kat.

V slid on the backpack and banderole. "To think these were fields," she said, sliding onto the bike, behind Kat.

"The breadbasket and cotton belt of America," Kat glanced over her shoulder, "and now ..."

"Now it's the Sahara," said V. She leaned against Kat and wrapped her arms – and claws – around Kat's waist.

Kat gently accelerated, as silently as possible – better, if possible, in the darkness, not to draw the attention of those *things*; if it could be avoided.

They drove through the broken barrier of barbed wire and on and on and on. The sandstorm was long past. The sun went down; the stars came out; the moon was bright in the crystal-clear sky.

So far there were no zombie-bats. The bike raced across the silver-tinted dunes and valleys and plains.

They came to a paved country highway; it was drifted over with ribbons and dunes of sand. They followed the highway hoping it would lead to some sort of shelter, perhaps an old silo or a barn or a village or town, maybe an abandoned shopping mall or mega-church.

Then in the distance, they saw a tall thin farmhouse that leaned slightly to one side. V mused: it looked like the classic haunted house. Of course, it might be sheltering zombie-bats or other monsters of the desert, but ...

"Maybe we stay there?" Kat shouted over her shoulder.

"Better than nothing," said V. They skidded to a stop about half a mile away.

"It looks like a haunted house in some old horror film," said Kat.

"Yes," said V, "and, Kat, we are not alone."

Zombie bats were zooming out of the sky, circling the old homestead, dive-bombing, gathering, squawking, screaming ... The front of the old house was black with the creatures, fighting, clustering ... dozens of them ...

"They're gathering for a feast," Kat said.

"Or they're already feasting," said V, her fangs gleaming grimly in the moonlight.

PART THREE – ORIGINAL SIN

CHAPTER 10 – APOTHEOSIS

The Great High Priest rubbed his hands. It had been a sublime night! It had been a time of transformation, the greatest day perhaps in the whole of the Religion of Dolly. The sacrifice had been sublime! Truly sublime! And the lessons learned would mark them all, every single mutant, he was absolutely sure of it, as long as they lived. It had been an apotheosis – an angel and a god had come among them! He turned to brother Toad, "Are all things ready for tonight's feast?"

"Yes, all is ready, Great High Priest!"

"Wonderful! The Goddess must find that all is to her taste!"

"The Goddess will be pleased, I am sure," said Brother Toad.

"Then you can begin," said the Great High Priest.

As he hurried away on his hallowed mission, Brother Toad's mind flashed back to what had happened, many hours before, and how, in a few minutes, the whole world had been turned upside down. Even before the revelation, Brother Toad had had an intimation of *something, something immense and mysterious and sacred*. But even he had had no idea what lay before them.

It was a revolution and a revelation – truly.

And it all happened so fast!

The Cosmos woman, the whore, the mother of the other Cosmos whore, had just been dragged out of the crowd which in its frenzy had tried to tear her limb-from-limb and which had scratched and clawed and bit at her, while she fought desperately to free herself.

The bear-warriors had plunged bravely – heroically – into the fray to rescue the Cosmos Sacrifice, pushing, shoving, and using their truncheons left and right. And finally, fighting all the way, they managed to seize her and to get her free of the surging crowd.

They brought the Cosmos Sacrifice back up to the altar, and there she was, as she stood before them, in all her naked Cosmos splendor, as she had already been stripped when the crowd burst through and grabbed her.

"This is strange," croaked Brother Toad. He stroked his mottled toad-like quadruple jowls with his webbed three-fingered hand, his bulging yellow eyes blinking at the Cosmos and dark bubbles forming on his thick lips.

"What is strange, Brother Toad?" Brother Rat blinked at him.

"This Cosmos shows no marks, no scratches, and no bruises from the man-handling, from the crowd. I saw Big Bear Hans dig his claw into the flesh of her shoulder when he was trying to free her from the furies, and, yet, look! Gaze upon the Cosmos, Brother Rat, and tell me – what do you see?"

"Nothing, oh Brother Toad, Dolly be blessed, I see nothing but the per-fection of Cosmos; like immaculate white marble in the Parthenon is this Cosmos! The Cosmos consume everything – all vitamins, all wealth, all life-forms, all cheeses, so their healing powers are great. It is most natural she should be immaculate and without mortal stain."

"Indeed. Such is the evil power and beauty of Cosmos."

Nikki was standing totally naked and absolutely still, waiting for the next step in what was obviously to be her destiny.

The little girl with the curved horns asked, "Ready?"

"Ready, she is ready," said Brother Toad, still feeling puzzled. He was not entirely satisfied with Brother Rat's explanation. The healing of the Cosmos had been too quick; or perhaps the claws and bites and blows had, from the beginning, made no impression on the Cosmos, leaving no mark whatsoever, which, if that were true, was equally strange, most passing strange.

"Yes, I am ready," said Nikki. She stepped up to the free-standing ceremon-ial white bathtub with lions feet and the rusty showerhead, and accepting the little girl's offered hand, she stepped into the bathtub, and placed herself under the showerhead.

"Ready?" said the little girl.

"Yes, I am ready," said Nikki.

The little girl pulled the chain, and out spurted rusty cold water.

"Brrrhhh!"

Nikki shivered. But at least it was water; it cascaded down, carrying away the last vestiges of Scav's amorous excesses, the clots and splotches and seed of his romantic yearnings.

Nikki tilted her face upwards; the water splashed over her forehead, and down her cheeks; she ran her fingers through her hair; the water was rusty, but it felt good. She really wondered at the hatred all these souls felt for the Cosmos. The Cosmos, isolated in their domed cities and protected by conscripted and mercenary armies and by the elite Centurions, had absolutely no idea of the intensity of the hatred that existed outside the Cosmos elite and against the Cosmos elite! When the uprising came, if it ever did, it would be devastating!

The water dribbled to a stop. Nikki blinked away the last drops. She glanced at the little girl. The little girl bowed – light reflecting off her two curved horns – and indicated that Nikki should step out of the shower.

So, still dripping wet, Nikki stepped out of the shower. She shook her head and ran her fingers through her hair and glanced at the priests: *Now, what's next?*

"Dolly's will be done!"

"Now the oil."

"Ah! The oil! The crowd cried out, "Ah, the oil!"

A vat of oil was rolled forward on a rickety wooden trolley by two of the large bear-like creatures. They huffed and puffed. The crowd screamed.

"The Oil!"

"The Oil!"

"Extra Virgin First Cold Pressing Esso Engine Oil," one of the priests chanted in warbling hierophantic falsetto, lifting up a bucket of the stuff, and, in a much deeper voice, he again intoned, "Extra Virgin First Cold Pressing Esso Engine Oil."

"Extra Virgin First Cold Pressing Esso Engine Oil!" the vast choir of mutants responded, "Extra Virgin First Cold Pressing Esso Engine Oil!"

"Lube!"

"Lube!"

Nikki wondered how long she should put up with this. Rusty water was one thing; filthy engine oil was quite another. But reason must prevail. Patience was a virtue. She had to gain time for Miranda and for Caliban. So far, they must have survived and escaped; there had been no triumphal return with Miranda and Caliban in chains. She would just have to grin and bear it. Besides it would be difficult – maybe impossible – to fight her way out of the crowded cave, and then she would have to catch up with Caliban and Miranda – and first she would have to find them – in the desert landscape up there. Those bear guardians looked pretty strong and pretty fast.

"Lube her!"

"Lube her!"

"We will make her one of us!"

"We will make her one of us!"

"We anoint the sacrifice, now," said the rat-faced priest. "Here! The flesh of Cosmos is to be consumed. It will make us whole; all the qualities of Cosmos are to be assumed in our flesh, to make us whole and to give us, inwardly, the beauty of Cosmos! Eat now cf Cosmos, for this is her essence, her flesh, her blood."

One of the assistant priests – the large, obese, toad-like fellow – waddled to the fore. From a brass tripod stand, he lifted up a large red metal coffee pot with an elegantly curved spout. He lifted the pot high above his head and showed it to the crowd. They went wild, cheering, jumping for joy. Banners, flags, and effigies danced above the throng. The air throbbed with feverish hysteria. With great solemnity, the priest dipped the pot into the vat of engine oil – letting it drink its fill. The crowd let out one long, wave-like sigh of anticipation and awe. He lifted the pot into the air. He hesitated. The suspense was palpable. The crowd grew quiet.

He held the spout right over Nikki.

Nikki looked up; then she looked down. Suspense and silence reigned. Nikki felt the heavy breathing of Brother Toad. Yes, she thought, that was his name and title, *Brother Toad.* He was visibly overcome by emotion, laboring under an excess of feeling. She caught his eye. And, still holding the coffee pot aloft he caught her eye; his bulging toad-like eyes were impassive, but not unfriendly. She allowed her glance to be amiable, almost a smile, an understanding, forgiving smile. Time stopped. She heard water dripping somewhere. She heard a cough. She heard the shuffling of limbs and feet. She heard far away shouts – a fishmonger somewhere in the main cavern shouting, "Gob fish, Gob fish! Gob fish!" She heard a breeze whispering, ever so gently, murmuring, making its way through the vaulted cathedral. Tall candles flickered, thin high flames swayed, curls of waxy brown smoke, rising in the luminous foggy dimness, bent darkly. Succumbing to the breeze; chains rattled, barely making a whisper; cables swayed; one of the overhead iron walkways groaned.

Brother Toad began to tilt the pot.

Oh, oh, Nikki gritted her teeth; her muscles tensed.

From the crowd there came a massive intake of breath.

Glug, glug, glug! Thick black machine oil spurted from the spout – it splashed over Nikki's shoulders, gushed over her head, streaming into her hair.

The crowd gasped. A few isolated shouts and screams of ecstasy rang out. Then, like a giant's damp breath, an immense wave of emotion swept through the cavernous cathedral. The shouts and voices merged into a crescendo of rhythmic beating cries, thunderous waves of a rising sea. The great stone walls echoed. The lofty ogive vaults sent back the cry. The metal stands and walkways rattled and trembled. The banners and flags flapped and fluttered. Pandemonium exploded. Worshipers fell on their knees, flung themselves down, prostrate, leaped into the air. Some danced in whirling circles, dervishes possessed by the Spirit of Dolly.

"Hallelujah!!"

"Hallelujah!!"

"We will make you one of us!"

"We will make you one of us!"

"Consume Flesh of Cosmos!!"

"Consume Flesh of Cosmos!!"

Brother Toad had refilled the pot and once again he lifted it and once again he poured forth the holy engine oil. It came down in thick sticky streams, black as night, thick as molasses.

Nikki shivered. She looked down, bowing her head, and she took a deep breath, hoping against hope that this would all end soon, that …

The Great High Priest – a tall, bent figure – had been standing on the altar rostrum, right under the giant effigy of Dolly Crucified. He neighed once, and shuffled closer, coming down a few of the holy dais steps. He seemed to be staring at Nikki; another gush of oil splashed down over her shoulders, it tickled, a particularly cool dribble snaking its way down her spine, all the way. It gave her the shivers. It was like being violated by a wet, lazy, disorganized, lascivious octopus.

Blinking through the veil of sacred engine oil, which was sticking in bright black bead-like drops to her eyelashes, Nikki suddenly realized that the Great High Priest was blind. Was this good or bad?

He stood there, looking puzzled. He was an impressive figure, perhaps seven feet tall. He had the face of a goat – with two horns – and, yes, he was probably – Nikki thought – a descendant of the victims of the "Caprine Caper," an experiment carried out in the 2090s, when goat DNA and Human

DNA were mixed together, fused into a new recipe, in an effort to create super-hardy, mountain climbing warriors, who could live at high altitudes with little oxygen, much ultra-violet radiation, and on a cheap diet of thistles and thorns.

As the oil was running, in thick glutinous waves, over her shoulders and belly and dribbling in long stringy lines down her legs, Nikki glanced around. All these creatures were victims in a sense, victims of the Faustian ambitions of humans – the unlimited god-like ambition of humans and Cosmos to change and transform and possess and subdue the world and all the living beings in it.

Yes, the Great High Priest was blind.

His nostrils twitched. He smelt something; he suspected something. He was visibly uneasy. He shuffled forward. Then he stopped. He stood still. Again he looked puzzled, standing alone, high up, next to the giant cross which soared far above him, bearing the huge carved effigy of Dolly the Goddess, which stared down, mournfully, gazing from her great dark eyes on the clamorous multitude.

Nikki was entirely coated in black oil. She blinked to keep it out of her eyes. It stung. She stared at the Great High Priest: *Perhaps he senses something. If he does sense something, then all of this will be much easier.*

The central fire, just under the great altar, roared. Sparks flamed up, small yellow stars, flying up in front of Dolly's great innocent sheep eyes, and reflecting in the depths of those eyes, making it seem that, within the statue of Dolly, the Spirit of Dolly was indeed alive.

"Oh, Holy Spirit of Dolly," an individual ran up, threw himself down, prostrating himself; then he got up and ran back, disappearing into the crowd.

The metal crucifixion cross was prepared.

Branding irons were all lined up in a row and glowing red hot.

The meat cleavers hung sparkling from hooks.

The assistant priests, all wearing gloves, seized Nikki's by now slippery and slick arms and legs. She was lifted and guided up to the metal cross that was tilted back at a forty-five-degree-angle. She was lowered onto it. She didn't resist.

The crowd cheered. Banners waved. Drums and cymbals began a rhythmic beat, a slow-building crescendo – *boom, boom, boom, clash, clash, clash!*

All the priests' eyes stared at her, curiously, but flat, dead to any empathy. After all, she was a Cosmos, the Enemy, the Exploiter and Devastator and Consumer of the Whole World and all the Creatures in it.

Nikki's hands and her feet were bound to the trunk and beam of the cross – thick sharp-edged metal bands that locked in place, dug into her ankles and wrists. Thus the Cosmos Sacrifice was locked to the cross.

The racket spread, overwhelming – cries, shouts, screams, chants, songs, the ringing of bells and the beating of drums.

The crowd, circling the altar, was exalting, wild – chanting, linking limbs, swaying in unison, stirring the smoky dark air of the immense cavern. The tension rose. Nikki faced her apotheosis and death.

She was lifted up, as the Cross was raised; in a second or two, it would be locked in the vertical position.

The flames flared high.

The crowd shouted, "Hallelujah!"

The sacrifice was about to be consummated!

From the back of the crowd, clinging to a metal support column, Scav looked up at his idol, dripping black oil, crucified on the cross, about to be burned to a crisp. He blinked. He closed his eyes. He was surprised at himself. He didn't want to watch. He didn't want to see this. He did not want to see the Cosmos die.

Still wearing Nikki's jacket, Muffle Shimmer Lazar, Nikki's first mutant fan, pulled the lapel closer, fingered the soft light material. She felt a chill, as if of ice – a feeling which she had never felt before. Ice coated her body, ate into her bones. She shivered and pressed her delicate seven-fingered hand to the lapel of the sacred jacket. The crowd around her was wild, but she and her friends were subdued, terrified, huddled at the far end of the cathedral, next to the entrance. Shimmer could not believe that the goddess-like Cosmos Nikki was going to be sacrificed. It was not possible that such a creature – who had been so kind, so brave, who had faced humiliation with such dignity and fortitude – could die! In female mutant garble talk, having three forked tongues made English pronunciation difficult, Shimmer whispered to her friends, "This is a tragedy, this cannot be happening!" Her friends blinked at her, balefully, and shook their heads, "But it is already happening," said Tracy Plume, the super-pretty bird girl, whose body was covered in a rainbow of feathers. "And we cannot stop it. No one can stop it." And then they wailed, a melodic, soaring, lamentation. But their wailing and keening was buried, lost in the overwhelming celebratory clamor of the crowd.

Ida Bones – her black and gold striped fur glittering in the torch-light – her slender, tufted tail wagging impatiently – and her prehensile claws sparkling as they clutched at outcroppings and protuberances – had climbed up onto the statue of the Prophet Aldous Huxley to get a better view. She was perched there, peeking over the Prophet's shoulder. She trembled with eagerness to see the sacrifice consummated. It was marvelous that such a thing should come to pass. Now, the Cosmos was naked. Now, she was covered in shimmering oil. Now, the Cosmos bowed her head, humbled and humiliated as every Cosmos must be humbled and humiliated. Now, Ida watched eagerly as the Cosmos was lifted onto the metal cross, and then as the cross was levered upwards, so that the Cosmos, manacled, naked, and helpless on the vertical cross, hung above the crowd. In a few moments, the Cosmos would be set alight. She would go up in flames and scream as her soul was torn from her body. She would go up in a column of waxy black smoke. Then the flames would be doused and the flesh carved up and the boiled blood or what was left of it would be drunk, and the skull would be placed in its own little niche and … Ida sighed. Ecstasy overwhelmed her. She knew that thirst for vengeance was evil and that delight in revenge was unworthy of her, but she could not resist. When she was a teenager, she had seen her mother and father and sisters hunted and shot down by Cosmos warriors and by mercenaries who worked for the Cosmos. All of her family vaporised – in the space of a few seconds. Everybody she loved – gone! She only survived because she had fallen down and had been splashed all over with her mother's blood and she lay quiet, pretending to be dead. The Cosmos officer came, and putting the toe of his highly polished boot under the small of her back, he had lifted her up, her back arching, arms and legs dangling, and, suspecting she was alive, he drew his pistol, and was about to shoot her, when someone called to him. He shifted his boot. She fell back. He turned away and was gone … When hours later she struggled to her feet, she was alone under the moon in a welter of blood, smoking gore, and charred bones, all that was left of everyone she had ever loved in the whole wide world. And now, upon the cross and gleaming wet with oil was the Cosmos. The Cosmos soon would die in horrible agony, and then the Cosmos would be eaten, and drunk, and "She would become one of us." Ida's tail swung back and forth, impatient for that final moment – painful and ecstatic, and wicked and good.

Outside the great iron door, the sandstorm raged, and battered and rattled everything that was loose. The bear guards paced just inside the door. They could hear, faintly and in the far distance, the roar of the crowd, the exaltation. One of the guards turned to another and whispered, "It is too bad, brother." "Yes," replied the other, "It is too bad – she and her daughter were good Cosmos, if there can be such a thing as a good Cosmos."

"And the daughter has escaped."

"Yes, she has escaped with Caliban my friend, my brother."

"Caliban was a brother to us all."

"True, true, he was, but now …"

"Now they are both, the beautiful young Cosmos and Caliban, they are both undoubtedly dead."

"Yes," the bear listened for a moment to the horrible roaring of the sandstorm, the great door trembled, "Yes, yes, they must be dead by now."

"We will make you one of us!"

"We will make you one of us!"

The cross was almost erect.

So, this is what it is like. Nikki gazed at the crowd. She had admired many crucifixion scenes in various museums and churches around the world; and she had wondered at the idea of Jesus of Nazareth, sacrificing himself so that the sins of God's creatures, of his creations, could be redeemed. A God, who sacrifices Himself, in the person of his Son, it was a sublime myth. That the scapegoat and outcast, the lowest of the low, should also be the Highest of the high, the Creator himself, or His son, was paradoxical, and hence transcendent, as a myth, truly sublime. And she had often wondered what Jesus thought in those last few seconds … She had always wondered if he had really cried out …

"My God, My God, why hast Thou forsaken me?"

Nikki's eyes were wide open, lined with black as if with kohl, blinking away the tar-like oil that had turned her face into a mask. Her teeth were bright, lined with black. She smiled.

Teetering, tottering, the vertical cross – with Nikki hanging from it – was wheeled into place, just behind the roaring sacrificial fire.

Within moments, Nikki would be set ablaze.

The gasoline, a rare and sacred commodity, was at hand, in jerry cans, ready to be sprayed over the sacrifice.

Then the torch would be applied.

And then …

Around the fire, the mutants danced, some of them seemingly human, some of them mixtures of creatures, experiments gone wrong, or gone right, who knows what they were meant to be.

Nikki's body, gleaming with black oil in the rippling light of the fire, was as dark as anthracite. In dancing, golden squiggles, every curve of her body gleamed with light from the flaring torches hanging from the walls, flaming sentinels, far above the crowd.

Already Nikki was an icon.

She was no longer human, no longer Cosmos.

She was an image, beyond life, beyond death.

The air echoed with screaming voices, waving claws, hands, paws, tentacles, with hideous faces, weird contorted and wonderful bodies, wearing multi-colored masks, hairy and smooth faces, animal faces, and half-human faces, all looking up, all swaying at once. There was even what looked like a few humans among them.

"We will make you one of us!"

"We will make you one of us!"

"Oh, Our Dolly, Who Art in Embryo!"

"Oh, Our Dolly from which all New Life sprang."

"Our Dolly, from whom Eternal Life forever springeth!"

"The Lamb is the Godhead and the Spirit which floats upon the waters," bellowed the Great High Priest, still high above them all, on his platform; but turning, for the first time, towards Nikki. He wore a sheep's head on his own head in guise of a miter. He had a long beard and saturnine caprine features and Nikki reckoned that, yes, certainly, he would have an acute sense of smell.

"Oh, Holy," the crowd changed, "Oh, Dolly, Most Holy Dolly!"

"Here now for sacrifice we offer up this Cosmos to Thee, Oh Dolly, Oh Goddess," the Great High Priest intoned in a high whinnying goatish voice. He approached the altar.

"Oh, Unique and Holy One, and now shall she burn," chanted the assistant priests. Only Brother Toad stared at her and licked his fat lips; Nikki felt the confusion – and even empathy – in his gaze. He suspects, she murmured, he suspects something.

"The Cosmos will Burn!" cried the crowd.

"The Cosmos will Burn!"

"We will make her one of us!"

"We will make her one of us!"

The crowd – feathered creatures, porcine giants, and bear-warriors, naked humanoids with wildly painted or tattooed or patterned bodies and faces, cow's heads on human bodies – everybody shouted and hollered.

Nikki blinked out over the throng. Poles with effigies of mutants were hoisted high, bobbed wildly, danced above the crowd – they represented a woman with an owl's face and feathers, a pig-man, a dog-faced man, a beautiful Renaissance Madonna, decked out with antlers; and there was a serpent man, and a cavorting satyr with high-kicking hooves and curved horns, and a neighing, rearing centaur, puffing steam from his human nostrils ...

All this swirled up in the thick, clammy smoke, the burgeoning, thickening, glowing haze, heavy with the sweet-spicy smell of burnt dung, of human and animal sweat, of phosphorescent mushrooms, and of torches hanging from the stone walls, and large free-standing candelabra, braziers of fire everywhere glowing red. The place, thought Nikki, was a tinder-box. Colored banners bounced up and down: "Burn the Cosmos!" "The Cosmos is the Devil!" "All Hail, Dolly!"

The chanting continued.

"Eat! Eat! Eat!"

"Feast! Feast! Feast!"

The priest's assistants gathered around Nikki, looking up upon her eagerly like bloodthirsty surgeons about to perform a particularly cruel operation; she imagined them getting out their scalpels, cleavers, needles, blow-torches, machetes, and bottles of acid.

One of the priests had a skeletal face, where bones showed through; his eyes were deep caverns. Another was covered in hair; with big droopy sad eyes, rather like a depressed Spaniel. Brother Toad stood slightly apart, near the Great High Priest.

Now, with the cross erect and close to the fire, the sharp-edged metal straps were cutting deeper into Nikki's flesh at the wrists and ankles.

She blinked away the pain. She bit her lip, twisted it.

She switched the pain off. She thought about other things. She thought about Miranda and Caliban and how they might be faring. And she watched the Great High Priest closely.

He was tall and gaunt and he swirled around in his priestly robes, a long cotton canary yellow housedress, with over-sized red polka dots, and a purple terrycloth belt, loosely tied, around the robe, both relics from a supermarket fire sale, 90% discount, from some by-gone age; it had probably – Nikki speculated – been looted from one of the burned-out, sand-buried towns and cities and malls of the Great Southern Desert about the time the First Universal Church of the Revealed Wal-Mart and Shopping Religion was torn apart by internecine strife and theological civil war.

Nikki sighed. The mechanisms of history were fascinating. How the commercial brands of the past had become the mystical icons of today; how pure happenstance had created forms of faith; how the flotsam and jetsam of the industrial and post-industrial ages had been abandoned on the shores of the desert, and, weirdly, had become fodder for idolatry. She really would like to discuss some of these thoughts with somebody – before she died.

If she died, which, in truth, she did *not* intend to do.

The ceremonial torches approached, carried by acolytes and seminarians, burning aloft, columns of smoke rising up, and flattening thickening into swirling clouds trapped by the high arched ceiling of the cathedral.

The moment was imminent.

The rat-like priest lifted the jerry can of gasoline.

Nikki tensed every muscle in her body – perhaps, just perhaps, she could break her bonds or, slippery with oil, she might be able to squeeze out of them. It was a hope, to cling to. She began to test the metal bonds – they were thin, and rather brittle. One was loose, perhaps loose enough. She took a deep breath. And now I prepare myself, and now I …

The Great High Priest came down the steps, closer to her and to the cross. It was the first time he had approached Nikki.

"Is this a truly beauteous Cosmos?" He blinked his clouded, whey-colored, unseeing eyes towards her, where she was hanging suspended a few feet away, naked, oil dripping like thick black blood from her fingers and toes.

His assistants gathered around. "She is most beauteous, High Priest," they chanted, "She is most apt for sacrifice, the very image and paragon of Cosmos perfection, now oiled up, lacquered, revved, fully lubed, Esso Extra Sacred Virgin, and ready to go."

"I have not heard her voice," said the Great High Priest, "I have not heard her sobs, her cries, her supplications, her prayers to Prada, to Apple, to Big Mac, to Armani, to Gucci, and to the Cola Deities."

"No, Great High Priest, she is not sobbing, crying, or supplicating. She is silent."

"Silent?"

"Yes, Great High Priest, she is silent."

"What? Silent? Why silent? How silent? She does not beg? All humans – even the mighty Cosmos – beg for their lives. In spite of their pride, Cosmos are spoiled and corrupt. In their final moments, they always pray to the Idolatrous gods that consume the world!"

"She is silent, oh Great High Priest. She has not mentioned shopping."

"She has not mentioned shopping?"

"No, Great High Priest, not a word!"

"Is she tied to the cross?"

"Yes, Oh, High Priest, she is bound tightly to the cross and the cross is risen up; the metal cuts her limbs – yet she begs not."

"And she laments not?"

"No, she laments not, oh, Great High Priest, she seems to be smiling."

"Smiling?"

"Yes, Oh Great High Priest, she is smiling."

"Let her speak!" The Great High Priest came closer. "Speak, Oh, Cosmos, Speak!"

Nikki cleared her throat. "What do you wish me to say, Oh, Great High Priest?"

"I wish to hear the music of your voice, Oh, Cosmos of Little Faith, Oh, Pagan idolater! Oh, Babylonian Shopping Mall Whore! Oh, ransacking shopping bag Jezebel Slut who has filled the fair air with dark magic CO_2, with sulfides, and turned the soil to dust and emptied the nitrogen-soaked seas of life!"

"Oh, Great High Priest, I can whistle a number of tunes, patriotic and romantic, and lamentations can I recite, I can sing in several tongues, I can recite poetry and the sacred texts of a dozen religions, and commercial jingles from several centuries, Oh, Great High Priest."

"Your voice, your voice is alluring and magical, Oh, Cosmos," said the Great High Priest.

"Thank you, Oh Great High Priest, you are most kind."

"I must come close to you."

He came close. He sniffed and sniffed again. He laid his long hairy waxen fingers with the uncut and dirty pointed yellow nails on her skin, on her thigh, her belly, and, pushing away the film of black oil, he stroked her skin up to her ribcage to the undercurve of her breasts. "Ah! Ah! Ah!" he sighed. He bent over, bringing his wide goatish nostrils close to her breasts; he sniffed, and he sniffed again. The nostrils quivered. Each nostril glowed with glassy mucus; each dark lozenge-like nostril quivered, separately, richly. His blind cataract-clouded eyes grew round and large. The corners of his thin-lipped mouth turned down. His four-fingered hand trembled and went to his fore-head, knocking his goatish miter awry, pushing one of his longish furry ears sideways.

"Oh, horror," the Great High Priest cried out, "Oh, sacrilege!"

"What?" the assistant priests surged back in fear. Brother Toad's eyes caught Nikki's eyes. Blinking away the oil, she smiled her oil-rimmed smile. Brother Toad's eyes went wider.

"Oh Sacrilege, Oh, Horror!" screaming – almost as if in pain, the Great High Priest started back. He dropped his scepter, which bounced and rolled away, tumbling off the Crucifixion Platform. He fell to his knees before the Cross of Nikki. "Oh, Goddess, forgive us, forgive me, let us worship!"

All of the assistant priests retreated further back, their mouths open in shock. "Oh, High Priest, what is it, what will become of us, what is it that thou fearest, what is it that thou thinkest!?"

"Fools, fools, fools," the Great High Priest rose to his feet and raged blindly around the altar, he was losing his balance. Any minute now and he would fall into the flames. "Free her, free her now! Fools free her! See that no harm comes to her. Oh, this is terrible! Oh, we are doomed! We are lost! Her wrath will be horrendous to see!"

"Oh!" a huge frightened cry went up from the crowd. Then silence fell, with a few cries, here and there, of "Oh, woe is me", or "Oh, the end is nigh!" The hush spread like terror. All the faces looked up, towards the Great High Priest, and towards the living effigy hanging on the cross.

The priests rushed forward; in confusion, the torches retreated; the jerry cans brimming with gasoline were tucked away. The priests tried to crank the cross down; the mechanism jammed. The cross was stuck at a thirty-degree angle. Smoke began to rise. The gears groaned and clicked. Nikki wiggled a bit, and helped by the oil, and by Brother Toad who loosened the ankle straps, she climbed down from the inclined cross and stood before the Great High Priest. The Great High Priest fell to his knees.

"So – you are that which was promised, oh, Goddess!"

"Please don't kneel, Great High Priest."

"Oh, Goddess!"

"I would help you up myself, but I am covered in sacred Esso True Lube Extra Virgin Engine Oil and I would not want to profane your sacred raiment or your exalted person with my oily hands. Perhaps Brother Toad will help you."

Brother Toad rushed forward and helped the Great High Priest, who was trembling in fear and adoration, to his feet.

"Oh, Goddess, thank you, you should not pollute your hands with my filthy mutant flesh, Oh, Goddess …"

The Great High Priest's extra sensitive foxy and goatish olfactory sense had clearly caught the DNA markers. It was a miracle and it almost – but not quite – made Nikki believe in magic. Well, really, as she well knew, it was science that saved her, and science that had built her – science.

"Will you now take your revenge on us?" the Great High Priest bowed his head.

"Revenge? Revenge? Goddess, Oh, Goddess," the assistants cried out, and they shrank back, fear and awe imprinted on every muzzle and snout and trunk and face.

"Goddess?" shouted half the crowd.

"Cosmos?" shouted half the crowd.

"She is no Cosmos," the Great High Priest thundered, turning to the crowd, hammering his wand on the floor, his polka dot dress swirling around him, the ends of the terrycloth belt swinging wildly, "She is No Cosmos!"

"No?"

"She is not a Cosmos; she is not human," he shouted, his voice taking on a raucous roaring quality, echoing from the distant walls and vaulted roofs, "She is the original!" His voice echoed from the vast ceilings of the cave.

"The Original!" the crowd hollered.

"The Original!" the roof echoed.

The Great High Priest took a deep breath, his furry chest – brown with a white stripe billowed out (visible now as his priestly robe had fallen half away), "She is the founder," he roared, "She is a Synthetic Individual, she is a SIN, she is the Original SIN!"

"SIN, SIN, ORIGINAL SIN!" The crowd took up the cry.

"SIN, SIN, ORIGINAL SIN!"

"Oh, oh, oh!" The assistants fell to their knees, gazing up in fear and adoration: their sacrifice, whom they had stripped of her raiment, covered in oil, and strapped to the cross, was the Highest of the High, a *Synthetic Individual*, and she was the Original Synthetic Individual, or SIN, the source of all mutant life, the original human replicant created in a laboratory in the mythical times, long ago before the Fall, and next in holiness to Dolly Herself!

And now she stood before them, exposed, alone, stripped naked, covered in oil, defiled, abased, insulted! Oh, woe, woe, woe! What would become of them?

The marks left by the metal that had been twisted into her flesh had already faded and her flesh and skin under the dripping black oil – and it was really thick and dripping down her belly and legs and like blood, running off the tips of her fingers.

"Oh, Goddess," the Great High Priest was again on his knees, quivering at her feet, "Are you angry, oh, Goddess, will you bring your wrath down upon us?"

"No, no," said Nikki, "Don't worry, Great High Priest. I'm not feeling like wrath right now, not at the moment."

"Oh, Goddess," they all moaned. Such magnanimity from a divinity was not to be expected – perhaps she was about to play a divine trick. The divinities were known to be sneaky and capricious.

"But I wouldn't mind a quick shower and getting my clothes back."

"Yes, yes, yes. Bathe the goddess! Clothe the goddess!"

"But we must have a sacrifice," the rat-faced monk was visibly furious, "We must sacrifice to our Goddess Original Sin – and she would do!" He pointed his rat-like finger at the little shower girl who had been standing patiently by the sacred bathtub watching events unfold. "The girl Tara whose beauty is exceptional would make an ideal sacrifice!!"

"Yes, yes, yes," the crowd shouted, "Sacrifice! Sacrifice! Sacrifice!"

Nikki raised a hand.

The crowd fell silent.

"No sacrifice," said Nikki, "No sacrifice, not now. And, as for the girl," Nikki, still blinking through the veil of oil, turned to her, "As for the girl, I want her! With your worships' permission, she shall be mine!"

"She is yours, oh, Sin, Oh, Original Sin!"

"She is yours!"

"Just as my personal assistant, you understand!" Nikki put an imperious tone into her voice. If she were too magnanimous, they would take her for a wimp. Gods may be many things, but they are not wimps. Her divinity would suffer. She roared, "The girl is mine!"

"Yes, yes, yes, Goddess, she is yours!"

"Now my little girl, WHO BELONGS TO ME, will help me shower! Is everyone agreed?"

"We agree, we agree!" The shout thundered from all corners of the vaulted cathedral. Priests and monks cowered, backed way, this Goddess had a way of looking at you that would brook no refusal, no nonsense; it was clear she was divine.

The little shower girl – her skin golden and the two tan-colored horns on her forehead gleaming in the flaming smoky light – stepped forward, bowed graciously from the waist, and said, without the slightest trace of fear or trembling, "Goddess, oh, Sublime Original SIN, if you will deign to step under the shower, I shall provide. And there is a bucket of soap at the side, right there."

"Thank you, my darling. And what is your name?" Nikki stepped into the bathtub, positioned herself under the sacred showerhead; the little girl pulled the chain. Rusty water gushed down over Nikki.

"My name is Tara Capricorn, oh, Goddess."

"I'm very pleased to meet you, Tara Capricorn," said Nikki, blinking out from between the cascade of oil and water.

"I am honored, Goddess." Tara Capricorn smiled shyly and covered her mouth because her smile was just too wide to show to the Goddess. She handed Nikki a small bottle which said, "Golden Lemon Shampoo," and she began to sponge Nikki's back with a soap-soaked ancient cloth – embossed with "Hilton Hotels" – a religious relic from "The Time Before."

It took a while and almost the whole bucket of soap – and the whole bottle of shampoo – to get rid of the oil, but soon Nikki was sparkling clean, a gleaming ivory statue.

"Do you feel better now, Goddess?" Tara Capricorn asked as, standing on a stool, she toweled Nikki's hair.

"I feel much better, thank you, Tara Capricorn."

"Oh, Goddess, oh, Sublime Original SIN, step forth." The Great High Priest was trembling in fear and ecstasy.

"Oh, Goddess," the crowd breathed as one; they were all bent down – in awe in the presence of a Goddess, the true ancestor, the founder of the race of mutants and genetically engineered species, the Original SIN!

"SIN, SIN, ORIGINAL SIN!"

"SIN, SIN, ORIGINAL SIN!"

A few minutes later, attended by Tara Capricorn and clothed once again in her own clothes – pleated skirt, dark stockings, black patent leather high-heels, and moiré silk T-shirt, all of which had been kept under priestly custody as sacred relics and thus were in surprisingly pristine shape considering the generally murky, muddy, filthy, smoky nature of the place – but not the jacket which she had given to Muffle Shimmer Lazar – Nikki was conferring in private with the High Priest and his Counsellors.

With Tara Capricorn sitting to her right, she told them her history – leaving out some bits, but basically, she told them how she had come into existence as the first complete post-human. She told them how she had been designed in the mythical city of Paris, France – yes, it really did exist – and she lived there many decades ago, in fact, more than 150 years ago; how her human parents, who were both scientists – or, in theological terms, *Makers of Magic* – and who had no children of their own, decided, when they saw her beginning to take shape, to give her a name – so she became Marie-Josée Duval – and a history, and to give her the illusion that she too was human – implanting borrowed and manufactured memories in her brain – so that for the first year of her life, she thought she was 19 years old, and that she had already lived 19 years, but then with the help of a fellow university student, a human girlfriend, Valda Weber, she had discovered that she was not human, that her history was a fabrication, that her very personality and all her memories were constructs, created by her father from fragments of a dead girl's life. At first, she was totally disoriented and wanted to die. But Valda said, "You are you. It doesn't matter if you were born yesterday. I was your friend yesterday, I'm your friend now; and I will be your friend tomorrow."

"That woman was a human saint," said the Great High Priest, "a Cosmos Saint, one of the just."

"Yes, she was," said Goddess Nikki, smiling, thinking that her bohemian Existentialist Left-Bank Gauloise-smoking, turtleneck-wearing friend Valda would have been very amused to discover that she had been elevated to sainthood. Nikki could see the ironic smirk – and at the image a shaft of painful tenderness and nostalgia shot through her heart.

"I confronted my mother and father."

"Oh."

"I was angry. I said some terrible things."

"Oh."

"Unforgivable things, really; I blush when I think back on it."

"But, oh Goddess, you were right ..."

"I'm not sure. I wanted to be loved."

"Loved?"

"Yes, loved. And they did love me and they accepted me – and they had given me life and consciousness and freedom – and so I loved them and accepted them and I began to live as a 'person' and I had many adventures; but, when others grew old, I did not grow old, and so I continued, and now here I am. I am come among you."

"Oh, Goddess, and we are thankful you have come to us!"

Nikki was pleased that the Great High Priest understood what she was, what she had been. She felt herself in most respects fully human; but it often happened that she was glad that she wasn't human – but a copy, in fact, and, inadvertently almost, accidentally, by a serendipitous accident in her father's laboratory, she was the prototype of something entirely new – and gifted with a life and with powers that were far beyond human.

"I consider myself a Daughter of Dolly," she said, which was true, cloning had opened the door to replicants, and knowledge of DNA had opened the door to the bottom-up total redesign of life forms.

"Oh, Daughter of Dolly, thou art most High," the Great High Priest said, and his counselors all agreed.

In fact, they were awed by the beauty and frankness of the Goddess who, in the guise of the most beauteous of Cosmos, and though a divinity, spoke to them most gently and in the wisest of terms.

"Now, Great High Priest, at the first light of dawn we shall go to search for Caliban and Miranda," Nikki said.

"Yes, oh, Goddess," said the Great High Priest, "But what am I to do with Caliban – though he saved your daughter, he betrayed his trust. I loved him – I love him – like a son, and ..." A tear ran down the Great High Priest's cheek.

"Dear Great High Priest, please forgive Caliban. His love for you is without limit; but I was the one who ordered him – at the risk of his own life – to rescue Miranda and to escape with her. They will return, Oh, Great High Priest. Have no fear!"

The Great High Priest trembled; tears flooded his eyes. "You are most gracious, Oh, Goddess, you have poured balm into my heart. Of course, I shall forgive Caliban; there is, now, nothing to forgive. If anything, it is he who must forgive me!"

Nikki told the Great High Priest that she liked the cave where she and Miranda had been held prisoner; it was very comfortable, and it had running water. So, if there were no objections, and there were none, that was where she, as Goddess Nikki, would set up her Court and Headquarters.

So soon Nikki was installed for the night in the same cave where she and Miranda had spent several delightful days and nights pretending to be in a spa. But now the barred gates were not locked, though bear-warriors stood on guard, they were now there as an Honor Guard to protect the Goddess. As for Tara Capricorn, it turned out she was an orphan – which was why she had been given the sacred role in the ceremonies – so Tara Capricorn came to stay the night with Nikki in the cave and to attend to the Goddess as her very special personal servant.

Then, just as they were about to settle down, with the Honor Guard outside the cave, the sirens went off.

The flying monsters of the night had penetrated the cave.

"These are the monsters you told me about," Nikki said to one of the bear warriors – a member of her Honor Guard – who came running.

"Yes, they are, Goddess, the winged monsters."

"Then, come! Let us defeat them. And you, Tara, stay here with this guard. And keep the bars of the cave shut!"

"Yes, Goddess," said Tara Capricorn, and bowed her head. "Good luck, Goddess," she added, boldly.

"I've always liked a good fight," said Nikki, rubbing her hands, smiling at Tara, and then glancing at the bear.

"Yes, Goddess, me too," said the Bear Hans.

"Good," said Nikki, "And victory will be ours!"

Leaving Tara Capricorn in the safety of the cave, Goddess Nikki and her warriors ran to meet a new challenge – the monsters of the night.

CHAPTER 11 – LAST STAND

So now we are going to die, Miranda thought. Well, then we shall die, we shall die making a stand worthy of Cosmos!

Hail Cosmos!

Hail Cosmos!

Hail, all Hail!

We who are about to die, we salute you, our Leader, our President!

Hail, all Hail!

And so the battle roared on and on, with Miranda and Caliban fighting against impossible odds.

Then, in the midst of the slashing and struggling, bat blood spurting all over the place, in the midst of the squealing and screaming of the bats, and the whimpering of the ghouls, and the slash, slash of Caliban's scimitar, and amid Caliban's cursing a string of beautifully colorful pirate curses from centuries past, Miranda, who had discovered she was really rather good, excellent in fact, at wielding a machete, heard something: the roar of a motor – *A motor*, my God, what was that? It couldn't be a *motor!*

A motor?

Where did a *motor* come from?

A motor?

The two bats that were attacking her, had almost cornered her, and were poised for a simultaneous final strike, squawked and turned. For a second, they were distracted. Still holding the machete in her left hand, Miranda leaped, and with her right fist, she punched one of them in the side of the head, as hard as she could, without even thinking.

The Bat's head exploded in a cloud of foul bloody goo. It was a slow-motion cloud, or so it seemed to Miranda as her adrenalin raced and as time slowed down, it was a lazy, air-borne ballet of feathers and fur and blood and bone and a sort of green-gray goo gush or geyser – which must be brains, or whatever stood in for brains, in those creatures – and, at the same time, it seemed to Miranda that she was standing outside herself, a real *out-of-body experience*: She could see herself, floating in slow motion, rising into the air, rising slowly, legs kicking out, punching, her arm stretched out, going full-throttle, and her right hand, a perfect expression of Cosmos battle training, fingers curling into a fist, ramming into the Bat's head, exploding it, and all the bits and pieces that, a mere second before, had been the bat's head, but were now just a cloud of muck floating away. It was like she had all the time in the world. *What a punch! How did I do that?*

She swung around, and, again without thinking, smashed her fist sideways into the neck of the other zombie-bat, and she heard, again as if in slow-motion, a crunching, cracking sound. The zombie-bat's head flipped back; its neck was broken! *Is this possible? Am I this strong?*

The Bats – dozens of them, and more were gathering – fell back, and behind them, sparkling brightly and coming over the bright moonlit dunes, was a weird and incredible sight.

Miranda backed up, pressing against Caliban. If she had to die, she wanted to die in his arms. The three ghouls clustered close. Bounce clung to her legs. For Miranda, now, the ghouls were family.

Caliban stopped slashing with his scimitar – He had just sliced through the wings of one of the bats, leaving it screeching and roiling back in a bloody blur of flapping, of flailing broken stumps of wings and arms and legs.

"Look," said Miranda. Caliban turned towards the roar of the motor. He had never heard such a sound in his life.

He tried again with the AK. Miraculously, it freed up, the lock moved smoothly. He flipped a new magazine out of his backpack. The magazine slid smoothly and clicked into place. Now, he was ready for anything. He put his arm around Miranda, his muddied, naked, bloodied, beautiful prisoner, and Queen and Princess.

"Look," she pointed.

It – the thing – *the motor* – was fast approaching.

"Yes," he said; he had to clear his throat. Miranda had that effect on him. She somehow threw his voice out of kilter, made it all clogged and foggy. It was part of the spell she cast. Was his princess a witch?

Bounce whimpered, clung tighter to Miranda's legs. Deep and Daisy, trembled, crouching, pressed against Caliban.

The zombie-bats had fallen back. Their screeching stopped. Now, dark hulks, they clustered under the moon, diabolic wings folded, waiting, fluttering, scheming. Others, even more of them, newcomers, circled in the sky, casting sharp black moon shadows on the silver sand.

In the sudden silence, in the moonlight, Miranda could see it. It was a vision, descended from heaven: a powerful ultra-tech Cosmos Centurion motorbike was roaring over the sand, a dark outline of Imperial Cosmos Power.

"Oh, Cosmos, this is the greatness of Cosmos, Oh Caliban, Oh, Cosmos – Forever Cosmos!" Miranda cried out, "It's a Centurion Bike – the Imperial United States Centurion Guard! They have come to save us!"

Hail, Hail, all Hail!

The bike bounced and leaped over the waves of sand; it was heading straight for them, straight for the farmhouse.

Hail, Hail, all Hail!

As the bike raced towards them – Miranda started back. Gosh! It's coming right at us; it's going to kill us!

Suddenly, at the very last instant, the bike swerved, skidded in a spray of sand, and bounced right up next to the veranda – and came skidding to a full stop, only three feet away, a mere meter, at the foot of the steps.

Off leaped two warriors, and, oh, my God …

Miranda and Caliban's hearts, in unison, skipped a beat.

The two warriors were …

"Oh, my God," said Miranda.

Caliban swung his AK, taking aim at the two.

"Don't shoot," whispered Miranda, as she took Caliban by the arm, and leaned into him.

'Friends," said the first of the warriors, raising a gloved hand, the palm flat towards them. Yes, she was an Imperial Centurion, part of the elite, the defenders of Cosmos; she had the uniform, the weapons, the wraparounds, the boots, the defiant stance, her legs slightly apart, arms tensed and ready for action. The breast and belly plate of her uniform had been shattered, her skin was visible, muscular, glowing black and rippled with silver in the moonlight; she had not raised her weapon, not yet, but now she did, and pronouncing clearly the words, "Peace!" then, louder but still in a calm even voice "Watch out!" She turned and from her automatic laser gun, a bright green and yellow beam shot out and vaporized first one bat and then another as, gliding in unseen from the sky, they swept down towards Miranda and Caliban. A sprinkling of blood and gristle and flesh rained down, splattering on the veranda and on the sandy steps.

But if the Centurion was amazing – how did a sole Centurion end up out here in the middle of the Dead Lands – much more amazing was her passenger, who was now standing beside the bike, holding it gently balanced with one claw. "Oh, by all the Gods," whispered Miranda again.

"Yes," whispered Caliban.

The ghouls, crouching, whimpered.

A few of the bats had moved back and were crouching on the sand. Most of the bats now circled overhead, blotches, blackening out a portion of the sky; but they were keeping their distance; for the moment, they were keeping their distance, a huge dark flapping flock of rabid monsters.

"It's a *hybrid*," whispered Miranda, "Oh, the Gods!"

"Yes," Caliban gripped the AK; the AK was good and solid and he was Long John Silver of the Dunes and he was Tarzan of the Desert, but he didn't think he and Miranda – and their ghoul-like friends – would stand much chance against a Centurion and a hybrid. But the situation was very strange. Centurions were the sworn enemies of hybrids and hunted mutants and hybrids; and, as for hybrids, well, hybrids were almost mythical creatures, absolute evil, they were known to hunt and kill everything and anything efficiently, effectively, and without hesitation or mercy. Nothing, it was whispered in the mutant kingdom, could match a hybrid, not even the Centurions.

"Why are they together?" It seemed to Miranda that time was standing still, that everything was happening very slowly, very deliberately.

"Centurions hunt hybrids," whispered Caliban, "And hybrids, I've heard, hunt everything."

"Yes," whispered Miranda, "They can kill almost anything. I mean, if they exist that is, I really didn't believe it, not until now … but …"

The ghouls pressed closer. Deep growled, Daisy whimpered, Bounce licked his lips, splashing splotches of moon-glow saliva on the veranda's floorboards.

This was frightening – a hybrid! My God! Miranda's heart seemed to have stopped and – at the same time – to be beating extra fast. The hybrid was turquoise and gold and her scales and fangs glittered in the moonlight; her enormous eyes glowed a yellowish gold. She was holding the bike erect with one claw, the other claw was on her hip, as she stared at them. She seemed to emanate a sense of calm; she was slender, even delicate, an exquisite shining metallic statue of a humanoid female, except of course she was not human; she was humanity's and Cosmos' worst enemy. It seemed to Miranda that she was beautiful, which was undoubtedly part of her danger – she could seduce and she could kill. Had she taken the Centurion prisoner? Or was she the Centurion's prisoner? Miranda noticed, to her surprise, that the hybrid was wearing a hip holster and a banderol – with a machine gun – and that it had on its back a Centurion black military backpack.

The hybrid was staring at Miranda in a very intense, very special way, the serpent-like eyes flashing. It gave Miranda the shivers, but not in an unpleasant way, in fact, she felt a flush of warmth flood through her; she felt, somehow, a shock of recognition; it was as if, in some mysterious way, she already knew the hybrid, but that was impossible; she tightened her grip on Caliban's hand. Perhaps the hybrid had already decided that Miranda was a choice morsel – the first on the menu for tonight. *Yum, yum, I've come to eat you, my dear!*

"We don't have much time, friends," said the Centurion; she motioned with the laser gun at the bats circling overhead, "What do you say, Major?"

Major? Miranda wondered what it the world was happening, *Major?*

The hybrid glanced at the Centurion, and for the first time she spoke, a very pleasant voice, a slight British-European Trans-Oceanic Imperial Cosmos accent, reminiscent of Nikki's way of speaking when she was tapping her fingers on her desk and getting just a wee bit impatient. "Lieutenant, I say we get the bike and all our friends inside before those creatures of darkness come for us all."

And as she spoke the "creatures" squealed and screamed and began a dive-bombing run – streaming down, en masse, heading directly for the porch.

"Go!" the hybrid said it softly, almost in a whisper, but it was truly an imperative, "Go!" And she pushed the bike up onto the veranda and along it, ramming it past two zombie-bats that had just landed – sweeping them aside as if they were made of straw, and pushing the bike towards the farmhouse door.

The Centurion had swung her weapon towards the incoming bats. Its green-yellow beam exploded them in mid-air. Still firing, she said, "Well, folks, are you coming or not?"

"We're coming," said Miranda, leaping forward and helping the hybrid with the bike.

"Well, Cosmos Child," said the hybrid, giving Miranda a look, up and down, scanning her nakedness.

"Well, hybrid," said Miranda, tossing her head haughtily, looking down her nose, and tightening her grip on the bike. A Cosmos is the pride of the universe; a Cosmos bows down before no man, no woman; a Cosmos bows down before absolutely nothing – a Cosmos will boldly defy anything – even a hybrid!

As they pushed the bike into the farmhouse, the hybrid held out, with one claw, a torn rag: the remains of Miranda's prison tunic.

"Oh," Miranda blushed; she took the rag, slung it over her shoulder.

"It *is* warm weather, even for a Cosmos," said the hybrid, her fangs glowing in what seemed like a smile.

They rolled the bike through the door, through the corridor, into the front parlor.

With Miranda helping to hold the bike upright, the hybrid kicked the bike stand into place, and now the bike was parked, free-standing, against a wall of the farmhouse parlor.

Miranda stood back and tried to put the prison sheath on, but it was too torn; only a ragged strip remained; she wrapped the shreds around her waist and tied a quick double-bow, the Cosmos Scouts *Our Leader's Health and Freedom* knot – Now, she too had a loincloth, not as elegant as Caliban's, and it covered hardly anything at all, but still, it did have a nifty rakish double knot, right over her left hipbone.

Hail, Hail, all Hail!

She took a quick breath and glanced around. Today – or tonight – was chock full of epiphanies. The bike, now standing in the front parlor, shimmered through its patina of dust; it looked, Miranda thought, like a painting by some ancient surrealist artist: This smooth, glossy, though dusty, ultra-killer Centurion bike, glowing with cutting-edge technological power, perched in the ancient farmhouse, next to the ghostly rocking chair, the ancient table, the massive dog-eared Bible, the smashed family photograph, and the spindly reading lamp – with the turquoise glowing hybrid and her backpack – it was all very spooky.

"So, Cosmos child," the hybrid said, as she unlatched two laser guns from the bike. She handed one to Miranda, "You know how to use this?"

"Yes of course, I'm a Cosmos First Class."

"And this nakedness, Cosmos Child First Class Presidential Gold Medal Winner, how did that come about?"

"Well, Ms. Hybrid, the truth is I ate some mushrooms," Miranda tested the weapon's safety mechanism – Yep, it worked, it was smooth – and she spoke in a breathless rush, suddenly overpowered by a need to confide in the mythical hybrid, to confess all her secrets, "I was having a mystical experience with Bounce and Daisy and Mr. Deep ..."

"Bounce and Daisy and Mr. Deep ..." The hybrid tilted its head to one side, its eyes opened wider.

"I gave the ghouls names so I could tell them apart. Anyway the mushrooms – it must have been the mushrooms – made me feel I wanted to be at one with the universe – the stars and galaxies and pebbles and beetles and earthworms and dust and HO_2 and CO_2 and quarks and protons and neutrinos and the clouds that are in the sky, and so on, and suchlike, and etc. I didn't want any barriers between me and the fluid divinity of material and universal existence ...

"... *the fluid divinity of material and universal existence*," repeated the sparkling hybrid. She seemed, to Miranda, to radiate light.

"Yes, Ms. Hybrid, I do know it sounds pretentious and overblown and just a bit highfalutin, but that was definitely the way I felt, I wanted to melt into the vast everything, to strip off the old social me, my old ego, and all its trappings, so I took off all my clothes – really just the prison tunic – there was nothing else – I was a prisoner in a mutant colony – organized mutants, they are a different kind of mutants from Bounce and Daisy and Mr. Deep, but still they are mutants – and I sat down naked – despoiled of everything, and feeling pure and sacred – on the veranda steps out there with Bounce sitting next to me – he had the most tremendous erection I ever saw and it just wouldn't go away – and I was united to the moon and the stars and the very farthest galaxies and the very edges of this universe and I plunged into consciousness of other universes, swimming in the interstices between universes, and then Caliban came ... and ..."

"Caliban ...?"

"Oh, Caliban," Miranda sighed, her heart rising like a tipsy canoe on a bright breathless tide, a tsunami of moonlit love and yearning, "He's Long John Silver a land pirate and Tarzan too – he took me and my mother Nikki prisoner – and he's read ever so many books – real books, ancient books, books made of paper and with pages and print that he keeps stored in a secret niche – and all this has stimulated his imagination, perhaps excessively, mind you, for one living out here in the desert among mutants ... But I love it! He sometimes doesn't know if he's in Elizabethan times, or in the 18th century, or if he's Tarzan King of the Jungle or a South Seas Pirate, like Long John Silver or somebody, or a cowboy maybe, or an Iroquois or Blackfoot, and he gets confused as to whether I'm his prisoner and slave or his friend and his princess, and we are very much in love, and I think this is very interesting because I've never been in love before – though I have a very special Sub friend, Kit – and I've never met a hybrid before, I mean you really are a hybrid, aren't you, Ms. Hybrid, and hybrids are outlawed and evil – I thought you were extinct – and you eat people and things like that and drink their blood and gobble humans up and we Cosmos are not even allowed to *think* of hybrids let alone mention them – the Mind Censor goes into a total meltdown at the mere mention of the word 'hybrid' – so this is very exciting – *totally awesome* – if you see what I mean – I used to have dreams I mean nightmares about hybrids, one of them looked just like you, Ms. Hybrid, exactly the same color scheme, I hope you aren't offended, you do see what I mean, don't you?"

"Absolutely," moonlight from outside glinted on the hybrid's fangs, "I totally see what you mean, Cosmos Child First Class, Miranda Hughes." The hybrid laid her claw on Miranda's shoulder – and again Miranda had the impression that time had slowed down – that in the flurry and storm of activity with Giant Zombie Bats wheeling and battering against the windows and walls – and with Caliban and the Centurion firing their weapons – rat-tat-tat – and zip-zip-zip – and with the three ghouls hurrying in the door, she had the impression that she and the hybrid were in a timeless little bubble, all by themselves, with all the time in the world, and that they had found each other at last, that they would never be separated, not really separated, ever again. Then she realized that the hybrid had called her by her name. *How did she know that?* Somehow, it didn't matter. "What's your name, Ms. Hybrid?" she asked.

"V," said the hybrid, "V is my name."

"V," repeated Miranda, some ancient memory surfacing, tales of the Mother of all hybrids, the super hybrid, the hybrid alien goddess from pagan times, the mythical source of all evil, the gateway to other worlds and to ancient rites, the blood-drinking extra-terrestrial hybrid who …

"You're the one they whisper about, you're the …"

"Yes, Miranda, yes, Cosmos Child, I'm the one they whisper about; but right now, we have a war to fight."

"Yes."

"Time is racing."

"Yes." Miranda was suddenly aware of the roaring storm of activity around them; time accelerated, zoomed, and galloped, head-down, full-speed. There was not an instant to lose. "There's a basement, there's a tunnel. I think there are caves."

"Go, we go!" V shouted, "Kat, the basement, tunnels, a cave!"

"The Centurion is called Kat?"

"Yes, she is," said V, "Let's go!"

Caliban and Kat the Centurion were fighting shoulder to shoulder, as they backed through the doorway, their guns blazing at the Bats outside. "You're good," the Centurion said to Caliban. "You too, Centurion," Caliban said. The dragon tattoo on Caliban's back glowed. The dragon flared its crest, blew crimson fire. Caliban's shoulders were broad; they gleamed, ribbons of silver flowing in the moonlight.

"Oh, what a man," thought Miranda, "What a pirate!"

V and Miranda herded the ghouls towards the basement. "Okay, folks, get down there, keep moving," shouted the Centurion, still blazing at the giant Bats who were thumping down on the porch, flashing claws and jaws, trying to force their way in through the door.

The ghouls, led by Miranda, started down the cellar stairs, but at the last minute, Mr. Deep, the old ghoul, the father ghoul with the wispy Biblical beard, broke loose with a growl, and he scrambled back up the stairs, pushing past the Centurion who, with Caliban, was still blazing away.

"What the hell?"

Miranda bolted up the stairs to try to grab Mr. Deep. She couldn't let him die in the claws and fangs of those creatures.

Just as Mr. Deep ran into the parlor, heading for the Bible and the photograph, two huge bats came smashing in through the two large parlor windows, crashing to a landing, rolling, and then standing upright, their wings folded, but their claws out, their fangs eager, ready to snatch up Mr. Deep and tear him to pieces. They plunged. The old ghoul dodged, ducked, grabbed the smashed photograph and the thick worn old Bible, and he scrambled, crawling, but the first of the Bats reached for him, snatching him up in its claws.

Miranda was ready to charge, when …

The Bat dropped Mr. Deep and screeched and the Bat's head was gone, swept from its neck by the clean blow of V's claws.

V swirled around and snapped the neck of the other Bat, a clean snap that sounded like a gun shot.

"Boy, oh, boy," said Miranda; she hadn't even had time to raise the laser gun.

"Come, friend," V said to the ghoul. He was whimpering and drooling, and he'd dropped the Bible and he was groping blindly for it – and V realized that he was almost blind.

"And, Miranda," V said, "Get downstairs quick; the others need you!"

"Yes, of course," Miranda leaped downstairs, but before she disappeared, she caught a glimpse of what was happening in the parlor.

The hybrid had noticed the Bible which had fallen just outside the brilliant sliver square made by the moonlight coming through the shattered windows, just outside the flickering clarity of the moon as other Bats crowded outside the windows, their shadows fighting to get in and the hybrid swooped down into the shadows and picked up the Bible, saying to Deep, "Here it is, let's go!"

The cowering frantic old ghoul looked up at the hybrid – this super being and at the Holy Book she was holding. He scrambled to his feet and followed V – she had also rescued the family photograph – as she led Deep past the Centurion and Caliban – shoulder to shoulder and still blasting away, defending the doorway – and Deep scrambled down the stairs.

Miranda looked up.

V, still holding the Bible and photograph was silhouetted by moonlight at the top of the stairs, and V shouted, "Come Kat, come Caliban, let's go!"

V stood aside as Kat and Caliban leaped down the stairs and rushed into the tunnel. Kat waited at the mouth of the tunnel for V. V was the last to come down the stairs and reach the tunnel.

A zombie-bat had already started to wiggle down the stairs; V saw that the zombie-bats were very clumsy in narrow spaces and on the ground, so the tunnel, though dark and friendly for the zombie-bat species, would be a good place to hide.

V shot the zombie-bat with her laser gun

It sizzled. A flash went up; it left a gaping smoking hole.

The zombie-bat toppled down the stairs.

V and Kat slid into the narrow tunnel – too narrow for the zombie-bats and their wings – and V pulled the big sheet of plywood back over it.

In the tunnel, crawling bent over, Miranda, who was leading the way, came to a small chapel-like cave. There was just room to stand up.

Miranda crawled out of the tunnel, stood up in the cave, and stretched – oh, it felt good! Glowing mushroom clusters hung from the ceiling like giant bunches of grapes, pulsating, emanating greenish light.

Soon everyone crowded into the little chapel.

V handed the Bible to Mr. Deep and she gave the family photograph to Daisy. Daisy gazed at the photograph, leaned over it, and began to whimper.

Mr. Deep crouched low, looking up at V, drooling, and he held the precious Holy Book pressed close to his chest, behind him soared up a wall decorated with human bones and, at one end of the chapel, Miranda noticed, there was a high pyramid of human skulls.

"Oh, boy, look at that!"

Caliban put his arm around her. It felt good, strong and warm and smooth. "What is this place? What happened here?"

"This is their *new* religion, I'll bet," said Kat, her gloved hands at her waist, thumbs hooked in her belt, the greenish lichen and moss light reflecting in pulsating lines on her black leather armor, sleek skintight armored leggings, on her dark wraparounds and helmet, on her full glossy black lips and her bright white teeth. "They worship the people they've eaten."

All along one wall skulls and bones were piled up in pyramids. The three mutants bowed down before the skulls, and banged their foreheads on the packed-down earth floor.

"They eat humans," said V, "And Cosmos."

"Gosh," said Miranda, nostrils twitching; she smelled something, something overpowering, coppery, bitter-sweet, and delicious! What was it? She was suddenly filled with yearning, with hunger, with …

"Blood: the ground is soaked with blood," said V, turning to Miranda with a strange sad reptilian smile, "This chapel is their slaughterhouse." V put down her backpack, pulled out a magazine, and reloaded her laser gun, "This place is soaked in human blood and mutant blood."

"Oh, boy!" Miranda sniffed again, nostrils quivering; it was old blood, it was not fresh at all; it was at least four days old; it was … Then she saw that there was a banjo lying in one corner, and a ukulele.

"Look at this, Caliban," Miranda picked the banjo up and twanged one string, a vibrant note.

Bounce waddled over and reached out his claw.

"You want it?"

"Grrrhhh!"

Miranda glanced at V and Kat. The hybrid and the Centurion both nodded. Miranda handed the banjo to Bounce.

The ghoul plucked a few strings and then he settled on his haunches and he began to play. Daisy and Deep settled on their haunches too; and they began to sing: "You are my sunshine, my only sunshine."

They had good voices. They sounded like a barbershop quartet from 1911, though the song itself dated from 1939, as Miranda's American Pop Cult Implant told her. She suddenly saw them as they must have been before they had been transformed. As they sang, they got excited, bobbing up and down on their haunches; Miranda was amazed: could ghouls smile? They seemed to be smiling. And then, Bounce changed tunes, and they really began to sing, with brio, spraying phosphorescent saliva all over the floor, over themselves, and everywhere: "Give me the old-time religion!"

"How did they become like this?" Miranda asked. Caliban was holding her close, his arm around her shoulders.

"Well," said Kat, the Centurion, pushing up her wraparounds; revealing clearly now that she was a gorgeous black woman, with the most beautiful eyes. "Well," she said, "It's a new contagion. I don't think anybody really knows what it is or how it spreads, not yet we don't anyway." The Centurion slipped her wraparounds down and crouched next to Bounce. He stopped playing and began banging his forehead on the ground. "You do eat humans, don't you?"

Bounce turned to Kat and looked up at her, drool spilling from his mouth, and he kneeled in front of her and kissed her glove. "Grrrhhh," he growled, licking her glove, drool spilling over.

"But I don't understand," Miranda frowned, "I'm human. I'm even a Cosmos. But they didn't eat me. They didn't even try," Miranda watched Bounce kneel before the Centurion, "They got down on hands and knees, like he's doing now. It was like they worship us. So how can that be? I mean we are human; I mean some of us are humans and Cosmos, aren't we …?"

V turned. The green phosphorescence of the clusters of mushrooms brightly sculpted her turquoise and gold scales, curves and shadows and relief, in gentle pulsating light. She really was like a bejeweled idol from some cave temple in India. Miranda sucked in her breath: V was definitely not human, not Cosmos.

V crouched, almost worshipfully, in front of Miranda. "Cosmos Child, it will soon be dawn. I think we had better go and save your mother."

CHAPTER 12 – GODDESS

The sun had come up a few hours before

Using an ancient pair of binoculars Nikki scanned the horizon; next to her stood an honor guard of bear-warriors.

The battle of the night before had been epic. The mutants had never met anything like the zombie-bats before and had no idea how to handle them.

At the beginning of the skirmishes, Nikki noticed the bats were terrified of fire. She ordered an attack involving torches. The bats floundered in confusion. They tried to escape. And as they tried to escape, they revealed the way they had come in, so Nikki, with the assent of the Great High Priest, had the old side drift sealed off, and cemented up. The few remaining zombie-bats, isolated, and without a way of escaping, were trapped and destroyed. The populace exulted. *Hail to the Goddess, hail, hail, hail, all hail …*

So, all in all, it had been a good night indeed.

Nikki spotted a plume of dust on the horizon – it was a bike, a Cosmos Centurion motorbike. "Friends, I do believe they are friends," said Nikki to the bear-warriors and to Tara Capricorn who was standing just behind her mistress, Goddess Nikki

And that is how it happened.

The bears were uneasy – a Cosmos bike-weapon! It was a symbol of the enemy, the all-powerful Cosmos. Might this be a Cosmos attack?

But the Goddess had spoken.

She even laid her hand upon the arm of one of the guards and said, "Do not worry, Yan, they are friends. They come in peace."

"Ours to obey," said Yan, bowing his head, and thrilled that the Goddess had deigned bless him with her touch.

Several hours later they were all reunited, Prince Caliban, Princess Miranda, V and Nikki and Kat and the Great High Priest, and Scav, and all the others.

Miranda was astounded.

Not only did V seem to know Nikki, it was also clear that Nikki knew V – they greeted each other like the best of old friends – but also, and this was totally, but totally, astounding, her mother, Nikki was now a Goddess – Good Grief! How had that happened? Nikki was the Goddess of the Mutants.

How in the world had mother pulled that off?

"Mother, how in the world did you become their Goddess, and their ruler, I mean, I know you are charming, and persuasive, and capable of winning any argument whatsoever, and everything, but …"

"I shall tell you shortly, Miranda," said Nikki, her arm around her daughter and glancing at V, who nodded, "but perhaps we've all had enough excitement and epiphanies for one day."

"And Kat and I have a mission," said V.

Kat nodded.

"Of course," said Nikki, "I understand."

And so, a few hours later, at dawn of the next day, after a grand feast in honor of the guests, there were tearful farewells …

Yes, there tearful farewells, as V and Kat, both now in Centurion bodysuits, and V in human form – Miranda's reaction to V's morph into human was, "Oh, My God! She's beautiful, utterly beautiful!"

They stood outside the Main Door of the great mutant colony. It was dawn. V and Kat had a whole day's travel before them. The desert sand was swirling in small dust devils. The sun was rising into a bone-dry cloudless sky. The heat hovered at 112 degrees Fahrenheit. It was at least a day's distance to the mythical Camp Terminus, and V had insisted they leave immediately. And Kat, the Centurion, agreed.

V embraced both Nikki and Miranda – giving Miranda a fabulously warm hug – and to Caliban she had said, while shaking his hand, "Well, young man, you have certainly chosen a handful!" Caliban smiled nervously and then he did something he rarely did, he put his arms around the hybrid, in her human form such a beautiful woman, such a perfect Cosmos, like Nikki, and he held her tight.

Then they mounted the bike, Kat driving and V clinging to her waist, and they waved, and the bike sped off.

Miranda watched them go, disappearing through the ruined mine buildings, then lost in a plume of dust, riding over a dune, and, invisible for a moment, then briefly visible on another dune, and then gone, beyond the horizon.

Miranda reached out – one hand in Nikki's hand and another in Caliban's hand.

"They'll be back, Miranda," Nikki said, "We'll all be together again."

"I have not been in the sun for many decades," said the Great High Priest, turning his blind goatish face towards the brilliance, "Oh, thank you, Goddess, Thank you!"

"Can't stay long, can't stay long," Scav was bouncing up and down, gazing at Nikki in adoration, "Sun burns, sun burns!"

"Yes, they cannot stay in the light," said Tara Capricorn, who had taken a great shining to Miranda – she had never, aside from the Goddess Nikki, seen such a beautiful female human before.

"Yes, Scav's right," said Nikki, "You can't stay too long in the sun. Let us return, Great High Priest, to your Kingdom."

"It is your kingdom now, Goddess," said the Great High Priest.

"It is our kingdom," Nikki declared, "All of us."

And they all entered the Great Door. The last to leave was Miranda.

Little Tara Capricorn, with Nikki's hand on her shoulder, lingered just inside the door; she yearned to watch over Miranda whom she had decided she worshipped. Caliban, always careful of his Princess, stood next to them.

"You like her?" Nikki said.

"Oh, yes," said the little girl.

"And you, Caliban?" said Nikki.

Caliban cleared his throat, "I …" he cleared his throat again, "I love her, yes, I love her, I wish to ask, Goddess, I wish to ask …"

"Not yet, Caliban," said Nikki, she put her hand on his arm, "The time is almost ripe for you to ask, but not yet, not just yet …"

Miranda stood alone, gazing at the distant horizon where waves of sand marched on and on and on. One tear rolled down her cheek. It was all so mysterious! Why did the hybrid V and the Centurion Kat seem so important to her? It was as if she were losing her oldest dearest friends. There was an ache in her heart.

"It is difficult to say good-bye, is it not, Princess?" said one of the Bear guardians, coming up to her, his pike upright and glittering in the sun, his breastplate glowing like liquid gold. He was the Bear who had chased her up the staircase: oh, it seemed now like eons ago.

"Yes, it is," said Miranda, "It is difficult, Yorick. Thank you!"

"Come now, Princess, it is time."

"Yes, you are right, Yorick, it is time."

Still Miranda lingered. It looked like there was just a whiff of a plume of dust on the farthest dune – many miles away – maybe it was them, V and Kat, racing forward on that lone bike lost in the immensity of emptiness, racing forward towards that mythical dark place, a dark satanic mill, a rumored inferno, Camp Terminus.

"Goddess Nikki and Prince Caliban are waiting, Princess."

"Yes, Yorick, you're right. I'm sorry. I'm being silly." She wiped at the one tear with the knuckles of her hand. The hot breeze rippled across her skin-shirt. Below the cliff, in the ruined mining camp, a rusty crane clanked – the steel beams shifting slightly in the wind. Looped and hanging chains rattled.

"Come, Princess." Another bear-warrior bowed.

"Yes, thank you, Peter."

Miranda entered the Door and Yorick and his fellow guard, Peter, slowly closed it, and then locked it, lowering the three great bars and turning the giant wheel so it locked into place and everyone was safe.

"Come on, you two," said Nikki, tousling Miranda's and Caliban's hair; she put her arms around them both. "They'll be back – and we'll all be together again, and forever. Meantime, Tara Capricorn and I shall look after you!"

"And we will live happily ever after – everybody living happily together, forever and ever, that's what you want, mother?" Miranda still didn't understand how her mother had become a goddess. After all, the mutants had intended to sacrifice her ... and ...

"Yes, Miranda, that's what I want."

"Me too," said Miranda.

"Me too," said Tara, nodding, the light reflecting in ripples on her two curved horns.

Miranda leaned down; she kissed little Tara on the forehead.

"And, Miranda, there is something I have to tell you. It will be difficult, Miranda, and you may want to pout or throw a fit, but I am sure that, in the end, you will understand." Nikki put her hands on Miranda's shoulders and looked deep into her daughter's eyes.

"Yes, mother?"

"Well, Miranda, you see, the truth is …"

Outside, as the door clanged shut, dusty brown as it was, it blended in perfectly with the rocks of the escarpment and with the gently blowing sand. The second it closed, it seemed as if there was nothing there, nothing at all.

The sun shone overhead, just as it shone over the abandoned and ruined cities of the interior of what had once been the United States of America.

Sand rustled and murmured in the ruined buildings and rusty machinery. Small brown reptiles skittered here and there.

A mottled six-foot-long rattlesnake slithered over a half-buried ribcage, which had been uncovered by the shifting sands; it raised its head, searching, and then flattened itself and zigzagged onward, tongue flickering, eyes alert, and sensing for heat differences; there was little left to eat.

V and Kat rode onwards, over the arid dusty plain, following the sun as it arched through the sky and headed down towards the horizon where, soon it would disappear.

With night, of course, would come terrors, yet new terrors …

NEXT: VOLUME 6 IN THE
ADVENTURES OF V

EXTINCTION

BOOK 2
REVOLT OF THE ANGELS

by
GILBERT REID

TWIN RIVERS
PRODUCTIONS

EXTINCTION BOOK 2:
REVOLT OF THE ANGELS

Camp Terminus – the end of the line.

"Bugs!!" Hilly Loritz tossed back and forth – writhing on his side of the king-size bed, its thin mattress, its creaking, rusty springs. "Bugs! Fuck! Bugs!"

Click, click, click …

On the ceiling, the rusty paddles of a sixty-year-old fan rotated, ticking off a sluggish, rhythmic *click-click-click* and casting a flickering shadow. It never stopped, *click, click, click …*

"Damn it!" Jane Fox turned on her right side, then on her left. "Damn it!" She flipped over and lay flat on her back. She stared at the rotating fan. She exhaled a ragged sigh. It was fucking impossible to sleep!

Stretching her body out full length, straining every sinew, she arched her back into the air. Taut as a violin string, she shook herself and yawned. It was past midnight. Inside the bedroom, it was at least 105 degrees Fahrenheit – 40 degrees Celsius. The air-conditioning had given up the ghost, sputtering into silence, four months, three days, and two hours ago, if Jane's reckoning was accurate. Jane possessed, perched inside her head, a sort of pitiless, scrupulous, time-keeper accountant. It took note of every passing minute, every passing second.

"Bugs!! Bugs!! Oh, God – Bugs!" Hilly screamed.

"Fuck! Hilly," Jane whispered, in a quiet, carefully controlled, clinical voice, "You're driving yourself nuts." She yawned and licked her lips. Yuk! Cruddy, salty, dry lips – dehydrated – disgusting! She picked at the flakes of crud. "You're driving me nuts too!"

She stretched her arms above her head, wrists slack, as if handcuffed, pressed against the metal bars of the ancient brass headboard. She stared at the ceiling. It had been cream-colored. Now, it was a dun gray, flaking, peeling. She counted the rotation of the ceiling fan's paddles – *one, two, three, four* … Laboriously, they clicked their way around the infernal circle, creating hardly any breeze at all, *click, click, click* … Worse than useless!

Jane left the handcuffed fantasy behind – her body helpless and offered up to pleasure – and levered herself up on her elbows. She glanced at her tummy. The flat, tense, sweaty midriff rippled with oily reflections. Great washboard abs! Neat, cupcake tits too. Pretty good shape! She sniffed and blinked at the gray darkness. *Fuck!* How many hours had she been lying there, naked, beaded in gluey sweat, crucified, on top of the sheets? Giving up, she had tossed and turned, tense as a twanging violin. Desperate for sleep. Fucking impossible! No, she was not going to get any sleep, not tonight. Goddamn it to Hell!

"Bugs!" The man screamed.

"Hilly!" Jane growled, evenly, between her teeth, "Shut the fuck up!"

Exiled to his half of the bed, Camp Commandant, Hilmar Loritz – his buddies called him "Hilly" – well, that was when Hilmar Loritz still had buddies – had kicked and thrashed, groaning and screaming – the whole goddamn night.

"Fuck!" Jane swiveled around, and sat up, the soles of her bare feet touching down on the rough unvarnished wooden planks of the floor. Even the wood sizzled. Dripping sweat, hunched forward, sitting on the edge of the bed, she stared into space. Her fists clutched the mattress so hard her knuckles turned white. What a dreary fucking godforsaken place!

The pithead and security perimeter lights glared through the torn, fly-spotted muslin curtain. Everything in the room was cast in a gray-silver ghostly hue. Jane glanced down. Her legs were pasty chalk – pale, vampire-like, the skinny legs of an anemic virgin. *A virgin! Now that would be something! A virgin! Pshaw!*

"I can't help it!" Hilly groaned. Even if the man did fall asleep, he still thrashed, fighting the bugs. The damned things crawled all over him. Every inch of the man's skin swarmed with bugs.

Maybe half an hour ago it was: He leaped out of bed, tore off his underpants, scampered around the goddamn room, stark naked, out his fucking mind. His voice had zipped up a few octaves, shrill, totally unlike the old Hilly. He scratched everywhere, jumping up and down, some strange high-kick dance, screaming, "Bugs, bugs, bugs, bugs!"

"Goddamn it, Hilly," Jane had sighed. "Enough already! It's all in your goddamn head! There are no bugs!"

The man saw bugs everywhere, and reported his sightings to Jane in gory sadomasochistic detail. A glistening drop of water running along a pipe was a scurrying, skittering, flesh-eating centipede. A wrinkle in the sheets was a marching line of bed bugs, each equipped with huge jaws and a stinger an inch long. Bugs popped out of the corner of Hilly's eyes. When he slapped them, they scattered into his hairline.

Bugs rippled through what little hair he had left. Their itchy, sticky, little feet beat out a tattoo on his cadaverous, waxy scalp, native tom-toms in some entirely imaginary heart of darkness. The bugs were underneath his skin. They moved in ripples in his flesh, nibbling like a cancer at his sphincter. They tunneled into his anus. They wiggled up inside his penis. They spiraled into his brain.

How to cure Hilly? Jane had no idea. She was a fucking flesh-and-bones doctor, not a goddamn psychotherapist.

She stood up, stretched, and walked to the window. She was acutely aware of herself – barefoot, naked, edgy, pissed off, soaked in sweat, dog-tired, but, even now, her body quivered with energy. It was a wiry, thin body, smooth and chalk-white, with neat little buttocks, perfect champagne-glass breasts, shapely legs, a tight, muscular belly, and a narrow, stubborn back.

She wiggled her shoulders. That damned stiffness in her neck! She pushed aside the tattered curtain. Above the dark buildings, the monstrous pit-head towered. A line from one of William Blake's poems rose up from some obscure forgotten place in her mind: *And was Jerusalem builded here, among these dark satanic mills?*

Fuck!

Jane put her finger on the window pane. William Blake was a goddamned prophet: *And they built a hell in heaven's despite …*

ACKNOWLEDGMENTS

Thanks to the many people who made the *Adventures of V: Return of the Goddess* possible: Adrienne Clarkson, Andra Sheffer, André Kirchberger, Anna Porter, Bernice Landry, Bernie Lucht, Beverly Topping, Bob Ramsay, Chuck Shamata, Claudia Neri, Denise Jacques, Diana Leblanc, Diane Shamata, Dianne Rinehart, Dorothy Vreeker, Duncan Derry, Ed Cowan, Elena Solari, Florence Treadwell, Heather Reid, Irene Spampinato, Irene Tudisco, Jacqueline Baker, Jacqueline Park, Jacqueline Swartz, Janie Yoon, Jennifer Hambleton, Jennifer Puncher, Jim Downs, John McGreevy, John Pearce, John Ralston Saul, Josephine Khu, Jules Cashford, Julia Belluz, Julia Hambleton, Marie-Christine Dunham-Pratt, Mark Fenwick, Martine Matus Siebert, Norm Barber, Norm Christie, Nuala Fitzgerald, Paola Pugliatti, Peter Williamson, Ramsay Derry, Sandra Martin, Simona Barabesi, Susan Mahoney, Susan S. Senstad, Tony Robinow, Trisha Jackson, Wendy Trueman, and many others too numerous to name. I owe an infinite number of literary debts, too, but in particular to Joyce Carol Oates, Justin Cronin, and Stephen King.

TITLES IN THE
ADVENTURES OF V

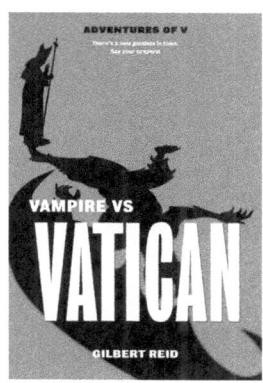

GILBERT REID

To receive a free book or novella
And to learn more about V and get notes on writing and other topics:

Sign up at

https://gilbertreid.com

Please write a short review!
Just two or three lines.
And post it to Goodreads or Amazon
or any other book group you may belong to.

Or send it to me!
At: gilbert@gilbertreid.com

GILBERT REID is the author of two short story collections: *So This is Love: Lollipop and Other Stories* (2004, 2019) and *Lava and Other Stories* (2019). He also co-authored, with Jacqueline Park, the historical novel *Son of Two Fathers* (2019). He has written extensively for television and radio. Most notably he researched, wrote, and narrated two five-hour radio series: *Gilbert Reid's Italy* and *Gilbert Reid's France* for CBC's flagship radio program IDEAS. His many television series include *Paths of the Gods*, *For King and Empire*, *For King and Country*, and *Sir Peter Ustinov in Burma: Road to Mandalay*. After thirty years in Europe working as an economist, university lecturer, diplomat, script doctor, journalist, and adventure travel guide, Gilbert now lives in Toronto.